Spain for the Sovereigns

SPAIN FOR THE SOVEREIGNS

JEAN PLAIDY

LARGE PRINT

Oxford

Copyright © Jean Plaidy, 1960

First published in Great Britain 1960
by
Robert Hale and Company

Published in Large Print 2009 by ISIS Publishing Ltd.,
7 Centremead, Osney Mead, Oxford OX2 0ES
by arrangement with
The Random House Group Company

British Library Cataloguing in Publication Data
Plaidy, Jean, 1906–1993.
    Spain for the sovereigns
    1. Inquisition - - Spain - - Fiction.
    2. Spain - - History - - Ferdinand and Isabella,
    1479–1516 - - Fiction.
    3. Historical fiction.
    4. Large type books.
    I. Title
    823.9'14–dc22

ISBN 978–0–7531–8346–5 (hb)
ISBN 978–0–7531–8347–2 (pb)

Printed and bound in Great Britain by
T. J. International Ltd., Padstow, Cornwall

CONTENTS

CHAPTER
ONE

Ferdinand

It was growing dark as the cavalcade rode into the silent city of Barcelona on its way to the Palace of the Kings of Aragon. On it went, through streets so narrow that the tall grey houses — to which the smell of sea and harbour clung — seemed to meet over the cobbles.

At the head of this company of horsemen rode a young man of medium height and of kingly bearing. His complexion was fresh and tanned by exposure to the wind and sun; his features were well formed, his teeth exceptionally white, and the hair, which grew far back from his forehead, was light brown with a gleam of chestnut.

When any of his companions addressed him, it was with the utmost respect. He was some twenty-two years old, already a warrior and a man of experience, and only in the determination that all should respect his dignity did he betray his youth.

He turned to the man who rode beside him. "How she suffered, this city!" he said.

"It is true, Highness. I heard from the lips of the King, your father, that when he entered after the siege he could scarce refrain from weeping — such terrible sights met his eyes."

Ferdinand of Aragon nodded grimly. "A warning," he murmured, "to subjects who seek to defy their rightful King."

His companion replied: "It is so, Highness." He dared not remind Ferdinand that the civil war which had recently come to an end had been fought because of the murder of the rightful heir — Ferdinand's half-brother Carlos, his father's son by his first wife. It was a matter best forgotten, for now Ferdinand was very ready to take and defend all that his ambitious father, all that his doting mother, had procured for him.

The little cavalcade had drawn up before the Palace in which John of Aragon had his headquarters, and Ferdinand cried in his deep resonant voice: "What ails you all? I am here. I, Ferdinand, have come!"

There was immediate bustle within. Doors were flung open and grooms ran forward surrounding the party. Ferdinand leaped from his horse and ran into the Palace, where his father, who had heard his arrival, came to meet him, arms outstretched.

"Ferdinand! Ferdinand!" he cried, and his eyes filled with tears as he embraced his son. "Ah, I knew you would not delay your coming. I knew you would be with me. I am singularly blessed. I was given the best of wives, and although she has now been taken from me, she has left me the best of sons."

The seventy-eight-year-old King of Aragon showed no signs of failing. Still strong and energetic — in spite of recent operations which had restored the sight of both eyes — he rarely permitted himself to show any weakness. But there was one emotion which he always failed to hide; that was the love he had for his dead wife and his son by her: Ferdinand.

His arm about Ferdinand's shoulder, John led his son into a small apartment and called for refreshment. When it was brought and they were alone Ferdinand said: "You sent for me, Father; that was enough to bring me hastening to your side."

John smiled. "But such a newly married husband, and such a charming wife!"

"Ah, yes," said Ferdinand, with a complacent smile. "Isabella was loth to lose me, but she is deeply conscious of duty, and when she heard of your need, she was certain that I should not fail you."

John nodded. "And all is well . . . in Castile, my son?"

"All is well, Father."

"And the child?"

"Healthy and strong."

"I would your little Isabella had been a boy!"

"There will be boys," said Ferdinand.

"Indeed there will be. And I will say this, Ferdinand. When you have a son, may he be so like yourself that all will say: 'Here is another Ferdinand come among us.' I cannot wish you better than that."

"Father, you think too highly of your son." But the young man's expression belied the charge.

John shook his head. "King of Castile! And one day . . . perhaps not far distant, King of Aragon."

"For the second title I would be content to wait all my life," said Ferdinand. "As for the first . . . as yet it is little more than a courtesy title."

"So Isabella is the Queen and you the Consort . . . for a time . . . for a time. I doubt not that very soon you will have brought her to understanding."

"Mayhap," agreed Ferdinand. "It is regrettable that the Salic law is not in force in Castile as in Aragon."

"Then, my son, you would be undoubted King and Isabella *your* Consort. Castile should be yours through your grandfather and namesake but for the fact that females are not excluded from the Castilian throne. But Isabella, the female heir, is your wife, my dearest son, and I am sure that this little difficulty is only a temporary one."

"Isabella is very loving," Ferdinand replied with a smile.

"There! Then soon all will be as we could wish."

"But let us talk of your affairs, Father. They are of greater moment, and it is for this purpose that I have come to you."

King John looked grave. "As you know," he said, "during the revolt of the Catalans it was necessary for me to ask help of Louis of France. He gave it to me, but Louis, as you know, never gives something for nothing."

"I know that the provinces of Roussillon and Cerdagne were placed in his custody as security, and that now they have risen in revolt against this foreign yoke."

"And have called to me for succour. Alas, the Seigneur du Lude has now invaded Roussillon with ten

4

thousand infantry and nine hundred lances. Moreover, he has brought supplies that will keep his armies happy for months. The civil war has been long. You know how it has drained the exchequer."

"We must raise money, Father, in some way."

"That is why I have called you. I want you to go to Saragossa and by some means raise the money for our needs. Defeat at the hands of France would be disastrous."

Ferdinand was silent for a few seconds. "I am wondering," he said at length, "how it will be possible to wring the necessary funds from the estates of Aragon. How do matters stand in Saragossa?"

"There is much lawlessness in Aragon."

"Even as in Castile," answered Ferdinand. "There has been such strife for so long that civil affairs are neglected and rogues and robbers spring up all around us."

"It would seem," John told him, "that a certain Ximenes Gordo has become King of Saragossa."

"How can that be?"

"You know the family. It is a noble one. Ximenes Gordo has cast aside his nobility. He has taken municipal office and has put himself into a position of such influence that it is not easy, from this distance, to deal with him. All the important posts have been given to his friends and relations and those who offer a big enough bribe. He is a colourful rogue and has in some manner managed to win the popular esteem. He makes a travesty of justice and I have evidence that he is guilty of numerous crimes."

"His trial and execution should be ordered."

"My dear son, to do so might bring civil strife to Saragossa. I have too much on my hands. But if you are going to raise funds for our needs a great deal will depend on Ximenes Gordo."

"The King of Aragon dependent on a subject!" cried Ferdinand. "That seems impossible."

"Does it not, my son. But I am in dire need, and far from Saragossa."

Ferdinand smiled. "You must leave this matter to me, Father. I will go to Saragossa. You may depend upon it, I will find some means of raising the money you need."

"You will do it, I know," said John. "It is your destiny always to succeed."

Ferdinand smiled complacently. "I shall set off without delay for Saragossa, Father," he said.

John looked wistful. "So shortly come, so soon to go," he murmured. "Yet you are right," he added. "There is little time to lose."

"Tomorrow morning, at dawn, I shall leave," Ferdinand told him. "Your cause — as always — is my own."

On his way through Catalonia to Saragossa there was one call which Ferdinand could not deny himself the pleasure of making.

It must be as far as possible a secret call. There was one little person whom he longed to see and who meant a great deal to him, but he was determined to go to great lengths to conceal his existence from Isabella.

He was beginning to realise that it was going to be somewhat difficult to live up to the ideal which his wife had made of him.

He and his followers had rested at an inn and, declaring that he would retire early, he with two of his most trusted attendants went to the room which had been assigned to him.

As soon as they were alone, he said: "Go to the stables. Have the horses made ready and I will join you when all is quiet."

"Yes, Highness."

Ferdinand was impatient when they had left him. How long his party took to settle down! He had to resist an impulse to go to them and demand that they retire to their beds immediately and fall into deep sleep.

That would be folly, of course, since the great need was for secrecy. He was not by nature impulsive. He knew what he wanted and was determined to get it; but experience had taught him that it was often necessary to wait a long time for success in one's endeavours. Ferdinand had learned to wait.

So now he did so, impatient yet restrained, until at last his servant was at the door.

"All is quiet, Highness. The horses are ready."

"That is well. Let us be off."

It was pleasant riding through the night. He had wondered whether to send a messenger ahead of him to warn her. But no. It should be a surprise. And if he found her with a lover, he did not greatly care. It was not she — beautiful as she was — who called him, it

7

was not merely for her sake that he was ready to make this secret journey, news of which might be brought to the ears of Isabella.

"Oh, Isabella, my wife, my Queen," he murmured to himself, "you will have to learn something of the world one day. You will have to know that men, such as I am, who spend long periods away from the conjugal bed, cannot be denied a mistress now and then."

And from love affairs such as that which he had enjoyed with the Viscountess of Eboli there were often results.

Ferdinand smiled. He was confident of his powers to obtain what he would from all women — even his sedate, and rather alarmingly prim, Isabella.

He was remembering the occasion when he and the Viscountess had become lovers. It was during one of those spells when he was away from Castile, in Catalonia on his father's business. It was Isabella who had insisted that he leave her. "It is your duty to go to your father's aid," she had said.

Duty! he thought. It was a word frequently recurrent in Isabella's vocabulary.

She would never fail to do her duty. She had been brought up to regard it as of paramount importance. She would risk her life for the sake of duty; she did not know, she must not guess that, when she had allowed her husband to depart into Catalonia, she had risked his fidelity to their marriage bed.

It had happened. And now here he was at the Eboli mansion; the house was stirring and the cry went forth: "He is come! The Master is within the gates."

When he had given his horse to the waiting groom, he said: "Softly, I pray you all. This is an unofficial visit. I am passing on my way to Aragon and I but pause to pay a friendly call."

The servants understood. They knew of the relationship between their mistress and Don Ferdinand. They did not speak of it outside the household. They knew that it was the wish of Don Ferdinand that this should be kept secret, and that it could be dangerous to offend him.

He had stepped into the house.

"Your mistress?" he asked of two women who had immediately dropped deep curtsies.

"She had retired for the night, Highness. But already she has heard of your coming."

Ferdinand looked up and saw his mistress at the head of the staircase. Her long dark hair fell in disorder about her shoulders; she was wearing a velvet robe of a rich ruby colour draped round her naked body.

She was beautiful; and she was faithful. He saw the joy in her face and his senses leaped with delight as he bounded up the stairs and they embraced.

"So . . . you have come at last . . ."

"You know that I would have been here before this, could I have arranged it."

She laughed, and keeping her arms about his neck, she said: "You have changed. You have grown older."

"A fate," he reminded her, "which befalls us all."

"But you have done it so becomingly," she told him.

They realised that they were being watched, and she took his arm and led him into her bedchamber.

There was a question which he wanted to ask above all others. Shrewdly he did not ask it . . . not yet. Much as she doted on the child, she must not suspect that it was for his sake that he had come and not for hers.

In her bedchamber he parted the velvet gown and kissed her body. She stood as though her ecstasy transfixed her.

He inevitably compared her with Isabella. Any woman, he told himself, would seem like a courtesan compared with Isabella. Virtue emanated from his wife. It surprised him that a halo was not visible about her head. Everything she did was done as a dedicated act. Even the sexual act — and there was no doubt that she loved him passionately — appeared, even in its most ecstatic moments, to be performed for the purpose of begetting heirs for the crown.

Ferdinand made excuses to himself for his infidelity. No man could subsist on a diet of unadulterated Isabella. There must be others.

Yet now, as he made love to his mistress, his thoughts were wandering. He would ask the all-important question at precisely the right moment. He prided himself on his calmness. It had been the admiration of his father and mother. But they had admired everything about him — good and bad qualities. And there had been times when he had been unable to curb his impetuosity. They would become fewer as he grew older. He was fully aware of that.

10

Now, satiated, his mistress lay beside him. There was a well-satisfied smile on her lips as he laced his fingers in hers.

"You are superb!" whispered Ferdinand. And then, as though it were an afterthought: "And . . . how is the boy?"

"He is well, Ferdinand."

"Tell me, does he ever speak of me?"

"Every day he says to me: 'Mother, do you think that this day my father will come?'"

"And what do you say to that?"

"I tell him that his father is the most important man in Aragon, in Catalonia, in Castile, and it is only because he is such an important man that he has not time to visit us."

"And his reply?"

"He says that one day he will be an important man like his father."

Ferdinand laughed with pleasure. "He is sleeping now?" he said wistfully.

"Worn out by the day's exertions. He is a General now, Ferdinand. He has his armies. You should hear him shouting orders."

"I would I could do so," said Ferdinand. "I wonder . . ."

"You wish to see him. You cannot wait. I know it. Perhaps if we were very quiet we should not wake him. He is in the next room. I keep him near me. I am always afraid that something may happen to him if I let him stray too far from me."

"What could happen to him?" demanded Ferdinand suddenly fierce.

"Oh, it is nothing, merely the anxieties of a mother." She had risen and put her robe about her. "Come, we will take a peep at him while he sleeps."

She picked up a candlestick and beckoned to Ferdinand, who threw on a few clothes and followed her to a door which she opened quietly.

In a small cot a boy of about three years was sleeping. One plump hand gripped the bedclothes, and the hair which curled about the well-shaped head had a gleam of chestnut in its brown.

This was a very beautiful little boy, and Ferdinand felt an immense pride as he looked down on him.

He and Isabella had a daughter, but this was his son, his first-born son; and the chubby charm and the resemblance to himself filled Ferdinand with an emotion which was rare to him.

"How soundly he sleeps!" he whispered; and he could not resist stooping over the bed and placing his lips against that soft head.

In that moment an impulse came to him to pick up the sleeping child and to take him from his mother, to take him into Castile, to present him to Isabella and say to her: "This is my son, my first-born son. The sight of him fills me with joy, and I will have him brought up here at Court with any children you and I may have."

He could never do such a thing. He imagined Isabella's reactions; and one thing he had learned since his marriage was the necessity of respecting Isabella in all her queenly dignity.

What a foolish thought when what he had to do was prevent Isabella's ever hearing of this child's existence.

The little boy awakened suddenly. He stared up at the man and woman by his bedside. Then he knew who the man was. He leaped up and a pair of small hot arms were about Ferdinand's neck.

"And what is the meaning of this?" cried Ferdinand in mock anger.

"It means my father is come," said the child.

"Then who are you?" asked Ferdinand.

"I am Alonso of Aragon," was the answer, and spoken like a Prince. "And you are Ferdinand of Aragon." The boy put his face close to Ferdinand's and peered into it; with his forefinger he traced the line of Ferdinand's nose.

"I will tell you something," he said.

"Well, what will you tell me?"

"We are something else too."

"What is that?"

"You are my father. I am your boy."

Ferdinand crushed the child in his arms. "It is true," he said. "It is true."

"You are holding me too tightly."

"It is unforgivable," answered Ferdinand.

"I will show you how I am a soldier now," the boy told him.

"But it is night and you should be asleep."

"Not when my father has come."

"There is the morning."

The boy looked shrewd and at that moment was poignantly like Ferdinand. "Then he may be gone," he said.

Ferdinand's hand stroked the glossy hair.

"It is his sorrow that he is not with you often. But tonight I am here and we shall be together."

The boy's eyes were round with wonder. "All through the night," he said.

"Yes, and tomorrow you will sleep."

"Tomorrow I will sleep."

The boy leaped out of bed. He was pulling open a trunk. He wanted to show his toys to his father. And Ferdinand knelt by the trunk and listened to the boy's chatter while his mother looked on and ambition gleamed in her eyes.

After a while the boy said: "Now tell me a story, Father. Tell me of when you were a soldier. Tell me about battles . . . and fighting and killing."

Ferdinand laughed. He sat down and nursed the boy in his arms.

And Ferdinand began to tell a story of his adventures, but before he was halfway through his son was asleep.

Ferdinand laid him gently in his bed, then with the boy's mother he tiptoed out of the room.

She said with a sudden fierceness: "You may have legitimate sons, princes born to be kings, but you will never have a child whom you can love as you love that one."

"I fear you may be right," said Ferdinand.

The door between the two rooms was fast shut, and Ferdinand leaned against it, looking at his mistress in the candlelight; she was no less beautiful when her eyes shone with ambition for her son.

"You may forget the love you once had for me," she went on, "but you will never forget me as the mother of your son."

"No," answered Ferdinand, "I shall never forget either of you."

He drew her to him and kissed her.

She said: "In the morning you will have gone. When shall I see you again?"

"Soon I shall be passing this way."

"And you will come," she answered, "to see the boy?"

"To see you both." He feigned a passion he did not altogether feel, for his thoughts were still with the child. "Come," he said, "there is little time left to us."

She took his hand and kissed it. "You will do something for him, Ferdinand. You will look after him. You will give him estates . . . titles."

"You may trust me to look after our son."

He led her to the bed and deliberately turned his thoughts from the child to his passion for the mother.

Later she said: "The Queen of Castile might not wish our son to receive the honours which you as his father would be ready to bestow upon him."

"Have no fear," said Ferdinand a little harshly. "I shall bestow them nevertheless."

"But the Queen of Castile . . ."

A sudden anger against Isabella came to Ferdinand. Were they already talking in Catalonia about his subservience to his wife? The Queen's Consort! It was not an easy position for a proud man to find himself in.

"You do not imagine that I will allow anything or anyone to come between me and my wishes for the boy!" he exclaimed. "I will make a promise now. When the Archbishopric of Saragossa falls vacant it shall be bestowed upon him . . . for a beginning."

The Viscountess of Eboli lay back, her eyes closed; she was the satisfied mistress, the triumphant mother.

Early next morning, Ferdinand took a hurried leave of the Viscountess of Eboli and kissed their sleeping son; then he sent one of his attendants back to the inn to tell his men who had slept there that he had gone on ahead of them and that they should overtake him before he crossed the Segre and passed into Aragon.

And as he rode on with his few attendants he tried to forget the son from whom he must part, and concentrate on the task ahead of him.

He called one of his men to ride beside him.

"What have you heard of this Ximenes Gordo who, it seems, rules Saragossa?"

"That he is a man of great cunning, Highness, and, in spite of his many crimes, has won the support of the people."

Ferdinand was grave. "I am determined," he said, "to countenance no other rulers but my Father and myself in Saragossa. And if this man thinks to set himself against me, he will discover that he is foolish."

16

They rode on in silence and were shortly joined by the rest of the party. Ferdinand believed that none of them was aware of the visit he had paid to the Viscountess of Eboli. Yet, he thought, when it is necessary to bestow honours on the boy there will be speculation.

He felt angry. Why should he have to pay secret calls on a woman? Why should he demean himself by subterfuge? He had never been ashamed of his virility before his marriage. Was he — Ferdinand of Aragon — allowing himself to be overawed by Isabella of Castile?

It was an impossible situation; and Isabella was like no other woman he had ever known. It was strange that when they had first met he had been most struck by her gentleness.

Isabella had two qualities which were strange companions — gentleness and determination.

Ferdinand admonished himself. He was dwelling on domestic matters, on love and jealousy, when he should be giving all his thoughts to the situation in Saragossa, and the all-important task of raising funds for his father.

Ferdinand was welcomed at Saragossa by its most prominent citizen — Ximenes Gordo. It was Gordo who rode through the streets at the side of the heir to the crown. One would imagine, thought Ferdinand, that it was Ximenes Gordo who was their Prince, and Ferdinand his henchman.

Some men, young as Ferdinand was, might have expressed displeasure. Ferdinand did not; he nursed his resentment. He had noticed how the poor, who gathered in the streets to watch the procession, fixed their eyes admiringly on Gordo. The man had a magnetism, a strong personality; he was like a robber baron who held the people's respect because they both feared and admired him.

"The citizens know you well," said Ferdinand.

"Highness," was the bland answer, "they see me often. I am always with them."

"And I am often far away, of necessity," said Ferdinand.

"They rarely have the pleasure and honour of seeing their Prince. They must content themselves with his humble servant who does his best to see that justice is administered in the absence of his King and Prince."

"It would not appear that the administration is very successful," Ferdinand commented dryly.

"Why, Highness, these are lawless times."

Ferdinand glanced at the debauched and crafty face of the man who rode beside him; but still he did not betray the anger and disgust he felt.

"I come on an urgent errand from my father," he announced.

Gordo waited for Ferdinand to proceed — in a manner which seemed to the young Prince both royal and condescending. It was as though Gordo were implying: You may be the heir to Aragon, but during your absence I have become the King of Saragossa.

Still Ferdinand restrained his anger, and continued: "Your King needs men, arms and money — urgently."

Gordo put his head on one side in an insolent way. "The people of Saragossa will not tolerate further taxation, I fear."

Ferdinand's voice was silky. "Will not the people of Saragossa obey the command of their King?"

"There was recently a revolt in Catalonia, Highness. There might be a revolt in Saragossa."

"Here . . . in the heart of Aragon! The Aragonese are not Catalans. They would be loyal to their King. I know it."

"Your Highness has been long absent."

Ferdinand gazed at the people in the streets. Had they changed? he wondered. What happened when men such as Ximenes Gordo took charge and ruled a city? There had been too many wars, and how could kings govern their kingdoms wisely and well when they must spend so much time away from them in order to be sure of keeping them? Thus it was that scoundrels seized power, setting up their evil control over neglected cities.

"You must tell me what has been happening during my absence," said Ferdinand.

"It shall be my pleasure, Highness."

Ferdinand had been several days in the Palace of Saragossa, yet he had made no progress with his task. At every turn, it seemed, there were Ximenes Gordo and his friends to obstruct him.

They ruled the town, for Gordo had placed all his adherents in the important posts. All citizens who were possessed of wealth were being continually robbed by him; his power was immense, because wherever he went he was cheered by the great army of beggars. They had nothing to lose, and it delighted them to see the industrious townsfolk robbed of their possessions.

Ferdinand listened to all that his spies told him. He was astounded at the influence Gordo exercised in the town. He had heard of his growing power, but he had not believed it could be so great.

Gordo was not perturbed by the visit of the heir to the throne, so convinced was he of his own strength, and he believed that, if it came to a battle between them, he would win. His friends, who profited from his unscrupulous ways, would certainly not want a return to strict laws and justice. He had only to call to the rabble and the beggars to come to his aid and he would have a fierce mob to serve him.

Ferdinand said: "There is only one course open to me; I must arrest that man. I must show him and the citizens who is master here. Until he is imprisoned I cannot begin to raise the money my father needs, and there is no time for delay."

"Highness," he was told by his advisers, "if you arrest Gordo, the Palace will be stormed by the mob. Your own life might be in danger. The scum of Saragossa and his rascally friends stand behind him. We are powerless."

Ferdinand was silent; he dismissed his advisers, but his thoughts were not idle.

Gordo was with his family when the message arrived from the Prince.

He read it and cried: "Our haughty little Prince has changed his tune. He implores me to visit him at the Palace. He wishes to talk with me on an urgent matter. He has something to say to me which he wishes to say to no other."

Gordo threw back his head and laughed aloud.

"So he has come to heel, our little Ferdinand, eh! And so it should be. This young bantam! A boy! What more? They say that in Castile he is the one who wears the skirt. Well, as Dona Isabella can keep him in order in Castile, so can Ximenes Gordo in Saragossa."

He waved a gay farewell to his wife and children, called for his horse and rode off to the Palace.

The people in the streets called to him: "Good fortune, Don Ximenes Gordo! Long life to you!"

And he answered these greetings with a gracious inclination of the head. After all, he was King of Saragossa in all but name.

Arriving at the Palace he flung his reins to a waiting groom. The groom was one of the Palace servants, but he bowed low to Don Ximenes Gordo.

Gordo was flushed with pride as he entered the building. He should be the one who was living here. And why should he not do so?

Why should he not say to young Ferdinand: "I have decided to take up my residence here. You have a home in Castile, my Prince; why do you not go to it? Dona Isabella, Queen of Castile, will be happy to welcome her Consort. Why, my Prince, it may well be that there is a happier welcome awaiting you there in Castile than you find even here in Aragon."

And what pleasure to see the young bantam flinch, to know that he realised the truth of those words!

The servants bowed to him — he imagined they did so with the utmost obsequiousness. Oh, there was no doubt that Ferdinand was beaten, and realised who was the master.

Ferdinand was waiting for him in the presence chamber. He looked less humble than he had expected, but Gordo reminded himself that the young man was arrogant by nature and found it difficult to assume a humble mien. He must be taught. Gordo relished the thought of watching Ferdinand ride disconsolately out of Saragossa, defeated.

Gordo bowed, and Ferdinand said in a mild and, so it seemed, placating voice: "It was good of you to come so promptly at my request."

"I came because I have something to say to Your Highness."

"First," said Ferdinand, still mildly, "I shall beg you to listen to me."

Gordo appeared to consider this, but Ferdinand had taken his arm, in a most familiar manner, as though, thought Gordo, he accepted him as an equal. "Come," said Ferdinand, "it is more private in my ante-chamber, and we shall need privacy."

Ferdinand had opened a door and gently pushed Gordo before him into a room. The door had closed behind them before Gordo realised that they were not alone.

As he looked round that room Gordo's face turned pale; in those first seconds he could not believe that his eyes did not deceive him. The room had been converted into a place of execution. He saw the scaffolding, the rope and a masked man whom he knew to be the public hangman. Beside him stood a priest, and several guards were stationed about the room.

Ferdinand's manner had changed. His eyes glittered as he addressed Gordo in stern tones. "Don Ximenes Gordo, you have not long to make your peace, and you have many sins on your conscience."

Gordo, the bully, had suddenly lost all his swaggering arrogance.

"This cannot be . . ." he cried.

"It is to be," Ferdinand told him.

"That rope is for . . . for . . ."

"You have guessed right. It is for you."

"But to condemn me thus . . . without trial! Is this justice?"

"It is my justice," said Ferdinand coolly. "And in my father's absence I rule Aragon."

"I demand a trial."

"You would be better advised to concern yourself with the salvation of your soul. Your time is short."

"I will not submit . . ."

Ferdinand signed to the guards, two of whom came forward to seize Gordo.

"I beg of you . . . have mercy," he implored.

"Pleasant as it is to hear you beg," said Ferdinand, "there will be no mercy for you. You are to die, and that without delay. This is the reward for your crimes." Ferdinand signed to the priest. "He has urgent need of you and the time is passing."

"There have been occasions," said Gordo, "when I have served your father well."

"That was before you became puffed up by your arrogance," answered Ferdinand, "but it shall not be forgotten. Your wife and children shall receive my protection as reward for the service you once gave my father. Now, say your prayers or you will leave this earth with your manifold sins upon you."

Gordo had fallen to his knees; the priest knelt with him.

Ferdinand watched them.

And after an interval he signed to the hangman to do his work.

There was silence in the streets of Saragossa. The news was being circulated in the great houses and those haunts frequented by the rabble. There had been arrests, and those who had been seized were the more prominent of Gordo's supporters.

Then in the market-place the body of a man was hung that all might see what befell those who flouted the authority of the rulers of Aragon.

Gordo! It seemed incredible. There was the man who a few days before had been so sure of his ability to rule Saragossa. And now he was nothing but a rotting corpse.

The young Prince of Aragon rode through the streets of Saragossa; there were some who averted their eyes, but there were many to cheer him. They had been mistaken in him. They had thought him a young boy who could not even take first place in Castile. They had been mistaken. Whatever happened in Castile, he was, in the absence of his father, master of Aragon.

The volume of the cheers began to increase.

"Don Ferdinand for Aragon!"

Ferdinand began to believe that he would successfully complete the task which he had come to Saragossa to perform. He had been ruthless; he had ignored justice; but, he assured himself, the times were harsh and, when dealing with men such as Gordo, one could only attack with weapons similar to their own.

So far he had succeeded; and success was all that mattered.

The money so desperately needed was coming in, and if it was less than he and his father had hoped for that was due to the poverty of the people, not to their unwillingness to provide it.

Soon he would rejoin his father; and on the way he would call and see his little Alonso.

Messengers from Castile came riding into Saragossa. They had come in great haste, fearing that they might arrive to find Ferdinand had already left.

Ferdinand had them brought to him immediately.

He was thoughtful as he read what his wife had written. It was all the more effective because Isabella was by nature so calm.

She was asking him to return without delay. There was trouble about to break in Castile. An army was gathering to march against her, and many powerful nobles of Castile had gone over to the enemies' camp.

These men were insisting that she was not the rightful heir to the crown. It was true she was the late King Henry's half-sister, and he had no son. But he had a daughter — whom many believed to be illegitimate, and who was even known as La Beltraneja because her father was almost certainly Beltran de la Cueva, Duke of Albuquerque.

Those who had set themselves against Isabella now sought to place La Beltraneja on the throne of Castile.

There was a possibility that Portugal was giving support to their enemies.

Castile was in danger. Isabella was in danger. And at such a time she needed the military skill and experience of her husband.

"It may well be," wrote Isabella, "that my need of you at this time is greater than that of your father."

Ferdinand thought of her, kneeling at her *prie-Dieu* or with her advisers carefully weighing the situation. She would not have said that, had she not meant it with all her heart.

He shouted to his attendants.

"Prepare to leave Saragossa at once. I shall need messengers to go to my father and let him know that what he needs is on its way to him. As for myself and the rest of us, we must leave for Castile without delay."

CHAPTER
TWO

Isabella

Isabella, Queen of Castile, looked up from the table at which she sat writing. There was a quiet pleasure in her serene blue eyes, and those who knew her very well wondered if what they suspected was true. She had been, these last weeks, a little more placid than usual, and through that placidity shone a certain joy. The Queen of Castile could be keeping a secret to herself; and it might be one which she would wish to remain unknown until she could share it with her husband.

The ladies-in-waiting whispered together. "Do you think it can be true? Is the Queen pregnant?"

They put their heads together and made calculations. It was only a few weeks since Ferdinand had ridden away to join his father.

"Let us pray that it is true," said these ladies, "and that this time it will be a son."

Even as she dealt with the papers on her table, Isabella too was saying to herself: "This time let it be a son."

She was very happy.

That destiny for which she had been prepared was being fulfilled; she was married to Ferdinand after years of waiting, after continual hazards and fears that the marriage which had been planned in their childhood might not take place.

But, largely due to her own determination — and that of Ferdinand and his family — the marriage had taken place; and on the death of Ferdinand's father, when Ferdinand would be King of Aragon, the crowns of Aragon and Castile would be united; and, apart from that small province still occupied by the Moors, Isabella and Ferdinand could then be said to rule over Spain.

It was certainly the realisation of a dream.

And Ferdinand, her husband, a year younger than herself, handsome, virile, was all that she had hoped for in a husband — or almost. She had to admit that he did not accept with a very good grace the fact that she was Queen of Castile and he her Consort. But he would in time, for she had no intention of letting a rift grow between them. Theirs was to be a marriage, perfect in all respects. She was going to ask his advice in all matters; and if it should ever be necessary for her to make a decision with which he did not agree she would employ the utmost tact and try to persuade him in time to agree with her.

She smiled fondly.

Dear Ferdinand. He would hate this separation as much as she did. But it was his duty to go to his father's help when he was called upon to do so. And as her good confessor, Tomás de Torquemada, used to tell her — in those days when he had undertaken her religious instruction — no matter what the rank, duty came first.

Now she smiled, for her attendant was announcing that Cardinal Don Pedro Gonzalez de Mendoza was begging an audience.

She asked that he be brought to her without delay.

The Cardinal came to her and bowed low.

"Welcome," said Isabella. "You look disturbed, Cardinal. Is aught wrong?"

The Cardinal let his eyes rest on those of her attendants who remained in the apartment.

"I trust all is well with Your Highness. Then all will be well with me," he said. "Your Highness appears to be in excellent health."

"It is so," said Isabella.

She understood. Soon she would dismiss her attendants because she guessed that the Cardinal had something to say which could not be said before others; also he did not wish it to be known that his mission was one of great secrecy.

Isabella felt herself warming to this man, and she was surprised at herself.

He was Cardinal of Spain and, although he was the fourth son of the Marquis of Santillana, so talented was he, and to such a high position had he risen, that he was now at the head of the powerful Mendoza family.

To his Palace at Guadalaxara he could draw the most influential men in Spain, and there persuade them to act for or against the Queen.

These were dangerous times, and Isabella's great desire was to promote law and order in Castile. She had been brought up to believe that one day this duty might be hers; and she, with that conscientiousness which was a part of her nature, had determined to rule her country well. There was one condition which brought a country low and that was war. She wished with all her heart to be able to lead her country to peace; and she believed that she could do so through the support of men such as Cardinal Mendoza.

He was an exceptionally handsome man, gracious and charming. About forty years old, in spite of his association with the Church he had not lived the life of a churchman. He was too fond of the luxuries of life, and he deemed it unwise for a man to deny himself these.

Abstinence narrowed the mind and starved the soul, he had said. Hypocrisy was lying in wait for the man who denied his body the daily food it craved; and the man who indulged himself now and then was apt to be more lenient with other men; he would find a kindly tolerance growing within him to replace that fanaticism which could often find an outlet in cruelty.

Thus he soothed his conscience. He liked good food and wine, and he had several illegitimate children.

These sins, thought Isabella, sat lightly upon him. She deplored them, but there were times — and these would become more frequent — when she must compromise and suppress her natural abhorrence for the good of the country.

She knew that she needed this charming, tolerant and brilliant man on her side.

When they were alone, he said: "I have come to warn Your Highness. There is one who, while feigning to be your friend, is making plans to desert you for your enemies."

Isabella nodded slowly. "I think I know his name," she said.

Cardinal Mendoza took a step closer to her. "Alfonso Carillo, Archbishop of Toledo."

"It is hard to believe," Isabella spoke sadly. "I remember how he stood beside me. There was a time when I might have become the prisoner of my enemies. It would have meant not only incarceration but doubtless in time a dose of poison would have ended my life. But he was there to save me, and I feel I should not be alive, nor be where I am today but for the Archbishop of Toledo."

"Your Highness doubtless owes much to this man. But his object in helping you to the crown was that, although you wore it, he should rule through you."

"I know. Ambition is his great failing."

"Have a care, Highness. Watch this man. You should not share matters of great secrecy with him. Remember that he is wavering now. This time next week . . . perhaps tomorrow . . . he may be with your enemies."

"I will remember your words," Isabella assured him. "Now I pray you sit here with me and read these documents."

The Cardinal did so, and watching him, Isabella thought: Have I gained the support of this man, only to lose that of one who served me so well in the past?

Impatiently, Alfonso Carillo, Archbishop of Toledo waited.

It was intolerable, he told himself, that *he* should be kept waiting. It should be enough that the Queen knew he wished to see her for her to dismiss any other person that she might receive him.

"Ingratitude!" he murmured, as he paced up and down. "All that I have done in the past is forgotten. Since that young cockerel, Ferdinand, sought to show his power over me, he has poisoned her mind against me. And my place beside her has been taken by Mendoza."

His eyes narrowed. He was a man of choleric temper whose personality would have been more suited to the military camp than to the Church. But as Archbishop of Toledo he was Primate of Spain; he was determined to cling to his position; and although he prided himself on having raised Isabella to the throne, if she failed to recognise that the most important person in Castile was not its Queen, nor her Consort, nor Cardinal Mendoza, but Alfonso Carillo, he, who had helped her to reach the throne, would be prepared to dash her from it.

His eyes were flashing; he was ready for battle.

And so he waited; and, when at length he was told that the Queen was ready to receive him, he met Cardinal Mendoza coming from her apartments.

They acknowledged each other coolly.

"I have been waiting long," said the Archbishop reproachfully.

"I crave your pardon, but I had state matters to discuss with the Queen."

The Archbishop hurried on; it would be unseemly if two men of the Church indulged in violence; and he was feeling violent.

He went into the audience chamber.

Isabella's smile was apologetic.

"I regret," she said placatingly, "that you were forced to wait so long."

"I also regret," the Archbishop retorted curtly.

Isabella looked surprised, but the Archbishop considered himself especially privileged.

"The waiting is over, my lord. I pray you let us come to business."

"It would seem that Your Highness prefers to discuss state matters with Cardinal Mendoza."

"I am fortunate in having so many brilliant advisers."

"Highness, I have come to tell you that I can no longer serve you while you retain the services of the Cardinal."

"I suggest, my lord, that you go too far."

The Archbishop looked haughtily at this young woman. He could not help but see her as she had been when as a young Princess she asked for his help. He remembered how he had set up her young brother Alfonso as King of Castile while Henry IV still lived; he remembered how he had offered to make Isabella Queen on Alfonso's death, and how she had gently reminded him that it was not possible for her to be Queen while the true King, her half-brother Henry, still lived.

Had she forgotten what she owed to him?

"I pray," murmured the Archbishop, "that Your Highness will reconsider this matter."

"I should certainly not wish you to leave me," said Isabella.

"It is for Your Highness to choose."

"But I choose that you should remain and curb your animosity towards the Cardinal. If you will be the Cardinal's friend I am assured that he will be yours."

"Highness, it is long since I visited my estates at Alcalá de Henares. I may shortly be asking your permission to retire there from Court for a while."

Isabella smiled sweetly. She did not believe that the Archbishop would willingly go into retirement.

"You are too important to us for that to be allowed," she told him; and he appeared to be placated.

But the Archbishop was far from satisfied. Every day he saw Cardinal Mendoza being taken more and more into his mistress's confidence and, a few weeks after that interview with the Queen, he made an excuse to retire from Court.

He had, however, no intention of retiring to his estates. He had decided that, since Isabella refused to be his puppet, he must set up one in her place who would be.

He was well aware that there were certain men in Spain who were dissatisfied with the succession of Isabella and would be ready to give their allegiance to the young Princess Joanna La Beltraneja, who many preferred to believe was not illegitimate — for if she were the legitimate daughter of the late King, then she, not Isabella, should be Queen of Castile.

He called to his house certain men whom he knew to be ready to rebel. Among these was the Marquis of Villena, son of the great Marquis, the Archbishop's nephew who, before his death, had played as big a part in his country's politics as the Archbishop himself. The present Marquis might not be a brilliant intriguer like his father, but he was a great soldier, and as such thirsted for battle. He was very rich, this young Marquis, and because he owned vast estates in Toledo and Murcia he could raise support from these provinces.

There were also the Marquis of Cadiz and the Duke of Arevalo.

When these men were gathered together the Archbishop, making sure that they were not overheard, announced his plans to them.

"Isabella has assumed the crowns of Castile and Leon," he said, "but there appears to be some doubt throughout this land as to whether she has a right to them. There are many who would rejoice to see the Princess Joanna in her place."

There were murmurs of approval. None of these men had received great honours from Isabella and, if the young Princess Joanna were accepted as Queen of Castile, since she was only twelve years old, there would be a Regency and high places for many of them.

Eyes glittered, and hands curled about sword hilts. A Regency would be a very desirable state of affairs.

"I strongly suspect these efforts to declare the Princess Joanna illegitimate," stated the Archbishop; and nobody reminded him that not very long ago he was one of the most fiery advocates of Joanna's illegitimacy and Isabella's right to the throne.

The circumstances had changed. Ferdinand had sought to curb his power; Isabella had transferred her interest to Cardinal Mendoza. Therefore the Archbishop had decided to change his mind.

"My lord Archbishop," said Villena, "I pray you tell us what plans you have for dethroning Isabella and setting up Joanna in her place."

"There is only one way of bringing this about, my friend," replied the Archbishop, "and that is with the sword."

"It would be necessary to raise an army," suggested Arevalo. "Is that possible?"

"It must be possible," said the Archbishop. "We cannot allow a usurper to retain the throne."

He smiled at the assembly. "I know what you are thinking, my friends. Isabella has won the allegiance of many. Ferdinand is related to many Castilian families. It might be difficult to raise an army, you are thinking. Yet we will do it. And I have other plans. They concern the Princess Joanna. Do not forget that young lady has her part to play in our schemes."

"I cannot see the young Princess riding into battle," said Villena.

"You take me too literally, my dear Marquis," answered the Archbishop. "You cannot believe that I would have brought you here unless I had something to put before you. The Princess will be the bait we have to offer. Then I think we can draw powerful forces into the field. I propose to dispatch an embassy immediately. My friends, let us put our heads close together and lower our voices, for even here there may be spies. I will now acquaint you with my plans. They concern Portugal."

Many of those present began to smile. They could see whither the Archbishop's plans were leading.

They nodded.

How fortunate, they were thinking, that the Archbishop was on their side. How careless of Isabella to have lost his friendship, when such a loss could lead to a much greater one: that of the throne of Castile.

Alfonso V of Portugal had listened with great interest to the proposals which had been brought to him from the secret faction of Castile, headed by the Archbishop of Toledo.

He discussed this matter with his son, Prince John.

"Why, Father," said the Prince, "I can see that naught but good would come of this."

"It will mean taking war into Castile, my son. Have you considered that?"

"You have been successful in your battles with the Barbary Moors. Why should you not be equally so in Castile?"

"Have you considered the forces which could be put into the field against us?"

"Yes, and I have thought of the prize."

Alfonso smiled at his son. John was ambitious and greedy for the good of Portugal. If they succeeded, Castile and Portugal would be as one. There might be a possibility of the Iberian Peninsula's eventually coming under one ruler — and that ruler would be of the House of Portugal.

It was a tempting offer.

There was something else which made Alfonso smile.

There had been a time when he had thought to marry Isabella. His sister, Joanna, had married Isabella's half-brother, Henry IV of Castile. Joanna was flighty. He had often warned her about that. It was all very well for a queen, married to a husband like Henry, to take an occasional lover, but she should have made sure that there was no scandal until long after the birth of the heir to the throne. Joanna had been careless, and, as a result, his little niece — another Joanna — was reputed to be the daughter, not of Henry the King, but of Beltran de la Cueva, Duke of Albuquerque; and so strong was this belief that young Joanna had been dubbed "La Beltraneja", and the name still clung to her. And because Joanna had been declared illegitimate, Isabella was now Queen of Castile. But that state of affairs might not continue; and if he decided to go to war it should not prevail.

He had been very angry with Isabella. He recalled how he had gone to Castile to become betrothed to her, and she had firmly refused him.

It was an insult. On one occasion she had declared her unwillingness to accept him as a suitor and had sought the help of the Cortes in averting the marriage. It was too humiliating for a King of Portugal to endure.

Therefore it would be a great pleasure to turn Isabella from the throne and set the crown on the head of his little niece.

John was smiling at him now. "Think, Father," he said. "When little Joanna is Queen of Castile and your bride, you will be master of Castile."

"She is my niece."

"What of that! The Holy Father will readily give the dispensation; especially when he sees that we can put a strong army in the field."

"And but twelve years old!" added Alfonso.

"It is unlike a bridegroom to complain of the youth of his bride."

Alfonso said: "Let us put this matter before the Council. If they are in agreement, then we will give our answer to the Archbishop of Toledo and his friends."

"And if," said John, "they should be so misguided as to ignore the advantages of such a situation, it must be our duty, Father, to insist on their accepting our decision."

Little Joanna was bewildered. From her earliest childhood she had known there was something strange about herself. Sometimes she was called Highness, sometimes Infanta, sometimes Princess. She was never quite sure what her rank was.

Her father had been kind to her when they met, but he was dead now; and she had not seen her mother for a long time when the call came for her to go to Madrid.

When her father had died she had heard that her aunt Isabella had been proclaimed Queen of Castile; and Isabella had said that she, Joanna, was to have her own household and an entourage worthy of a Princess of Castile. Isabella was kind, she knew; and she would be good to her as long as she did not allow anyone to say that she was the King's legitimate daughter.

But how could a girl of twelve prevent people from saying what they wished to say?

Joanna lived in fear that one day important men would come to her, disturbing her quiet existence among her books and music; she was terrified that they would kneel at her feet, swear allegiance and tell her that they were going to serve her with their lives.

She did not want that and all it implied. She wanted to live in peace, away from these awe-inspiring men.

And now she was on her way to Madrid because her mother had sent for her.

She had heard many stories of her mother. She was very beautiful, it was said; and when she first came into Castile to be the wife of the King, although her manner had been frivolous by Castilian standards, no one had guessed that she would be responsible for one of the greatest and most dangerous controversies which had ever disturbed the succession of Castile.

And she, the Princess Joanna, was at the very heart of that controversy. It was an alarming thought.

She had often met the man who was reputed to be her father. He was tall and very handsome; a man of great importance and a brave soldier. But he was not

40

her mother's husband, and therein lay the root of the trouble.

When she saw her mother on this occasion she would ask her to tell her sincerely the truth; and if Beltran de la Cueva, Duke of Albuquerque, was indeed her father she would make this widely known and in future refuse to allow anyone to insist on her right to the throne.

It was a big undertaking for a twelve-year-old girl, and Joanna feared that she was not bold or very determined; but there must be some understanding if she were ever to live in peace.

And, now that she was going to her mother's establishment in Madrid, she trembled to think what she might discover there. She had heard whispers and rumours from her servants of the life her mother led in Madrid. When she had left the King she had kept a lavishly extravagant house where, it was said, parties of a scandalous nature frequently took place.

Joanna had several brothers and sisters, she believed. They, however, were more fortunate than she was. They shared the stigma of illegitimacy, but nobody could suggest that they had even a remote claim to the throne.

She was alarmed to contemplate what sort of house this was to which she was going; and as she, with her little company, rode along the valley of the Manzanares the plain which stretched about them seemed gloomy and full of foreboding. She turned her horse away from the distant Sierras towards the town, and as they entered it they were met by a party of riders.

The man at the head of this party rode up to Joanna and, bowing his head, told her that he had been watchful for her coming.

"I am to take you to the Queen, your mother, Princess," he told her. "She has gone to a convent in Madrid, and it would be advisable for you to join her there with all speed."

"My mother . . . in a convent!" cried Joanna; for it was the last place in which she would expect to find her gay and frivolous mother.

"She thought it wise to rest there awhile," was the answer. "You will find her changed."

"Why has my mother gone to this convent?" she asked.

"She will explain to you when you see her," was the answer.

They rode into the town, and eventually they reached the convent. Here Joanna was received with great respect by the Mother Superior, who immediately said: "You are fatigued, Princess, but it would be well if you came to see the Queen without delay."

"Take me to her, I pray you," said Joanna.

The Mother Superior led the way up a cold stone staircase to a cell, which contained little more than a bed and a crucifix on the wall; and here lay Joanna, Princess of Portugal, Queen to the late Henry IV of Castile.

Joanna knelt by her mother's bed, and the older Joanna smiled wanly. Kneeling there, the Princess knew that it was the approach of death which had driven her mother to repentance.

* * *

Joanna sat by her mother's bed.

"So you see," said the Dowager Queen of Castile, "I have not long to live. Who would have thought that I should follow Henry so soon?"

"Oh, my mother, if you live quietly, if you rest here, you may recover and live for many more years."

"No, my child. It is not possible. I am exhausted. I am worn out. I have lived my life fully, recklessly. Now the price is demanded for such a life. I am repentant, yet I fear that if I were young again, if I felt life stirring within me, I should find the temptation which beckoned me irresistible."

"You are too young to die, Mother."

"Yet my life has been full. I have had lovers . . . my child . . . so many lovers that I cannot recall a half of them. It was an exciting life . . . a life of pleasure. But now it ebbs away."

"Mother, Castile has paid dearly for your pleasure."

Over the Dowager Queen's face there spread a smile of amusement and mischief.

"I shall never be forgotten. I, the wayward Queen, had a hand in shaping the future of Castile, did I not?"

Young Joanna shivered.

"Mother, there is a question I must ask you. It is important that I know the truth. So much depends on it."

"I know what is on your mind, my child. You ask yourself the same question which all Castile asks. Who is your father? It is the most important question in Castile."

"It is the answer that is important," said Joanna softly. "I would know, Mother. If I am not the King's daughter, I think I should like to go into a convent like this and be quiet for a very long time."

"A convent life! That is no life at all!"

"Mother, I beg of you, tell me."

"If I told you that Henry was your father what would you do?"

"There is only one thing I could do, Mother. I should be the rightful Queen of Castile, and it would be my duty to take the throne."

"What of Isabella?"

"She would have no alternative but to relinquish the throne."

"And do you think she would? You do not know Isabella, nor Ferdinand . . . nor all those men who are determined to uphold her."

"Mother, tell me the truth."

The Dowager Queen smiled. "I am weak," she said. "I will tell you later if I can. Yet, how could even I be sure? Sometimes I think you are like the King; sometimes you remind me of Beltran. Beltran was a handsome man, daughter. The handsomest at Court. And Henry . . . Oh, it seems so long ago. I look back into mists, my child. I cannot remember. I am so tired now. Sit still awhile and I will try to think. Give me your hand, Joanna. Later it will come back to me. Who . . . who is my Joanna's father. Was it Henry? Was it Beltran?"

Joanna knelt by the bedside and her eyes were imploring. "I must know, Mother. I must know."

But the Dowager Queen had closed her eyes, and her lips murmured: "Henry, was it you? You, Beltran, was it you?"

Then she slipped into sleep; her face was so white and still that Joanna thought she was already dead.

The Dowager Queen of Castile had been laid in her tomb and Joanna remained in the convent. The bells were tolling and as she listened to their dismal notes she thought: I shall never know the answer now.

The peace of the convent seemed to close in around her, sheltering her from the outside world in which a mighty storm was rising; it was a storm which she could not escape. It was for this reason that the peace of the convent seemed doubly entrancing.

Each morning she thought to herself: Will this be the last day that I am allowed to *enjoy* this peace?

And as the weeks passed she began to wonder whether she had been unnecessarily anxious. Isabella had been proclaimed in many towns of Castile as Queen. The people admired Isabella; she, with Ferdinand, was so suited to become their Queen. Perhaps the people of Castile did not wish for trouble any more than she did. Perhaps they would now be content to forget that Joanna, wife of Henry IV of Castile, had had a daughter who might or might not be the King's.

One day two noblemen came riding to the convent. They came on a secret mission and they wished for an audience with the Princess Joanna.

As soon as they were brought to her and announced themselves as the Duke of Arevalo and the Marquis of Villena she knew that this was the end of her peace.

They bowed low and humbly.

"We have great news for you, Princess," they told her; and her heart sank, for she knew the purport of this news before they told her. She interpreted the ambitious glitter in their eyes.

"Princess," said Arevalo, "we have come to tell you that you are not forgotten."

She lowered her eyes lest they should read in them that it was her dearest wish to be forgotten.

"This is news to set Your Highness's heart soaring with hope," went on Villena. "There is a powerful force behind us, and we shall succeed in turning the impostor Isabella from the throne and setting you up in her place."

"There is great news from Portugal," added Arevalo.

"From Portugal?" Joanna asked.

"The King of Portugal, Alfonso V, asks your hand in marriage."

"My . . . mother's brother!"

"Have no fear. His Holiness will not withhold a dispensation if we can show him that we have the means to oust Isabella from the throne."

"But my uncle is an old man . . ."

"He is the King of Portugal, Highness. Moreover, he has an army to put into the field. We cannot fail with Portugal behind us. Highness, we shall succeed, and in succeeding we shall bring you a crown and a husband."

Joanna felt unable to reply. She was struck dumb with horror. That ageing man, her uncle, as a husband! War . . . with herself as the reason for it!

She turned to these men, about to protest, but she did not speak, because, when she looked at their hard ambitious faces, she knew that it was useless. She knew her personal feelings were of no account. She was to be the figurehead, the symbol, and they would declare that they fought for her sake.

For my sake, she thought bitterly. To give me a throne which I do not want. To give me for a husband an ageing man who terrifies me!

Isabella was frowning over documents which were spread on a table before her in her private apartments in the Madrid Alcazar.

These documents told a desperate story, for to study them was to learn how ill-equipped for battle were the armies of Castile.

It seemed to her that, should there be a rising in Castile, she would not have more than about five hundred horse to attempt to quell it; and she was not even sure on which towns she could rely.

The Archbishop of Toledo had retired to his estates in Alcalá de Henares and she was not sure how far he was ready to go in order to betray her. The loss of his friendship wounded her deeply; and the practical side of her nature deplored it even more. In those stormy days which had preceded the death of her brother she had come to learn something of the resourcefulness of this man; and that at such a critical time he had ceased to be her friend hurt her. That he might become her active enemy horrified her.

War was what she dreaded more than anything. She needed long years of peace that she might restore order to Castile. She had taken over a bankrupt kingdom rent by anarchy, and she was determined to make it rich and law-abiding. Yet if at this stage she were plunged into war, how would she fare?

She had so little at her disposal. Her good friend Andres de Cabrera, who, in the Alcazar at Segovia, had charge of the treasury, had warned her that the royal coffers were almost empty. No war could be waged without men and equipment; and now it seemed that reckless men in her kingdom were ready to plunge Castile into war.

She needed strong men about her at this time; and most of all she needed Ferdinand.

Then even as she sat looking at these depressing figures, she heard the clattering of horses' hoofs below; she heard the shouts of voices raised in welcome and, forgetting her dignity, she leaped from her chair and ran to the window.

She stood there, clutching the hangings to steady herself, for the sight of Ferdinand after a long absence never failed to move her deeply. There he was, jaunty and full of vigour, coming to her as she had known he would, the moment he received her call for help.

She loved him so much, this husband of hers, that at times she was afraid of her own emotions, afraid that they would betray her into an indiscretion which would be unworthy of the Queen of Castile.

In a short time he was standing before her; and those attendants who knew something of the depth of her feelings for this man retired without orders, that Isabella might be alone with her husband.

At such times Isabella laid aside the dignity of queenship. She ran to Ferdinand and put her arms about him; and Ferdinand, never more delighted than at these displays of affection, embraced her with passion.

"I knew you would come without delay," she cried.

"As always when you needed me."

"We need each other at this time, Ferdinand," she told him quickly. "Castile is threatened."

He accepted the implication that the affairs of Castile concerned him as much as her.

"My love," he said, "joyous as I am to be with you, before we give ourselves to the pleasure of reunion we must explore this desperate situation in which we find ourselves."

"You have heard?" Isabella asked. "There are rumours that Villena and Arevalo are rebelling in favour of La Beltraneja, and that they are gathering partisans throughout Castile."

"That child!" cried Ferdinand. "The people will never accept her."

"It will depend on what forces our enemies can muster, Ferdinand. Our treasury is depleted; I have discovered that we have no more than five hundred horse which we could put into the field."

"We must raise more men; we must find the means to fight these rebels. We shall do it, Isabella. Have no fear of that."

"I knew you would say that. Yes, Ferdinand, we shall do it. Oh, how glad I am that you have come. With you beside me, what seemed an insuperable task becomes possible."

"You need me, Isabella," said Ferdinand fiercely. "You need me."

"Have I ever denied it?" She was aware of a sudden fear within her. Was he going to demand once more that he be accepted in Castile on equal terms with herself? This was not the time for dissension between them. "Ferdinand," she said quickly, "I have news for you. I am with child."

She watched the frown change to a smile on Ferdinand's face.

"Why, Isabella, my Queen! That is great news. When will our son be born?"

"It is too early yet to say. But I am sure I am with child. I hope that by the time this child is born our troubles will be over and we shall have prevented this threatened rebellion from taking place."

Ferdinand had taken her hands in his; he bent swiftly to kiss them. When he was in Isabella's presence he could not help but admire her.

"Come," he said, "let us examine our position. What men could be put into the field?"

She answered: "I have been studying these matters." She led him to the table. "Ferdinand, my husband, I pray you examine these figures and tell me what, in your opinion, is best to be done."

She knew that Ferdinand was alert to the danger; that he would allow no friction to arise between them while it existed. She had been right to believe she could rely on him. There was not a man in Spain who was more suited to stand beside her in this fight for the crown. And if, on occasions, his desire for supremacy over her sullied their relationship, making it a little bitter, how could it be otherwise where a man as strong, as entirely masculine as Ferdinand was concerned.

While they worked a messenger arrived at the Alcazar. He came from the King of Portugal.

As soon as Isabella knew that he was in the Palace she had him brought to her. Ferdinand stood beside her and, as the man bowed and held out the dispatches, he lifted a hand to take them. But Isabella, who had anticipated this move, was anxious to take them as unobtrusively as possible — for she knew that with regard to this matter of supremacy she dared not give way even in the smallest matters. She took them before it was evident to any others that Ferdinand had attempted to do so.

She dismissed the messenger and glanced at the papers.

Then she lifted her eyes to Ferdinand's face.

"He asks us to resign our crowns," she said, "that the Princess Joanna may ascend the throne."

"He must be an imbecile," retorted Ferdinand.

Isabella turned to the table on which the documents were still spread out.

"I am informed," she said, "that he could put five thousand six hundred horse and fourteen thousand foot into the field. Perhaps he would say that we were imbeciles to oppose him."

Ferdinand's eyes glittered. "Yet we *shall* oppose him, and we shall defeat him. You know that, Isabella."

"I do know it, Ferdinand."

"We have our daughter to fight for and our unborn son."

"And we have each other," she added, and smiled brilliantly. "I know, Ferdinand, that while we are together we cannot fail. And we must be together, Ferdinand, always. You feel that, as I do. Where is Isabella without Ferdinand? No matter what should befall, we shall always stand together."

"You speak truth," said Ferdinand, and his voice was gruff with emotion.

"And together we shall be invincible," she went on.

Then solemnly they embraced. Isabella was the first to withdraw.

"And now," she said, "to business. We shall ignore these demands; but we must decide how we, with the few resources at our disposal, can defeat the might of Portugal."

In spite of the ceremonial robes in which her women had dressed her, Joanna looked what she was, a child of barely thirteen.

There was an expression of mingled resignation and despair on her face. She was to be affianced to a man who was thirty years older than herself, and the prospect terrified her. But this was even more than a distasteful marriage; it was a prelude to war.

Her women had chattered as they prepared her for this important ceremony.

"Why, Alfonso is the bravest of kings. They say he is called the African because of his exploits against the Moors of Barbary. He is a great soldier."

"He must be quite an old man," said Joanna.

"No, Princess, it is you who are so young. You will not think of his age. He is the King of Portugal and he comes here to make you his Queen."

"And to make himself King of Castile."

"Well, only because he will make you Queen."

"I do not wish . . ."

But what was the use of stating her wishes? Joanna had lived through so many conflicts that she had long realised the futility of words.

Her friends were imploring her to enjoy her prospects. A king was coming to claim her hand. She should be joyful, they told her; because they did not understand.

And when she was robed and made ready she was taken to meet the man who had come to this town of Placencia for the purpose of the betrothal, and to take Castile from Isabella and Ferdinand and bestow it upon herself.

All about the Palace were encamped the armies of her future husband, so that she could not be unaware of his might.

And when she stood before him and lifted her eyes to his eager ones, she saw a man in his forties; and that seemed to her very old. She was trembling, but she smiled and greeted him as though with pleasure. All the time she was aware of those two men who had determined to set her on the throne — the Duke of Arevalo and the Marquis of Villena.

Alfonso took her hand and led her to two ornate chairs which had been set side by side. As they took their seats he said: "My dear Princess, you must not be afraid of me."

"I am so young for marriage," Joanna answered.

"Youth is a blessing, compared with which the experience which comes with age is but a small compensation. Do not deplore your youth, my dear one, for I do not."

"Thank you, Highness," she whispered.

"You look uneasy. Do you so fear me?"

"We are very closely related. You are my mother's brother."

"Have no fear, my dear. A messenger is being dispatched to the Pope. He will send us a dispensation without delay."

She could not endure his inquiring tender gaze, and she feigned relief.

Alfonso felt happy. He was a man who must for ever pursue some cause, and he preferred it to be a romantic one. He had had great success against the Moors, but fighting the Moors was a commonplace occupation in the Iberian Peninsula. Now here was a young girl — his own niece — in need of a champion. To some she was the rightful heiress to the throne; to others the late Queen's bastard. Her cause appealed to him because she was young and he, a widower, could make her his bride. This was the most romantic cause in which he had ever fought, and it delighted him — particularly as victory could bring such benefit to him.

He was not a man to bear a grudge, but he could not forget his meeting with the proud Isabella, who had shown so openly her distaste for marriage with him — King though he was.

It was not unpleasant therefore to contemplate the discomfiture of the haughty Isabella when she found herself ousted from the throne by the man whom once she had so recklessly refused.

He was smiling as he took Joanna's hand, and those assembled, led by Villena and Arevalo, proceeded to declare Alfonso and Joanna Sovereigns of Castile.

As soon as the dispensation from the Pope arrived they would be married. Joanna prayed that the dispensation might be delayed.

In the meantime, the betrothal was celebrated, and on this and all occasions she must sit side by side with Alfonso and accept his tender attentions.

After some days Alfonso and his army, Joanna travelling with them, left Placencia for Arevalo.

Being aware of the sad state of the Castilian armies and that Isabella and Ferdinand had inherited a bankrupt state, Alfonso anticipated a victory which would be easy to complete.

At Arevalo he paused in his journey, and it seemed as though he halted there to prepare himself for the attack.

★ ★ ★

Isabella and Ferdinand were together when news was brought to them of Alfonso's arrival at Placencia and of his betrothal to Joanna.

Ferdinand received the news gloomily. "This means he is prepared to risk his armies in her cause," he said.

"She is his niece," cried Isabella, "and but a child."

"What cares he for either fact! He thinks she will bring him Castile and, if he is successful, depend upon it the Pope will not long deny him the dispensation he needs."

"*If* he is successful. He shall not be successful! I promise you that."

"Isabella, what do you know of war? And how can we prevent him?"

"I know," she said, her eyes flashing, "that I was born to be Queen of Castile."

"Well, you have had your brief glory."

"I have done nothing of what I intend to do. I know I shall succeed."

Ferdinand took her gently by the arm and led her to a table on which a map was spread.

He pointed to South Castile. "Here," he said, "the friends of Alfonso are waiting. They are numerous and they have men and arms at their disposal. Arevalo, Villena, Cadiz . . . they are his men. They will give all they have to drive us from the throne and set up Joanna and Alfonso. He has only to turn south tomorrow and there traitors will be ready for him. Town after town will freely give itself into his hands. And we . . . we shall find ourselves unable to attack, for on his march through Castile he will grow richer and richer as important towns pass into his possession."

"Ferdinand," Isabella reproved him, "I do not understand you. Have we not *our* friends?"

"There are waverers."

"Then they shall cease to be waverers."

"They will cease to be when they see the might of Alfonso's army!"

"They must be converted to our cause."

"But who shall convert them?"

"I shall. I . . . their Queen."

Ferdinand looked at her with mild surprise; there were times when he felt that even now he did not know Isabella. She seemed so dedicated to her cause, so certain of her ability to fight and win in this unequal struggle, that Ferdinand believed her.

It was at times like this that he forgave her for insisting on her supremacy, when he was glad that he had not returned to Aragon in a fit of pique because she had been determined to be supreme in Castile.

"You forget, Isabella," he said gently, "you are in no fit state to conduct a campaign. You have our unborn son to think of."

"It is because of our unborn son that I must be doubly sure that none shall rob me of the throne," she told him.

Isabella had lived through many hazards, but she felt that never had she faced danger so great as that which threatened during the months that followed. The days were full and she worked far into the night. She spent a great deal of time at prayer, for she was sure that she had previously been granted Divine protection and that it would be afforded her again.

Yet, even while she prayed, she never forgot that if she were to win heavenly aid she must neglect nothing of which her human strength was capable.

She would sit during the night receiving from and sending messages to the pitiably few troops she possessed. That was not all. She had decided that she herself must visit those towns which, she feared, were waiting to see which was the stronger party before bestowing their allegiance.

She set out on a tour of these towns. Riding was difficult; the roads were rough and the hours she was forced to spend in the saddle were very irksome, as with each passing week her pregnancy became more apparent.

It was impossible for the townsfolk to see Isabella and listen to her without being deeply affected. Isabella was inspired; she believed in her destiny; she knew she could not fail, and she conveyed this certainty to many of those whom she had come to rally to her standard.

Ferdinand was with her army endeavouring to prepare it for the attack, which, for some strange reason, Alfonso was hesitating to make. Each day both Ferdinand and Isabella expected to hear that Alfonso was on the march; they dreaded to hear that news.

"Give us a few more weeks," prayed Isabella. "Then we shall not be so vulnerable."

"A month . . . two months of preparation," declared Ferdinand to his generals, "and, if the Queen continues to rally men to our cause as she has begun to do, I think we shall give a very good account of ourselves and soon send Alfonso marching back across the frontier. But we need those weeks ... we need them desperately."

So while they worked they watched anxiously for Alfonso to move; yet he remained at Arevalo awaiting, he said, the arrival of his Castilian supporters, so that when he attacked there should be one decisive battle.

"How could such a man have scored such successes against the Moors?" wondered Ferdinand. "He must be in his dotage. Castile lies open to him now — and he hesitates. If he will but hesitate a few weeks longer we have as good a chance as he has of winning this war."

And as Isabella neared Toledo on her journey through the kingdom she thought of that old ally, Alfonso Carillo, Archbishop of Toledo, without whose support she could never have attained the throne.

She believed that if she could meet him, if she could reason with him, she would win him back to her cause; and if the Archbishop were on her side she would have secured the most important man in Spain as her ally. It was difficult to believe that a man of his intelligence could desert her out of pique, yet first he had resented Ferdinand, and then Cardinal Mendoza. She had not realised that, although he was capable of great valour and possessed political skill, he could also be capable of petty jealousy.

She called to one of her servants and said to him: "We are near Alcalá de Henares, and the Archbishop of Toledo is in residence there. Go to him and tell him that I propose calling at his palace, as I wish to talk with him."

When her messenger returned from his visit to the Archbishop he came almost shamefacedly into Isabella's presence.

"What news?" she asked. "You saw the Archbishop?"

"Yes, Highness. I saw the Archbishop."

"I pray you do not hesitate," said Isabella gently. "Come, what is his answer?"

"The Archbishop replied, Highness, that even though Your Highness wishes to see him, he does not wish to see you; and if you should enter his palace by one door he will go out by another."

Isabella's expression scarcely changed.

"I see that it was a fruitless errand. But perhaps not entirely so. We have discovered an enemy where we thought to have a friend. You have my leave to retire."

When she was alone she went to a chair and sat down heavily. She felt sick through her pregnancy and with fear for the future. Had the Archbishop believed she had the slightest chance of beating Alfonso he would never have dared send her such a message. Quite clearly he believed her to be on the brink of defeat.

She felt the child move within her, and with her awareness of this other life she longed to go to her bed and stay there, to give up this weary pilgrimage through her kingdom, to trust in God and her destiny and to be able to say to herself: If I lose the Kingdom of Castile I shall then be merely Queen of Aragon, and I shall devote myself to my husband, the child we already have and the children which will surely be ours. That would be so easy; and the churlish conduct of one who had once been so firm an ally filled her with such despair that she wanted nothing so much as the peace of her own apartments.

But there were dispatches to be sent off to Ferdinand, telling him of her progress; there were more towns to be visited.

There was one important factor. Others would know of the rebuff she had received from the Archbishop; she must wear an even bolder face; she must be even more certain of success.

She ignored the stirring life within her, the great desire for rest.

Never for one moment must she forget her destiny, nor the fact that only if she were worthy to wear the crown of Castile could she hope for Divine favour.

Isabella was reading a dispatch from Ferdinand.

"The position has changed for the better, thanks to your efforts. I now have at my disposal four thousand men-at-arms, eight thousand light horse and thirty thousand foot. We lack equipment, and many of these men know little of soldiering, but my confidence grows daily. And should Alfonso attack us now he will find he has missed the great chance which was his two months ago."

Isabella looked up and smiled.

They had worked a miracle. They had found men ready to fight for them; and if these men were as yet inexperienced that would be remedied. She had Ferdinand as the commander of her army, and

Ferdinand was experienced in war; he was young and Alfonso was old. Ferdinand would win.

Isabella's smile became tender.

Her great friend, Beatriz de Bobadilla, wife of Andres de Cabrera, believed that she idealised Ferdinand, that she saw him as a god among men.

It was not entirely true nowadays. The years of marriage had changed that. Yet when he had first come to Castile she had thought him wonderful. She loved him no less; but she was aware of the vanity, the arrogance, the signs of cupidity which were all part of Ferdinand's character. She did not forget the sulkiness he had displayed when he had realised that, for all her love, she was not prepared to give him control of Castilian affairs. Yet these faults made her the more tender, even as did those of her young daughter Isabella. And if Ferdinand at times had the faults of a boy, he had also the attributes of a man. She trusted his generalship; she knew she could rely on him to fight her cause — perhaps because it was also his own — more than she could rely on any other man in the kingdom. But the disaffection of the Archbishop of Toledo had made her realise how unwise she would be to put complete trust in anyone.

She rose from her table, and as she did so her body was racked with a pain so violent that she could not repress a cry.

One of her women who had been in the apartment came hurrying to her side.

"Highness . . ." The woman gasped at the pallor of Isabella's face, and caught her in her arms, for she believed the Queen was on the point of fainting. She called to others, and in a few seconds Isabella was surrounded by her women.

She put out a hand to steady herself against the table. She knew the violent pain was coming again.

"Help me . . ." she murmured. "Help me to my bed. I fear my time has come . . . and it is so soon . . . too soon."

So it was over.

There would be no child. Isabella felt limp and defeated. Should she have considered the child? If she had done so there would not be that army under Ferdinand's generalship; Castile would lie open to the invader.

And because it had been necessary to rally men to her cause — and only she, the Queen, could do it — she had lost her child, the son she and Ferdinand were to have made the heir to Castile and Aragon.

She felt bitter.

It was time they had more children; but what chance had they of being parents while they lived this troubled life.

She lay thinking of the journeyings over rough roads, the jolting, the uncomfortable nights often spent in humble beds in roadside inns.

And so . . . she had lost her child. But in doing so she had formed an army.

She smiled briefly.

There would be other children. Once this weary matter of La Beltraneja's right to the throne was settled, she and Ferdinand would be together always; they would have many children.

She dozed a little, and when her women came to see how she fared she was smiling peacefully. She murmured a little in her sleep, and when one of the women stooped to hear what she said she heard not the lament for the lost child but the words: "Eight thousand light horse."

CHAPTER
THREE

The Prince Of The Asturias

Isabella came riding to the Alcazar of Segovia.

More than a year had passed since she had lost her child and raised men and arms to fight the invading Alfonso. It had been an arduous period.

Yet Isabella had quickly recovered from her miscarriage; indeed, many said that it was her spirit which had proved the best doctor. There had been no time during that dark period to lie abed and woo back her health; Isabella had very soon to be on horseback, riding through her kingdom, calling a Cortes at Medina del Campo and by her eloquence moving all so deeply that she had raised the money she so badly needed.

That had been after the disasters at Toro and Zamora, which had both fallen to Alfonso, and when, had Alfonso been wise, he would have thrown in his full force against the inferior Castilian army of Ferdinand and Isabella.

But Alfonso had been timid; he had hesitated again, even when the Archbishop of Toledo, considering Alfonso's gains at Toro and Zamora to be decisive, not only openly allied himself with the King of Portugal but took with him five hundred lancers to join his new friend in the fight against his old one.

But now the Castilian army had been vastly improved and was ready to do battle with the enemy; and on her journeys through her kingdom Isabella gave herself up to the pleasure of a short respite where she would enjoy the hospitality of her dearest friend.

When the news was brought to Beatriz de Bobadilla that the Queen was in the Alcazar she hurried to greet Isabella, and the two women embraced without formality.

"This makes me very happy," said Beatriz emotionally. "I would I had known I might expect the honour."

"There would then have been no surprise." Isabella smiled.

"But think of the anticipation I have missed!"

"Beatriz, it is wonderful to see you. I would like to be alone with you as we used to be in the past."

"I will have food and wine sent to us, and we will take it in my small private chamber. I long to hear what has been happening to you."

"Pray lead me to that small private chamber," said Isabella.

Beatriz laid her hand on the Queen's arm as they went together to the small room of which Beatriz had spoken.

"I pray Your Highness sit down," said Beatriz. "Soon we shall be served, and then . . . we will talk in comfort." Beatriz called: "Food and wine, for the Queen and myself . . . with all speed."

Isabella, smiling, watched her. "You have not changed at all," she said. "They all hold you in great awe, I'll swear."

"Why should they not? They are my servants," said Beatriz, falling into the familiarity which had often existed between them.

"And your husband, Andres too — do you still command him?"

Beatriz laughed. "Andres obeys me, he says, because he values peace and it is the only way to get it. And Ferdinand? He is well?"

"He is very well, Beatriz. What should I do without him?"

Beatriz looked at the Queen, her head on one side, a smile playing about her mouth. So, thought Beatriz, she continues to adore that man. But not completely. Beatriz knew that Ferdinand had been disappointed not to have taken full authority from Isabella. Beatriz applauded the Queen's resistance.

"He fights for his kingdom as well as yours," said Beatrix, "for although you are Queen of Castile, he is your Consort."

"He has been magnificent. Beatriz, I do not believe there has ever been a soldier in Spain to compare with Ferdinand."

Beatriz laughed aloud; then her servants appeared with refreshments and her manner changed. Now the utmost respect must be paid to the Queen, and Beatriz dropped the easy familiar manner.

But when they were alone again Beatriz said: "Isabella, you are looking a little tired. I hope you are

67

going to stay here for some time that I may look after you, as I used to in the old days when we were together."

"Ah, those old days," sighed Isabella. "I was not a queen then."

"But we had some anxious times, nevertheless." Beatriz smiled reminiscently. "At least we do not have to worry that you will be snatched from Ferdinand and given to some husband who would be unacceptable to you!"

"Thank God for that. Oh, Beatriz, I am a little worried about this battle that must soon take place."

"But you put your trust in Ferdinand."

"I do, indeed I do. But there are mighty forces against us."

"Ferdinand will succeed," said Beatriz. "He is a good soldier."

Beatriz was thoughtful for a few seconds. A better soldier than a husband, she was thinking; and he will be determined to succeed. He will not allow himself to be driven from Castile.

"I was very sad," went on Beatriz, "when I heard that you had lost your child."

"It seems long ago."

"But a bitter blow."

"As the loss of a child must be. But there was no time to brood. It was all-important that we should get an army together; and we did it, Beatriz, even though it may well be due to that that the child was lost."

"It might have killed you," said Beatriz gruffly.

"But I am strong, Beatriz; have you not yet learned that? Moreover, I am destined to be Queen of Castile."

"You *are* Queen of Castile."

"I have never really reigned yet. Since my accession there has been this trouble. Once it is settled I shall be able to do for Castile what I always longed to do."

"Castile will prosper when you are firmly on the throne, Isabella."

Isabella's eyes were shining with purpose. She looked full of vitality at such times, thought Beatriz; it was rarely that those outside her intimate circle saw her so unreserved.

"First," she was saying, "I shall abolish this disastrous anarchy. I shall bring law and order back to Castile. Then, when I have a law-abiding country, I shall do all in my power to make good Christians of my subjects. You remember Tomás de Torquemada, Beatriz?"

Beatriz grimaced. "Who could forget him?"

"You were harsh with him, Beatriz."

"He was too harsh with us all, including himself."

"He is a good man, Beatriz."

"I doubt it not. But I cannot forgive him for trying to suppress our laughter. He thought laughter was sinful."

"It was because he realised how necessary it was for me to avoid frivolous ways. I remember that one day, after confession, he made me promise that if ever it were in my power I would convert my kingdom to the true faith."

"Let us hope that in converting them you will not make them as lean and wretched looking as friend Tomás."

"Well, Beatriz, there is another task of mine when all is at peace. I will endeavour to free every inch of Spanish soil from Moslem rule; I will raise the flag of Christ over every Alcazar, over every town in Spain."

"I am sure you will do it," said Beatriz, "but only if you have some little regard for your health. Stay with me a while, dear Isabella. Give me the pleasure of looking after you myself. Please. I beg of you."

"How I should enjoy that!" said Isabella. "But there is work to do. I have stolen these few short hours from my duty because I was in the neighbourhood of Segovia and could not resist the joy of seeing you. But tomorrow I must be on my way."

"I shall do my utmost to persuade you to stay."

But Isabella was not to be persuaded; the next day she set out for Tordesillas.

The battlefield was between Toro and Zamora, along the banks of the glittering Douro. The armies were now equally matched; Alfonso was old compared with Ferdinand, but his son, Prince John, had joined him and was in command of the cavalry.

Ferdinand, surveying the enemy, determined to succeed or die in the attempt. Alfonso lacked Ferdinand's zeal; it was characteristic of him to tire quickly of the causes for which he had originally been so enthusiastic. He had been long in Castile, and his presence was needed in his own country; his men were restive; they too had been a long time away from home. Alfonso had intended to make speedy war in Castile, drive Isabella, whom he called the usurper, from the throne and put his betrothed Joanna in her place. But the affair had been long drawn out; and already he was tiring of it. His son John was enthusiastic, but John had not much experience of war; and Alfonso longed for the end of this day's battle.

Ferdinand, riding between the Admiral of Castile and the Duke of Alva, cried aloud: "St James and St Lazarus!" which was the old cry of Castile; and those Castilians in the Portuguese ranks who heard it, trembled. It was as though Ferdinand were reminding them that they were traitors.

There was one riding furiously towards the enemy, who cared not for the old cry of Castile. The Archbishop of Toledo enjoyed battle, and he was determined to exploit this opportunity to the full.

The battle had begun, and furiously it raged; it was as though every soldier in those armies knew what depended upon its issue.

Ferdinand shouted to his men. They must fight. In the name of Isabella, they must fight. Their future and the future of their Queen, the future of Castile, depended on them.

There were many who remembered the Queen; they thought of the pregnant woman who had endured great discomfort to come to them that she might move them with her eloquence, that she might remind them of their duty to Castile. They remembered that these men who fought against them were their old enemies, the

Portuguese, and those Castilians who had seen fit to fight against their own Queen.

Lances were shattered, and swords were drawn; and men grappled hand to hand with one another in the melee.

And Ferdinand's heart leaped with joy, for he knew that the outcome of this day's battle would be victory for him.

But there were a few men in the Portuguese Army who were determined that it should not be so. Edward de Almeyda, the Portuguese flag bearer, was an example to all. He had snatched the Portuguese Emblem from Castilian soldiers who were about to trample it in the dust and, with a shout of triumph, held it aloft, a sign to all Portuguese that the day was not lost for Alfonso.

But even as he rode away a Castilian soldier had lifted his sword and cut off the right arm which held the flag. But as it would have fallen, Almeyda, ignoring the loss of his right arm, had caught it in his left hand.

"Joanna and Alfonso!" he shouted as swords hacked at the arm which now held the flag aloft.

With both arms shattered and bleeding he managed to transfer the standard to his mouth; and he was seen riding among his defeated fellow countrymen, armless, the standard in his mouth, for some minutes before he was unhorsed.

Even such heroism could not save the day. Prince John was missing. Alfonso had also disappeared.

Ferdinand found himself master of the field.

★ ★ ★

In the castle of Castro Nufio, some miles from the battlefield, the young Joanna waited in apprehension. She knew that this battle would prove decisive, and she believed that her affianced husband would be the victor.

Then all hope of a peaceful existence for her would be over. She did not believe that Isabella would ever quietly stand aside and allow her to take the throne.

What would happen to her if Isabella's armies were victorious she could not imagine; all she knew was that neither solution could bring her much joy; and she greatly wished that she could have been allowed to stay in the Madrid convent, living a life which was governed by bells.

All day she had waited for news. She had placed herself at a window in the fortified castle where she could command a good view of the surrounding country.

Soon, she knew, a rider would appear, perhaps several; she would know then whether the result of the conflict was defeat or victory for Alfonso.

It was almost dusk when her vigil was rewarded, and she saw a party of riders coming towards the castle. She stood alert, her eyes strained, and as they came nearer she recognised the leader of the party. It was Alfonso, and with him were four of his men.

She knew what this must mean; for Alfonso did not come riding to Castro Nuno as a victor; it was obvious from his demeanour that he came as a fugitive.

She hurried down, calling as she went: "The King is riding to the castle. He will be here in a few minutes."

From all over the castle men and women came hurrying into the hall, and Joanna was in the courtyard when Alfonso and his party rode in.

Poor Alfonso! Indeed, he looked an old man today. He was dishevelled and dirty, his face grey; and for the first time she felt tender towards him.

He leaped from his horse and threw the reins to a groom, crying: "The army is routed. We must leave almost immediately for Portugal."

"I am to go to Portugal?" stammered Joanna.

Alfonso put a hand on her shoulder. His eyes were suddenly alight with that quixotic expression which was not unendearing.

"Do not despair," he said. "It is a defeat. A temporary defeat. I will win your kingdom for you yet."

Then he took her hand and they went into the castle.

A few hours later, when Alfonso and his party had refreshed themselves, they left Castro Nuno and rode westward over the border into Portugal; and Joanna went with them.

Isabella was at Tordesillas when the news was brought to her. Ferdinand triumphant! The King of Portugal and his son John in flight! Through great endeavour and fervent prayer she had overcome yet another ordeal which in the beginning had seemed impassable.

Never before had Isabella been so sure of her destiny as now.

At the Convent of Santa Clara she gave thanks to God for this further proof of His favour. There in that beautiful building which had once been the palace of a king's mistress she remained in her cell, on her knees, while she reminded herself that she owed this victory to the intervention of God. The atmosphere of the Convent of Santa Clara suited her mood. She, the triumphant Queen of Castile, was prostrated in humility, in that beautiful building with its Moorish baths which had once been the delight of Dona Maria de Padilla, who herself had delighted Pedro the Cruel; these walls, which must once have been the scene of voluptuous entertainments, now enclosed the refuge of silent-footed nuns.

Isabella wanted all to know that the victory was due to Divine guidance. All her subjects must understand that she was now the undoubted ruler of Castile.

The next day, in a loose and simple gown, her feet bare, Isabella led a procession to the Church of St Paul, where, in the greatest humility, she gave thanks to God for this victory which could leave no doubt that she, and she alone, was Queen of Castile.

Although the battle which had been fought between Toro and Zamora was decisive, it did not bring complete peace to Castile.

Louis XI of France, who had come to the aid of Alfonso, was still giving trouble, and Ferdinand could not disband his army; and when Isabella studied the effect of the war, following on the disastrous reigns of her half-brother and her father, she knew that her task had hardly begun.

It was September before she was able to spend a few days in Ferdinand's company.

She was in residence at the Madrid Alcazar and, when messengers brought her news that he was on the way, she set her cooks to prepare a banquet worthy of the victor.

Isabella was not by nature extravagant and she knew that Ferdinand was not. How could they be when they considered the state of the exchequer; when they had had to work so hard to get together the means to fight their enemies? But although Isabella was cautious in spending money, she knew that there were times when she must put aside that caution.

Those about her must understand the importance of this victory. They must not whisper among themselves that the Queen of Castile and her Consort were a parsimonious pair who did not know how to live like royalty.

This would be the first real celebration she and Ferdinand together had had since the Battle of Toro, and everyone must be aware of its importance.

Ferdinand came riding in triumph to the Alcazar, and Isabella was waiting to receive him.

As she stood, surrounded by her ministers and attendants, and Ferdinand came towards her, her heart beat faster at the sight of him. He had aged a little; the lines were more deeply marked on his face; that alertness of his eyes was accentuated. But even in those first few seconds the rivalry was there between them. Ferdinand in battle was the supreme leader. Here in the Alcazar he was merely the Queen's Consort. He had to adjust himself, and the adjustment was somewhat distasteful.

He took Isabella's hand, bowed over it and put his lips against it.

"Welcome, my husband," she said, and her voice had lost its habitual calm. "Welcome, my dearest husband."

The heralds blew a few triumphant notes on their *trompas* and the drummers beat their *baldosas*.

Then Isabella laid Ferdinand's hand on her arm, and this was the signal for them to enter the castle.

There was feasting and music, and Isabella was happier than she had been for a very long time.

Ferdinand did not leave her side during the banquet and the ball which followed, and she believed that he had such an affection for her that he ceased to fret because in Castile she was supreme.

Isabella almost wished that she were not a queen on that night, and that she and Ferdinand could have retired in peace from their guests and spent an hour or so with their little seven-year-old Isabella.

When the ball was at last over and they had retired to their apartments she reminded him that it was eight years almost to the month since they had married.

"It is difficult to believe it is so long," said Isabella, "for in that eight years we have seen far too little of each other."

"When the kingdom is at peace," Ferdinand answered, "there will not be these separations."

"I shall be so much happier then. Oh, Ferdinand, what should I have done without you? You have brought victory to Castile."

"It is only my duty," he said. She saw the faintly sullen lines beginning to form about his mouth, and she went swiftly to him and put an arm about his shoulders.

"We have a great task before us, Ferdinand," she said, "but I thank God that we are together."

He was a little mollified. "Now it is our task to deal with the French," he told her.

"You think it will be difficult, Ferdinand?"

"No, I do not think so. Louis has his hands full with the trouble between himself and Burgundy, and now that we have driven Alfonso back where he belongs he'll have little heart for this fight."

"Soon, then, we shall have peace, and then, Ferdinand, begins our real task."

"I have news for you. Arevalo has made advances. I think he is prepared to forget the claims of Joanna and offer his allegiance to you."

"That is excellent news."

"It shows which way the wind blows, eh?"

"And the Archbishop of Toledo?"

"He will follow doubtless."

"Then victory will indeed be ours."

Ferdinand seized her hands and drew her to her feet. She was comely; she was a woman; and here in the bedchamber he was no longer merely the Consort of the Queen.

"Have we not fought for it, sacrificed for it?" he demanded. "Why, Isabella, you might have lost your life. You were very ill when you lost our child."

"It is a great grief to me . . . a continual grief. Yet our crown depended on the army I could raise."

"And all these months," went on Ferdinand, "I have scarcely seen you." He drew her towards him. "We are young, eh, Isabella. We are husband and wife. The quickest way to forget our sorrow is to have a son who will replace the child we lost. We have won a great victory, Isabella, and this should not be beyond our powers."

Then he laughed and lifted her in his arms. That cold dignity dropped from her as though it were a cloak which he had loosened. And there was Isabella, warm, loving, eager.

It was during Ferdinand's stay at the Madrid Alcazar that their son was conceived.

From his residence at Alcalá de Henares, Alfonso de Carillo, the Archbishop of Toledo, grimly reviewed the situation.

King Alfonso had fled with Joanna into Portugal. There were victories all over Castile for Ferdinand. Many of the Archbishop's possessions had already passed into the hands of Ferdinand, and very soon he himself would do so.

Ferdinand would have no mercy on him. Was this the end, then, of an exciting and glorious career?

His only hope lay with the Queen, and Isabella, after all, was the ruler of Castile.

He would write to her reminding her of all she owed him. It was true that he had boasted of having raised her up and that he would cast her down. He had been wrong. He had not understood the force of her character. He had believed her to be steadfast and firm in her determination to support what she believed to be right. So she was. But she was shrewd also; or was it that her belief in her destiny was so strong that she forced others to share that belief even against their will?

The Archbishop of Toledo, statesman and soldier, was forced to admit that he had been foolish in allying himself with the wrong side.

Now he must humble himself. So he wrote to Isabella offering her his allegiance. He reminded her of all that he had done for her in the past. He asked pardon for his folly and arrogance.

Ferdinand, who was with Isabella when this plea arrived, laughed scornfully. "This is the man who, when you were risking your life to ride about the country pleading for funds, took five hundred lances and rode at the head of them to serve our enemy. He must think we are fools."

Isabella was thinking of that occasion when she had called at his palace and the Archbishop had said that if she entered by one door he would go out at the other. It was hard to forget such an insult. It was also hard to forget that occasion when she had been threatened with capture at Madrigal, and the Archbishop of Toledo had come galloping to her rescue.

She smiled. He was a fiery old man, whose dignity must be preserved at all costs. And he had been piqued by her reliance on Ferdinand and Cardinal Mendoza.

"We should not be too harsh with the old Archbishop," mused Isabella.

Ferdinand looked at her in amazement.

"Public execution should be his lot."

"Once he was my very good friend," she reminded him.

"He was also our very bad enemy. It will be good for the people to see what happens to those who work against us."

Isabella shook her head. "I should never agree to the execution of the Archbishop," she said.

"You are a sentimental woman."

"That may be, but I cannot forget all he once did for me."

Ferdinand snapped his fingers. "There was a time, Isabella, when defeat stared us in the face. If Alfonso had been a better general we should not be rulers of Castile at this moment. Fugitives we should be. Or you might. I should doubtless have died on the field of battle."

"Do not speak of it," said Isabella.

"Then I pray you be reasonable. This man is dangerous."

"This man is old and broken in spirit."

"Such as he is never accept age; their spirit is unbreakable."

"I would rather have him my friend than my enemy."

"Then send him where he can be neither."

"I could not do that, Ferdinand."

"Nevertheless . . ."

Gently she interrupted: "I *shall* not do it, Ferdinand."

She watched the slow flush spread over Ferdinand's face. He clenched his hands and said between his teeth:

"I intrude. I had forgotten. *You* are the Queen. I ask Your Highness's permission to retire."

With that he bowed and left her.

It was not the first of such scenes. Isabella sighed. She feared it would not be the last. But she was right — she knew she was right.

She must rule Castile with that dignity and calm of which she — and so few others — was capable. Anger and resentment could never go hand in hand with justice.

The Archbishop had been her bitter enemy, she knew; but he had also been her friend.

She had decided how he should be dealt with. He should buy his pardon. He was rich, and the royal exchequer was low. He should remain in exile at Alcalá de Henares for the rest of his life.

He would be saddened, of course, by his exile from Court. But he was ageing, and he would find plenty to occupy him at Alcalá de Henares. He was an alchemist of some ability, and he would turn his immense energy into that field for the years that were left to him.

Isabella wrote the order which decided the future of the Archbishop of Toledo, and when she had dispatched it she sat silent for a few moments, and a sad wistful smile touched her mouth.

She was thinking of Ferdinand.

Isabella was riding towards Arevalo. Beside her was her friend Beatriz de Bobadilla and a few of her attendants.

It was early spring, and soon Isabella would be too heavy to trust herself on horseback.

Beatriz would stay with her until after the confinement. Isabella turned to smile at her friend. Beatriz had declared her intention of resuming her old position with the Queen as chief maid of honour until the baby had been born; she was going to see that no undue exertion threatened the life of this one. And Beatrix was a forceful woman. Once she had stated her intention, Andres, her husband, must allow her to leave him; and Isabella, her Queen, must be ready to receive her.

"Your Highness is amused?" asked Beatriz.

"Only by your determination to look after me."

"Indeed I will look after you," said Beatriz. "And who better than one who loves you as I do?"

"I know, Beatriz. You are good, and it gives me great pleasure to have you with me. I am sorry though for poor Andres."

"Do not be. He has his work to do. Mayhap he is glad of a little respite from my tongue. This journey is too much for Your Highness."

"You tried hard to dissuade me from making it," said Isabella. "But I fear that in the next few weeks I shall feel still less inclined to do so."

"After this you must rest more frequently."

There was a frown between Beatriz's well-marked brows. She knew Isabella as well as anyone knew her; she was aware of that firm spirit behind the serene facade. She knew that she could only appear to persuade Isabella when the Queen had made up her own mind. That was why she had ceased to rail against this journey to Arevalo, once she realised that Isabella was quite determined to make it.

But Beatriz was not only worried by the effect this journey might have on Isabella; she was wondering how much the Queen would have to suffer during her stay at the castle of Arevalo.

Beatriz had made up her mind that their stay there should be as brief as she could make it.

Isabella turned to her friend. "I always feel deeply moved when I come to Arevalo," she said. "There are so many memories."

"Perhaps we should have delayed the journey until after the child is born."

"No, it is long since I have seen my mother. She may be growing anxious. It is very bad for her to be anxious."

"I would rather she was anxious because you were absent than that I and Ferdinand, and all who love you, should be because of your state of health."

"You fret too much, Beatriz. It is all in the hands of God."

"Who would have as little patience with us now as He had last time," retorted Beatriz.

"Beatriz, you blaspheme."

Isabella was really shocked, and Beatriz seeing the horror in the Queen's face, hastened to apologise.

"You see, Highness," she murmured, "I am as I always was. I speak without thinking."

A gentle smile crossed Isabella's face. "It is on account of your care for me, I know. But I would hear no more of the hazards of this journey and your disapproval of our visit to my mother."

"I see I have offended Your Highness, and crave pardon."

"Not offended, Beatriz, but please say no more."

It was an order and, as they rode on to Arevalo, Beatriz was silent for a while; and Isabella's thoughts went back to the day when she, with her mother and young brother, had hurried away from her half-brother's Court to live for so many years in obscurity in the castle of Arevalo.

Isabella knelt before the woman in the chair. This was her mother, also Isabella, Queen-widow of King John II of Castile.

And as Isabella knelt there she felt an urge to weep, for she remembered so well those days when she had watched her mother's face for a sign of the madness which could be terrifying to a small daughter.

The long thin fingers stroked her hair and the woman said: "Who is this who has come to see me?"

"It is Isabella."

"I am Isabella."

"It is that other Isabella, Highness. Your daughter."

"My daughter Isabella." The blank expression lifted and the eyes became more bright. "My little child, Isabella. Where is your brother, Isabella? Where is Alfonso?"

"He is dead, Mother," answered Isabella.

"One day he could be King of Castile. One day he shall be King of Castile."

Isabella shook her head and the tears stung her eyes.

The old Queen put her face close to her daughter's, but she did not seem to see her. She said in a husky whisper: "I must take them away while there is time. One day Alfonso could be King of Castile. And if aught should happen to him, my little Isabella would be Queen."

Isabella took the trembling fingers and laid her lips against them.

"Mother, so much time has passed. I am your Isabella and *I am* Queen of Castile. That makes you happy, does it not? Is it not what you always wanted?"

The old Queen rose in her chair, and Isabella stood up and quickly put her arms about her.

"Queen . . ." she murmured. "Queen of Castile?"

"Yes, Mother. I . . . your little Isabella. But little no longer. Mother, I am married to Ferdinand. It was the match we always wanted, was it not? And we have a daughter . . . yet another Isabella. A sweet and lively child. And, Mother, there is another soon to be born."

"Queen of Castile . . ." repeated the old Queen.

"She stands before you now, Mother, your own daughter."

There was a smile about the twitching lips. She had understood and she was happy.

How glad I am that I came, thought Isabella. She will be at peace now. She will remember.

"Come, Mother," she said, "let us sit down. Let us sit side by side, and I will tell you that the war is over and there is no more danger to my crown. I will tell you how happy I am with my kingdom, with my husband and my family."

She led her mother to her chair, and they sat side by side. They held hands while Isabella talked and the old woman nodded and from time to time said: "Isabella . . . my little daughter, Queen of Castile."

"So now, Mother, you know," said Isabella. "There is no need for you to be sad any more. As often as I can I will come to Arevalo and we will talk together. You can be happy now, Mother."

The old Queen nodded.

"I shall rest here for a few days," said Isabella, "then I shall go. I do not wish to stay too long at this time because of my condition. You understand, Mother?"

Old Isabella went on nodding her head.

Isabella put her lips to her mother's forehead. "While I am here we shall be together often. That makes me happy. Now I shall go to my apartment and rest awhile. It is necessary, you see, because of the child."

The old Queen put out a hand suddenly. She whispered: "Have a care."

"I will take great care," Isabella assured her.

"*He* will never get a child," said her mother. "It is the life he has led." She laughed suddenly. It was an echo of that wild laughter which had once terrified the young Isabella when she had first become aware of the taint of insanity in her mother. "He will try to foist the Queen's child on the people, but they'll not have it. No, they'll not have it."

She was talking of her stepson, King Henry IV, who had been dead for some years. She still at times lived in the past.

She gripped Isabella's hand. "I must keep the children away from him. A pillow over their mouths . . . that is what it would be. Poison mixed with their food. I do not trust them . . . neither Henry nor his Queen. They are evil . . . evil, and I have my babies to protect. My little Alfonso could be King of Castile . . . my little Isabella could be Queen."

So all that she had said had left only a momentary impression on that poor dazed mind.

Isabella felt the sobs about to choke her as she took a hurried leave of her mother.

She lay on her bed, and slowly the tears ran down her cheeks. This was weakness. She, the Queen of Castile, to be in tears! No one must see her thus.

It was so tragic. That poor woman, who cared so much, who had planned for her children, whose unbalanced state had no doubt been aggravated by her anxieties for them, might now see one of her dearest dreams realised; but her poor mind could not grasp the truth.

"Poor sad Highness!" murmured Isabella. "Dearest Mother! Is there any sickness worse than that of the mind?"

Beatriz had come into the apartment.

"I did not send for you," said Isabella.

But Beatriz had thrown herself on her knees beside the bed.

"Highness, you are unhappy. When you are so, if I could comfort you in the smallest measure, nothing would keep me from you."

Beatriz had seen the tears; it was no use hiding the distress. Isabella put out a hand, and Beatriz took it.

"It makes me weep; it is so sad," said Isabella.

"It is not wise that you should upset yourself."

"You were right, I think, Beatriz. I should not have come. There is no good I can do her. Or is there? I fancy she was pleased to see me."

"The little good you may do her by your visit might mean a lot of harm to your health."

"I have been thinking about the child, Beatriz. I am a little upset this day, because my thoughts are melancholy."

"There is nothing to fear. You are healthy. The miscarriage was due to your exertions. There will be no more miscarriages."

"It was not a miscarriage that I feared, Beatriz."

"You feared for your own health. But you are strong, Highness. You are young. You will bear many children yet."

"It was seeing *her*, Beatriz. How did she become like that? Why was she born with a mind that could plunge into darkness? I can tell you the answer, my dear friend. It is because others in her family have suffered so."

"What are you thinking?" cried Beatriz aghast.

"That she is my mother . . . even as I am the mother of this life which stirs within me now."

"These are morbid thoughts. It is bad for a pregnant woman to harbour such."

"It is a sudden fear grown up within me, Beatriz, like an evil weed in a plot of beautiful flowers. There were

89

others before her who were afflicted thus. Beatriz, I think of my child."

"It is folly. Forgive me, Highness, but I must say what I think. The Princess Isabella is a beautiful child, her mind is lively and quick. This darkness has come to your mother because of the sad life she led. It has nothing to do with her blood."

"Is that so, Beatriz? Do you believe it?"

"Indeed I do," lied Beatriz. "I will tell you something else. It will be a boy. I know it from the way you carry it."

"A boy, Beatriz. It is what Ferdinand wants. Do you know he would like our heir to be a boy? He thinks that sovereigns should be male."

"We ourselves have seen Castile under two kings, and we are not greatly impressed by masculine rule. Now we have a Queen, and I'll warrant that in a very short time Castile will have good reason to be thankful for that."

"Perhaps," said Isabella, "I should appoint you as my Primate."

"Nay," said Beatriz, "I would prefer to be the power behind the throne. Do you think we could leave tomorrow?"

"Our stay has been so short."

"Isabella, my dearest mistress, she does not know who you are nor why you are here. Let us leave tomorrow. It would be better for you . . . and the child."

"I believe you are right," said Isabella. "What good can we do by staying here? But when my child is born

I shall come again and see her . . . I shall come often. There are times when her mind clears a little. Then she understands and is happy to see me."

"She is as happy here as she could be. You are her very dutiful daughter. It is enough, Isabella, that she is cared for. You must think of the child."

Isabella nodded slowly.

She *was* thinking of the child. A new dread had come into her life. She believed that it would always be haunted by a shadow.

She would think often of those wild fits of laughter which used to overtake her mother; she would think of the poor dazed mind, lost in a half-world of darkness; and in the future she would watch her children, wondering and fearful. Her mother had brought the seeds of insanity from Portugal. It was possible that they had taken root and would break into hideous flower in the generations to come.

Meanwhile Alfonso of Portugal had not been idle. No sooner had he returned to his country in the company of the young Joanna than he was eager to make another attempt to win for her and himself the crown of Castile, for although he had tired of the old campaign, he was very eager to begin a new one.

He discussed this with his son John.

"Are we to allow the crown of Castile to slip from our grasp?" he demanded. "What of our young Joanna — this lady in distress? Is she to be deprived of what is hers by right?"

"What do you propose to do, Father? We have lost the best of our army in Castile. We are not equipped to go to war again."

"We should need help," Alfonso agreed. "But we have our old ally. Louis will help us."

"At the moment he is deeply involved with Burgundy."

Alfonso's eyes were glittering with a new purpose.

"He will help if our ambassadors can persuade him of the justice of our cause."

"And the profit our success might bring to him," added John cynically.

"Well, Louis will see that there is profit in it for himself."

"Whom shall we send into France? You had someone in mind?"

Alfonso was restless. His desire for adventure did not leave him with advancing years. He wished to enjoy his youthful bride, but he could not marry a girl — however young, however charming — who might be illegitimate and have no claim to a crown whatsoever. There was only one way in which he could deal with this matter. He must set a crown on his little Joanna's head. Then he would marry her; then Castile would be under the sway of Portugal.

He could not bear to wait for what he wanted. He must be on the move all the time.

He thought of the long journey into France, of his ambassadors trying to set the case before Louis, whose mind would be on the threatened war with Burgundy.

There was only one man in Portugal, he felt sure, who could explain to Louis what great good could come to France and Portugal through an invasion of Castile and the setting up of Joanna in place of Isabella.

He looked as eager as a boy as he turned to John. "I myself will go to Louis," he said.

It was a triumphal progress which Alfonso made through France with the retinue of two hundred which he had taken with him.

Louis XI had given the order: "The King of Portugal is my friend. Honour him wherever he should go."

Thus the people of France gave a warm welcome to this friend of their King's, and those in the country villages threw flowers at his feet and cried "Long life" to him as he went on his way.

Louis himself, seeming so honest in his shabby fustian doublet and battered old hat, in which he wore a leaden image of the Virgin, took Alfonso in his arms and kissed him on both cheeks before a large assembly, to assure all those who did not know Louis of his friendship and esteem for his ally.

There was a meeting between the two kings, when they sat opposite each other in the council chamber surrounded by their ministers and advisers. Louis was as affable as ever, but his friendly words were couched in cautious phrases and he did not offer that which Alfonso had come to France to obtain.

"My dear friend and brother," said Louis, "you see me here in a most unhappy state — my kingdom plunged in war, my resources strained to their limit in this conflict with Burgundy."

"But my brother of France is master of great resources."

"Great!" The eyes of the King of France flashed with fire rarely seen in them. Then he smiled a little sadly, stroking his fustian doublet as though to call attention to his simple and shabby garments that the King of Portugal might compare them with his own finery. He shook his head. "Wars deplete our treasury, brother. I could not burden my poor people with more taxes than they already suffer. Nay, when I have brought this trouble with Burgundy to an end . . . then . . . why then I should be most happy to come to your help, that together we may defeat the usurper Isabella and set the rightful heiress on the throne of Castile. Until then . . ." Louis lifted his hands and allowed a helpless expression to creep over his cunning features.

"Wars have a way of dragging on," said Alfonso desperately.

"But until this conflict has been brought to a satisfactory conclusion you will stay in my kingdom as my guest . . . my very honoured guest."

Louis had leaned forward in his chair, and certain of the Portuguese retinue shivered with distaste. Louis reminded them of a great spider in his drab garments, his pale face brightened only by those shrewd, alert eyes.

"And it may well be," went on the King of France, "that by that time His Holiness can be persuaded to give you the dispensation you need for marriage with your niece."

It was a further excuse for delay. The marriage could not take place without the dispensation from the Pope, and was he likely to give it while Isabella was firmly on the throne of Castile?

If the journey through France had delighted the King of Portugal, his meeting with France's King could only fill him with foreboding.

Alfonso had been right to feel apprehensive. As the months passed, although the French continued to treat him with respect, Louis, on every occasion when the purpose of his visit was mentioned, became evasive.

Burgundy! was the answer. And where was the dispensation from the Pope?

A whole year Alfonso lingered in France, for, having made the long journey, how could he face a return without having achieved what he had come for?

The unhappy figure of the King of Portugal at the Court of France had become a commonplace. He was looked upon as a hanger-on whose prestige waned with each passing week.

The Duke of Burgundy had died and Louis had invaded his dominions. The Pope had given the dispensation.

Still there was no answer for Alfonso.

He began to grow melancholy and to wonder what he should do, for he could not stay indefinitely in France.

And one day, after he had been a year in Louis's dominions, one of his retinue asked to speak to Alfonso privately; and when they were alone he said to the King: "Highness, we are being deceived. Louis has no intention of helping us. I have proof that he is at this time negotiating with Ferdinand and Isabella, and seeking a treaty of friendship with them."

"It is impossible!" cried Alfonso.

"There is proof, Highness."

When he was assured that he had been told the truth Alfonso was overcome with mortification.

What can I do? he asked himself. Return to Portugal? There he would become the object of ridicule. Louis was not to be trusted, and he, Alfonso, had been a fool to think he could bargain with such a man. Louis had never intended to help him; and it was obvious that, since he sought the friendship of Isabella and Ferdinand, he believed them to be secure on the throne of Castile.

He called to three of his most trusted servants.

"Prepare," he said, "to leave the Court immediately."

"We are returning home, Highness?" asked one eagerly.

"Home," murmured the King. "We can never go home again. I could never face my son, nor my people."

"Then where shall we go, Highness?"

Alfonso looked in a bewildered fashion at his servants.

"There is a little village in Normandy. We will make for that place, and there we shall live in obscurity until I have made up my mind what I had best do."

★ ★ ★

Alfonso stared out of the window of the inn at the fowls which scrabbled in the yard.

I, he mourned, a King of Portugal to come to this!

For several days he had lived here, like a fugitive, incognito, afraid to proclaim his identity lest even these humble people should be laughing at him.

At the Court of France his retinue would be asking themselves what had become of him; he did not care. All he wanted now was to hide from the world.

In Portugal Joanna would hear of his humiliation; and what would become of her? Poor child! A sad life hers, for what hope had she now of ever attaining the throne of Castile?

He had dreamed of a romantic enterprise. A fair young girl in distress, a gallant king to her rescue, who should become her bridegroom; and here he was, an ageing man in hiding, perhaps already known to the world as a fighter of lost causes.

What is left to me? he asked himself. What is left to Joanna? A convent for her. And for me?

He saw himself in coarse robe and hair shirt. He saw himself barefoot before some shrine. Why not a pilgrimage to the Holy Land and, after that, return home to the monastic life? Thus if he could not procure the crown of Castile he could make sure of his place in heaven.

He did not pause long to consider. When had he ever done so?

He called for pen and paper.

"I have a very important letter to write," he said.

"My son, [he wrote] I have decided to retire from the world. All earthly vanities which were once within me are dead. I propose to go on a pilgrimage to the Holy Land and after that devote myself to God in the monastic life.

"It is for you to hear this news as though it were of my death, for dead I am to the world. You will assume the sovereignty of Portugal. When you receive this letter Alfonso is no longer King of Portugal. I salute King John . . ."

Isabella lay in her bed awaiting the birth of her child. It would not be long now, and she was glad that Beatriz was with her. The Queen's journeyings had brought her to Seville. It was the month of June, the heat was intense and the sweat was on Isabella's brow as the intermittent pain tortured her body.

"Beatrix," she murmured, "are you there, Beatriz?"

"Beside you, my dearest."

"There is no need to worry, Beatriz. All will be well."

"Indeed all will be well!"

"The child will be born in the most beautiful of my towns. Seville, *La Tierra de Maria Santisima*. One understands why it is so called, Beatriz. Last night I sat at my window and looked out on the fertile vineyards. But how hot it is!"

Beatriz leaned over Isabella, moving the big fan back and forth.

"Is that better, my dearest?"

"Better, Beatriz. I am happy to have you with me."

A frown had puckered Isabella's brow, and Beatriz asked herself: "Is she thinking of the woman in the castle of Arevalo? Oh, not now, my dearest, not at this time. It would be wrong. It might work some evil. Not now . . . Isabella, my Queen, when the child is about to come into the world."

"It is the pain," said Isabella. "I should be able to endure it better than this."

"You are the bravest woman in Castile."

"When you think what it means! Our child is about to be born . . . mine and Ferdinand's. This child could be King or Queen of Castile. That was what my mother used to say to us . . ."

Isabella had caught her breath, and Beatriz, fanning more vigorously, said quickly: "The people are already gathering outside. They crowd into the *patios* and in the glare of the sun. They await news of the birth of your child."

"I must not disappoint them, Beatriz."

"You will never disappoint your people, Isabella."

Beatriz held the child in her arms. She laughed exultantly. Then she handed it to a nurse and went to kneel by Isabella's bed.

"The child?" said Isabella.

"Your Highness has borne a perfect child."

"I would see the child."

"Can you hear the cries? Loud . . . healthy . . . just as they should be. Oh, this is a happy day! Oh, my dearest mistress, your son is born."

Isabella lay back on her pillows and smiled.

"So it is a son."

"A Prince for Castile!" cried Beatriz.

"And he is well . . . quite well . . . in all ways?"

"He is perfect. I know it."

"But . . ."

She was thinking that, when her mother had been born, doubtless there had been no sign of the terrible affliction which was to come to her.

"Put unhappy thoughts from your mind, Highness. They are doubly bad at such a time. All is well. This is a beautiful child, a fine heir for Castile. Here he is." She took him from the nurse and laid him in Isabella's arms.

And as she looked at her son, Isabella forgot her fears.

He was born at last — the son for whom she and Ferdinand had longed.

"He shall be John . . . Juan," she said, "after Ferdinand's father. That will delight my husband."

She kissed the baby's brow and whispered: "Juan . . . my little son, born in the most beautiful of my towns, welcome . . . welcome to Castile."

CHAPTER
FOUR

Isabella And The Archbishop Of Saragossa

Alfonso gave himself up to dreaming. He would sit in the room overlooking the inn yard, dreaming of the life he would lead in the monastery of his choosing. He had decided that he would become a Franciscan because their simple way of life best fitted his present mood. How different would existence at a Franciscan monastery be compared with that of a royal Court!

First, there would be his pilgrimage. He closed his eyes and saw himself, pack on back, simply clad in a flowing garment, the sun beating upon him, suffering a hundred discomforts. Imaginary discomforts were so comforting.

And as he sat dreaming there he heard the clatter of horses' hoofs in the lane and started out of his world of imagination to see that several members of his retinue, whom he had left behind at the Court of France, had arrived at the inn.

He went down to greet them.

They bowed before him. "God be praised, Highness," said their leader, "that we have found you."

"Call me Highness no more," said the King. "I have relinquished my rank. Very soon I shall be nothing more than the humblest friar."

His followers looked aghast, but he saw that they were already aware of his intended abdication; and it was for this reason that they, discovering his hiding-place, had come to him with all haste.

"Highness," said one, "it is imperative that you return to Portugal with all speed. If there is any delay it may well be that the Prince, your son, will have become King."

"It is what I intended."

"There is also the Princess Joanna, who expects to be your bride."

Alfonso looked pained. He had allowed the thought of Joanna to slip from his mind. But she was so young, so helpless. She would be a charmingly innocent bride.

The Franciscan robe lost some of its charm then; thinking of the soft body of the Princess Joanna, he was reminded of the hardship of the hair shirt.

A princess in distress, and he was sworn to rescue her! How could he desert her?

He remembered the Court — its balls and banquets, its fetes, all its pleasures. The life of a king was his life; he had been brought up to expect it.

"It is too late," he said. "I have already written to my son. When he receives my letter he will make ready for his coronation. Once he is crowned King of Portugal, there will be no place there for me."

"Highness, it is not too late. Louis has offered a fleet of ships to carry you back to Portugal. We should leave without delay. And if we are fortunate we may reach Portugal before the coronation of Prince John."

Alfonso shook his head. "But no," he said. "I have decided." He smiled. This would be the most quixotic adventure of them all. The charms of Joanna were appealing; the court life had its attractions; but he could not abandon the Franciscan habit as easily as this.

"Highness," went on the chief of his advisers, "you cannot give up your crown. The Princess Joanna awaits you. She will be longing for your return. All Portugal will wish to see their King again. You cannot abandon the Princess Joanna. You cannot abandon your people."

He told himself they were right.

My beautiful Joanna, my little niece-bride. Of course I could not abandon you.

Yet he remained aloof from their argument, for his dignity would not allow him to give way too easily.

They knew that; they also knew that in time they would persuade him to give up this dream of retirement; they would make him see it as the chimera it was.

Ferdinand faced Isabella in that apartment where they were alone with their children. Ferdinand was dressed for a long journey.

"It grieves me to leave you," he was saying, "but you understand that it must be so."

"Indeed I understand. You must always go to your father when he needs you . . . as I must to my mother."

Ferdinand thought that the one was not to be compared with the other. His father, the great warrior statesman, and Isabella's mother, the insane creature of the Castle of Arevalo! But he did not comment on this. Isabella was, of course, referring to their duty.

"At least," she said, "you have happier news for him than when you were last with him. Although we must not forget that we are not yet completely safe."

"I shall always be wary of Alfonso," he said. "How can one know what mad scheme he will think of next? The idea of giving up his throne to his son! He talks of going into a monastery!"

Isabella smiled. "He has been humiliated by Louis, and he cannot face his countrymen. Poor Alfonso! He is unfit to wear a crown."

"You will take care of yourself and our children while I am away."

Isabella smiled at him fondly. "You can trust me to do so, Ferdinand."

"Care for them as assiduously as you care for Castile."

"I will, Ferdinand."

"There is a large enough force on the frontier to withstand an attack from Portugal should it come."

"Have no fear."

"You are a wise woman, Isabella. I regret I must leave my family. But the time is passing."

"You must say goodbye to the children," Isabella reminded him. She called to her daughter. "Isabella, my dear. Come. Your father has to leave us now."

104

The eight-year-old Infanta Isabella came running at her mother's call. She was a pretty though delicate child, and in her abundant hair was that hint of red which she had inherited from her Plantagenet ancestors. Even at eight she lacked the serenity of her mother.

She knelt before Ferdinand and Isabella, but Ferdinand swing her up in his arms and, holding her tightly against him, kissed her.

"Well, daughter," he said, "are you going to miss me?"

"So much, dear Father," she answered.

"I shall soon be with you again."

"Please come back soon, Father."

Isabella looked at them fondly.

"You will not," said the Infanta, "look for a husband for me, Father."

"That had not been my intention."

"Because," said young Isabella, playing with the ornament on his doublet, "I shall never wish to leave you and the Queen to go to France and be the daughter of the French King."

"You shall not leave us for many years," Ferdinand promised.

And Isabella threw her arms about her father's neck and hugged him tightly.

The Queen, watching them, found herself praying silently. "Preserve them both. Bring them happiness . . . the greatest happiness in life. If there are afflictions to be borne I will bear them. But let these two know perfect happiness."

They seemed to her like two children. Ferdinand, who was so often like a spoilt boy, for all his valour in battle, for all his dignity; and dear Isabella, whose desire at this time was never to leave the heart of her family.

Isabella thrust away her emotion and said: "You should not forget your son, Ferdinand. He will wish to take his leave of you."

"He is too young to know our father," said young Isabella, pouting slightly, not wishing to share her parents' attention with the baby who, she considered, usually had an unfair portion of it.

"Yet your father will wish to take his leave of him," said the Queen.

So they went to the royal nursery. The nurses curtsied as they approached and stood back from the cradle, where little Juan crowed and smiled as though to show off his prowess to the spectators.

Ferdinand lifted him in his arms and kissed the small forehead, young Juan showing a mild protest; but he was a healthy, happy baby. A quiet baby, thought Isabella exultantly.

And so the farewells were said and Ferdinand left his wife and children to ride into Aragon.

He was shocked to see how his father had aged. John of Aragon was almost eighty-three years old, but, although he looked ill, his mental powers had not diminished in the least; moreover, his agility belied his years.

Ferdinand had no need to complain of any lack of respect shown to him in Aragon. Here his father insisted on treating him not only like a king, but a greater king than he was himself.

"Ferdinand, King of Castile!" cried John as he embraced his son. "It does my heart good to see you. Oh, no . . . no. I shall walk on your left. Castile should take precedence over Aragon."

"Father," said Ferdinand, deeply moved, "you are my father and always should take precedence."

"Not in public any more, my son. And I pray you do not kiss my hand. It is I who shall kiss yours on all public occasions. Oh, it does me good to see you thus. King of Castile, eh?"

"Consort to the Queen, Father."

"That little matter? It is of no account. King of Castile you are, and as such worthy of the utmost respect."

It was a delight to John to be alone with his son. He would hear all the news. So he was grandfather to two children now. That delighted him. And Ferdinand had a son. Juan! They had thought to delight him to the utmost by giving him that name. "May it be long before he comes to the throne of Castile," cried John emotionally.

He wanted news of Isabella. "She still refuses to allow you equal rights then? She is a strong woman."

"To understand Isabella one must be with her constantly," mused Ferdinand. "And even then perhaps one does not know her really well. She has the strongest character in Castile and the mildest manners."

"She is highly respected throughout all Spain, and France too, I believe. It is of France that I wish to speak to you, my son. I have been in communication with Louis, and he is prepared to relinquish his friendship with Portugal, to give no more support to the cause of La Beltraneja and to make an alliance with you and Isabella, that there shall be perpetual peace between France and Castile."

"If this could be effected, Father, it would lift great anxieties from our minds."

"If it should be effected! Do you not know your old father? It *shall* be effected."

Ferdinand felt happy to be in Aragon.

"There is something in one's native air," he said to his attendants, "that lifts the spirits. How I miss my family! I long to see the Queen and my children. But nevertheless I could not be entirely unhappy while I am in Aragon."

There were certain delights in Saragossa, but Ferdinand must enjoy them in secret.

He left his father's palace and rode out at dusk. His destination was a house in the city, where he was received by a dignified lady who gave way to expressions of pleasure when she saw who her visitor was.

"I have business," said Ferdinand, "with the Archbishop of Saragossa. I pray you take me to him."

The lady bowed her head and led the way up a staircase. Ferdinand noted the expensive furnishings of the house and said: "It delights me that my lord Archbishop lives in a manner fitting to his rank."

"My lord is happy to enjoy the benefits of his rank," was the answer.

She opened a door on to a room where a boy of about seven years old was taking a fencing lesson.

He did not look up as the two stood in the doorway, but his tutor turned.

"On guard!" cried the boy.

"Pray continue," said Ferdinand; and he smiled to watch the boy's skill with the sword.

The tutor, no doubt thinking that the lesson should be brought to an end, with a flick of his wrist sent the boy's sword spinning out of his hand.

"How dare you! How dare you!" cried the boy. "One day I will run you through for that."

"Alonso, Alonso," said the lady. She turned to Ferdinand. "He has such high spirits. He excels at most sports and cannot bear not to shine." She signed to the tutor to leave them, and when they were alone she said: "Alonso, your father has come."

The boy stood for a few seconds, staring at Ferdinand; then he came forward, knelt, took Ferdinand's hand and kissed it.

"So my lord Archbishop is glad to see his father?"

"The Archbishop has great pleasure in welcoming the King."

Ferdinand's lips twitched at the corners. This boy, with his flashing dark eyes and bold manners, was very dear to him. For his sake he had risked unpleasant scandal by bestowing on him, when he was only six years old, the Archbishopric of Saragossa, with all its attendant revenues, so the child was one of the richest people in Aragon.

"He would wish," went on the boy, "that he was more often given the opportunity of doing so."

Ferdinand smiled at the boy's mother, who was clearly delighted with her son's precocity.

"It is a matter of deep regret to the King also," said Ferdinand. "But let us endure it, for the time being. There may come a day when we shall be more frequently in each other's company."

The boy's eyes sparkled. His dignity deserted him and he was an eager child begging for a treat. He had seized Ferdinand's arm and was shaking it. "When, Father, when?" he demanded.

"One day. Have no fear of that." Ferdinand pictured this boy at the Court of Castile. Isabella would have to know. Well, she must accept the fact that kings such as Ferdinand must be expected to have an illegitimate son here and there. He would insist on Isabella's accepting this fact. Here, under the admiring gaze of his mistress and his son, he did not doubt that he would be capable of dealing with Isabella.

"I shall come to Court."

"Certainly you shall come to Court. By the saints, what a dashing courtier you will make, eh?"

"I shall be brave," said the boy. "And I shall be very important. All men will tremble at my approach."

"Will you be as fierce as all that?"

"I shall be the King's son," said Alonso simply.

Ferdinand replied solemnly: "You have learned much, Alonso — to strut like a courtier, to fence a

110

little. But there is one thing you have not learned, and that is humility."

"Humility? You mean you would have me humble?"

"It is a lesson we all have to learn at some time or other, whether we be archbishops or king's sons. You lost your temper when your tutor showed more skill with the sword than you. Come, let me take his place."

The Viscountess of Eboli stood aside, watching her son and lover fencing together.

Again and again Ferdinand sent the boy's sword spinning out of his hand. Alonso was disconsolate, yet Ferdinand noticed with pleasure that the boy returned again and again to the play, always with the hope that this time it would not happen.

At last Ferdinand said: "That is enough." He threw aside his sword and put a hand on the boy's arm. "You will be a great swordsman one day, my son," he said, "providing you learn your lesson. I want you to excel in all things which you attempt. But I would have you understand that while you must have complete confidence in your ability to succeed, you must always be prepared to learn from those who have greater experience. That is the true humility, Alonso — and the only sort worth having."

"Yes, Father," said the boy, a little subdued.

"Now you shall tell me what you have been doing during my absence. There is little time left to us. My visit, as usual, must be brief."

The boy's face puckered in distress, and Ferdinand put his arm about him impulsively and embraced him.

"Perhaps, my son," he said fervently, "it will not always be so."

Alfonso of Portugal had arrived in his own country. Like most of his ventures, his arrival was ill-timed. As he set foot on the shores of his native land two items of news were brought to him, both of them disturbing.

His son John had been crowned King of Portugal five days before; and Pope Sixtus IV had been induced by Isabella and Ferdinand, and the conduct of Alfonso himself, to withdraw the dispensation which he had previously given to make the marriage between Alfonso and Joanna possible.

"What an unhappy man I am," mourned Alfonso. "You see, my friends, the hand of God is turned against me. I promised myself that I would return to my country, that I would marry the Princess Joanna, that I would rule more wisely than I have in the past. You see, I am not to marry nor to rule. What is left to me? Oh, why did I allow myself to be dissuaded from living the monastic life! What is left to me . . . but that!"

He travelled to Lisbon, and he felt that, as he passed through the towns, people watched him furtively. They did not know how to receive him. He was a king and yet not a king. He had brought poverty to Portugal with his wild enterprises; he had brought more than poverty — humiliation.

His son John received him with affection.

"You are the King of Portugal now," said Alfonso, kissing his hand. "You take precedence of your father. I

112

was wrong to have come back to Court. I think I shall soon be leaving it."

John answered: "Father, if it were possible to retrace our steps, would you have kept the crown for yourself?"

Alfonso looked sadly at his son. "There is no place at Court for a king who has abdicated. He only makes trouble for his successor."

"Then what will you do, Father?"

"I think the monastery is the only answer."

"You would not long be happy in a monastery. The novelty would soon disappear, and you have been used to such an active life. How could you endure it?"

"I should learn to live a new life."

"Father, you regret abandoning the crown to me, do you not?"

"My son, I wish you all success."

"There comes a day when a son should take the crown from his father, and that is when his father is in his tomb."

"What do you mean, John?"

"I mean, Father, that as you gave your crown to me, I now abdicate and give it back to you. My time to wear it has not yet come. I trust it will not come for many years."

Alfonso smiled at John with tears in his eyes.

John felt relieved. He had been alarmed when his father had bestowed the crown upon him. He considered what often happened when there were two kings with only one crown between them. His father had abdicated, but there would almost certainly arise a faction which desired to put him back on the throne, whether he wished it or not.

John was happier waiting to inherit the crown on his father's death than wearing it while he was still alive.

So Alfonso forgot his humiliating adventure in France and accepted the crown at the hands of John.

As for the people of Portugal, they had grown accustomed to the eccentricities of their King, and after a while they ceased to talk of the two abdications.

Alfonso sent for the Princess Joanna.

She was growing into a charming young woman, and it distressed him that Sixtus had withdrawn the dispensation.

"My dear," he said, taking her hand and making her sit beside him, "how very unsettled life is for you."

"I am learning to be happy here, Highness," Joanna told him.

"I am glad. But I cannot be happy while our marriage is delayed."

"Highness, we accept what is."

"Nay, my dear, we will not accept it. We will marry. I am determined on that."

Joanna drew back in alarm. "We could not," she said, "without the dispensation."

"The dispensation!" cried Alfonso. "Sixtus declares that he withdrew it because we did not give him the true facts. We know how much truth there is in that! He withdrew it because Isabella and Ferdinand insisted that he should; and they are supreme in Castile . . . at the moment."

114

"Yes," said Joanna, "the people accept Isabella as their Queen. They want no other."

"They are successful at the moment," said Alfonso. "But remember I say at the moment. This does not mean that they will always be so."

"We have tried," said Joanna, "and we have failed."

"My dear, your future husband never accepts failure. I have a plan."

"Not . . . not to go into Castile again?" stammered Joanna.

"We have failed once. But he wins who is successful in the last battle. That is the important one, my dear."

"You could not thrust the people of Portugal into war again."

The dreamlike expression was creeping over Alfonso's face.

"We must fight," he said, "we must fight for the right."

Ferdinand had returned from Aragon, and Isabella had prepared a banquet to welcome him.

She had wished it to be an elaborate feast. Not that Ferdinand was given to excessive eating or drinking any more than she was; not that he would care to see so much money spent, any more than she would; but he would appreciate the fact that his return was of such importance to herself and Castile.

Isabella carefully watched the expenditure of the treasury, but she was the first to admit that there were occasions when it was wise to spend; and this was one of them.

Ferdinand looked well, but she noticed a change in him. He was experiencing mingling anxiety and excitement. She felt she understood. His father's health must be giving him that cause for anxiety, while it gave him equal cause for excitement.

Ferdinand was fond of his father; he would never cease to be grateful to him; but at the same time King John's death would make Ferdinand King of Aragon; and, once that title was bestowed upon him, he would feel that he could stand in equality beside Isabella.

Isabella knew that all Ferdinand's emotions must be mingled with his love of possessions, so that even the death of a beloved parent could not be entirely deplored if it brought him a crown.

When she had received him and they were at last alone she said to him: "And your father, Ferdinand? How fares your father?"

"He is pleased with what we have done here in Castile; but he is ailing, I fear. He forgets that he is nearly eighty-three. And I think we forget it too."

"He has caused you to worry, Ferdinand."

"I cannot help feeling that his end is near."

"Yet it is largely due to him that this treaty of St Jean de Luz, between ourselves and the French, has been made."

"His mind will be active till the end, Isabella. But I fear I may never see him again."

"Come, Ferdinand, I will call our daughter. She will turn your thoughts from this melancholy subject."

116

But even as Isabella called for her daughter she knew that the subject was not an entirely melancholy one; and the thought disturbed her.

It was early in the following year when the news came from Aragon.

The fierce winds of January, sweeping across the plain from the Guadarramas, penetrated the Palace, and in spite of huge fires it was difficult to keep it warm.

As soon as the messenger entered his presence, Ferdinand knew the nature of the news he had brought. It was evident, in the man's attitude as he presented the message, that he was not merely in the presence of the heir to the throne but in that of the monarch himself.

The colour deepened in Ferdinand's bronzed cheeks.

"You bring news of the King of Aragon?"

"Long live Don Ferdinand, King of Aragon!" was the answer.

"It is so?" said Ferdinand, and he drew himself up to his full height while he tried to think of his sorrow and all that the loss of one of the best friends he could ever have would mean to him. He turned away as though to hide his emotion. But the emotion was not entirely grief, and he did not want the man to see how much it meant to him to have inherited the throne of Aragon.

He turned back and put his hand over his eyes. "I pray you leave me now," he said quietly.

He waved his hand, and those who had been with him retired also.

He sat down at a table and buried his face in his hands. He was trying to think of his father, who had schemed for him — murdered for him — and all those occasions when John of Aragon had given him advice and help. He remembered his father at his mother's bedside when she had been afraid because she believed that the ghost of Carlos, Ferdinand's murdered stepbrother, had been there at the bedside. Carlos had died, it was generally believed, at the hands of his father and stepmother, so that their son Ferdinand might find no one to stand in his way to the throne.

This man was dead now. Never again could Ferdinand turn to him for guidance. The father who had loved him, surely as few were loved, was now no more. Every action of his had been for the advancement of Ferdinand; not only was Ferdinand his idolised son but the son of the woman whom he had loved beyond all else in the world.

Even in dying he gave Ferdinand a crown.

Isabella had heard the news and came in haste to the apartment.

He glanced up as she approached. She looked grave; and he thought then that there could not be a woman in the world who disguised her feelings as successfully as Isabella.

She knelt at his feet; she took his hand and kissed it. She was offering him solace for the loss of his father and at the same time homage to the King of Aragon.

"It has come, Isabella," he said, "as I feared." He might have added, and as I hoped. For he had certainly longed to feel the crown upon his head.

He felt a flicker of irritation against her because, being aware of his own mercenary feelings at this time, he could blame Isabella for them. It was Isabella's determination to remain supreme in Castile that made it so necessary for him to be a king in his own right — not merely of Sicily, but of the great province of Aragon.

Now that had happened and, when he should be grieving for his father, he found himself elated.

"You must not grieve," said Isabella. "He would not have it so. Ferdinand, this is a great occasion. I am Queen of Castile; you are King of Aragon. All that I have is yours; all that you have is mine. Now almost the whole of Spain is united."

"The whole of Spain apart from that accursed Moorish kingdom — ours . . . ours, Isabella."

"We have a son who will be King of Spain, Ferdinand. I remind you of this, because I know how you suffer at this moment."

Ferdinand was suddenly aware of his loss. He said: "He was so good to me. No one ever had a better father."

"I know," she said; and she lifted her kerchief to her eyes.

But she was thinking: Castile and Aragon — we reign over almost the whole of Spain. Our destiny is being fulfilled. We are God's chosen rulers.

And he was thinking: I am a king . . . a king in my own right. King of Aragon, to stand side by side with the Queen of Castile.

119

★ ★ ★

The King of Aragon was no longer quite so insistent on the deference which must be paid to him. It was clear that he was the King . . . the King in his own right. He had a crown which he did not owe to his wife.

Isabella was delighted to see this change in him. She believed it augured well for their future. Ferdinand would not now grudge her her power in Castile.

If the war for the Succession could only be settled once and for all, Isabella would be ready to set her kingdom in order; but as long as Alfonso boasted of his intention to set Joanna on the throne of Castile in place of Isabella there could be no peace.

Yet her hopes for the future were high. She had her family — her charming Isabella, her healthy little Juan, so normal, both of them — and she for a brief spell had Ferdinand with her, a contented Ferdinand no longer looking for slights: Don Ferdinand, the King of Aragon.

It was during those spring months that Isabella once more discovered that she might expect a child.

Isabella found it necessary to visit the fortified towns on the borders of Castile and Portugal.

As she travelled from place to place she brooded on the sad state of her kingdom. Robbers were still numerous on the road. The Hermandad was doing good work, but while war threatened it was impossible to find the necessary funds to keep the organization going. The position was not as serious as it had once been, but there must be continual vigil in the frontier towns.

Beatriz came from Segovia to be with her.

"You should rest," said Beatriz. "Eight months after the birth of Juan and you become pregnant again!"

"It is a queen's duty, Beatriz," Isabella reminded her friend with a smile, "to ensure that the royal line is continued."

"And to take care of herself that she may perform this duty," retorted Beatriz. "Has Your Highness forgotten another occasion, when you lost your child?"

Isabella smiled. She allowed Beatriz to speak to her in this rather hectoring manner because she knew that it was the outward sign of a great affection. Perhaps no one in Castile loved her, reflected Isabella, as did this forthright, bold Beatriz de Bobadilla.

"It is not for me to think of the peril to myself," she said calmly. "If I am timid, how can I expect my friends to be otherwise?"

Beatriz attempted once more to dissuade Isabella from making these journeys, which were not only arduous but dangerous; but Isabella firmly implied that she wished to hear no more; and although Beatriz was by nature overbearing and Isabella so calm, Beatriz always realised when the moment had come to say no more and to drop the role of privileged friend for that of humble confidante.

It was while Isabella was inspecting the border fortifications that she received a communication from the Infanta Dona Beatriz of Portugal. The Infanta, who was Isabella's maternal aunt, deplored the fact that Castile and Portugal, whose sovereigns were so closely related, should be continually at war. She would be grateful, she wrote, if Isabella would meet her, and if

121

together they could discuss some means of making peace between the two countries.

Isabella was eager for the meeting, and she immediately agreed to it.

Meanwhile, with Ferdinand and her counsellors, she drew up the peace terms.

Isabella, not yet incapacitated by pregnancy, rode to the border town of Alcantara, where Dona Beatriz of Portugal was waiting for her.

The ladies embraced and, because each was so eager to bring about peace, they wasted no time in celebrations but began their discussions immediately.

"My dear Dona Beatriz," said Isabella, as they sat together in the council chamber, "the Portuguese Army was beaten in the field, and should it come against us once more we should be confident of annihilating it."

"That is true," said Dona Beatriz, "but let us not consider the possibility of war. Let us turn our thoughts to peace."

"By all means," was the answer. "The first clause that we should insist on would be that Alfonso gives up the title and armorial bearings of Castile which he has assumed."

"That is reasonable. I feel sure he will agree to that."

"There must be no more claims from or on behalf of Joanna, and the King must no longer consider himself betrothed to her. Moreover, he must never again aspire to her hand."

Dona Beatriz frowned. "He has a great fondness for Joanna," she said.

"And for the crown of Castile," replied Isabella dryly, "to which he pretends to believe she has a claim."

"I can put this clause before him," said Beatriz. "It will be for me to persuade him to accept it."

"You are convinced of the justice of it?"

"I am convinced that there must be peace between Castile and Portugal."

"Between Castile *and* Aragon and Portugal," said Isabella with a smile. "We are stronger now."

"I will remind the King of that also."

"As for Joanna," went on Isabella, "she must either leave Portugal or be betrothed to my son, Juan."

"Juan! He is not yet a year old . . . and she . . . she is now a young woman."

"It is a condition," said Isabella. "We will give her six months to decide whether she will leave Portugal or be betrothed to my son. If, when he reaches a marriageable age, she prefers to enter a convent, I shall not stand in her way. If she did enter a convent it would be necessary for her to take the veil."

Beatriz looked long into the smiling face of Isabella, and she thought: We are discussing the life of a young girl who, although she has been a menace to Isabella, is in herself innocent. Yet Isabella, herself so happy in her marriage and her family, is so determined to be secure upon the throne, that she is not only denying this girl any hope of the crown but of the normal life of a woman. The face Isabella showed to the world was completely enigmatic. It would be well not to be deceived by that gentle façade.

"It is a hard choice for a young girl," mused Beatriz. "Betrothal to a baby or the veil!"

"It is an important condition," said Isabella.

"I can put these terms before Joanna," said Beatriz, "and before the King. I can do no more."

"That is understood," said Isabella. "All Castilians who have fought with the King of Portugal for Joanna will be pardoned and, to show that I and my husband wish for friendship with Portugal, my daughter, the Infanta Isabella, shall be betrothed to Alonso, son of the Prince of Portugal."

"So these are your conditions," said Beatriz. "I do not think it will be easy to obtain the King's consent to all of them."

"I deplore war," Isabella told her. "But it will be necessary for the King to agree to *all* these conditions if we are to have peace. He must remember that he was defeated in the field. He will know that, eager as Castile is for peace, it does not need it so desperately as does Portugal."

The two ladies took their leave of each other, Beatriz travelling westward to Lisbon, Isabella eastward to Madrid.

Isabella waited. The conditions were hard, but they were necessarily so, she told herself, to secure lasting peace. She was sorry for Joanna, who had been a helpless puppet in the hands of ambitious men, but the comfort and happiness of one young woman could not be considered when the prosperity of Castile was at stake.

Isabella was large with her child when news came that Alfonso had accepted her terms.

Her spirits were high. The War of the Succession, which had lasted four years, was over.

And very soon another child would be born to her and Ferdinand.

The city of Toledo was set high on a plateau of stone which appeared to have been carved out of the surrounding mountains in the gorge of the Tagus. Only on the north side was it accessible by a narrow isthmus which connected it with the plain of Castile. In no other city in Isabella's Castile was there more evidence of Moorish occupation.

Isabella could never visit her city of Toledo without reiterating the vow that one day she would wrest from the Moors those provinces of Spain which were still under their domination, and that the flag of Christian Spain should float over every city.

But, to remind her of the state of her country, not far from this very palace of Toledo in which she now lay was that great rock, from which it was the custom to hurl alleged criminals. Many would meet their fate at the rock of Toledo before Castile would be safe for honest men and women to live in.

A tremendous task lay before her, and as soon as she had left this childbed she must devote herself to stabilising her country. Nothing should be spared, she had decided. She would be harsh if harshness were needed, and all her honest subjects would rejoice. She had sworn to rid Castile of its criminals, to make the roads safe for travellers by imposing such penalties on offenders that even the most hardened robber would think twice before offending.

But now there was the child about to be born.

It would be soon, and she was unafraid. One grew accustomed to childbearing. The pains of birth she could bear stoically. She had a daughter and son, and she no longer had any uneasy feelings regarding a child she would bear. Her mother was living in a dark world of her own at Arevalo, and the dread that the children should be like her had disappeared. Why should they be? Isabella was in full possession of her mental powers. No one in Castile was more balanced, more controlled than the Queen. Why, then, should she fear?

The pains were becoming more frequent. Isabella waited a while before she called to her women.

It was some hours later when, in the fortress town of Toledo, Isabella's second daughter and third child was born.

She called her Juana.

Joanna knew herself to be deserted. Alfonso had agreed to Isabella's terms, and she had been offered her choice: a marriage with a boy who was still a baby, or the veil.

Joanna knew that only would that marriage take place if by the time Prince Juan was in his teens there were still people to remember her cause in Castile. She wondered what sort of marriage she could hope for with a partner so many years younger than herself.

126

The peace of the cloister seemed inviting; but to take the veil, to shut herself off from the world for ever! Could she do that?

Yet what alternative was Isabella offering her? Shrewd Isabella who, so gently and with seeming kindness, could drive a poor bewildered girl into a prison from which there was no escape!

She must resign herself. She would take the veil. It was the only way to end conflict. How unhappy were those who, by an accident of birth, could never be allowed to live their lives as they would choose to do.

"I think," she said to her attendants, "that I will prepare myself to go to the convent of Santa Clara at Coimbra."

The visiting embassy called upon her when her decision was made known.

The leaders of this embassy were Dr Diaz de Madrigal, a member of Isabella's Council, and Fray Fernando de Talavera, her confessor.

Talavera gave Joanna his blessing.

"You have chosen well, my daughter," he said. "In the convent of Santa Clara you will find a peace which you have never known outside the convent walls." Joanna smiled wanly.

She knew then how fervent had been Isabella's wish that she would take this course.

Alfonso came to her to take his last farewell.

"My dearest," he said, taking both her hands and kissing them. "So this is the end of all our hopes."

"It is perhaps better so," said Joanna. "Many seem to be of that opinion."

"It leaves me desolate," declared Alfonso. "My dearest Joanna, I had made so many dreams."

"Too many dreams," said Joanna wistfully.

"What shall I do when you are immersed in your convent? What shall I do when there is an impenetrable barrier between us?"

"You will govern your country and doubtless make another marriage."

"That I shall never do," cried Alfonso. His eyes kindled, and Joanna guessed that he was conceiving a new plan to marry her in spite of the Pope, in spite of the agreement he had made with Isabella.

Joanna shook her head. "You have agreed to these terms," she said. "There can be no going back. That would result in a war which might prove disastrous to Portugal."

"Must I let you go?"

"Indeed you must."

Alfonso's looks became melancholy. He had abandoned the idea of defiance. He now said: "Since you are to incarcerate yourself in a convent, I shall spend the rest of my days in a monastery. As it must be the veil for you, it must be the Franciscan habit for me."

She smiled at him sadly. "You remember, Alfonso," she said, "that on a previous occasion you came near to entering a monastery. On that occasion, you changed your mind."

"This time I shall not change," said Alfonso, "for this is the only way I can bear the loss of my lady Joanna."

Never before had Isabella felt so confident, never so sure of her powers.

She had summoned a Cortes to meet at Toledo, and here new laws had been discussed and introduced. Isabella had made it clear that she intended to crush the power of the nobles and to eliminate crime in her dominions as far as possible.

The Santa Hermandad must be extended; only if it were efficient could crime be dealt with, and Isabella was certain that only harsh punishment, meted out to proved offenders, could deter others from following their example. Officers of the Hermandad were sent to every village in Castile, where they took up residence so that order there might be maintained. Two *alcaldes* were set up in every village. This had to be paid for, and a house tax of 18,000 *maravedis* was imposed on every hundred householders.

But Isabella was fully aware of the fact that she could not punish with great severity those who carried out their crimes in a small way and allow those who offended on a larger scale to escape.

During the reigns of her father and half-brother many sinecures had been created, and those men who had supported these kings had received large incomes as a reward. Isabella was determined that such drains on the exchequer should cease. Those who supported her must do so for love of their country, not for monetary reward. Thus Isabella deprived Beltran de la

Cueva of a yearly income of a million and a half *maravedis*, in spite of the fact that he had turned from Joanna, alleged to be his daughter, to offer his services to Isabella; the Duke of Alva lost 600,000 *maravedis*, the Duke of Medina Sidonia 180,000 and Ferdinand's relative, Admiral Henriquez, 240,000.

This caused discontent among these nobles, but they dared not protest; and thus these large sums, which they had been squandering, helped to support the Santa Hermandad; and the effect of Isabella's stern rule soon began to be noticed throughout the land.

She was confident that in a few years' time she would transform the anarchical kingdom, which Castile had been when she had become its Queen, into a well-ordered state; she believed that the empty coffers of the treasury would be filled.

And once she had set her own house in order she would look farther afield.

Her eyes were on the Kingdom of Granada, and Ferdinand was beside her in this. He yearned to go into battle against the Moors, but she, the wiser one, restrained him for a while.

When they went into battle there should be victory for them. But they would not engage in war until there was peace and prosperity at home.

In spite of her preoccupation with state affairs, Isabella tried not to forget that she was a wife and mother. She deplored her own lack of education. Often she thought of those years at Arevalo, where she lived with her mother and her brother Alfonso, and where she was taught that one day she might be Queen, but little Latin, Greek or any other language which would have been useful to her. Her children should not suffer similarly; they should have the best of tutors. Most important of all was their religious instruction. That should certainly not be neglected.

There were occasions when she liked to escape to the nursery to forget the magnitude of the task of governing a kingdom which until recently had been on the verge of decay.

She liked to sit and sew with a few of her women as though she were a simple noblewoman, and talk of matters other than those concerned with the state. There was little time for this, and greatly she treasured those brief hours when she could indulge in it.

It was on one of these occasions, when her women were chattering together, that one of them who had recently come from Aragon talked of a ceremony she had seen there.

Isabella listened idly to the conversation. ". . . such a ceremony! The churchmen, brilliant in their vestments. And the one who attracted most attention was, of course, the Archbishop of Saragossa. An Archbishop only ten years old . . . certainly little more. Such a handsome little fellow . . . with all the dignity required of his rank."

"An Archbishop, ten years old?" said Isabella.

"Why yes, Highness, the Archbishop of Saragossa. He cannot be much more."

"He is very young to have attained such a post. The Archbishop of Saragossa must be a remarkable person indeed."

Isabella changed the subject, but she kept in mind the young Archbishop of Saragossa.

Isabella was discussing that ever-present problem with Ferdinand — the state of the treasury; and she said: "I am determined to divert the wealth of the great Military and Religious Orders to the royal coffers."

"What?" cried Ferdinand. "You will never do that."

"I think I shall."

"But how?"

"By having you elected Grand Master of each of them when those offices fall vacant."

Ferdinand's eyes took on that glazed look which the contemplation of large sums of money always brought to them.

"Calatrava, Alcantara, Santiago . . ." he murmured.

"All shall fall gradually into our hands," said Isabella. "When I contemplate the wealth in the possession of these Orders — the armies, the fortresses — it is inconceivable that they should exist to threaten the crown. We should be able to rely on the loyalty of these Orders without question, to use their arms and their wealth as we need it. Therefore they should be the property of the crown. And when you are Grand Master that will be achieved."

"It is a brilliant idea," agreed Ferdinand gleefully, and he gave his wife a glance of admiration. At such times he did not resent her determination to stand supreme as ruler of Castile.

"You shall see it achieved," she told him. "But it will be when the time is ripe."

"I believe," said Ferdinand, "that our struggles are behind us. A glorious future will be ours, Isabella, if we stand together."

"And so we shall stand. It was what I always intended."

He embraced her, and she drew back from his arms to smile at him.

"Castile and Aragon are ours! We have three healthy children," she said.

Ferdinand caught her hands and laughed. "We are young yet," he reminded her.

"Our little Isabella will be Queen of Portugal. We must arrange grand marriages for the others."

"Never fear. There will be many who will wish to marry with the children of Ferdinand and Isabella."

"Ferdinand, I am glad they are young yet. I shall suffer when they are forced to go from us."

"But they are still children as yet. Why, our little Isabella is but eleven years old."

"Eleven years old," mused Isabella. "But perhaps that is not so young. I hear you have an Archbishop in Saragossa of that age."

Ferdinand's face grew a little pale and then flushed. His eyes had become alert and suspicious.

"An Archbishop . . ." he murmured.

"You must have had your reasons for sanctioning the appointment," she said with a smile. "I wondered what great qualifications one so young could have."

She was unprepared for Ferdinand's reaction. He said: "You have made the affairs of Castile yours. I pray you leave to me those of Aragon."

It was Isabella's turn to grow pale. "Why, Ferdinand . . ." she began.

But Ferdinand had bowed and left her.

Why, she asked herself, should he have been so angry? What had she done but ask a simple question?

She stared after him and then sat down heavily. Understanding had come to her.

To have made a boy of that age an Archbishop, Ferdinand must have a very special reason for favouring him. What reason could Ferdinand have?

She refused to accept the explanation which was inevitably forcing itself into her mind.

He would have been born about the same time as their . . . first-born, little Isabella.

"No!" cried Isabella.

She, who had been so faithful to him in every way, could not tolerate this suspicion. But it was fast becoming no longer a suspicion. She now knew that Ferdinand was the lover of other women, that they had given him children — children whom he must love dearly to have risked exposure by making one of them Archbishop of Saragossa.

There was nothing that could have hurt her more. And this discovery had come to her at a time when all that she had hoped for seemed to be coming her way.

Her marriage was to have been perfect. She had known that he was jealous of her authority, but that she had understood. This was different.

She felt numb with the pain of this discovery. She felt a longing to give way to some weakness, to find Ferdinand, to rail against him, to throw herself onto her bed and give way to tears — to rage, to storm, to ease in some way the bitterness of this knowledge which wounded her more deeply than anything had ever done before.

Her women were coming to her.

She set her face in a quiet smile. None would have guessed that the smiling face masked such turbulent emotions and jealous humiliation.

CHAPTER
FIVE

Tomas De Torquemada

In a cell in the Monastery of Santa Cruz in the town of Segovia, a gaunt man, dressed in the rough garb of the Dominican Order, was on his knees.

He had remained thus for several hours, and this was not unusual for it was his custom to meditate and pray alternately for hours at a time.

He prayed now that he might be purged of all evil and given the power to bring others to the same state of exaltation which he felt that he himself — with minor lapses — enjoyed.

"Holy Mother," he murmured, "listen to this humble supplicant . . ."

He believed fervently in his humility and, if it had been pointed out to him that this great quality had its roots in a fierce pride, he would have been astonished. Tomás de Torquemada saw himself as the elect of Heaven.

Beneath the drab robe of rough serge he wore the hair shirt which was a continual torment to his delicate skin. He revelled in the discomfort it caused; yet after years of confinement in this hideous garment he had grown a little accustomed to it and he fancied that it was less of a burden than it had once been. The thought disturbed him, for he wanted to suffer the utmost discomfort. He slept on a plank of wood without a pillow. Soft beds were not for him. In the early days of his austerity he had scarcely slept at all; now he found that he needed very little sleep and, when he lay on his plank, he fell almost immediately into unconsciousness. Thus another avenue of self-torture was closed to him.

He ate only enough to keep him alive; he travelled barefoot wherever he went and took care to choose the stony paths. The sight of his cracked and bleeding feet gave him a similar pleasure to that which fine garments gave to other men and women.

He gloried in austerity with a fierce and fanatical pride — as other men delighted in worldly glitter.

It was almost sixty years ago that he had been born in the little town of Torquemada (which took its name from the Latin *turre cremata* — burnt tower) not far from Valladolid in North Castile.

From Tomás's early days he had shown great piety. His uncle, Juan de Torquemada, had been the Cardinal of San Sisto, a very distinguished theologian and writer on religious subjects.

Tomás had known that his father, Pero Fernandez de Torquemada, hoped that he would make the care of the family estates his life work, as he was an only son, and Pero was eager for Tomás to marry early and beget sons that this branch of the family might not become extinct.

Tomás had inherited a certain pride in his family, and this may have been one of the reasons why he decided so firmly that the life he had been called upon to lead, by a higher authority than that of Pero, should be one which demanded absolute celibacy.

At a very early age Tomás became a Dominican. With what joy he cast aside the fine raiment of a prosperous nobleman! With what pleasure he donned the rough serge habit, even at that age refusing to wear linen so that the coarse stuff could irritate his skin! It was very soon afterwards that he took to wearing the hair shirt, until he discovered that he must not wear it continually for fear that he should grow accustomed to it and the torment of it grow less.

He had become Prior of Santa Cruz of Segovia, but the news of his austere habits had reached the Court, and King Henry IV had chosen him as confessor to his sister Isabella.

He had refused at first; he wanted no soft life at Court. But then he had realised that there might be devils to tempt him at Court who could never penetrate the sanctity of Santa Cruz; and there would be more spiritual joy in resisting temptation than never encountering it.

The young Isabella had been a willing pupil. There could rarely have been a young princess so eager to share her confessor's spirituality, so earnestly desirous of leading a rigidly religious life.

She had been pleased with her confessor, and he with her.

He had told her of his great desire to see an all-Christian Spain and, in an access of fervour, had asked that she kneel with him and swear that, if ever it

138

were in her power to convert to Christianity the realm over which she might one day rule, she would seize the opportunity to do so.

The young girl, her eyes glowing with a fervour to match that of her confessor, had accordingly sworn.

It often occurred to Tomás de Torquemada that the opportunity must soon arise.

Torquemada had kept the esteem of the Queen. She admired his piety; she respected his motives; in a Court where she was surrounded by men who sought temporal power, this ascetic monk stood out as a man of deep sincerity.

As Torquemada prayed there was a thought at the back of his mind: now that Castile had ceased to be tormented by civil war, the time had come when the religious life of the country should be examined, and to him it seemed that the best way of doing this was to reintroduce the Inquisition into Castile, a new form of the Inquisition which he himself would be prepared to organise, an Inquisition which should be supervised by men like himself — monks of great piety, of the Dominican and Franciscan orders.

But another little matter had intruded into Torquemada's schemes, and he had been diverted. It was because of this that he now prayed so earnestly. He had allowed himself to indulge in pleasure rather than duty.

A certain Hernan Nuñez Arnalt had recently died, and his will had disclosed that he had named Tomás de Torquemada as its executor. Arnalt had been a very rich man, and had left a considerable sum for the purpose of building a monastery at Avila which should be called the Monastery of Saint Thomas.

To Tomás de Torquemada had fallen the task of carrying out his wishes and he found great joy in this duty. He spent much time with architects and discovered a great love of building; but so great was this pleasure that he began to be doubtful about it. Anything that made a man as happy as the studying of plans for this great work made him, must surely have an element of sin in it. He was suspicious of happiness; and as he looked back to that day when he had first heard of the proposed endowment, and that he had been entrusted to see the work carried out, he was alarmed.

He had neglected his duties at Santa Cruz; he had thought only occasionally of the need to force Christianity on every inhabitant of Castile; he had ceased to consider the numbers who, while calling themselves Christians, were reverting to the Jewish religion in secret. These sinners called for the greatest punishment that could be devised by the human mind; and he, the chosen servant of God and all his saints, had been occupying himself by supervising the piling of stone on stone, by deciding on the exquisite line of the cloisters, by taking sensuous enjoyment in planning with sculptors the designs for the chapel.

Torquemada beat his hands on his breast and cried: "Holy Mother of God, intercede for this miserable sinner."

He must devise some penance. But long austerity had made him careless of what his body suffered. "Yet," he said, "the Monastery will be dedicated to the glory of God. Is it such a sin to erect a building where men will live as recluses, a spiritual life, in great simplicity and austerity, and so come close to the Divine presence? Is that sin?"

The answer came from within. "It is sin to indulge in any earthly desire. It is sin to take pleasure. And you, Tomás de Torquemada, have exulted over these plans; you have made images of stone, works of exquisite sculpture; and you have lusted for these earthly baubles as some men lust for women."

"Holy Mother, scourge me," he prayed. "Guide me. Show me how I can expiate my sin. Shall I cut myself off from the work on the monastery? But it is for the glory of God that the monastery will be built. Is it such a sin to find joy in building a house of God?"

He would not visit the site of Avila for three weeks; he would look at no more plans. He would say: "My work at Santa Cruz demands all my energy. Castile is an unholy land, and I must do all in my power to bring sinners back to the Church."

He rose from his knees. He had decided on the penance. He would shut his beautiful monastery from his mind for three weeks. He would live on nothing but dry bread and water; and he would increase his hours of prayer.

As he left his cell a monk came to him to tell him that two Dominicans from Seville had arrived at Santa Cruz, and they had come to speak with the Sacred Prior, Tomás de Torquemada.

★　★　★

Torquemada received the visitors in a cell which was bare of all furniture except a wooden table and three stools. On a wall hung a crucifix.

"My brothers," said Torquemada in greeting, "welcome to Santa Cruz."

"Most holy Prior," said the first of the monks, "you know that I am Alonso de Ojeda, Prior of the monastery of Saint Paul. I would present our fellow Dominican, Diego de Merlo."

"Welcome, welcome," said Torquemada.

"We are disturbed by events in Seville and, knowing of your great piety and influence with the Queen, we have come to ask your advice and help."

"I shall be glad to give it, if it should be in my power," was the answer.

"Evil is practised in Seville," said Ojeda.

"What evil is this, brother?"

"The evil of those who work against the Holy Catholic Church. I speak of the *Marrams*."

Torquemada's face lost its deathlike pallor for an instant, and his blood showed pale pink beneath his skin; his eyes flashed momentarily with rage and hatred.

"These *Marrams*," cried Diego de Merlo, "they abound in Seville . . . in Cordova . . . in every fair city of Castile. They are the rich men of Castile. Jews! Jews who feign to be Christians. They are *Conversos*. They are of the true faith; so they would imply. And in secret they practise their foul rites."

142

Torquemada clenched his fists tightly and, although his face was bloodless once more, his eyes continued to gleam with fanatical hatred.

Ojeda began to speak rapidly. "Alonso de Spina warned us some years ago. They are here among us. They jeer at all that is sacred . . . in secret, of course. Jeer! If that were all! They are the enemies of Christians. In secret they practise their hideous rites. They spit upon holy images. You remember what Spina wrote of them?"

"I remember," said Torquemada quietly.

But Ojeda went on as though Torquemada had not spoken: "They cook their food in oils, and they stink of rancid food. They eat *kosher* food. You can tell a Jew by his stink. Should we have these people among us? Only if they renounce their beliefs. Only if they are purified by their genuine acceptance of the Christian faith. But they cheat, I tell you."

"They are cheats and liars," echoed Diego de Merlo.

"They are murderers," went on Ojeda. "They poison our wells; and worst of all they show their secret scorn of the Christian faith by committing hideous crimes. Only recently a little boy was missing from his home . . . a beautiful little boy. His body was discovered in a cave. He had been crucified, and his heart cut out."

"So these outrages continue," said Torquemada.

"They continue, brother; and nothing is done to put an end to them."

"Something must be done," said de Merlo.

"Something *shall* be done," replied Torquemada.

"There should be a tribunal set up to deal with heretics," cried Ojeda.

"The Inquisition is the answer," replied Torquemada; "but a new Inquisition . . . an efficient organization which would in time rid the country of heresy."

"There is no Inquisition in Castile at this time," went on Ojeda. "And why? Because, brother, it is considered that there are not enough cases of heresy existing in Castile to warrant the setting up of such an institution."

Torquemada said: "There are Inquisitors in Aragon, in Catalonia and in Valencia. It is high time there were Inquisitors in Castile."

"And because of this negligence," said Ojeda, "in the town of Seville these knaves flourish. I would ask for particular attention to the men of Seville. Brother, we have come to ask your help."

"Readily would I give it in order to drive heresy from Spain," Torquemada told them.

"We propose to ask an audience of the Queen to lay these facts before her. Holy Prior, can we count on your support with Her Highness?"

"You may count on me," said Torquemada. His thin lips tightened, his eyes glistened. "I would arrest those who are suspect. I would wring confessions from them that they might implicate all who are concerned with them in their malpractices; and when they are exposed I would offer them a chance to save their souls before the fire consumed them. Death by the fire! It is the only way to cleanse those who have been sullied by partaking in these evil rites." He turned to his guests. "When do you propose to visit the Queen?"

"We are on our way to her now, brother, but we came first to you, for we wished to assure ourselves of your support."

"It is yours," said Torquemada. His eyes were shining. "The hour has come. It has been long delayed. This country has suffered much from civil war, but now we are at peace and the time has come to turn all men and women in Castile into good Christians. Oh, it will be a mighty task. And we shall need to bring them to their salvation through the rack, hoist and faggot. But the hour of glory is about to strike. Yes, yes, my friends, I am with you. Every accursed Jew in this kingdom, who has returned to the evil creed of his forefathers, shall be taken up, shall be put to the test, shall feel the healing fire. Go. Go to the Queen with my blessing. Call on me when you wish. I am with you."

When his visitors had gone, Torquemada went to his cell and paced up and down.

"Holy Mother," he cried, "curse all Jews. Curse those who deny the Christ. Give us power to uncover their wickedness and, when they are exposed in all their horror, we shall know how to deal with them in your holy name and that of Christ your son. We will take them. We will set them on the rack. We will tear their flesh with red-hot pincers. We will dislocate their limbs on the hoist. We will torture their bodies that we may save their souls."

"A curse on the *Marranos*. A curse on the *Conversos*. I hate all practising Jews. I suspect all those who call themselves New Christians. Only when we

145

have purged this land of their loathsome presence shall we have a pure Christian country."

He fell to his knees and one phrase kept hammering in his brain: I hate all Jews.

He shut his mind to thoughts which kept intruding. It was not true. He would not accept it. His grandmother had *not* been a Jewess. His family possessed the pure Castilian blood. They were proud of their *limpieza*.

Never, never would Alvar Fernandez de Torquemada have introduced Jewish blood into the family. It was an evil thought; it was like a maggot working in his brain, tormenting him.

It was impossible, he told himself.

Yet, during the period in which his grandfather had been married, persecution of the Jews was rare. Many of them occupied high posts at Court and no one cared very much what blood they had in their veins. Grandfather Alvar Fernandez had carelessly married, perhaps not thinking of the future trouble he might be causing his family.

Tomás de Torquemada refused to believe it. But the thought persisted.

He remembered early days. The sly knowledge and sidelong looks of other boys, the whispers: "Tomás de Torquemada — he boasts of his Castilian blood. Oh, he is so proud of his *limpieza* — but what of his old grandmother? They say she is a Jewess."

What antidote was there against this fear? What but hatred?

146

"I hate the Jews!" he had said continually. He forced himself to show great anger against them. Thus, he reasoned, none would believe that he was in the slightest way connected with them. Thus he could perhaps convince himself.

Alonso de Spina, who, almost twenty years before, had tried to arouse the people's anger against the Jews, was himself a *Converso*. Did he, Tomás de Torquemada, whip himself to anger against them for the same reason?

Torquemada threw himself onto his knees. "Give me strength," he cried, "strength to drive all infidels and unbelievers to their death. Give me strength to bring the whole of Castile together as one Christian state. One God. One religion. And to the fire with all those who believe otherwise."

Torquemada — who feared there might be a trace of Jewish blood in his veins — would emerge as the greatest Catholic of Castile, the punisher of heretics, the scourge of the Jews, the man who worked indefatigably to make an all-Christian Castile.

Ferdinand was with Isabella when she received Alonso de Ojeda and Diego de Merlo.

Isabella welcomed the monks cordially and begged them to state their business.

Ojeda broke into an impassioned speech in which he called her attention to the number of *Conversos* living in Seville.

"There are many *Conversos* throughout Castile," said Isabella quietly. "I employ some of them in my own service. I rejoice that they have become Christians. It is what I would wish all my subjects to be."

"Highness, my complaint is that while many of these Conversos in Seville profess Christianity they practise the Jewish religion."

"That," said Isabella, "is a very evil state of affairs."

"And one which," put in Diego de Merlo, "Your Highness would doubtless wish to end at the earliest possible moment."

Isabella nodded slowly. "You had some project in mind, my friends?" she said.

"Highness, the Holy Office does not exist in Castile. We ask that you consider installing it here."

Isabella glanced at Ferdinand. She saw that the pulse in his temple had begun to hammer. She felt sad momentarily, and almost wished that she did not understand Ferdinand so well. He was possessed by much human frailty, she feared. It had been a great shock to discover that not only had he an illegitimate son but that he had appointed him, at the age of six, Archbishop of Saragossa. That boy was not the only child Ferdinand had had by other women. She had discovered that a noble Portuguese lady had borne him a daughter. There might be others. How should she hear of them?

Now his eyes glistened, and she understood why. The Inquisition had been set up in Aragon and because of it the riches of certain condemned men had found their way into the royal coffers. Money could make Ferdinand's eyes glisten like that.

"Such procedure would need a great deal of consideration," said Isabella.

"I am inclined to believe," said Ferdinand, his eyes still shining and with the flush in his cheeks, "that the installation of the Holy Office in Castile is greatly to be desired."

The monks had now turned their attention to Ferdinand, and Ojeda poured out a storm of abuse against the Jews. He spoke of ritual murders, of Christian boys, three or four years old, who had been kidnapped to take part in some loathsome rites which involved the crucifixion of the innocent child and the cutting out of his heart.

Ferdinand cried: "This is monstrous. You are right. We must have an inquiry immediately."

"Have the bodies of these children been discovered?" asked Isabella calmly.

"Highness, these people are crafty. They bury the bodies in secret places. It is a part of their ritual."

"I think it would be considered necessary to have proof of these happenings before we could believe them," said Isabella.

Ferdinand had turned to her. She saw the angry retort trembling on his lips. She smiled at him gently. "I am sure," she said quietly, "that the King agrees with me."

"An inquiry might be made," said Ferdinand. His voice sounded aloof, as it did when he was angry.

"An inquiry, yes," said Isabella. She turned to the monks. "This matter shall have my serious consideration. I am indebted to you for bringing it to my notice."

She laid her hand on Ferdinand's arm. It was a command to escort her from the chamber.

When they were alone, Ferdinand said: "My opinion would appear to count for little."

"It counts for a great deal," she told him.

"But the Queen is averse to setting up the Inquisition in Castile?"

"I have not yet given the matter sufficient consideration."

"I had always believed that it was one of your dearest wishes to see an all-Christian Castile."

"That is one of my dearest wishes."

"Why, then, should you be against the extirpation of heretics?"

"Indeed I am not against it. You know it is part of our plans for Castile."

"Then who is best fitted to track them down? Surely the Inquisitors are the men for that task?"

"I am not sure, Ferdinand, that I wish to see the Inquisition in Castile. I would wish first to assure myself that, by installing the Inquisition here, I should not give greater power to the Pope than he already has. We are the sovereigns of Castile, Ferdinand. We should share our power with no one else."

Ferdinand hesitated. Then he said: "I am sure we could set up our Inquisition — our own Inquisition which should be apart from Papal influence. I may tell you, Isabella, that the Inquisition can bring profit to the crown. Many of the *Conversos* are rich men, and it is one of the rules of the Inquisition that those who are

150

found guilty of heresy forfeit land . . . wealth . . . all possessions."

"The treasury is depleted," said Isabella. "We need money. But I would prefer to replenish it through other means."

"Are the means so important?"

She looked at him almost coldly. "They are of the utmost importance."

Ferdinand corrected himself quickly. "Providing the motive is a good one . . ." he began. "And what better motive than to bring salvation to poor misguided fools? What nobler purpose than to lead them into the Catholic Church?"

"It is what I would wish to see, but as yet I am inclined to give this matter further consideration."

"You will come to understand that the Inquisition is a necessity if you are to make an all-Catholic Castile."

"You may be right, Ferdinand. You often are." She smiled affectionately. Come, she seemed to be saying, let us be friends. This marriage of ours has brought disappointments to us both. I am a woman who knows she must rule in her own way; you hoped I would be different. You are a man who cannot be faithful to his wife; I hoped *you* would be different. But here we are — two people of strong personalities which we cannot change, even for the sake of the other. Let us be content with what we have been given. Do not let us sigh for the impossible. For our marriage is more than the union of two people. What matters it if in our hearts we suffer these little disappointments? What are they, compared with the task which lies before us?

She went on: "I wish to show you our new device. I trust it will please you, for it gives me so much pleasure. I am having it embroidered on a banner, and I did not mean to show you until it was finished; but soon it will be seen all over Castile, and when the people see it they will know that you and I stand together in all things."

He allowed himself to be placated; and she called to one of her pages to bring the piece of embroidery to her.

When it was brought she showed him the partly finished pattern.

She read in her quiet voice, which held a ring of triumph: "*Tanto monta, monta tanto — Isabel como Fernando.*"

She saw a slow smile break out on Ferdinand's face. As much as the one is worth, so much is the other — Isabella as Ferdinand.

She could not say more clearly than that how she valued him, how she looked upon him as her co-ruler in Castile.

Still he knew that in all important matters she considered herself the sole adjudicator. Whatever their device, whatever her gentleness, she still remained Queen in her own right. She held supreme authority in Castile.

As for the installation of the Inquisition, thought Ferdinand, in time she would agree to it. He would arrange for Torquemada to persuade her.

With Ferdinand on one side to show what material good the Inquisitors could bring them, with Torquemada on the other to speak of the spiritual needs of Castile — they would win. But it would not be until they had convinced Isabella that the Inquisition was necessary to Castile.

Isabella sent for Cardinal Mendoza and commanded that it should be a completely private audience.

"I pray you sit down, Cardinal," she said. "I am deeply disturbed, and I wish you to give me your considered opinion on the matter I shall put before you."

The Cardinal waited respectfully; he guessed the matter was connected with the visit of the two Dominicans.

"Alonso de Ojeda and Diego de Merlo," began Isabella, "are deeply concerned regarding the behaviour of *Marrams* in Seville. They declare that there are many men and women who, proclaiming themselves to be Christians, cynically practise Jewish rites in secret. They even accuse them of kidnapping and crucifying small boys. They wish to set up the Inquisition in Castile. What is your opinion of this, Cardinal?"

The Cardinal was thoughtful for a few seconds. Then he said: "We have fanatics in our midst, Highness. I am deeply opposed to fanaticism. It warps the judgement and destroys the peace of the community. Through the centuries the Jewish communities have been persecuted, but there is no evidence that such persecution has brought much good to the countries in which it was carried out. Your Highness will remember that in the fourteenth century Fernando Martinez preached against the Jews and declared that they were responsible for the Black Death. The result — pogroms all over Spain. Many suffered, but there is no evidence of any good that this brought. From time to time rumours spring up of the kidnapping and crucifixion of small boys, but we should ask ourselves what truth there is in these rumours. It was not very long ago that Alonso de Spina published his account of the evil doings of *Conversos*. Strange, when he himself was a *Converso*. One feels that he wished it to be widely known that he was a good Catholic . . . so good, so earnest that he was determined to expose his fellows. Very soon afterwards rumours of kidnappings and crucifixions occurred again. I think, Highness, knowing your desire for justice, that you would wish to examine these rumours with the utmost care before accepting them as truth."

"You are right. But should they not be examined? And in that case, who should be the examiners? Should this task not be the duty of Inquisitors?"

"Can we be sure, Highness, that this desire to set up the Inquisition in Castile does not come from Rome?"

Isabella smiled faintly. "It is as though you speak my thoughts aloud."

"May I remind you of the little controversy which recently occurred?"

"There is no need to remind me," answered Isabella. "I remember full well."

Her thoughts went to that recent incident, when she had asked for the appointment of one of her chaplains, Alonso de Burgos, to the bishopric of Cuenca; but because the nephew of Pope Sixtus, Raffaele Riario, had desired the post it had gone to him. As Isabella had on two previous occasions asked for appointments for two of her protegés — which had gone to the Pope's candidates — she was angry and had recalled her ambassador from the Vatican. With Ferdinand's help she had proposed to get together a council, that the conduct of the Pope might be examined. Sixtus, alarmed that his nepotism would be exposed in all its blatancy, gave way to Isabella and Ferdinand, and bestowed the posts they had demanded on their candidates.

It was quite reasonable to suppose therefore that Sixtus would have his alert eyes on Isabella and Ferdinand and would seek some means of curbing their power. How could this be done with greater effect than by installing the Inquisition — an institution which was apart from the state and had its roots in Rome? The Inquisition could grow up side by side with the state, gradually usurping more and more of its power. It could be equivalent to a measure of Roman rule in Spain.

Isabella looked with grateful affection at the Cardinal, who had been thinking on the same lines and who saw the issues at stake as clearly as she did herself.

"I know Your Highness will agree with me that we must be continually watchful of the power of Rome. Here in Castile Your Highness is supreme. It is my urgent desire that you should remain so."

"You are right as usual," answered Isabella. "But I am disturbed that some of my subjects should revile the Christian faith."

The Cardinal was thoughtful. In his heart — although this was something he could never explain to Isabella, for he knew she would never understand him — he believed in taking his religion lightly. He was aware that belief — to be real belief — must be free. It was something which could not be forced. This was contrary to the accepted notion, he was fully aware, and for this reason he must keep his thoughts to himself. He wished life to be comfortably pleasant and, above all, dignified. The Inquisition in Aragon, Valencia and Catalonia was, he realised, at this stage a lethargic institution. Its officers lived easily and did not much concern themselves with the finding of heretics. If such were discovered they could, no doubt, by the means of a little bribery and diplomacy, escape disaster.

But when he thought of this earnest young Queen who, by her single-minded purpose and strict punishment of all offenders, had changed a state of anarchy into one of evergrowing law and order, he could imagine what such a new and terrifying institution as the Inquisition could become under the sway of Isabella and such men as Tomás de Torquemada, whom it was almost certain, Isabella would nominate — perhaps with himself — as her chief adviser if she should establish the Inquisition in Castile.

Isabella and Torquemada were stern with themselves; they would be more dreadfully so with others.

To a man who loved luxury, who cared for good living, who was devoted to the study of literature and enjoyed translating Ovid, Sallust and Virgil into verse, the thought of forcing opinions on men who were

156

reluctant to receive them, and would only do so under threat of torture and death, was abhorrent.

Cardinal Mendoza would have enjoyed calling to his presence those men of different opinion, discussing their views, conceding a point, setting forth his own views. To force his opinions on others was nauseating to a man of his culture and tolerance. As for the thought of torture, it disgusted him.

This he could not explain to Isabella. He admired Isabella. She was shrewd; she was earnest; she was determined to do what was right. But, in the Cardinal's opinion, she was uneducated; and he deplored her lack of education, which had resulted in a narrow mind and a bigotry which prevented her from meeting the Cardinal on his own intellectual level.

The Cardinal was going to fight against the installation of the Inquisition with certain enthusiasm. He could not, however, bring to bear the fervour of a Torquemada, for he was not of the same fervent nature. But he would certainly attempt to lead Isabella away from that line of action.

He said: "Highness, let us give a great deal of thought to this matter. Before we decide to bring in the Inquisitors, let us warn the people of Seville that they place themselves in danger by denying the faith."

Isabella nodded. "We will prepare a manifesto . . . a special catechism in which we will explain the duties of a true Christian. This could be set up in all churches in Seville and preached from all pulpits."

"Those who do not conform," said the Cardinal, "will be threatened with the fires of hell."

"It may well be," said Isabella, "that this will be enough to turn these men and women of Seville from their evil ways."

"Let us pray that it will serve," said the Cardinal. "Is it Your Highness's wish that I should prepare this catechism?"

"None could do it so well, I am sure," said Isabella.

The Cardinal withdrew, well pleased. He had — for the time at least — foiled the attempt of the Dominicans to install the Inquisition in Castile. Now he would produce his catechism, and he hoped that it would bring about the required effect.

Shortly afterwards Mendoza's *Catecismo de la Doctrina Cristiana* was being widely circulated throughout the erring town of Seville.

When Torquemada heard that Mendoza's *Catecismo* was being circulated in Seville he laughed aloud, and laughter was something he rarely indulged in. But this laughter was scornful and ironical.

"There is a great deal you have to learn about the wickedness of human nature, Cardinal Mendoza!" he murmured to himself.

Torquemada was sure that the heretics of Seville would pretend to study the catechism; they would feign belief in the Christian faith; then they would creep away and jeer at Mendoza, at Isabella, at all good Christians while they practised their Jewish rites in secret.

"This is not the way to cleanse Seville!" cried Torquemada; and he was on his knees asking for Divine help, imploring the Virgin to intercede for him, that he might be given the power to cleanse not only Seville but the whole of Castile of the taint of heresy.

In time, he told himself, understanding will dawn on the Queen — even on the Cardinal who, though a good Catholic himself, leads a far from virtuous life. Scented linen, frequent baths, *amours* . . . indulgence in the sensuous enjoyment of music and literature! The Cardinal would on his deathbed have to ask remission of many sins.

Torquemada embraced himself, pressing his arms round his torso so that the hair shirt came into even more painful contact with his long-suffering body. Secretly he thanked God and the saints that he was not as other men.

It seemed to him then that he had a glimmer of the Divine will. His time would come. The Cardinal would fail, and into the hands of Torquemada would be placed the task of bringing Castile to repentance.

Until then he might concern himself with the building of the monastery of St Thomas. So to Avila he travelled with a good conscience. He was sure that soon he would receive the call to desert pleasure for duty.

Isabella had journeyed to Seville.

It had been the custom of the Kings of Castile to sit in the great hall of the Alcazar and pronounce judgement on offenders who were brought before them.

Each day Isabella attended in the great hall. Occasionally Ferdinand accompanied her and they sat side by side administering justice.

These sessions were conducted in a ceremonial manner, and Isabella was sumptuously dressed for the purpose. She took little delight in fine clothes, but was always ready to see the need for splendour. It was imperative that she be recognised in this turbulent city as the great Queen of Castile; and in this place, where the inhabitants had lived among the remains of Moorish splendours, it was necessary to impress them with her own grandeur.

Isabella proved herself to be a stern judge.

Determined as she was to eradicate crime in her kingdom, she showed little mercy to those who were found guilty. She believed that the slightest leniency on her part might send certain of her subjects back to a life of crime, and that, she was determined, should not happen. If she could not make them reform for the love of virtue she would make them do so from the fear of dire punishment.

Executions were numerous, and a daily ceremony.

The people were beginning to understand that this woman, who was their Queen, was far stronger than the male rulers of the past years. Four thousand robbers escaped across the frontiers, while Isabella dealt with those who had been caught and found guilty. They would suffer as they had made others suffer, and they should be an example to all.

It was in the great hall of the Seville Alcazar that a party of weeping women, led by the Church dignitaries of Andalucia, came to her and implored her for mercy.

Isabella received them gravely. She sat in regal state, her face quite impassive, while she watched those women in their anguish.

They were the mothers and daughters of men who had offended against the laws of the land.

"Highness," cried their spokesman, "these people admit that their loved ones have sinned and that the Queen's rule is just, but they implore your mercy. Grant them the lives of their husbands and fathers on condition that they swear never to sin again."

Isabella considered the assembly.

To her there was only wrong and right — completely clear cut. She could condemn malefactors to great suffering and be quite unmoved; Isabella had not much imagination, and it would never occur to her to see herself in another's place. Therefore she could contemplate the utmost suffering unperturbed.

But her aim was not punishment in itself, but only as a means to law and order; and, as she studied these weeping women, it occurred to her that if they would be responsible for the good conduct of their men she had no wish to punish them.

"My good people," she said, "you may go your way in peace. My great desire is not to inflict harsh punishment on you and your folk, but to ensure for you all a peaceful land. I therefore grant an amnesty for all sinners — except those who have committed serious crimes. There is a condition. Those who are freed must give an undertaking to live in future as peaceful citizens. If they do not, and are again brought before myself or any of the judges, their punishment will be doubly severe."

A great cry went up in the hall. "Long live Isabella!" In the streets, the cry was taken up; and as a tribute to her strength they added: "Long live *King* Isabella!"

From Andalucia to Galicia went Ferdinand and Isabella. Galicia was a turbulent province, ready to give trouble to Isabella as Catalonia had given trouble to Aragon.

But how different was the state of the country! Already there were signs of prosperity where there had been desolation. Travellers no longer had their fear of robbers which had once made travelling a nightmare. The inns were looking prosperous and almost gay.

Isabella felt a wave of exultation as she rode through the countryside and received the heartfelt gratitude of her subjects.

Ferdinand, riding beside her, said: "We see a prosperous country emerging from the chaos. Let us hope that soon it will be not only a prosperous but an all-Christian country."

Isabella knew that this was a reference to her refusal to establish the Inquisition in Castile, but she feigned ignorance of the meaning behind his words. "I share that hope," she said gently.

"It will not be until we have defeated Muley Abul Hassan and have set the holy banner flying over Granada."

"I fear not, Ferdinand."

"He showed his defiance of us when he asked for a peace treaty and refused to pay the tribute I demanded on your behalf. Because he had paid none to your brother, that did not mean that we should allow him to pay none to you. You remember his insolent answer."

"I remember it very well," answered Isabella. " 'Tell the Queen and King of Castile that we do not coin gold but steel in Granada.' "

"An insolent threat," cried Ferdinand, "made by Muley Abul Hassan because he knew that we were not in a position to chastise him for it. But the position is changing, eh, Isabella."

She smiled at him. He was restive, always eager for action. It was as though he said: Since we cannot have the Inquisition installed in Castile let us make immediate war on Granada.

She said, continuing her thoughts aloud: "We have recently emerged from one war. There is nothing that saps a country's resources so surely as war, there is nothing so fraught with danger."

"This would be a holy war," said Ferdinand piously. "We should have Heaven on our side."

"A holy war," mused Isabella.

She was thinking of herself as a young Princess, kneeling with Tomás de Torquemada, who had said: "You must swear that if ever you have the power you will work with all your might to make an all-Christian Spain." And she had replied: "I swear."

"I swear," now said Isabella the Queen.

In Galicia Isabella dispensed justice with the same severity as she did in Castile. For those who had robbed and murdered she showed little mercy; and she dealt justice alike to rich and poor.

Often Ferdinand would be on the point of making suggestions to her. She did her utmost to avoid this; one of the things she hated most was to have to deny Ferdinand what he asked; yet she never hesitated to do so if she felt that justice demanded it.

It was thus in the case of Alvaro Yañez de Lugo. De Lugo was a very wealthy knight of Galicia who had been found guilty of turning his castle into a robber's den; travellers had been lured there to be robbed and murdered; and Isabella had judged that his punishment should be death.

She had left the judgement hall for her apartments when she heard that a man was imploring an audience with her on a matter of extreme importance.

Ferdinand was with her, and she asked that the man be brought to her presence immediately.

When he came, he looked furtively about him, and Isabella gave the order for all except Ferdinand to retire.

The man still looked apprehensive, and Isabella said: "I pray you tell me your mission. Have no fear, none but the King and myself will hear what you have to say."

"Highnesses," said the man falling on his knees, "I come from Don Alvaro Yañez de Lugo."

Isabella frowned. "The robber," she said coldly, "who is under sentence of death?"

"Yes, Highness. He has rich and powerful friends. They offer you a large sum of money if you will spare his life."

164

Isabella indignantly replied: "How could his life be spared when he has been justly sentenced to death?"

"How much money?" Ferdinand had found it impossible to prevent himself asking that question.

The answer came promptly. "Forty thousand *doblas* of gold."

"Forty thousand *doblas*!" Ferdinand echoed the words almost unbelievingly. "Have his friends so large a sum?"

"Indeed yes, Highness. And it is at your disposal. All that is asked in return is the life of Alvaro Yañez de Lugo."

"His is a very valuable life," said Ferdinand with a smile, and to her horror Isabella saw the acquisitive light in his eyes.

"In gold, Highness," whispered the man. "Half to be delivered on your Highnesses' promise, the other half when Don Alvaro is free."

Isabella spoke then. She said: "It seems to have been forgotten that this man is guilty of crimes so great that the death penalty has been imposed on him."

"That is why," explained Ferdinand, not without some impatience, "a great sum is offered for his release."

"It would seem to me," said Isabella quietly, "that this money, which is doubtless stolen property, would be highly tainted."

"We would wash it free of all taint," said Ferdinand, "if . . ."

"We shall not put ourselves to such pains," answered Isabella decisively. "You may return to your friends," she went on, addressing the man, "and tell them that this is not the way the Queen of Castile dispenses justice."

"Highness . . . you refuse!"

"The friends of Alvaro Yañez de Lugo do not know me, or they would not have dared bring such a dishonourable proposal to me. You should leave immediately before I decide to have you arrested for attempted bribery."

The man bowed and hurried from the apartment.

Ferdinand's face was white with anger.

"I see that you do not wish to pursue this holy war against the Moors."

"I wish it with all my heart," Isabella replied mildly.

"And as we are debarred from fighting this war because of the low state of the treasury you turn your back on forty thousand gold *doblas*!"

"I turn my back on bribery."

"But forty thousand *doblas* . . ."

"My kingdom shall be built on justice," Isabella told him simply. "How could that be if I brought to justice only those who could not buy their release?"

Ferdinand lifted his hands in an exasperated gesture. "We need money . . . desperately."

"We need honour more," she told him with dignity.

Ferdinand turned away from her. He could not trust himself to speak. Money . . . gold was in question; and Isabella was learning that her husband loved gold with a fervour he rarely bestowed on anything else.

166

★ ★ ★

Alonso de Ojeda had returned to the Monastery of St Paul in Seville a disappointed man. He had hoped by this time to have seen the Inquisition flourishing in Seville; and he feared that since Torquemada — who he knew desired, as much as he did himself, to see the Inquisition set up — could not persuade the Queen to it, there was little hope that anyone else could.

The fiery Ojeda stormed at his fellow Dominicans; he harangued the saints in his prayers. "How long, how long," he demanded, "must you look on at the sin of this city? How long before to us there is given a means of punishing these heretics that they may have a chance of salvation? Give me a sign . . . a sign."

Then — so Ojeda believed — came the sign, when there arrived at the monastery a young man who asked that he might be allowed an interview with the Prior, as he was deeply disturbed by something he had witnessed. He needed immediate advice.

Ojeda agreed to see him.

The man was young and good looking, and Ojeda, recognising him immediately as a member of the noble house of Guzman, took him into a small cell-like apartment.

"Now, my son," said the Prior, "you look distraught. What is this you want to confess, and why did you not take the matter to your own confessor?"

"Most Holy Prior, I feel this matter to be more than a confession. I feel it could be of the utmost importance. I know that you journeyed to Court recently and saw the Queen. For this reason, I believed I should come to you."

167

"Well, let me hear the nature of this confession."

"Holy Prior, I have a mistress."

"The lusts of the flesh must be subdued. You must do penance and sin no more."

"She is a *Marram*."

Ojeda's lids fell over his eyes, but his heart leaped with excitement.

"If she is a true Christian her Jewish blood should be of small account."

"Holy Prior, I believed her to be a true Christian. Otherwise I should never have consorted with her."

Ojeda nodded. Then he said: "She lives in the Jewish quarter?"

"Yes, Holy Prior. I visited her father's house in the *juderia*. She is very young, and it is naturally against the wishes of her family that she should take a lover."

"That is understandable," said Ojeda sternly. "And you persuaded her to defy her father's commands?"

"She is very beautiful, Holy Prior, and I was sorely tempted."

"How was it that you visited her father's house when he had forbidden her to take a lover?"

"I went in secret, Holy Prior."

"Your penance must be harsh."

"It may be, Holy Prior, that my sin will be readily forgiven me because had I not gone in secret I should never have discovered the evil that was going on in the house of my mistress."

Ojeda's voice shook with excitement. "Pray continue," he said.

"This is Holy Week," went on the young man. "I had forgotten that it was also the eve of the Jewish Passover."

"Go on, go on," cried Ojeda, unable now to suppress his eagerness.

"My mistress had secreted me in her room, and there we made love. But, Holy Prior, I became aware of much bustle in the house. Many people seemed to be calling, and this was not usual. There were footsteps outside the room in which I lay with my mistress, and I grew alarmed. It occurred to me that her father had discovered my presence in the house and was calling together his friends to surprise us and perhaps kill me."

"And this was what they were doing?"

"They had not a thought of me, Holy Prior, as I was to discover. I could no longer lie there, so I rose hastily and dressed. I told my mistress that I wished to leave as soon as I could, and she, seeming to catch my fear, replied that the sooner I was out of the house the better. So we waited until there was quietness on the stairs, and then we slipped out of her room. But as we reached the hall we heard sounds in a room nearby, and my mistress, in panic, opened a door and pushed me into a cupboard and shut the door. She was only just in time, for her father came into the hall and greeted friends who had just arrived. They were close to the cupboard in which I was hidden, and they did not lower their voices; so I heard all that was said. The friends had arrived at the house to celebrate the Passover. My mistress's father laughed aloud and jeered at Christianity. He laughed because he, a professing Christian, in secret practised the Jewish religion."

Ojeda clenched his fists and closed his eyes. "And so we have caught them," he cried; "we have caught them in all their wickedness. You did right, my friend; you did right to come to me."

"Then, Holy Prior, I am forgiven?"

"Forgiven! You are blessed. You were led to that house that you might bring retribution on those who insult Christianity. Be assured the holy saints will intercede for you. You will be forgiven the sin you have committed, since you bring these evil doers to justice. Now tell me, the name of your mistress's father? The house where he lives? Ah, he will not long live in his evil state!"

"Holy Prior, my mistress . . ."

"If she is innocent all will be well with her."

"I would not speak against her."

"You have saved her from eternal damnation. Living in such an evil house, it may well be that she is in need of salvation. Have no fear, my son. Your sins are forgiven you."

The *Marrano* family was brought before Ojeda.

"It is useless," he told them, "to deny your sins. I have evidence of them which cannot be refuted. You must furnish me with a list of all those who took part with you in the Jewish Passover."

The head of the house spoke earnestly to Ojeda. "Most Holy Prior," he said, "we have sinned against the Holy Catholic Church. We reverted to the religion of

170

our Fathers. We crave pardon. We ask for our sins to be forgiven and that we may be taken back into the Church."

"There must have been others who joined in these barbarous rites with you. Who were these?"

"Holy Prior, I beg of you, do not ask me to betray my friends."

"But I do ask it," said Ojeda.

"I could not give their names. They came in secrecy and they were promised secrecy."

"It would be wiser for you to name them."

"I cannot do it, Holy Prior."

Ojeda felt a violent hatred rising in his heart. It should be possible now to take this man to the torture chambers for a little persuasion. Oh, he could stand there very nobly defending his friends. How would he fare if he were put on the rack, or had his limbs dislocated on the hoist? That would be a very different story.

And here am I, thought Ojeda, with a miserable sinner before me; and I am unable to act.

"Your penance would be less severe if you gave us the names of your friends," Ojeda reminded him.

But the man was adamant. He would not betray his friends.

Ojeda imposed the penance, and since these *Marranos* begged to be received back into the Christian Church, there was nothing to be done but admit them.

When he was alone Ojeda railed against the laws of Castile. Had the Inquisition been effective in Castile, that man would have been taken to a dungeon; there he would have been questioned; there he would have betrayed his friends; and instead of a few penances, a few souls saved, there might have been hundreds. Nor would they have escaped with a light sentence. They would have been found guilty of heresy, and the true punishment for heresy was surely death . . . death by fire that the sinner might have a foretaste of Hell's torment for which he was destined.

But as yet the Inquisition had not been introduced into Castile.

Ojeda set out for Avila, where Torquemada was busy with the plans for the monastery of Saint Thomas.

He received Ojeda with as much pleasure as it was possible for him to show, for Ojeda was a man after his own heart.

Ojeda lost no time in coming to the point.

"I am on my way to Cordova, where the sovereigns are at this time in residence," he explained. "I have uncovered certain iniquity in Seville which cannot be passed over. I shall ask for an audience and then implore the Queen to introduce the Inquisition into this land."

He then told Torquemada what had happened in the house in the *juderia*.

"But this is deeply shocking," cried Torquemada. "I could wish that the young Guzman had gone to the house on a different mission — but the ways of God are inscrutable. In the cupboard he heard enough to condemn these people to death — if as much consideration had been given here in Spain to spiritual

172

life as has been given to civil laws. The facts should be laid before the Queen without delay."

"And who could do that more eloquently than yourself? It is for this reason that I have come to you now. I pray you accompany me to Cordova, there to add your pleas to mine."

Torquemada looked with some regret at the plans he had been studying. He forced his mind from a contemplation of exquisite sculpture. This was his duty. The building of a Christian state from which all heresy had been eliminated — that was a greater achievement than the finest monastery in the world.

Torquemada stood before the Queen. A few paces behind her stood Ferdinand, and behind Torquemada was Ojeda.

Ojeda had recounted the story of what the young man had heard in the cupboard.

"And this," cried Torquemada, "is an everyday occurrence in Your Highness's city of Seville."

"I cannot like the young man's mission in that house," mused Isabella.

"Highness, we deplore it. But his discovery is of the utmost importance; and who shall say whether or not this particular young man was led to sin, not by the devil, but by the saints? Perhaps in this way we have been shown our duty?"

Isabella was deeply shocked. To her it seemed sad that certain of her subjects should not only be outside the Christian faith but that they should revile it. Clearly some action must be taken.

She did not trust Sixtus. Yet Ferdinand was eager for the setting up of the Inquisition. She knew, of course, that his hope was that by its action riches would be diverted, from those who now possessed them, to the royal coffers. She knew that many of the New Christians were rich men, for the Jews had a way of enriching themselves. She needed money. But she would not so far forget her sense of honour and justice as to set up the Inquisition for the sake of monetary gain.

She hesitated. Three pairs of fanatical eyes watched her intently while the fate of Spain hung in the balance.

Ojeda and Torquemada believed that torture and death should be the reward of the heretic. Isabella agreed with them. Since they were destined for eternal Hell fire, what was a little baptismal burning on earth? Ferdinand was a fanatic too. When he thought of money and possessions his eyes flashed every bit as fiercely as Torquemada's did for the faith.

Isabella remembered the vow she had once made before Torquemada; he was reminding her of it now.

An all-Christian Spain. It was her dream. But was she to give the Pope more influence than he already had?

Yet, considering her recent victories over him, she believed she — and Ferdinand with her — could handle him, should the occasion arise. Therefore why should she hesitate to set up the Inquisition in Castile that the land might be purged of heretics?

She turned to Ferdinand. "We will ask His Holiness for permission to set up the Inquisition in Castile," she said.

The waiting men relaxed.

Isabella had decided the fate of Spain, the fate of thousands.

CHAPTER SIX

La Susanna

It was spring in Toledo. Isabella rode through the streets between the Moorish buildings, and with her was Ferdinand and her two-year-old son, Prince Juan.

This was an important occasion. The Cortes was assembled in Toledo.

Isabella, so simple in her tastes on ordinary occasions, displayed the utmost splendour when she took her place at affairs of state. Now she was dressed in crimson brocade which was embroidered with gold, cut away to show a white satin petticoat encrusted with pearls; and seated on her horse she made a beautiful picture.

The people cheered her. They did not forget that she had brought justice into the land. They recalled the reigns of her father and half-brother, when favouritism had ruled in the palace and anarchy on the highway. Yet this young woman with the serene and gentle smile had been responsible for the change.

The sight of the little Prince in brocade and satin, as fine as that worn by his parents, warmed their hearts. There he sat on his pony, smiling and accepting the applause of the crowd as though he were a man instead of a very small boy.

"Long live Isabella and Ferdinand! Long live the Prince of the Asturias!" cried the people.

The citizens of Toledo were sure that this little one, when he reached manhood, would be as wise as his parents.

Into the great hall they went, and the first duty of that Cortes was to swear allegiance to the young Prince and proclaim him heir to the throne.

Isabella watched her son, and her smile became even more gentle. She was so proud of him. Indeed, she was proud of all her children. She wished that she had more time to spend with them. It was one of her greatest regrets that her duties called her so continually from the company of her children.

But she was dedicated to a great task. She was already achieving that which she had set out to do; she had made of Castile a law-abiding state. Galicia and Leon were following Castile. Once she had made them a *Christian* state, perhaps she would be able to think a little more frequently of her own family. For the time being she must leave them in the care of others; and only on rare occasions could she be with them.

Now little Juan was the recognised heir to the thrones of Castile and Aragon. Isabella determined that, before he reached these thrones, she and Ferdinand would have done their duty, so that it would not only be Castile and Aragon that he inherited but the whole of Spain, including the kingdom of Granada.

177

The Cortes then discussed the finances of the country; and it was agreeable to realise that these had been placed on a much firmer foundation than had existed when Isabella had inherited the throne.

But the most important edicts of that Cortes were the rules against the Jews, which were being reinforced.

These were unanimously adopted.

"All Jews in the kingdom to wear a red circle of cloth on the shoulders of their cloaks that they may be recognised as Jews by all who behold them."

"All Jews to keep within the *juderias,* the gates of which shall be locked at nightfall."

"No Jew is to take up a profession as innkeeper, apothecary, doctor or surgeon."

The persecution had been renewed.

Alonso de Ojeda was on the scent. As he walked through the streets of Seville he promised himself that very soon these carefree citizens would see sights to startle them.

The Jews did not believe that the laws were to be taken seriously. They had found living easy for too many years, thought Ojeda grimly.

They were to be seen without their red circles; they continued to practise as surgeons and doctors, and many people patronised them — for they were noted as being very skilled in these professions. They were not keeping to their ghettos.

They shrugged aside the new law. They could be seen sunning themselves under the palms and acacias, or strolling with their families along the banks of the Guadalquivir.

They had not realised that the old sun-drenched life was fast coming to an end.

One of Ojeda's fellow Dominicans brought a pamphlet to him and, as Ojeda read it, he smiled cynically.

Some Jew who was a little too sure of himself had written this.

What, he demanded, were these new laws but an attack on the Jewish community? The country was under the spell of priests and monks. Was that the way to prosperity? The Christian religion sounded impressive in theory; but how was it in practice?

"Blasphemy! Blasphemy!" cried Ojeda, and hurried with all speed to Torquemada, who, when he had read the pamphlet, was in full agreement with Ojeda that something must be done immediately.

He went to see Isabella.

Isabella, reading the pamphlet, shared the horror of the Dominicans.

She sent for Cardinal Mendoza and Torquemada.

"You see, Cardinal," she said, "your plan of persuasion has failed."

The Cardinal answered: "Highness, dire punishment will prove no more effective than persuasion, I feel sure."

Torquemada's fiery eyes blazed in his emaciated face. "Persuasion has undoubtedly failed," he cried. "We will at least try dire punishment."

"I fear, Cardinal," said Isabella, "that the time has come to do so."

"What are Your Highness's orders?" Mendoza asked.

"I desire," said Isabella, "that you and Tomás de Torquemada appoint Inquisitors; and as the town of Seville would appear to be more tainted with heresy than any other in our dominion, I pray you begin there."

Tomás de Torquemada flashed a glance of triumph at the Cardinal. His way was to be the accepted one. The catechism had proved fruitless.

The Cardinal was resigned. He saw that there was nothing he could do to hold back the tide of persecution. That Jew and his pamphlet had caused his race a great deal of harm.

The Cardinal had no alternative but to go with the stream.

"My lord Cardinal," said Torquemada, "let us obey the Queen's command and appoint Inquisitors for Seville. I suggest two monks of my order — Miguel Morillo and Juan de San Martino. Do you agree?"

"I agree," said the Cardinal.

In the narrow streets of Seville, dominated by the buildings of a Moorish character, the people lounged. It was warm on that October day, and ladies wearing high combs and black mantillas sat on the balconies overlooking the crowds gathering in the streets.

This was in the nature of a feast day, and the people of Seville loved feast days.

A man and his family sat on the balcony of one of the handsomest houses in the town, overlooking the streets. With them sat a young boy strumming a lute and another with a flute.

People paused to glance at the balcony as they passed along the street. They had been looking at Diego de Susan, who was known as one of the richest merchants in Seville.

They whispered of him: "They say he owns ten million *maravedis.*"

"Is there so much money in all Spain?"

"He earned it himself. He is a shrewd merchant."

"Like all these Jews."

"He has something besides his fortune. Is it true that his daughter is the loveliest girl in Seville?"

"Take a look at her. There she is, on the balcony. La Susanna, we call her here in Seville. She is his natural daughter and he dotes on her, they tell me. She is well guarded; and needs to be. She is not only full of beauty but full of promise, eh?"

And those who glanced up at the balcony saw La Susanna beside her father. Her large black eyes were slumbrous; her small face an enchanting oval, her heavy black hair caught up with combs which sparkled in the sunshine; her white, ringed hands waved the scarlet and gold fan before her exquisite features.

Diego de Susan was much aware of his daughter. She was his delight, and his great regret was that she was not his legitimate child. He had not been able to resist the temptation to take her into his household and bring her up with all the privileges of one born in wedlock.

He was afraid for La Susanna. She was so beautiful. He feared that the fate of her mother might befall her; and so he guarded her well. This he intended to do until he could make a brilliant marriage for her, which he was sure he would do, since she was so beautiful and he was so rich.

But now his attention was turned to the events of this day.

He had felt a little uneasy when he had heard the proclamation read in the streets.

Great suspicion had been aroused concerning the secret habits of certain New Christians — those Jews who had embraced the Christians religion only to revert in secret to their own faith. This, went on the proclamation, was the worst sort of heresy, and Inquisitors had been appointed to stamp it out. It was the duty of all citizens to watch their neighbours and if they discovered aught that was suspicious they must report it to the Inquisitors or their servants with all speed.

That made Diego de Susan feel vaguely uncomfortable; and when he recalled that it was added that those who did not report such suspicious conduct would themselves be considered guilty, his fear took on a more definite shape.

Were neighbours being asked to spy on each other? Were they being told: "Report heretics, for if you do not you in your turn will be considered guilty!"

Diego tried to shrug aside such uneasy thoughts. This was Seville — this beautiful and prosperous town which had been made prosperous by men such as himself and his fellow merchants. Many of them were New Christians, for it was the Jewish community who by their industry and financial genius had brought prosperity to the town.

No, these priests could do no harm in Seville.

He looked at his daughter. Automatically the white hand worked the vivid fan back and forth. Her long lashes drooped. Did she look a little secretive? Was all well with La Susanna?

La Susanna was thinking: What will he say when he knows? What will he do? He will never forgive me. It is what he feared would happen to me.

She grew suddenly angry. She had a fiery temper which could rise within her and madden her temporarily. It is his own fault, she told herself. He should not have shut me away. I am not the kind to be shut away. Perhaps I take after my mother. I must be free. If I wish for a lover, a lover I must have.

Her expression did not change as she went on moving the fan.

She adored Diego, but her emotions were too strong to be controlled. She hated herself because she had deceived him, and because she hated herself she hated him.

It is his fault, all his fault, she told herself. He has no one to blame but himself.

Soon, she thought, I shall be unable to hide the fact from him that I am pregnant. What then?

She had been well guarded, but, with the help of her sympathetic maid, it had not been impossible to have her lover smuggled into the house. He was young and handsome, a member of a noble Castilian family, and she had been unable to repress her desire for him. She had not thought of the consequences. She had never thought of the consequences of her actions. She had been impulsive. Thus must her mother have been.

Now she sat on the balcony, only vaguely hearing the shouts in the streets, unaware of the new tension which was creeping over the city. She was thinking of her father, who had loved her so tenderly during the years of her childhood, who was so proud of the daughter known throughout Seville as *la hermosa hembra*. Oh, yes, she was indeed beautiful, but she was no longer a child; now she was a woman who must live her life as she wished to, who must escape from the rule of a father who, out of his very love for her, treated her with a strictness which, to one of her wild nature, was intolerable.

And what will he say, she asked herself again and again, when I present myself to him and say, "Father, I am with child"?

And where was her lover? She did not know. She had tired of him, and he had no longer been smuggled into her room. There was only the child within her to remind herself how much she had loved him.

A procession was now coming through the street, and the sight of it sent a shiver through the most thoughtless of the spectators. It was as though a warning cloud hung over the sunny streets.

On it came, headed by the Dominican monk who carried the white cross. There were the Inquisitors in their white robes and black hoods. With them walked their familiars, the *alguazils*, who would assist them in their work, and the Dominican friars, in their coarse habits, their feet bare.

It was a mournful procession, funereal and depressing. On it went to the Convent of St Paul, where the Prior, Alonso de Ojeda, was ready to instruct these men in the duties which lay before them, to whip them to fierce enthusiasm by his fiery denunciation of those who did not accept the rigid tenets of his own faith.

Even La Susanna, her mind full of her own impending tragedy, sensed the foreboding inspired by that grim band of men. She looked at her father and saw that he was sitting tense, watching.

Crowds of gipsies, beggars and children followed the procession to the convent, but they, who previously had been chattering, shouting and dancing as they went, had fallen silent.

A visitor had stepped onto the balcony. It was a fellow merchant and friend of Diego de Susan.

He was looking grave. He said: "I do not like the look of that, my friend."

Diego de Susan seemed to rouse himself and throw off his depression. "Why, they are trying to bring the Inquisition to Seville. They will not succeed."

"Who will prevent them?"

Diego had risen and laid his hand on the shoulder of his friend. "Men like you and myself. Seville prospers. Why? Because we have brought trade to it. Men such as ourselves rule Seville. We have only to stand together, and we shall soon make it clear that we will have no Inquisitors inquiring into our private lives."

185

"You think this possible?"

"I am sure of it."

Diego de Susan spoke in strong ringing tones; and one of the musicians on the balcony began to strum his lute.

La Susanna forgot the procession. She was saying to herself: How shall I tell him? How shall I dare?

In a back room of Diego de Susan's house many of the most important citizens of Seville were gathered together. Among them were Juan Abolafio, who was the Captain of Justice and Farmer of the Royal Customs, and his brother Fernandez Abolafio, the licentiate. There were other wealthy men, such as Manuel Sauli and Bartolomé Torralba.

Diego had all the doors closed and had posted servants whom he could trust outside, that none might overhear what was said.

Then he addressed the gathering. "My friends," he said soberly, "you know why I have asked you to assemble here this day. We have seen the procession on its way to the Convent of St Paul, and we know what this means. Hitherto we have lived happily in this town. We have enjoyed prosperity and security. If we allow the Inquisitors to achieve the power for which they are clearly aiming that will be the end of our security, the end of our prosperity."

"At any hour of the night we may hear the knock on the door. We may be hurried away from our families before we even have time to dress. Who can say what will happen to us in the dark dungeons of the

Inquisition? It may be that, once taken, we should never see our friends and families again. My friends, it need not be. I am convinced it need not be."

"Pray tell us, friend Diego, how you propose to foil these plots against us?" asked Juan Abolafio.

"Are they plots against us?" interrupted his brother.

Diego shook his head sadly. "I fear they may well be directed against us. We are the New Christians; we have wealth. It will be easy to bring a charge against us. Yes, my friends, I am certain that these plots are directed against ourselves. The Inquisitors have been shown great respect by the people of Seville; but their invitation to come forward and expose those whom they call heretic has not been taken up. Therefore they themselves will begin to look for victims."

"It has been announced that it is a sin for the people not to pass on any information that comes their way . . . in other words, the citizens are being subtly threatened that they must become spies, or themselves be suspected," said Bartolomé Torralba.

"You are right, Bartolomé," Diego replied. "We must consider the fate of those New Christians who fled from Seville and took refuge with the Marquis of Cadiz, the Duke of Medina Sidonia and the Count of Arcos."

"It is because you are considering these people," put in Sauli, "that you have asked us to come here this day, is it not, Diego?"

Diego nodded sadly. "You know, my friends, that these noblemen, who gave the fugitives refuge on their estates, have been ordered to hand them over to the Inquisitors of our town."

All the men looked grave.

He went on: "They have been threatened with ecclesiastical displeasure if they do not obey. More than that . . . they themselves will incur the displeasure of the Queen, and we know what this could mean. But do not let us be downhearted. Seville is our town. We will fight to preserve our rights and dignities."

"Can we do this?"

"I think we can. Once we show our determination to be strong, the people of Seville will be with us. We have their high regard. They know that we have brought prosperity to the town, and they ask that they may go on in that prosperity. Yes, if we show that we are strong and ready to fight for our liberty — and the liberty of conscience for all — they will be on our side. We are not poor men. I have brought you here to ask you how much money, how many men and arms you can put into this enterprise."

Diego drew papers towards him, and the conspirators watched him tensely.

From then on the conspirators met in the house of Diego de Susan.

There was great need, Diego impressed upon them, to preserve secrecy. Since the Inquisitors were continually reminding the people that it was their duty to spy, how could they be sure who, even among those servants whom they considered loyal, might not be on the alert?

188

It was a few days later when Diego came into his daughter's room without warning; he saw her sitting with her embroidery in her hand, staring before her with an expression on her face which Diego could only construe as fearful apprehension.

His mind was full of the conspiracy which was coming to its climax, and he thought: My dearest child, she has sensed what is about to happen and she is terrified of what will become of me.

"My darling," he cried, and he went to her and embraced her.

She threw herself into his arms and began to sob passionately.

He stroked her hair. "All will be well, my daughter," he murmured. "You should have no fear. No harm will come to your father. They frightened you, did they not . . . with their black hoods and their mournful chanting voices! I grant you they are enough to strike terror in any heart. But they shall not harm us. Your father is safe."

"Safe?" she murmured, in a bewildered voice. "You, safe . . . Father?"

"Yes, yes, daughter. This is our secret . . . not to be spoken of outside these walls. But you, who know me so well, have sensed what is happening. You know why the Captain of Justice and his friends come to the house. You have heard the injunctions from the Convent of St Paul. Yes, my child, we are going to rise against them. We are going to turn them out of Seville."

La Susanna had been so occupied with her personal tragedy that she had not given much thought to the new laws which had been brought to Seville. The conspiracy, of which her father was the head, seemed to her, in her ignorance — for she had always lived in the utmost comfort and luxury, sheltered in her father's house — a trivial affair. She could not conceive that her father, the rich and influential Diego de Susan, could ever fail in his dealings with the authorities; and this conspiracy seemed to her a childish game compared with her own dilemma.

She had never been able to restrain her feelings. Her wild and passionate nature broke forth at that moment, and she burst into loud laughter.

"Your conspiracy!" she cried. "You are obsessed with that and give no thought to me and what may be happening to me. I am in dire trouble . . . and you are concerned only with your conspiracy!"

"My dearest, what is this?"

She stood up, drew herself to her full height and, as he looked at her body, in which the first signs of pregnancy were beginning to be apparent, he understood.

She saw him turn pale; he was stunned with horror; she realised with triumph that for a moment she had made him forget his conspiracy.

"It is impossible," he cried out, angry and pathetic at the same time. He was refusing to believe what he saw; he was imploring her to tell him he was mistaken.

La Susanna's uncontrolled emotions broke out. She loved him so much that she could not bear to hurt him; and because she was self-willed, defiant and illogical she now hated herself for having brought this tragedy on him; and since she could not continue to hate herself, she must hate him because his pain made her suffer so.

"No!" she cried. "It is not impossible. It is true. I am with child. My lover visited me at night. You thought you had me guarded so well. I deceived you. And now he has gone and I am to have a child."

Diego groaned and buried his face in his hands.

She stood watching him defiantly. He dropped his hands and looked at her; and his face, she saw, was distorted with rage and grief.

"I have loved you," he said. "I could not have loved you more if you had been my legitimate daughter. I have cared for you . . . I have watched over you all these years, and this is how you repay me."

La Susanna thought: I cannot endure this. I am going mad. Is it not enough that I must bear my child in shame? How can he look at me like that? It is as though he no longer loves me. He thinks to rule me . . . to rule Seville . . . me with his strict rules; Seville with his conspiracy. I cannot endure this.

"So you regret taking me into your house! Have no fear. I shall ask nothing of you that you do not want to give."

She was laughing and crying as she ran from the room and out of the house. She heard his voice as he called her: "Daughter, daughter, come back."

But she went on running; she ran through the streets of Seville, her beautiful black hair escaping from its combs and flying out behind her.

191

She was thinking of her father whom she had loved so dearly. She could not forget the expression of rage and sorrow on his face.

"I love him no longer . . . I hate him. I hate him. I shall punish him for what he has made me suffer."

And, when she stopped running, she found herself outside the Convent of St Paul.

It was dusk, and still La Susanna had not returned to the house.

Diego was frantic. He had searched for her in the streets of Seville and beyond; he had wandered along the banks of the Guadalquivir calling her name, imploring her to come home.

But he could not find her.

He thought of her wandering in the country in the darkness of the night, at the mercy of robbers and bold adventurers who would have no respect for her womanhood. It was more than Diego could bear. His anxiety for her had made him forget temporarily the plan which was about to come to fruition to oust the Inquisitors from Seville.

He returned to the house, and when he heard that she had not come home he wandered out into the streets again, calling her name.

And at last he found her.

She was quiet now, and she walked through the streets as though she were unaware of everything, even herself.

He ran to her and embraced her; she was trembling and she could not find words to speak to him. But she was coming home.

He put his arm about her. "My little one," he said, "what anxiety you have caused me! Never run away from me. This has happened, but we will weather it together, my darling. Never run away from me again."

She shook her head and her lips framed the words: "Never . . . never . . ."

Yet she seemed distrait, as though her mind wandered; and Diego, who knew the wild impetuosity of her nature, feared that some harm had been done to her mind by the shock she had suffered.

He murmured tenderly as they came towards the house: "All is well now, my little one. Here we are at home. Now I shall nurse you back to health. We will overcome this trouble. Have no fear. Whatever happens, you are my own dear daughter."

They entered the house. It seemed unusually quiet. One of the servants appeared. He did not speak, but at the sight of his master and La Susanna he turned and hurried away.

Diego was astonished. He strode into the small parlour, and there he found that they had visitors, for several men rose silently as he entered.

They were the *alguazils* of the Inquisition.

"Diego de Susan," said one of them, "you are the prisoner of the Inquisition. You will accompany us to the Convent of St Paul for questioning."

"I!" cried Diego, his eyes flashing. "I am one of the leading citizens of Seville. You cannot . . ."

The *alguazil* made a sign to two guards, who came forward and seized Diego.

As they dragged him out of the house, Diego saw that La Susanna had fainted.

The news spread through Seville. Its leading citizens were lodged in the cells of St Paul's. What was happening to them there could be guessed. The Inquisitors were determined to show the citizens of Seville that a mistake had been made if it was thought they did not mean to carry out their threats.

Others were arrested. Did this mean that the cells of St Paul's had been turned into torture chambers?

La Susanna, who had collapsed at the sight of the *alguazils* who had come to arrest her father, had been lying on her bed in a dazed condition. When at length she arose, her grief was terrible. It was the grief of remorse.

It was she who had brought the *alguazils* to the house; it was she who, in a sudden uncontrollable rage, had run to the Convent of St Paul's and told the eager Inquisitors of the conspiracy which was brewing in her father's house and of which her father was the leader.

What were they doing to him and his friends now in the Convent of St Paul? There were terrible hints of torture, and if these were true, she and she alone was responsible.

There was only one way to cling to her sanity. She would refuse to believe these stories of the methods of Inquisitors. There would merely be gentle questionings; the plot would be unmasked; and then her father would return home.

194

She went out and stood in the shadow of the Convent of St Paul looking up at those stone walls.

"Father," she sobbed, "I did not mean to do it. I did not know. I did not think . . ."

Then she went to the gate and asked to be admitted.

"Let my father be freed," she implored. "Let me take his place."

"This girl is mad," was the answer. "Tell her to go away. There is nothing we can do for her here."

Then she beat with her hands on the stone walls, and she wept until she was exhausted and slumped down in her misery, her dark hair falling about her face so that she, *la hermosa hembra*, had the appearance of a beggar rather than of the one-time pampered daughter of the town's richest man.

As she crouched there a man who was passing took pity on her.

"Rise, my child," he said. "Whatever your sorrow, you cannot wash it away with tears."

"I deserve death," she answered, and she lifted her beautiful eyes to his face.

"What crime have you committed?"

"The greatest. That of betrayal. I have betrayed the one whom I loved best in the world, who has shown me nothing but kindness. He is in there and I do not know what is happening to him, yet some sense tells me that he is suffering greatly. I brought this suffering to him — *I* who have received nothing but good at his hands. That is why I weep and pray for death."

"My child, you should go home and pray for the man you have betrayed, and pray for yourself. Only in prayer can you find consolation."

"Who are you?" she asked.

"I am Reginaldo Rubino, Bishop of Tiberiades. I know who your father is. He is Diego de Susan, who has been guilty of plotting against the Holy Office. Go home and pray, my child, for he will need your prayers."

A great despair came to her then.

She knew this man spoke the truth. She knew that a tragedy had come to Seville which made her own problems but trifles in comparison.

In awe she returned to the house; and although she believed that she had reached the very depth of despair, she was silent and no longer wept.

The day had come.

It was to be as a feast day . . . a grim holiday when all the people must go into the streets to see the show.

The bells were tolling. This was the occasion of the first *auto de fé* in Seville.

La Susanna had not slept for several nights. She had awaited this day with a terror which numbed her. Yet she would be there; she would witness the results of her treachery.

She listened to the bells, and she wrapped her shawl tightly about her, for she did not wish to be recognised. All Seville knew who would be the chief victims in today's grizzly spectacle; and they would know who was the wicked one who had made this possible — the girl who had betrayed her own father.

But I did not know, she wanted to cry out. I did not understand. Did any of you understand what the coming of the Inquisition would mean to Seville? Once we were free. Our doors were left open and we did not dread a knocking on them. We had no fear that suddenly the *alguazils* would be among us . . . pointing at our loved ones. You . . . you and you . . . *You* are the prisoners of the Inquisition. You will come with us. And who could realise that that would be the last one saw of the dear familiar face.

For when one saw it again, the face would appear to be different. It would be unfamiliar. It would not be the face of one who had lived at peace for years among his family. It would be that of a man who had been torn from the family life he had once known, by a terrible experience of physical and mental pain and the brutal knowledge of the inhumanity of men towards their fellows. No, it would not be the same.

"I cannot look. I dare not look," she murmured. But she must look.

There was the Dominican monk leading the procession; he looked sinister in his coarse robes. He carried the green cross high, and about it had been draped the black crape. This meant that the Holy Church was in mourning because it had discovered in its midst those who did not love it.

La Susanna looked up at the sky and asked herself: "Perhaps it is all Heaven that is in mourning because men can act with such cruelty towards other men?"

197

Here they were — the dreary monks, the familiars of the Holy Office; and then the halberdiers guarding the prisoners.

"I cannot look, I cannot look," murmured La Susanna yet she continued to look; and she saw him — her beloved father, barefoot and wearing the hideous yellow *sanbenito*, and she saw that on it was painted the head and shoulders of a man being consumed by flames; there were devils with pitchforks, and the flames were pointing upwards.

With him were his fellow conspirators, all men whom she had known throughout her childhood. She had heard them laugh and chat with her father; they had sat at table with the family. But now they were strangers. Outwardly they had changed. The marks of torture were on them; their faces had lost their healthy colour; they were yellow — although a different shade from that of the garments they wore; and in their eyes was that look of men who had suffered horror, before this undreamed of.

The prisoners passed on, and following them were the Inquisitors themselves with a party of Dominicans, at the head of which was the Prior of St Paul's, Alonso de Ojeda . . . triumphant.

Ojeda looked down on the prisoners as he preached his sermon in the Cathedral.

His expression was one of extreme fanaticism. His voice was high-pitched with mingled fury and triumph. He pointed to the prisoners in their yellow garments. These were the sinners who had defiled Holy Church.

These were the men who would undoubtedly burn for ever in Hell fire.

All must understand — all in this wicked city of Seville — that the apathy of the past was over.

Ojeda, the avenger, was among them.

From the Cathedral the procession went to the meadows of Tablada.

La Susanna followed.

She felt sick and faint, yet within her there burned a hope which she would not abandon. This could not be true. This could not happen to her father. He was a rich man who had always been able to buy what he wanted; he was a man of great influence in Seville. He had so few enemies; he had been the friend of the people and he had brought prosperity to their town.

Something will happen to save him, she told herself.

But they had reached the meadows; and there were the stakes; and there were the faggots.

"Father!" she cried shrilly. "Oh, my father, what have they done to you?"

He could not have heard her cry; yet it seemed to her that his eyes were on her. It seemed that for a few seconds they looked at each other. She could scarcely recognise him — he who had been so full of dignity, he who had been a little vain about his linen — in that hideous yellow garment.

"What have they done to you, my father?" she whispered. And she fancied there was compassion in his eyes; and that he forgave her.

The fires were lighted. She could not look. But how could she turn away?

She heard the cries of agony. She saw the flames run up the hideous yellow; she saw her father's face through the smoke.

"No!" she cried. "*No!*"

Then she slid to the ground, and knelt praying there, praying for a miracle while the smell of burning flesh filled her nostrils.

"Oh God," she whispered, "take me . . . Let me not rise from my knees. Strike me dead, out of your mercy."

She felt a hand on her shoulder and a pair of kindly eyes were looking into hers.

It was the Bishop of Tiberiades who had spoken to her outside the Convent of St Paul.

"So . . ." he said, "it is La Susanna. You should not have come here, my child."

"He is dying . . . cruelly dying," she moaned.

"Hush! You must not question the sentence of the Holy Office."

"He was so good to me."

"What will you do now?"

"I shall not go back to his house."

"All his goods will be confiscated by the Inquisition, my child; so you would not be able to stay there long if you went."

"I care not what becomes of me. I pray for death."

"Come with me."

She obeyed him and walked beside him through the streets of the city. She did not notice the strained faces of the people. She did not hear their frightened whispers. She was unaware that they were asking themselves whether this terrible scene, which they had witnessed this day, could become a common one in Seville.

There was nothing for La Susanna but her own misery.

They had reached the door of a building which she knew to be one of the city's convents.

The Bishop knocked and they were admitted.

"Take care of this woman," said the Bishop to the Mother Superior. "She is in great need of your care."

And he left her there, left her with her remorse and the memory of her father at the stake, with the sound of his cries of anguish as the flames licked his body — all of which were engraved upon her mind for ever.

In the Convent of St Paul Ojeda planned more such spectacles. They had begun the work. The people of Seville had lost their truculence. They understood now what could happen to those who defied the Inquisition. Soon more smoke would be rising above the meadows of Tablada.

Seville should lead the way, and other towns would follow; he would show Torquemada and the Queen what a zealous Christian was Alonso de Ojeda.

He sent his Dominicans to preach against heresy in all the pulpits of the city. Information must be lodged against suspected heretics. Anyone who could be suspected of the slightest heresy must be brought before the tribunals and tortured until he involved his neighbours.

There were friars at St Paul's whose special duty it was on the Jewish Sabbath to station themselves on the roof of the convent and watch the chimneys of the town. Anyone who did not light a fire was suspect. Those whose chimneys were smokeless would be brought before the tribunal; and if they did not confess, the torture could be applied; it was very likely that, on the rack or the hoist or subjected to a taste of the water torture, these people would be ready not only to confess their own guilt but to involve their friends.

"Ah!" cried Ojeda. "I will prove my zeal to Tomás de Torquemada. The Queen will recognise me as her very good servant."

And, even as he spoke, one of his monks came hurrying to him to tell him that plague had struck the city.

Ojeda's eyes flashed. "This is the Divine will," he declared. "This is God's punishment for the evil-living in Seville."

The stricken people were dying in the streets.

"Holy Prior," declared the Inquisitor Morillo, "it is impossible to continue with our good work while the plague rages. It may be that men who are brought in for questioning will sicken and die in their cells. Soon we shall have plague in St Paul's. There is only one thing we can do."

"Leave this stricken city," agreed Ojeda. "It is the Divine will that these people shall be punished for their loose living; but God would not wish that we, who do His work, should suffer with them. Yes, we must leave Seville."

"We might go to Aracena, and there wait until the city is clean again."

"Let us do that," agreed Ojeda. "I doubt not that Aracena will profit from our visit. It is certain that it contains some heretics who should not be allowed to sully its purity."

"We should travel with all speed," said Morillo.

"Then let us leave this day."

When he was alone Ojeda felt a strange lethargy creep over him; he felt sick and dizzy.

He said to himself: It is this talk of the plague. It is time we left Seville.

He sat down heavily and tried to think of Aracena. The edict should be read immediately on their arrival, warning all the inhabitants that it would be advisable for them to report any acts of heresy they had witnessed. Thus it should not be difficult to find victims for an *auto de fé*.

One of the Dominicans had come into the room; he looked at the Prior, and his startled terror showed on his face.

He made an excuse to retire quickly, and Ojeda tried to rise to his feet and follow him, but he slipped back into his chair.

Then Ojeda knew. The plague had come to St Paul's; it embraced not only those who defied the laws of the Church but also those who set out to enforce them.

Within a few days Ojeda was dead; but the *Quemadero* — the Burning Place — had come to stay; and all over Castile the fires had begun to burn.

CHAPTER
SEVEN

The Birth Of Maria And The Death Of Carillo

Christmas had come and Isabella was enjoying a brief respite from her duties, with her family. It was rarely that they could all be together, and this union made the Queen very happy.

She could look back over the years of her reign with a certain pride.

There was peace in the kingdom. Alfonso of Portugal had died in the August of the previous year. He had been making preparations to resign the throne in order to go into residence at the monastery of Varatojo, and was travelling through Cintra when he was attacked by an illness which proved to be fatal. He had caused her a great deal of anxiety and she could only feel relieved that he could cause her no more.

She had punished criminals so harshly that she had considerably reduced their number; and she now proposed to punish heretics until none was left in her country.

She saw her friend Tomás de Torquemada infrequently now; he was obsessed by his work for the Holy Office. Her present confessor was Father Talavera, who was almost as zealous a worker for the Faith as Torquemada himself.

She knew she must not rest on her triumphs. Always she must remember the work that was left to be done. There was yet another great task awaiting her, for the setting up of the Inquisition, and the ridding her country of all heretics, was not all. There, she told herself, like a great abscess on the fair form of Spain, was the kingdom of Granada.

But for this Christmas she would indulge herself. She would be as an ordinary woman in the heart of her family.

She went to the nurseries to see her children.

As they stood before her and curtsied she felt a sadness touch her. She was a stranger to them, and she their mother. She suppressed a desire to take them in her arms and caress them, to weep over them, to tell them how she longed to be a gentle mother to them.

That would be unwise. These children must never forget that, although she was their mother, she was also their Queen.

"And how are my children this day?" she asked them.

Isabella, who was eleven years old, naturally spoke for the others. "They are all well, Highness; and they hope they see Your Highness in like state."

A faint smile curved Isabella's lips. What a formal answer to a mother's question! But it was the correct answer of course.

Her eyes dwelt on her son — her little three-year-old Juan. How could she help his being her favourite? Ferdinand had wanted a boy, because he had felt it was fitting that there should be a male heir to the throne; and for Ferdinand's sake she was glad.

And there was little Juana, a charming two-year-old, with a sparkle in her eyes.

"I am very happy, my dears," said Isabella, "because now your father and I can spare a little time from our duties to spend with our family."

"What duties, Highness?" asked young Juana.

The Infanta Isabella gave her sister a stern look, but the Queen said: "Nay, let her speak."

She sat down and lifted her youngest daughter onto her knee. "You would know what the duties of a king and queen are, my child?"

Juana nodded.

The Infanta Isabella nudged her. "You must not nod when the Queen speaks to you. You must answer."

Juana smiled enchantingly. "What must I say?"

"Oh, Highness," said the Infanta Isabella, "she is but two, you know."

"I know full well," said Isabella. "And now we are in our close family circle we need not observe too strictly the etiquette which it is necessary to maintain on all other occasions. But of course you must remember that it is only at such times as this that we can relax."

"Oh, yes, Highness," the young Isabella and Juan replied together.

Then the Queen told her children of the duties of king and queen, how they must travel from place to place; how it was necessary to call a Cortes to govern the country, how it was necessary to set up courts to judge evil doers — those who broke the civic law and the laws of God. The children listened gravely.

"One day," said Isabella, "Juan will be a King, and I think it very possible that you, my daughters, may be Queens."

"Queens?" asked young Isabella. "But Juan will be King, so how can we be Queens?"

"Not of Castile and Aragon, of course. But you will marry, and your husbands may be Kings; you will reign with them. You must always remember this and prepare yourselves."

Isabella stopped suddenly. She had had a vivid reminder of the past. She remembered those days at Arevalo where she and her young brother Alfonso had spent their childhood. She remembered her mother's hysteria and how the theme of her conversation was always: You could be King — or Queen — of Castile.

But this is different, she hastened to assure herself. These children will ascend thrones without trouble. It is not wild hysteria which makes *me* bid them prepare.

But she changed the subject abruptly and wished to know how they were progressing with their lessons. She would see their books and hear them read.

Then young Isabella read and, while she was doing so, the child began to cough.

"Do you cough often?" the Queen asked,

"Now and then, Mother."

"She is always coughing," Juan told his mother.

"Not always," Isabella contradicted. "At night sometimes, Mother. Then I am given a soothing syrup, and that makes me go to sleep."

Isabella looked grave. She would consult the Infanta's governess about the cough.

The two younger children were clearly healthy; she wished that Isabella did not look so fragile.

"Highness," said little Juana, "it is my turn to read."

"She cannot," said the Infanta Isabella.

"She points to the page and pretends to," Juan added.

"I do read. I do," cried Juana. "I do, Highness, Highness, I do! I do! I *do*!"

"Well, my little one, you must not become so excited; and you must not tell lies, you know. If you say you can read, and you cannot read, that is a lie."

"People who tell lies go to Hell and burn for ever," announced Juan. "They burn here too. There are lots of people who burn here. *They* tell lies. They don't believe in God . . . our God . . . so we burn them to death."

"So you hear these things?" the Queen asked.

"They are always listening to gossip, Highness," the Infanta Isabella told her.

"It does not matter that they burn," Juan announced. "They are going to burn for ever, so what do a few minutes on earth matter? The priest told me so."

"Now, my children," said Isabella, "you must not talk of these matters, for they are not for children. Juana has told me she can read, and I shall be very disappointed in her if she has told me a lie."

Juana's face puckered, and Juan, who was very kind, put his arm about her shoulder.

"She learns some words, Highness, and knows them by heart. She points to the book and *thinks* she is reading."

Juana stamped her foot. "I do not *think* I read. I *do* read."

"Silence, my child!" commanded Isabella.

"You forget," said the Infanta, to her little sister, "that you are in the presence of Her Highness the Queen."

"I can read. I *can* read!" sobbed the child.

Isabella tried to catch her, but she wrenched herself free; she began to run round the room shouting: "I can read. I can. I can . . ."

The elder children watched her in dismay and amazement.

Then little Juana began to laugh, and as she laughed her laughter turned to tears.

The Queen stared at her youngest child, and a terrible fear had come to her.

Ferdinand burst on the domestic scene. Isabella started up at the sight of him, because she saw from his expression that some disaster had come to them.

Juan ran to his father and threw himself into his arms, but although Ferdinand lifted the boy up and kissed his cheek, he was not thinking of his children.

210

"Now that the King has come, you must go back to your nursery," Isabella told the children.

"No!" cried the naughty Juana. "No! We wish to stay with Papa."

"But you have heard Her Highness's command," said young Isabella horrified.

"And she will obey them," put in Ferdinand, smiling down at his little daughter, who was pulling at his doublet, murmuring: "My turn, Papa. It was my turn to be kissed."

"This little one," said Ferdinand, "reminds me of my mother."

Those words delighted Isabella so much that she forgot to wonder what ill news Ferdinand had to impart to her. Like *his* mother, she thought — calm, shrewd, practical Joan Henriquez. Not like Isabella's own mother, the poor sad Queen living in darkness at Arevalo.

"Come little mother-in-law," said Isabella, "you must go now to your nursery."

"What is a mother-in-law?" Juana asked.

"It is the mother of a wife's husband or a husband's wife," Isabella told her daughter.

Juana stood very still, her bright eyes wide, repeating to herself: "*Suegra. Suegra* . . . the mother of a wife's husband."

"Go along, Suegra, at once, I said," the Queen reminded her daughter; and young Isabella took her sister's hand and forced her to curtsey.

Ferdinand and Isabella stood looking after the children as they retired.

"You have bad news, Ferdinand," she said.

"The Moors have surprised our fortress of Zahara; it has fallen into their hands."

"Zahara! But that is serious."

Ferdinand nodded. "It was my own grandfather who recovered it from the Infidel," he said, "and now it is theirs once more."

"It must not remain so," Isabella replied.

"It shall not, my dear. If we had funds at our command I would wage a mighty war against the Infidel; and I would not cease to fight until every Mussulman had been driven from our land."

"Or converted to our faith," said Isabella.

"I would see the Christian flag flying over every town in Spain," went on Ferdinand. And his eyes were brilliant, so that Isabella knew that he was thinking of the riches of Moorish cities; he was thinking of their golden treasures.

"It shall come to pass," she told him.

Ferdinand turned to her then and laid his hands on her shoulders.

"You are tired, Isabella. You should rest more."

"No," she told him, "I am but in my third month of pregnancy. You know how it is with me. I work up to the end."

"Have a care, my wife. Although we have three children, we do not wish to lose any newcomers."

"I will take care, Ferdinand. Have no fear of that. You consider the loss of this fortress very damaging to our cause?"

"I consider it as the beginning of the Holy War."

"There have been many beginnings of that war which has been waged over our land periodically for centuries."

Ferdinand's grip on her shoulders tightened. "This, my Queen, is the beginning of that Holy War which is to end all such wars. This is the beginning of a united Spain."

It was three months after the loss of Zahara, when Isabella was in the town of Medina. She was now six months pregnant and was finding journeys irksome indeed. Again and again she reminded herself — and her friends did also — of that time when, undertaking similar journeys, she had suffered a miscarriage.

When she passed through villages and saw mothers in the fields and vineyards with their children about them she was a little envious. She loved her children dearly, and one of the greatest sorrows of her life was that she saw so little of them.

But as long as they were in good health and well cared for she must not think too constantly of them; perhaps when she had completed her great tasks she would be able to spend more time with them.

By then, she admitted ruefully, they would probably be married. For the magnitude of the two tasks which lay before her she well understood: to purge her country of all heretics, to set the Christian flag flying over all Spanish territory — these were the meaning of life to her; and she did not forget that they had been attempted before in the past centuries. But no one, as yet, had succeeded in completing them.

"Yet, with God's help, I will," declared Isabella. "And Ferdinand and such men as Torquemada will make my task easier."

Her confessor, Fray Fernando de Talavera came to her, and she greeted him with pleasure.

Devoted to piety as she was, she had always had a special friendship for her confessors, and when she was on her knees with them, she rarely sought to remind them that she was the Queen.

The influence of Torquemada would always be with her; and Talavera equally enjoyed her esteem.

Talavera was a much milder man than Torquemada — indeed it would have been difficult to find anyone who could match his zeal with that of the Prior of Santa Cruz — yet he was fervent in his piety. Like Torquemada, he did not hesitate to reprimand either Isabella or Ferdinand if he felt it was right to do so; and, although Ferdinand might resent this, Isabella never did if she believed that she deserved that reprimand.

She remembered now the first time Talavera had come to her to hear her confess. She had knelt, and had been astonished that he remained seated.

"Fray Fernando de Talavera," she had said, "you do not kneel with me. It is the custom for my confessors to kneel when I kneel."

But Talavera had answered: "This is God's Tribunal. I am here as His minister. Thus it is fitting that I should remain seated — as I represent God — while Your Highness kneels before me to confess."

214

Isabella had been surprised to be so addressed; but considering this matter, she came to agree that, as God's minister, her confessor should remain seated while she, the Queen, knelt.

From that day she had begun to believe that she had found a singularly honest man in Talavera.

Now she confessed that she longed for a simpler life, so that she might take a larger part in the bringing up of her children, that she envied mothers in humbler stations, that on occasion she asked herself what she had done to be condemned to a life of continual endeavour.

Talavera took her to task. She was God's chosen instrument. She did wrong to complain or to rail against such a noble vocation.

"I know it," she told him. "But there is a continual temptation for a mother who loves her husband and children to long for a more peaceful life with them at her side."

She prayed with Talavera for strength to do her duty, and for humility that she might accept with grace this life of sacrifice which had been demanded of her.

And when they had prayed, Ferdinand came to them.

He said: "I come to you with all speed. There is exciting news. The fortress of Alhama has been captured by Christian troops."

Isabella stood very still, her eyes closed, while she thanked God for this victory.

Ferdinand looked at her with some impatience. Her piety at times irritated him. Isabella never forgot it; as

215

for himself he had long decided that his religion was meant to serve him, not he his religion.

"The place," said Ferdinand, his eyes agleam, "is a treasure house. Ponce de Leon, the Marquis of Cadiz, attacked the fortress, and it succumbed after a struggle. He and his men stormed the town. The carnage was great; bodies are piled high in the streets, and the booty is such as has rarely been seen."

Isabella said: "And Alhama is but five or six leagues from Granada."

"There is wailing throughout the Arab kingdom," Ferdinand told her gleefully. "I shall prepare to leave at once and go to the assistance of brave Ponce de Leon, who has entered Alhama and is now being besieged by the Moors."

"This is a great victory," said Isabella. She was thinking of wild Ponce de Leon, who was an illegitimate son of the Count of Arcos, but who, on account of his many attributes, had been legitimised and given the title of Marquis of Cadiz. He was one of the boldest and bravest soldiers in Castile.

"Alhama must never be allowed to fall again into Moorish hands," said Ferdinand. "We have it and we will hold it. It shall be the springboard for our great campaign."

He left Isabella with Talavera and, when they were alone, Isabella said: "Let us give thanks for this great victory." And confessor and Queen knelt side by side.

When they arose, the Queen said: "My dear friend, when an opportunity arises I shall reward you for your services to me."

"I ask for no reward but to remain in Your Highness's service," was the answer.

"But I am determined to reward you," said the Queen, "for the great good you have done me. I shall bestow upon you the bishopric of Salamanca when it falls vacant."

"Nay, Highness, I should not accept it."

Isabella showed faint surprise. "So you would disobey my orders?"

Talavera knelt and, taking her hand, put his lips to it. "Highness," he said, "I would not accept any bishopric except one."

"And that one?"

"Granada," he said.

Isabella replied firmly: "It shall be yours . . . before long, my friend."

Her voice rang with determination. There would be no holding back now. The war against the Moors must begin in earnest.

It was April, and Isabella had journeyed from Medina to Cordova, where Ferdinand was stationed. She was now large with her child and she knew that she could do little more travelling before it was born.

Yet she wished to be with Ferdinand at this time.

But when she arrived, Ferdinand had already left, as the siege of Alhama had now been raised and Ponce de Leon freed.

Ferdinand had gone into Alhama with members of the Church and there had taken place a ceremony of purification. The mosques were turned into Christian churches, and bells, altar-cloths and such articles which were so much a part of the Christian Church were pouring into the town.

There was great rejoicing throughout Castile; there was great wailing throughout Granada.

"What treatment must we expect at the hands of these Christians?" the Moors asked themselves; for when they had ridden to the defence of Alhama they had found the bodies of the conquered Moors of that town, lying outside the walls, where they had been thrown by the conquerors; and those bodies lay rotting and naked, half devoured by vultures and hungry dogs.

"Is there to be no decent burial for an honourable enemy?" demanded the Moors.

The Christian answer was: "But these are Infidels. What should honourable burial mean to them?"

Furious with rage and humiliation, the Moors had again gone savagely to the attack, but by this time more Christian troops had appeared, and their efforts were futile.

Thus the victory of Alhama was complete, and Moors as well as Christians believed that this might well be a turning point in the centuries-long war.

To the church of Santa Maria de la Encarnacion Isabella sent an altar-cloth which she herself had embroidered; and she announced her regret that she could not go barefoot in person to give thanks for this victory. She dared not risk danger to her child, even in such a cause.

218

June had come and Isabella lay in childbed.

Beatriz de Bobadilla had come to be with her at this time. "For," said Beatriz, "I trust no other to care for you."

Isabella could always smile at her forthright friend, and only to Beatriz could she speak of her innermost thoughts.

"I long to be up and active again," she told Beatriz; "there is so much of importance to be done."

"You are a woman, not a soldier," grumbled Beatriz.

"A queen must often be both."

"Kings are fortunate," said Beatriz. "They may give themselves to the governing of their kingdom. A queen must bear children while she performs the same tasks as a king."

"But I have Ferdinand to help me," Isabella reminded her. "He is always there . . . ready to take over my duties when I am indisposed."

"When this one is born you will have four," said Beatriz. "Perhaps that is enough to ensure the succession."

"I would I had another boy. I feel there should be more boys. Ferdinand wishes for boys."

"The conceit of the male!" snorted Beatriz. "Our present Queen shows us that women make as good rulers as men — nay, better."

"Yet I think the people feel happier under a king."

"Clearly they do not, since they will not have the Salic law here."

"Never mind, Beatriz. The next ruler of Castile and Aragon — and perhaps all Spain — will be my Juan."

"That," answered Beatriz, "is years away."

"Beatrix . . ." Isabella spoke quietly. "Have you noticed anything . . . unusual about my little Juana?"

"She's a lively little baggage. That's what I have noticed."

"Nothing more, Beatriz?"

Beatriz looked puzzled. "What should I have noticed, Highness?"

"A certain wildness . . . a tendency to be hysterical."

"A spirited little girl with a brother who is a year older, and a sister who is several years older! She would need to be spirited, I think. I should say she is exhibiting normal tendencies."

"Beatriz . . . are you telling me the truth?"

Beatriz threw herself onto her knees beside her mistress. "Pregnant women are notorious for their fancies," she said. "I am learning that queens are no exception."

"You are my comforter, Beatriz."

Beatriz kissed her hand. "Always at your service . . . ready to die there," she answered brusquely.

"Let us not talk of death, but of birth. I do not think it will be long now. Pray for a boy, please, Beatriz. That would delight Ferdinand. We have two girls and but one boy. Families such as ours grow nervous. Our children must be more than children; and they do not belong entirely to us but to the state. So . . . pray for a boy."

"I will," said Beatriz fervently.

A few days later, Isabella's fourth child was born. It was a girl: Maria.

In a convent in the town of Seville a young woman was on her knees in her cell. She listened to the tolling bells and thought: I shall go mad if I stay here.

There was no way of forgetting in this quiet place. Every time she heard the bells, she thought of a grim procession passing through the streets; she could hear the voice of the preacher in the Cathedral; she could see, among the yellow-clad figures, the face of one whom she had loved and betrayed, she could smell the hideous odour which she had smelt for the first time in the meadows of Tablada.

Assuredly, she told herself a thousand times, I shall go mad if I stay here.

But where should she go? There was nowhere. The house which had been her father's had been confiscated. All that he had possessed had passed into the hands of the Inquisition; they had taken his goods when they had taken his life; and they had taken his daughter's peace of mind.

If she had her child . . . But what could a nun in a convent do with a child? She had lost her child. She had lost her father; she was losing her freedom.

How can I forget? she asked herself. Perhaps there was a way. She thought of fine glittering garments to replace the coarse serge of the nun's habit. She thought of a soft bed shared with a lover, to take the place of a hard pallet in a cell.

Perhaps in a life of gaiety she could forget her unhappiness.

I must escape, she told herself, for I shall go mad if I stay here.

She was passing out of her novitiate. Soon she must take the veil, and that would be the end of her hopes. Her days would be passed in silent solitude. A nun's life for *la hermosa hembra*, a life of solitude for one who had been the most beautiful woman in Seville?

She ran her hand through her short curls. They would grow again in all their beauty. But she must act quickly, before it was too late.

It was dusk as she slipped out of the convent.

On an errand of mercy, it was believed. They did not know her secret thoughts.

And when she was outside those grey walls she made her way to her father's house.

It was a foolish thing to do. There was no one belonging to him there.

She stood looking at the house and, as she looked, a man passed by. He stared at her. Her hood had fallen back, showing her short, glistening curls; and her face was no less beautiful than it had been in the days when she had sat on her father's balcony and fanned herself.

"Forgive me," said the man. His voice and manner told her he was of the nobility. "You are in distress?"

"I have escaped from a convent," she told him. "I have nowhere to go."

"But why did you escape? Do you mean you have simply walked out and decided not to go back again?"

"I escaped because the life of a nun is not the life for me."

Then he looked at her face, at the slumbrous dark eyes, at the sensual lips.

He said: "You are very beautiful."

"It is long since I was told so," she answered.

"If you come with me I will give you shelter," he told her. "Then you can tell me your story and make your plans. Will you come?"

She hesitated for a moment. His eyes, though courteous, were bold. She knew she was taking a step along a certain path. She must make up her mind now whether she would continue on that road to which he was beckoning her.

Her hesitation was brief.

It was for this that she had left her convent. This man pleased her; and he was offering to be her protector.

"Yes," she said. "I will come with you."

She turned her back on the house which had been her father's, and she was smiling as she walked beside her new protector.

In his residence at Alcalá de Henares, Alfonso Carillo, the Archbishop of Toledo, had left his laboratories and retired to his own apartments.

He said to his servants: "I will go to my bed, for I am very tired."

They were astonished because they had never before seen him so resigned. It was as though all the militancy had gone out of him and that he had no longer any interest in the affairs of the country, nor in the discoveries he might make through the scientific experiments in the pursuit of which he had squandered his vast fortunes.

"I think it is time," he said, "for me to make my peace with God, for I am an old man and I do not think there is much time left to me."

So his servant hurried away to arrange for the last rites, and the old Archbishop lay back on his bed thinking of the past.

"She is a great Queen, this Isabella of ours," he murmured to himself. "She has set the fires burning all over Castile. She will rid Castile of heretics and, it may well be, of all infidels, for she is determined to drive the Moors from Granada, and I have a feeling that what our Isabella sets out to achieve she will.

"And but for me she would never have attained the throne. Yet here I live in disgrace, cut off from the affairs which were once the whole meaning of life to me. I have been foolish. I should have taken no offence at Ferdinand's treatment of me. I should have shown no rancour towards Mendoza, the sly old fox! They are only waiting for my death to make him Primate of Spain.

"Yes, I have been foolish. After raising her up, I thought I could dash her down. But I was mistaken. I did not know Isabella. I could not guess the strength of this woman. And who can blame me? Was there ever such gentleness disguising such strength?"

He fell into a doze and, when he awoke, he saw the priests at his bedside. They had come to administer Extreme Unction.

The end of his turbulent life was near.

Isabella was with her month-old baby, Maria, when news from Loja was brought to her.

Muley Abul Hassan, the King of Granada, had taken fright at the loss of Alhama, and throughout the city of Granada there had been great mourning. But the Arabs were a warlike people and they remembered defeats of the past which had been turned into victories.

So they rallied and met the Christians at Loja.

Perhaps the Christians had allowed the success of Alhama to go to their heads; perhaps they had underestimated the resourcefulness of their enemies.

At Loja, that July, there was such a rout of the Christian armies that, had reinforcements come more quickly from Granada, Muley Abul Hassan would have wiped out all that was left of Ferdinand's army.

Isabella received the news without changing her expression, although her heart was filled with anxiety.

She sent for Cardinal Mendoza and, when he was with her, she told him the news.

He bowed his head and there were a few seconds of silence.

Then Isabella spoke. "I think this may be sent as a warning to us. We were too confident; we believed that we owed our victories to our own arms and skill, and not to God."

Mendoza gave the Queen a look which she construed as conveying his agreement with her. But in fact Mendoza was marvelling at her ability to see the guiding hand of God in all that befell her.

225

All over Castile the dread Inquisition was establishing itself. In many towns the atmosphere had changed almost overnight. The people walked the streets, furtive and afraid. The Cardinal guessed that their nights were uneasy. For who could know when there would be that knock at the door, those dreaded words: "Open in the name of the Inquisition."

Yet if he asked her what had happened to her towns she would have answered: "They are being cleansed of heretics." And she would believe that she was carrying out the wishes of God by setting up the Inquisition in Spain.

She will succeed in all she does, pondered Mendoza. There is a fire and fervency beneath that gentle façade which is unbeatable. She does not question the rightness of what she does. She is Isabella of Castile, and therefore rules by Divine will.

"The Moors are strong," said the Cardinal. "The task before us would seem insuperable — except by our brave and wise Queen."

Isabella accepted the compliment. Mendoza was too gallant, too courteous. He lacked the honesty of men such as Talavera and Torquemada; but his company was perhaps more pleasant, and she must forgive him his light-mindedness. He was a wise man in spite of the life he led; and disapproving of that as she did, she was still ready to accept him as her leading minister.

In affairs of state, she told herself, one must not overlook people because of their licentious habits. This man was a statesman, shrewd and wise, and she had need of him.

She said: "We shall prosecute the war with success. And now, my friend, I have news from Alcalá de Henares for you. Alfonso Carillo is dead. Poor Alfonso Carillo, he has died deeply in debt, I fear. He could never restrain himself — neither in politics nor in his scientific experiments. It was always so. He did me great harm, yet I am saddened because I remember those days when he was my friend."

"Your Highness should not grieve. He was your friend when he felt it expedient to be so."

"You are right, Archbishop."

The Cardinal looked at her, and she smiled at him in her gentle way.

"Who but you should be Archbishop of Toledo, and Primate of Spain? Who else could be trusted at the head of affairs in the years before us?"

Mendoza knelt and took her hand.

He was an ambitious man and was overcome with admiration and respect for a Queen as bigoted as herself, who could choose a man of his reputation because she knew he was her ablest statesman.

Ferdinand was pacing up and down the Queen's apartment. The defeat at Loja had greatly upset him. He had believed that victory over the Moors was almost within their grasp; and he could not face setbacks with the calm which was his wife's.

But Isabella herself — although she did not show this — was uneasy on account of the latest item of news which had now been brought to them.

They had thought La Beltraneja safe in her convent. Had she not taken the veil?

Ferdinand cried: "How can one be sure what Louis will do next? He has his eyes on Navarre. Make no mistake about that. Navarre shall belong to us. It is mine . . . through my father."

Isabella considered the position. The first wife of Ferdinand's father, Blanche, daughter of Charles III of Navarre, had on her death left Navarre to her son Carlos, who had been murdered to make way for Ferdinand. Navarre had then passed to Blanche, elder sister of Carlos and repudiated wife of Henry IV of Castile. Poor Blanche, like her brother, had met an untimely death; this was at the instigation of her sister Eleanor, who wanted Navarre for her son, Gaston de Foix.

On the death of John of Aragon, who had retained the title of King of Navarre, Eleanor had greedily seized power, but her glory was short-lived, for she died three weeks after her father.

Eleanor had arranged the murder of her sister Blanche, that her son, Gaston de Foix, might inherit Navarre, but Gaston had been killed during a tourney at Lisbon some years before the death of Eleanor, and the next heir was Gaston's son, Francis Phoebus.

Gaston's wife had been the Princess Madeleine, sister of Louis XI of France; thus Louis had his eye on Navarre and was determined that it should not go back to the crown of Aragon.

Ferdinand now told Isabella the cause of his alarm.

"Who can guess what Louis plans next? He now suggests a marriage between Francis Phoebus, King of Navarre, and La Beltraneja!"

"That is quite impossible," cried Isabella. "La Beltraneja has taken the veil and will spend the rest of her days in the convent of Santa Clara at Coimbra."

"Do you think the vows of La Beltraneja will stop Louis's making this marriage if he wishes it?"

"You may be right," said Isabella. "Doubtless he wishes to put Navarre under French rule and then, if La Beltraneja were the wife of his nephew, Francis Phoebus, he would support her claims to my crown."

"Exactly!" agreed Ferdinand. "We plan to make war on the Moors. Louis knows this. Doubtless he has heard of what happened at Loja. The crafty old man is choosing the right moment to strike at us."

"We must stop him, Ferdinand. Nothing should now stand in the way of our campaigns in this Holy War."

"Nothing shall," said Ferdinand.

CHAPTER EIGHT

Inside The Kingdom Of Granada

The most beautiful and the most prosperous province of Spain was Granada. It contained rich resources; there were minerals in its mountains; its Mediterranean ports were the most important in the whole of Spain; its pasture lands were well watered; and the industry of its people had made it rich.

The most beautiful city in Spain was the capital of the kingdom, Granada itself. Enclosed in walls with a thousand and thirty towers and seven portals, it appeared to be impregnable. The Moors were proud of their city and had reason to be. Its buildings were exquisite; its streets were narrow and the lofty houses were decorated with metal which shone in sun and starlight, giving the impression that they were jewelled.

The most handsome building in Granada — and in the whole of Spain — was the mighty Alhambra, fortress and palace, set on a hill. Not only was this enchanting to the eye, with its brilliant porticos and colonnades, not only did it, with its *patios* and baths, speak of luxury and extravagance, it was also useful and could house, should the need arise, an army of forty thousand.

Granada had been the centre of Moorish culture since 1228, when a chieftain of the tribe of Beni Hud had decided to make himself ruler of this fair city and had received rights of sovereignty from the Caliph of Baghdad, that he might reign under the titles of Amir ul Moslemin and Al Mutawakal (the Commando of the Moslems and the Protected of God).

There had been many to come after him, and their reigns had been turbulent; there were continual affrays with the Christian forces, and in 1464 a treaty was made with Henry IV in which it was arranged that Mohammed, the reigning King, should put Granada under the protection of Castile, and for this protection should pay to the kings of Castile an annual tribute of 12,000 gold ducats. It was this sum that the acquisitive Ferdinand had sought to bring to the Castilian coffers, for, when the affairs of Castile became anarchical during the latter years of the disastrous reign of Henry IV, the Moors had allowed the tribute to lapse, and the Castilians had not been in a position to enforce it.

Mohammed Ismail died in 1466, and when his son Muley Abul Hassan came to the throne the affairs of Granada were becoming almost as turbulent as those in the nearby province of Castile.

Even so, the Moors were a warlike people and determined to defend what they considered to be theirs. It was seven hundred years since the Arabs had conquered the Visigoths and settled in Spain. After seven hundred years the Moors felt that they could call Granada their own country.

Unfortunately for the Moorish population of Spain they faced defeat, not only because of the enemy without but on account of their troubles within.

There was treason in the very heart of the royal family.

From behind the hangings the Sultana Zoraya, the Star of the Morning, looked out onto the *patio* where the Sultan's favourite slave sat trailing her fingers in the water. Zoraya was full of hatred.

The Greek was beautiful, with a strange beauty never seen before in the harem; and the Sultan visited her often.

Zoraya was not disturbed by this. Let the Sultan visit the Greek when he wished. Zoraya was no longer young, and she had lived long enough in the harem to know that the favour of Sultans passed quickly.

The great ambition of the Sultan's wives should be to have a son, and Zoraya had her son, her Abu Abdallah, known as Boabdil.

Her fear was that the Greek's son should be put above Boabdil; and that she would never allow. She would be ready to kill any who stood between her son and his inheritance, and she was determined that the next Sultan of Granada should be Boabdil.

It was for this reason that she watched the Greek; it was for this reason that she intrigued within the Alhambra itself — a difficult feat for a woman who, a wife of the Sultan, must live among women guarded by eunuchs.

But Zoraya was no humble Arab woman, and she did not believe in the superiority of the male.

She had been educated in her home in Martos, when she had been intended for a brilliant marriage, so it was surprising that she should have lived so many years of her life in a Sultan's palace.

Yet it had not been a bad life. She would have no regrets once she had set Boabdil on the throne of Granada.

It was not difficult to arrange for messages to be passed from the harem to other parts of the palace. She who had been such a beautiful woman in her youth was now a forceful one. And Muley Abul Hassan was growing old and feeble. It was his brother, who was known by the name of El Zagal, the Valiant One, whom she feared.

Zoraya was proud. She had had her way often enough with the old Sultan. She had demanded special privileges from the moment when she had been brought before him in chains, and Muley Abul Hassan had denied her little in those days.

She was allowed to visit her son, Boabdil, though it should have been clear to the old Sultan that she sought to set a new Sultan in his place.

She despised Muley Abul Hassan as much as she feared his brother.

Now, as she watched the Greek slave, she asked herself what she had to fear. The Greek was beautiful, but Zoraya had more than beauty.

She thought of the day she had been brought to the Alhambra. She, the proud daughter of the proud governor of the town of Martos.

A strange day of heat and tension, a day which stood out in her life as one in which everything had changed, when she had stepped from one life to another — from one civilization to another. How many women were destined to live the life of a sheltered daughter of a Castilian nobleman and that of one of several wives in the harem of a Sultan!

But on that day Dona Isabella de Solis had become Zoraya, the Star of the Morning.

All through the day the battle had raged, and it was in the late afternoon when the Moors had stormed her father's residence. In a room in one of the towers, which could only be reached by a spiral staircase, she had cowered with her personal maid, listening to the shouts of the invaders, the death-cries of men, the screams of the women.

"We cannot escape," she had said again and again. "How is it possible for us to escape? Will they not search every room, every corner?"

She was right. There was no escape. And when she heard footsteps on the spiral staircase she pushed her trembling maid behind her and confronted the intruder. He was a man of high rank in the Moorish army. He stood looking at her, his bloody scimitar in his hand, and he saw that she was beautiful. Her dignity — that ingrained Castilian quality — was not lost on her captor. He took her maid. She would be for him, but when he set the chains on the wrists of Dona

Isabella de Solis, he said to her: "You are reserved for the Sultan himself."

And so she was taken in chains to Granada, into the mighty fortress which was to be her home. And there, she stood before Muley Abul Hassan, as proud as a visiting queen.

This amused him. He had taken her to his harem. She should be one of his wives. It was clearly an honour due to a high-born lady of such dignity.

Then she became his Star of the Morning and she bore him Boabdil; and from that time she determined that the next Sultan of Granada should be her son.

She had no fear that this would not be so. But the Greek had come, and the Greek was full of wiles. She also had a son.

Boabdil stood before his mother. He had the face of a dreamer. He wished that life would run more peacefully.

"Boabdil, my son," said Zoraya, "you seem unmoved. Do you not understand that that woman plots against us?"

"She will not succeed, oh my mother," said Boabdil. "For I am the eldest son of my father."

"You do not know how women will fight for their children."

Boabdil smiled at her. "But do I not see you, my mother, fighting for yours?"

"I will find a means of removing her from the palace. We will trick her. We will lure her into a situation from which she cannot escape. She shall be slain in the manner of an unfaithful woman. Boabdil, where is your manhood? Why do you not wish to fight for what is yours?"

"When Allah decides, I shall be Sultan of Granada, my mother. If Allah wished me to be Sultan at this time, he would make me so."

"You accept your fate. That is your Moorish blood, my son. My people take what they want."

"Yet it was they who were taken," said Boabdil gently.

"You anger me," said Zoraya. She came closer to him: "Boabdil, my son, there are men in Granada who would take up arms for you if you set yourself in opposition to your father."

"You would ask me to take up arms against my father?"

"There is your uncle, El Zagal, whose plan it is to take the crown from you. Your father is weak. But you would have your supporters. You do not ask me how I know this, but I will tell you. I have my spies in the streets. Messages are brought to me. I know what we could do."

"You endanger your life by such action, my mother."

She stamped her foot and threw back her still handsome head. Boabdil looked at her with affection, admiration and exasperation. He had never known a woman like his mother.

She narrowed her eyes and whispered: "If I thought that any might succeed in taking the throne from you, I would put you at the head of an army . . . this very day."

"My mother, you talk treason."

Her eyes flashed. "I owe loyalty to none. I was taken from my home against my will. I was brought here in chains. I was forced to lead the life of an Arab slave. I . . . the daughter of a proud Castilian. I owe no loyalty to any. Others ruled my life; now I say my reward is a crown for my son. You shall be Sultan of Granada even if we must make war on your father to put the crown on your head."

"But why should we fight for that which must, when Allah wills it, be ours?"

"My foolish son," answered Zoraya, "do you not understand that others intrigue to take the crown of Granada instead of you? The Greek wants it for her son. She is sly. How can we know what promises she wrings from a besotted old man? Your uncle looks covetously towards the crown. He wants it for himself. Allah helps those who help themselves. Have you not yet learned that, Boabdil?"

"I hear voices."

"Go then and see who listens to us."

"I beg of you, my mother, do not speak treasonably in case any should hear."

But even as he spoke guards had entered the apartment.

Zoraya was shocked. She demanded: "What do you here? Do you not know what the punishment is for forcing your way into the apartments of the Sultana?"

The guards bowed low. They spoke to Boabdil. "My lord, we come on the command of Muley Abul Hassan, Sultan of Granada. We must humbly request you to allow us to put these chains upon you, for it is our unhappy duty to conduct you and the Sultana to the prison in the palace."

Zoraya cried: "You shall put no chains on me."

But it was useless; the guards had seized her. Her eyes flashed with contempt when she saw her son Boabdil meekly hold out his hands to receive the chains.

In her prison Zoraya did not cease to intrigue. As Sultana and mother of Boabdil, recognised heir to the crown of Granada, there were many to work for her. The rule of Muley Abul Hassan was not popular. It was well known throughout the kingdom that the Christian armies were gathering against Mussulmans and that the Castile of today was a formidable province — no less so because, through the marriage of Isabella with Ferdinand, it was allied with Aragon.

"The Sultan is old. He is finished. Can an old man defend Granada against the growing danger?" That was the message which Zoraya had caused to be circulated through Granada. And in the streets the people whispered: "We are a kingdom in peril and a kingdom divided against itself. Old men are set in old ways. Our future is in the hands of our youth."

Zoraya and her son, although prisoners, did not suffer any privations. They were surrounded by servants and attendants. Thus Muley Abul Hassan had made it easy for Zoraya to continue to work for his dethronement and the succession of her son, Boabdil.

She sent her spies into the streets to spread abroad the scandals of the palace, to whisper of the bravery of Zoraya and Boabdil whom others sought to rob of their inheritance. Here was a brave mother fighting for the rights of her son; they could depend upon it that Allah would not turn his back upon her.

News was brought to her that the people in the streets were no longer whispering but saying aloud: "Have done with the old Sultan. Give us the new!" And Zoraya judged the moment had come. She summoned all her servants and attendants to her. She made the women take off their veils, the eunuchs their *haiks*.

Then she, with Boabdil and a very few of her most trusted servants, tied these end to end, making a long rope, which they secured and hung from a window.

First she descended the rope, followed by Boabdil.

She had arranged that they should be expected. No sooner had Boabdil reached the ground than several of their supporters were on the spot greeting Boabdil as their Sultan, honouring Zoraya as the great Sultana and mother, a woman whose name, they believed, would be a legend in the history of the Mussulmans, because she, in her maternal love, by her bravery and resource, had delivered their new Sultan from the tyranny of the old one.

There was war in Granada. Thousands rallied to the cause of Boabdil.

In the streets of the beautiful city of Granada, Moor fought Moor and the battle was fierce.

Muley Abul Hassan was taken by surprise, first by the treachery of his family, then by the force of their supporters. And although the fortress of the Alhambra itself remained faithful to him, the city was against him. Chivalry turned the men of Granada to the brave Sultana and her young son. Prudence weighed the matter and decided that Muley Abul Hassan had had his day and that the times needed the vigour of a young Sultan; and Muley Abul Hassan was driven from Granada, whence he fled to the city of Malaga, which had declared itself for him.

Thus while the Christian armies were gathering against them there was civil strife in the kingdom of Granada.

Isabella was thoughtful as she sat at her needlework. This was one of the rare occasions when she could find a brief hour's escape from state duties; and it was pleasant to have Beatriz with her at such a time.

Beatriz had her duties to her husband and was not in constant attendance on Isabella, so that those opportunities of being together were especially precious.

Isabella was now thinking of Ferdinand, who had seemed to be brooding on some secret matter. She wondered if his thoughts were with the events in Granada as hers were; but perhaps they were with some woman, some family of his, which existed unknown to her. It seemed strange that Ferdinand might have other families, women who loved him, children who aroused his affection even as her Isabella, Juan, Juana and little

Maria did — a strange, disturbing and unhappy thought.

She looked at Beatriz, who, not with any great pleasure, was working on a piece of needlework. Beatriz was too active a woman to find delight in such a sedentary occupation. Isabella would have enjoyed talking of these matters which disturbed her to a sympathetic friend like Beatriz; but she refrained from doing so; not even to Beatriz would she speak of matters, so derogatory, she believed, to the dignity of herself and Ferdinand as sovereigns of Castile and Aragon.

Beatriz herself spoke, for on these occasions Isabella had asked her friend to dispense with all ceremony, and that they should behave as two good wives come together for a friendly gossip.

"How go affairs in Navarre?" asked Beatriz.

"They give us cause for anxiety," answered Isabella. "One can never be sure what tortuous plan is in Louis's mind."

"Surely even he could not arrange that the vows La Beltraneja has taken should be swept aside."

"He is very powerful. And I do not trust Pope Sixtus. We have had our differences. And bribes can work wonders with a man such as he is, I fear."

"Bribes or threats," murmured Beatriz. "Francis Phoebus is, I hear, a beautiful creature. They say that he is rightly called Phoebus and that his hair is like golden sunshine."

"Doubtless," answered Isabella, "they exaggerate. Phoebus is a family name. It may well be that he is handsome, but he is also a king, and the beauty of kings and queens often takes its lustre from their royalty."

Beatriz smiled at her friend. "My Queen," she said, "I believe your natural good sense is equal to your beauty — and you are beautiful, Isabella, Queen or not!"

"We were talking of Francis Phoebus," Isabella reminded her.

"Ah, yes, Francis Phoebus, who is as beautiful as his name. I wonder what he feels about marrying the released nun of doubtful parentage."

"If that marriage is made," said Isabella grimly, "there will be many to assure him that there is no doubt whatsoever of her parentage. Oh, Beatriz, the tasks before us seem to grow daily. I had hoped that ere long we should be making war . . . real war . . . on Granada. But now that it would seem favourable to do so, there is trouble in Navarre. If Louis suggests removing La Beltraneja from her convent, having her released from her vows and married to his nephew of Navarre, make no mistake about it, his first plan will be to take Navarre under the protection of France, and his second to win my crown for La Beltraneja."

"Even Louis would never succeed."

"He would not succeed, Beatriz, but there would be another bitter war. A War of the Succession has already been fought and won. I pray hourly that there may not be another."

"That you may devote your energies to the war against the Moors."

Isabella thoughtfully continued with her needlework.

It was shortly afterwards that Ferdinand entered her apartment. He came without ceremony, but Beatriz, realising that he would not wish her to greet him with the informality which Isabella allowed, was on her feet and gave him a deep curtsey.

Isabella saw that Ferdinand was excited. His eyes shone in his bronzed face and his mouth twitched slightly.

"You have news, Ferdinand, good news?" she asked. "Please do not consider the presence of Beatriz. You know she is our very good friend."

Beatriz waited for his dismissal, but it did not come.

He sat down on the chair beside the Queen, and Isabella signed to Beatriz that she might return to her chair.

Ferdinand said: "News from Navarre."

"What news?" asked Isabella sharply.

"The King of Navarre is dead."

An almost imperceptible look of triumph stole across Ferdinand's face.

Beatriz caught her breath. She had visualised so clearly the young man known as Francis Phoebus who had been likened to the Sun God himself, and only a few moments ago she had considered him in his golden beauty; now she must adjust the picture and see a young man lying on his bier.

"How did he die?" Isabella asked.

"Quite suddenly," said Ferdinand; and, try as he might to look solemn, he could not manage it. The triumph remained on his face.

Beatriz's eyes went to Isabella's face, but as usual the Queen's expression told her nothing.

What does she think of murder? wondered Beatriz. How can I know, when she does not betray herself? Does she accept the murder of a young man, as beautiful as his name implies, because his existence threatens the throne of Castile? Will she say Thank God? Or in her prayers will she ask forgiveness because, when she hears that murder has been done at the instigation of her husband, she has rejoiced?

"Then," said Isabella slowly, "the danger of a marriage between Navarre and La Beltraneja no longer exists."

"That danger is over," agreed Ferdinand.

He folded his arms and smiled at his Queen. He looked invincible thus, thought Beatriz. Isabella realises this; and perhaps she says to herself: Unfaithful husband though you are, murderer though you may be, you are a worthy husband for Isabella of Castile!

"Now who rules Navarre?" asked Isabella.

"His sister Catharine has been proclaimed Queen."

"A child of thirteen!"

"Her mother rules until she is older."

"There is one thing we must do with all speed," said Isabella. "Juan shall be betrothed to Catharine of Navarre."

"I agree," said Ferdinand. "But I have news that Louis has not been idle. He is making preparations to seize Navarre. In which case it may very well be that they will not accept our son for Catharine."

"We must act against Louis at once," said Isabella.

"Your short respite is over," Ferdinand told her ruefully.

"I will leave at once for the frontier," Isabella replied. "We must show Louis that, should he attempt to move into Navarre, we have strong forces to resist him."

Isabella folded up her needlework as though, thought Beatriz, she were a housewife, preparing to perform some other domestic duty.

She handed the work to Beatriz. "It must be set aside for a time," she said.

Beatriz took the work, and understanding that they wished to discuss plans from which she was excluded, she curtsied and left Ferdinand and Isabella alone together.

Boabdil rode into battle against the Christian army.

Muley Abul Hassan and his brother El Zagal were fighting their own war, also against the Christians. They had made several attacks near Gibraltar and had had some success.

The people of Granada were beginning to say: "It may be that Muley Abul Hassan grows old and feeble, but with El Zagal beside him he can still win victories. Perhaps it is not the will of Allah that we throw him aside for the new Sultan, Boabdil."

"Boabdil must go into action," cried Zoraya. "He must show the Arab kingdom that he can fight as poor Muley Abul Hassan, and even El Zagal, never could."

So it was that Boabdil rode into action against the Christians. He was confident of success. Brilliantly clad in a mantle of crimson velvet embroidered with gold, he was an impressive figure, for beneath the cloak his damascened steel armour caught and reflected the light and glistened.

Out of the town of Granada he rode to the cheers of the people; and those cheers were still ringing in his ears when he took the road to Cordova.

He met the Christian forces on the banks of the Xenil, and the fighting was fierce.

Boabdil had not been born to be a fighter. He was a man who longed for peace; and but for his forceful mother he would never have found himself in the position he was in that day. His men sensed the lack of resolution in their leader; and the Christians were determined.

And there on the banks of the Xenil, Boabdil saw his Moors defeated and, realising that he himself in his rich garments and on his milk-white horse was conspicuous as their leader, he sought a way to hide himself and escape death or what would be more humiliating, capture.

He saw his men mowed down, his captains slaughtered; and he knew the battle was lost.

The river had risen during the night and it was impossible for him to ford it; so he dismounted and, abandoning his horse, hid himself among the brush which bordered the river.

As he cowered there among the reeds, a passing soldier caught a glimpse of the bright scarlet of his cloak and came to investigate.

Boabdil stood up, his scimitar in his hand, and prepared to fight for his life. But his discoverer, a soldier named Martin Hurtado, realising that here was a man of high rank, yelled to his comrades and, at once, Boabdil was surrounded.

Now his scimitar was of no use against so many and, in an endeavour to save his life, he cried: "I am Boabdil, Sultan of Granada."

That made the soldiers pause. Here was a prize beyond their wildest hopes.

"Stay your swords, my friends," cried Martin Hurtado. "We will take this prize to King Ferdinand. I'll warrant we'll be richly rewarded for it."

The others agreed, although it went against the grain to relinquish that scarlet velvet cloak, that shining armour and all the other treasures which, it was reasonable to believe, such a personage might have upon him.

So in this way was Boabdil brought to Ferdinand a prisoner.

Isabella was at the frontier town of Logrono, when news was brought to her of the death of Louis.

She fell on her knees and gave thanks for this deliverance.

The King of France, she heard, had died in great fear of the hereafter, for he had committed many sins and the memory of these tortured him.

Yet, thought Isabella, he worked for his country. France was put first always. Perhaps his sins would be forgiven because of that one great virtue.

His son, Charles VIII, was a minor and there would be troubles enough in his country to keep French eyes off Navarre for some time.

It is yet another miracle, pondered Isabella. It is further evidence that I have been selected for the great tasks before me.

Now she need no longer stay on the borders of Navarre. She could join Ferdinand; they could prosecute the war against the Infidel with all their resources.

As she travelled towards Cordova more exhilarating news was brought to her.

The Moors had been routed on the banks of the Xenil, and Boabdil himself was Ferdinand's prisoner.

"Let us give thanks to God and his saints," cried Isabella to her attendants. "The way is being made clear to us. Our Inquisitors are bringing the heretic to justice. Now we shall drive the Infidel from Granada. If we do this we shall not have lived in vain, and there will be rejoicing in Heaven. Our sins will be as molehills beside the mountain of our achievements."

And she was smiling. For the first time since she had heard of it she was no longer disturbed by the thought of bright and beautiful Francis Phoebus, lying dead at the hand of a poisoner.

CHAPTER
NINE

The Dream Of Christoforo Colombo

In a small shop in one of the narrow streets of the town of Lisbon a man waited for customers, and on his face was an expression of frustration and sorrow.

"Will it always be thus?" he asked himself. "Will my plans never come to fruition?"

He had asked the question again and again of Filippa, his wife, and she had always replied in the same way: "Have courage, Christoforo. One day your dreams will be realised. One day you will find those who will believe you, who will make it possible for you to carry out your plan."

And he had said in those days: "You are right, Filippa; one day I shall succeed."

He had smiled at her because he had known that in her heart she was not displeased. When the great day came she would stand at the door of the shop, little Diego in her arms, waving to a husband who was going away on his great adventure, an adventure which would, more likely than not, end in death.

Yet she need not have feared on that account. She was the one who had gone to meet death — not on the high seas, but in the back room of this dark little shop which was crowded with charts and nautical instruments.

Little Diego came and stood beside him. Patient little Diego, who now had no mother to care for him, and tried so hard to understand the meaning of the dreams he saw in his father's eyes.

Few people came into the shop to buy. Christoforo was not a good salesman, he feared. If they came, if they were interested in sailing the seas, he would invite them into the room beyond and there, over a bottle of wine, they would talk while Christoforo forgot the need to sell his goods that he might provide food for himself and his son.

It was nearly ten years since he had come to Lisbon from Genoa. He was even then nearly thirty years old. He often talked now to little Diego, who had been his chief companion since Filippa had died.

Diego would stand, his hands on his father's knees, listening.

Diego thought his father the most handsome man in Lisbon, indeed in the world, for Diego knew nothing of the world beyond Lisbon. When his father talked his eyes would glow with a luminosity which Diego did not understand — and yet it thrilled his small body. His father talked as no others talked; and his talk was all of a land that lay somewhere across the oceans, a land which existed and yet about which no one on this side of the world knew anything.

Diego looked into the face of a man who saw visions. A tall man, a broad man, with long legs, blue eyes which seemed made for looking over long distances, and thick hair which had a touch of red and gold in it.

"Father," Diego would say, "tell me about the great voyage of discovery."

Then Christoforo would talk, and as he talked those light, luminous eyes swept across the past to the present and on into the future, and it was as though he saw clearly what had happened, what was happening and what the future held.

"I came to Lisbon, my son," he would begin, "because I believed that here in this country I might find more sympathy for my schemes than was given me in Italy. In Italy . . . they laughed at me. My son, I think they begin to laugh at me here."

Diego listened intently. They laughed at his father because they were fools. They did not believe in the existence of the great land across the water.

"Fools! Fools!" cried Diego, clenching his fists and bringing them down on his father's knees.

Then Christoforo remembered the youthfulness of his son and he was unhappy again, for he thought: What if they listened to me with serious attention? What if they smiled on me? What would become of this small boy?

It had been different when Filippa was alive. He could no longer see himself setting out while Filippa waved farewell with their son in her arms.

He would take the boy on his knee and tell him of the journeys he had made. He would talk of voyages to the coast of Guinea and Iceland, to the Cape de Verd Islands. He talked of the time when he had first come to Lisbon. Filippa had come with him; and she had known what he planned; he had made no secret of his ambitions. She had understood. She was her father's daughter and *he* had sailed the seas; *he* understood the desire of men to discover new lands. So Filippa Muñiiz de Palestrello understood also.

She had watched her husband and her father bending over the charts, growing excited, talking of what lay beyond the wastes of water so far unexplored by Europeans.

When her father died all his charts and all his instruments were left to Christoforo, who had by then married Filippa.

One day Christoforo, who had vainly been trying to interest influential men in his projects, heard that an adventurer was more likely to get a sympathetic understanding in the maritime port of Lisbon than anywhere else, for King John II of Portugal was interested in expeditions into the unknown world.

"Pack up what we have, Filippa," he had said. "This day we leave for Lisbon."

And so to Lisbon they had come, and found a home here among its seven hills. But Filippa had died, leaving him only Diego to remind him of her — Diego, that precious and beloved creature, who because of the dream must be an anxiety.

Wandering along the banks of the Tagus, walking disconsolately through the Alfama district, gazing up to the Castle of Sao Jorge set on the highest of the hills, he

252

dreamed continually of the day when he would leave Lisbon; for his dream had become an obsession which tormented him, and had grown to such proportions that it obliterated even the love of his wife and child.

"But one day, Diego, my son," said Christoforo, "they will not laugh. One day they will honour your father. Mayhap they will make him an Admiral and I shall ask a place at Court for you, my little son."

Diego nodded; he had no idea what a place at Court would mean to him, but he was pleased that his father did not forget him; for young as he was, Diego understood the force of his father's ambition.

"Father," he said, "will it be soon that you sail away?"

"Soon, my son. It must be soon. I have waited long. And while I am away, you will be good?"

"I will be good," said the boy, "but I shall long for your return."

Christoforo was smitten with remorse afresh. He lifted the boy in his arms and held him tightly. Little Diego had such confidence in his father who was preparing to leave him, and indeed longing to do so. He did not doubt that provision would be made for him during his father's absence, and in the event of his father's not returning at all.

And it shall be! Christoforo assured himself. Even if I have to take him with me.

Yet what sort of a father was he, to expose a tender child to the hazards of the sea!

I am not a father, Christoforo told himself, any more than I was a husband. I am an explorer-adventurer —

and there is little space in one lifetime to be more than that. Yet, I swear, Diego shall be cared for.

He set the boy on his knee and took out one of the charts which had been left to him by his father-in-law. He showed the boy where he believed the new land to lie, and as he talked he was railing against this fate which prevented him from making the voyage of his dreams. If he were but a rich man . . . But he was a poor adventurer who had to depend on the wealth of others to finance his venture; and in some ways he was a practical man; he knew that great wealth would have to be expended on an expedition such as he wished to lead. Only great nobles could help; only kings.

But nothing could be done without the approval of the Church; and the Church was inclined to laugh at his proposals. The Bishops wanted verification of his assumptions. What were the chances of success? Could they put their trust in the dream of an adventurer? They did not believe in the existence of this great undiscovered land.

Yet they had allowed him to hope.

It was while he sat with his son that a visitor called to see him. Christoforo's heart leaped as the man entered the shop. He knew that he had not come to buy nautical instruments, for he was in the service of the Bishop of Ceuta.

Christoforo rose hastily and pushed Diego from his knee.

"Leave us, my son," he said.

And Diego ran up the spiral staircase, but he did not enter the room above the shop; he sat on the top stair listening to the voices below. He could not hear what was said but he would know by the sound of his father's voice whether the news was good. Good news would be that his father might prepare immediately to make the voyage, and although Diego knew that would mean separation, no less than his father he longed to hear this news. For Diego, like Christoforo, there could only be real satisfaction when the dream became reality; and like his father, the boy was ready to endure any hardship if this should come to pass.

Meanwhile Christoforo had taken his visitor into the dark little room beyond the shop.

Christoforo's heart had sunk at the sight of the man's face; he had seen that expression on faces before, the faintly suppressed smile of superiority which men of small understanding, who thought themselves wise, gave to those who in their opinion bordered on imbecility.

"I come from my lord Bishop of Ceuta," said the man.

"And your news?"

The man shook his head. "Nothing more can be done. The voyage is impossible."

"Impossible!" cried Christoforo rising, his blue eyes blazing. "How can any say this of that which has not been proved?"

"It had been proved." The man's smile widened. "The Ecclesiastical Council decided that your project would be a hopeless one, but his lordship, the Bishop of Ceuta, did not dismiss your claims as lightly as did the others."

"I know," said Christoforo, "he promised me that ere long I should be equipped with all I needed to make the voyage."

"Meanwhile his lordship decided to put your theories to the test."

"But he has not done so. I have been here in Lisbon these many months . . . waiting . . . waiting, eternally waiting."

"But he has done this. He sent his own expedition. He equipped a vessel and sent her out in search of this new world which you are so sure exists."

Christoforo was fighting hard to restrain himself. He was not a meek man, and he wanted to crash his fist into the smiling face. They had cheated him. They had listened to his plans; they had studied his charts. It had been necessary to convince them that he had something to support his theories. Then they had deceived him. They had equipped a vessel for someone else.

"The ship returned, battered and almost unseaworthy. It is a miracle that she arrived back safely in Lisbon. She encountered such storms in the Saragossa Sea that it was impossible to continue the journey. In fact, the discovery has been made that the journey is impossible."

Christoforo's rage was tempered with relief. The failure of others did not affect his dream.

He held it intact, but he had made one important discovery. He could expect no help in Lisbon. He had wasted his time.

"You are now convinced that what you propose is impossible, I hope?" he was asked.

Christoforo's eyes were as hard and brilliant as aquamarines.

"I am convinced of the impossibility of getting help from Portugal," he said.

Now the visitor was smiling broadly. "I trust business is good?"

Christoforo lifted his hands in a gesture of despair. "What do you think, my good sir? Do you think that Lisbon is a city of adventurers who would be interested in my charts and instruments?"

"Sailors need them on their journeys, do they not?"

"But in Lisbon!" said Christoforo, his anger rising. "Perhaps the sale of such articles would be more profitable in towns where men do not set out to sea and then allow a storm or two to drive them back to port."

"You are an angry man, Christoforo Colombo."

"I should be less angry if I were alone."

The visitor rose abruptly and left him.

Christoforo sat down at the table and stared ahead of him. Little Diego crept down and stood watching him.

Diego longed to run to his father and comfort him, but he was afraid. He could understand and share the terrible disappointment.

Then Christoforo saw the small figure standing there, and he smiled slowly. He beckoned, and the boy ran to him. Christoforo took him into his arms, and for a while neither spoke.

Then Christoforo said: "Diego, let us start packing the charts and a few things that we shall need for a journey."

"A long journey, Father?"

"A very long journey. We are leaving Lisbon. Lisbon has cheated us. I shall not rest until I have shaken its dust from off my feet."

"Where shall we go, Father?"

"We have little money. We shall go on foot, my son. There is only one place we can make for."

Diego looked expectantly into his father's face. Then he saw the disappointment fade; he saw the rebirth of hope.

"They say Isabella, the Queen of Castile, is a wise woman. My son, let us prepare with all speed. We shall go to Spain and there attempt to interest Isabella in our new world."

The journey was long and arduous. They were often hungry, always footsore. But their spirits never flagged. Christoforo knew with absolute certainty that one day he would interest some wealthy and influential person in his schemes; as for eight-year-old Diego, he had been brought up with the dream and he too never doubted.

In his scrip Christoforo carried his charts; he also wore a dagger, for the way through the Alemtejo district was wild and infested with robbers.

It was late afternoon; they had left the province of Huelva behind them and were approaching the estuary of the Rio Tinto.

The month was January, and a cold wind was blowing in from the Atlantic.

"Diego, my son," said Christoforo, "you are weary."

"I am weary, Father," the boy admitted.

They had left the small town of Palos two or three miles behind, and Diego had wondered why they did not stop there and ask for shelter. Christoforo, however, had walked purposefully on.

"Soon we shall have a roof over our heads, my son. Can you keep up your spirits for another mile?"

"Why, yes, Father."

Diego threw back his shoulders and walked on beside his father. Then, as they trudged on in the direction of Cadiz and Gibraltar, and the wind caught the sand and flung it among the pine trees which grew sparsely here and there, he understood, for in the distance he saw the walls of a monastery and he knew that this was the place to which his father was taking him.

"There we will ask for food and shelter for the night," said Christoforo. He did not add that he hoped for more. He was now inside Spain; and in the monasteries were learned men who might listen to his talk of an undiscovered world.

If, however, he could interest no one at the Franciscan Monastery of Santa Maria de la Rabida he must pass hopefully on.

They approached the gate, and Christoforo addressed the lay brother whose duty it was to guard it.

"I come to beg food and shelter for myself and my child," he said. "We have come far; we are poor, weary and hungry. I believe you will not deny us charity."

The lay brother looked at them — the travel-stained man and the weary little boy. He said: "You are right, traveller, to expect charity from us. It is our boast that we never turn the weary and hungry from our gates. Enter."

Christoforo took Diego by the hand and they entered the monastery of Santa Maria de la Rabida.

They were taken to wash off the travel stains in the great trough, and when this was done they were led to the kitchens and set at a table where hot soup and bread were given them.

They fed ravenously; and while they ate, a young monk who was passing paused to look with curiosity at the man and boy and said: "Good day to you, travellers. Have you come far?"

"From Lisbon," answered Christoforo.

"And you have a long journey ahead of you?"

"We travel hopefully," answered Christoforo, "and it may be, if we are fortunate, to the Court of Isabella, the Queen."

The monk was interested. Occasionally travellers stopped at the monastery, but never before had he encountered a man with that almost fanatical light in his eyes; never had he seen such a shabby traveller on his way to visit the Queen.

Christoforo was determined to exploit the interest of the monk. It was not by chance that he had come to this monastery. He was aware that the Prior, Fray Juan Perez de Marchena, was a man of wide interests and a friend of Fernando de Talavera, who was confessor to, and in high favour with, the Queen herself.

So he talked to the monk of his ambitions; he patted his scrip and told him: "In here I have plans, I have charts ... If I could find the means to equip an expedition, I would find a New World."

It was fascinating talk to the monk who lived life within the quiet walls of the monastery, and he listened entranced while Christoforo entertained him with tales of his adventures off the coast of Guinea and Iceland.

Diego had finished his soup, and his father's was growing cold. The boy anxiously tugged his father's sleeve and nodded at the soup, whereupon Christoforo smiled and finished it.

The monk said: "And the child, he is to go with you to this New World?"

"There are hazards, and he is young," said Christoforo. "But if other provision cannot be made for him ..."

"You are a man of dreams," said the monk.

"Many of us are, and those who are not, should be. All that is accomplished on earth must begin as a dream."

The monk rose and hurried away to his duties, but he could not forget the strange talk of the traveller; he sought out the Prior and told him of the unusual guests who had sought comfort within their walls.

Diego lay on a pallet in a small cell. He was so tired that he was soon fast asleep.

Meanwhile the Prior of Santa Maria de la Rabida had sent for Christoforo.

In the small room with bare walls apart from a large crucifix, and by the light of two candles, Christoforo spread his charts on the table and talked to the Prior of his ambitions.

Fray Juan believed he understood men. He looked at that weather-beaten face with the bright seaman's eyes and he said to himself: This man has genius.

Fray Juan was fascinated. It was late, but he could not release the traveller. He must hear more.

And when they had talked for many hours he said suddenly: "Christoforo Colombo, I believe in you. I believe in your New World."

Then Christoforo covered his face with his hands and there were tears in his eyes. He was ashamed of himself, but so intense was his relief that he could not hide his emotion.

"You will help me to obtain an audience with the Queen?" he asked.

"I will do all in my power," answered Fray Juan. "You know it is not easy. She has little time. There has been trouble in Navarre, and it is the great wish of the Queen to see a Christian Spain. The war with Granada is imminent . . . in fact it has already begun. It may be that the Queen, with so much to occupy her thoughts, will have little patience with . . . a dream."

"You hold out little hope, Fray Juan."

"I implore you to have patience," was the answer. "But listen. I have a plan. I will not approach Fernando de Talavera. He is a good man, the Queen's confessor, and I know him well, but he is so anxious to make war on the Infidel that he might be impatient of your schemes. I will, however, give you an introduction to the Duke of Medina Sidonia, who is rich and powerful and could bring your case to the notice of the Court."

"How can I show my gratitude?"

"By discovering your New World. By justifying this faith I have in you."

"It shall be done," said Christoforo as though he were taking an oath.

"There is one matter which needs consideration," said Fray Juan. "I refer to the boy, your son."

Christoforo's face changed and anxiety took the place of exhilaration.

Fray Juan was smiling. "I wish to set your mind at rest concerning him. Go to the Queen, go and find your New World. While you do these things I will undertake the charge of your son. He shall remain with us here at Rabida, and we will clothe and feed him, we will shelter and educate him until your return."

Christoforo rose. He could not speak. The tears were visible in his eyes now.

"Do not thank me," said Fray Juan. "Let us get to our knees and thank God. Let us do that . . . together."

CHAPTER
TEN

The Royal Family

Throughout the kingdom of Granada there was mourning. Never before had a Moorish Sultan fallen captive to a Christian army. Nor was Boabdil the only prisoner in the hands of the enemy. Many of the captured were powerful men and, as the character of Ferdinand was beginning to be known throughout Granada, it was calculated that large ransoms would be demanded before they were allowed to return.

"Allah has turned his face from us," mourned the people. "The hostile star of Islam is scattering its malignant influences upon us. Can this mean the downfall of the Mussulman Empire?"

Muley Abul Hassan discussed the position with his brother, El Zagal.

"Boabdil must be released without delay. The effect of his captivity on the people is becoming disastrous."

El Zagal agreed with his brother. He was certain that Boabdil should be returned to them so that they might quash his rebellion.

"Offer a ransom," he said. "Offer a sum which Ferdinand will find it difficult to refuse."

"It shall be done," said Muley Abul Hassan.

The Sultana Zoraya was torn between anger and anxiety. Her son, the captive of the Christians! He must be released at once.

She raged against Boabdil, who had never been a warrior. When all was well she would devote herself to the upbringing of Boabdil's young son and make a warrior out of him.

It was imperative that Boabdil should not be allowed to remain in the hands of his captives. If he were, the people of Granada would forget they had called him their Sultan. She foresaw a return to the undisputed rule of Muley Abul Hassan. The Moors might, in their adversity, forget their differences. Then what would happen to Boabdil? Would he be left to fret in his Christian prison? What would happen to her?

When she heard that Muley Abul Hassan had offered a ransom, she was determined that further delay would be dangerous. Boabdil must not be delivered into the hands of his father.

"What ransom has Muley Abul Hassan offered?" she demanded to know. "No matter what it is, I must offer a greater."

Ferdinand was gleeful. This was an unexpected stroke of good fortune. Boabdil was in the hands of General the Count of Cabra, having been captured by some of his men.

"Highness," ran the Count's message, "Boabdil, King of Granada, is now a prisoner in my castle of Baena. Here I am according him all the courtesy which his rank demands while I await Your Highness's instructions."

Ferdinand sat with Isabella in the Royal Council Chamber, and the fate of Boabdil was considered.

Isabella knew that Ferdinand was thinking of the large ransoms offered by Muley Abul Hassan and the Sultana Zoraya, and that he longed to lay his hands on their gold.

Ferdinand addressed the Council, saying that the ransom should be accepted and Boabdil sent back to his people.

There was an immediate outcry. Send back such a valuable prisoner! The King of Granada himself in their hands, and he to be sent back on the payment of a certain sum!

Isabella listened to the impassioned pleading, to the clash of opinion.

The Marquis of Cadiz rose and said: "Your Highnesses and Gentlemen of the Council, our one thought should be to weaken our enemy, to prepare him to our advantage for the final battle. What we have to consider is whether Boabdil is of more use to us here as our prisoner than there, free to cause trouble in his own kingdom."

"He is our captive!" was the answer. "He, the leader, the King! What is an army without a leader?"

The Marquis answered: "But there were two leaders, other than Boabdil, in Granada — Muley Abul Hassan and El Zagal."

266

Ferdinand had begun to speak and, as she listened to him, Isabella rejoiced in his shrewdness.

"It is clear what must be done," said Ferdinand. "If Boabdil remains here there will soon be peace within Granada. Muley Abul Hassan will return to the throne with the support of his brother. There will only be one ruler . . . no longer the Old King and the Little King. By our capture of Boabdil we shall have ended civil war in Granada, and one of the greatest aids to our cause *is* the civil war in Granada."

Isabella lifted her hand then and said: "I am sure that the path we must take is clear to us all now. The King is right. Boabdil must be returned to his people. We must not help to make peace within the kingdom of Granada. Return Boabdil to his people, and once more there, civil war will be intensified."

"And we shall have the ransom money," added Ferdinand with a gay smile. "Zoraya's ransom money, for naturally he must be returned to his mother, who will help him to reorganise his forces against his father and uncle. And by God's good grace the ransom money which she offers is greater than that suggested by Muley Abul Hassan. Heaven is with us." The Council then declared itself to be in agreement with Ferdinand's suggestion; and Ferdinand took the Queen's hand and they, with a few of their highest ministers, retired to draw up the treaty with Boabdil.

Ferdinand received Boabdil at Cordova, determined to charm his captive into a ready acceptance of his proposals.

When Boabdil would have knelt, Ferdinand put out his hand to prevent his doing so.

"We meet as kings," said Ferdinand.

The two kings sat side by side in chairs which had been set for them.

"You are blessed with a mother who gives all she has for your sake," said Ferdinand.

"It is true," Boabdil replied.

"And, because she has pleaded with us so touchingly, the Queen and myself are inclined to grant her request."

"Your Highness is munificent," Boabdil murmured.

Ferdinand did not deny it. "I will tell you briefly what terms we have drawn up, and when you have agreed to them, and your mother has sent the ransom, we shall hold you here no longer, but shall allow you to depart; for if you give us your word that you will accept these terms we shall trust you."

Boabdil bowed his head in grateful thanks.

"We grant a truce of two years' standing to such territory within the kingdom of Granada which is under your dominion."

"I gratefully accept that," answered Boabdil.

"You have been captured in battle, and it will be necessary for you to make some reparation," said Ferdinand smoothly. "Our people would not be pleased if you did not."

"It is understandable," agreed Boabdil.

"Then you shall return to us four hundred Christian slaves for whom we shall pay no ransom."

"They shall be yours."

"You shall pay annually twelve thousand gold *doblas* to the Queen and myself."

Boabdil looked less pleased, but he had known that Ferdinand would require some such reward for his clemency, and there was nothing to be done but to grant it.

"We must ask you for a free passage through your kingdom, should we wish it while making war on your father and your uncle."

Boabdil was taken aback by this suggestion. Ferdinand was calmly suggesting that he should play the traitor to his own country; and although Boabdil was ready to make war on his father, he hesitated before agreeing to allow the Christians a free passage through his land.

Ferdinand passed on quickly: "Then you may go free; but should I wish to see you at any time to discuss the differences between our kingdoms, you must come immediately to my command; and I shall require you to give your son into my possession together with the sons of certain of your nobles, that we may hold them as sureties of your good faith."

Boabdil was stunned by these terms. But he saw the need to escape from captivity, and that there was nothing to be done but to accept them.

So Ferdinand took the ransom offered by the Sultana, and Boabdil returned to his people, bewildered, humiliated, aware that he had agreed to act as Ferdinand's pawn to be moved at his will; and he could be certain that those moves would be made for the aggrandisement of the Sovereigns and the detriment of his own people.

Boabdil, saddened and chastened, wished that he had never listened to his mother's advice, wished that he was now fighting the Christians on the side of his father.

Ferdinand was saying his farewell to Isabella before he set out on his journey to Aragon.

Isabella was doing her best to be patient, but it was not easy. They had made great strides in the war against the Moors; Boabdil could be said to be their creature, yet they lacked the means to continue the war against the Moors in a way which could be conclusive.

"Always," cried Ferdinand, "we are faced with this lack of money."

Isabella agreed that this was so and, agreeing, forgave Ferdinand his preoccupation with possessions. She knew there was a reproach in his words. She was in a position to replenish the royal coffers, yet she steadfastly refused to act. She was determined that her rule should be just, and that she would give no favours in exchange for bribes. Even though the moment seemed ripe for the attack on the Moors, she would not resort to dishonourable means of raising money. She was certain that God would turn His favour from her if she did.

"What can we do?" he demanded now. "Merely destroy their crops, merely attack their small hamlets, lay waste their land, set fire to their vineyards! This we will do, but until we have the means of raising a mighty army we can never hope for complete conquest."

"We shall raise that army," said Isabella. "Have no doubt of that."

"It is to be hoped that, by the time we do, we shall not have lost the advantage we now hold."

"If so, we shall gain others," answered Isabella. "It is the will of God that we shall rule over an all-Christian Spain, and I have never for a moment doubted it."

"And in the meantime we must tarry. We must show ourselves as being too weak, too poor, to prosecute the war."

"Alas that it should be so!"

"But it need not be."

Isabella gave him that firm yet affectionate smile. "When the time comes God and all Heaven will be beside us," she said. "Why, now your presence is needed in Aragon, so it is no bad thing that we had not planned to make our great attack on Granada."

Ferdinand was inclined to be sullen. This was one of those occasions when he blamed her methods as the cause of their inability to prosecute the war.

But she was convinced that she was right. She must act honourably and according to her own lights, or she would lose that belief in her destiny. God was with her, she was sure, and He would only support that which was just. If He had been slow in giving her the means of attacking the Moors, she must wait in patience, telling herself that the ways of Heaven were often inscrutable.

She wondered now whether she should tell Ferdinand that she hoped she was pregnant once more.

It was early yet, and perhaps it would be unwise to raise his hopes. He would begin to plan for another son. And of her four children only one was a boy, so perhaps her fifth would also be a girl.

No, she would keep this little matter to herself. She would watch him ride away with Torquemada into Aragon, whence reports had come that heretics abounded; Torquemada had been denouncing them and was eager that the methods which were being used in Castile should be put into force in Aragon. Away with the old easy-going tribunals! Torquemada's Inquisition should be taken to Aragon.

"It may well be," she told Ferdinand, "that God wishes to see how we bring tormented souls back to His kingdom, before He helps us to take possession of those of the Moors."

"It may be so," agreed Ferdinand. "Farewell, my Queen and wife."

Once more he embraced her, but even as he did so she wondered whether, when he reached Aragon, he would make his way to the mother of that illegitimate son, of whom he had been so besottedly fond that he had made him an Archbishop at the age of six.

During that summer Isabella found time to be with Beatriz de Bobadilla.

"It would seem," she said to her friend, "that it is only when I am about to have a child that I have an opportunity of being with my family and friends."

"Highness, when the Holy War is over, when the Moors have been driven from Spain, then you will have a little more time for us. It will be a great joy and pleasure to us all."

"To me also. And, Beatriz, I believe that day is not so far off as I once feared it might be. Now that the Inquisition is working so zealously throughout Castile, I feel that one part of our plan is succeeding. Beatriz, bring the altar-cloth I am working on. I will not waste time while we talk."

Beatriz sent a woman for the needlework and, when it was brought, they settled down to it.

Isabella worked busily with the coloured threads. She found the work very soothing.

"How do matters go in Aragon?" asked Beatriz.

Isabella frowned down at her work. "I hear that there is opposition there to the Inquisition, but Ferdinand and Torquemada are determined that it shall be established and that it shall become as effective as it is here in Castile."

"There are many New Christians in Aragon."

"Yes, and I believe they have been practising Jewish rites in private. Otherwise why should they fear the coming of the Inquisition?"

Beatriz murmured: "They fear that accusations may be brought against them, and that they may not be able to prove their innocence."

"But," said Isabella mildly, "if they are innocent, why should they not be able to prove it?"

"Perhaps torture might force a victim to confess not only what is true but what is completely untrue. Perhaps it is this they fear."

"If they tell the truth immediately, and name those who have shared their sins, the torture will not be applied. I expect we shall have a little trouble in Aragon, although I do not doubt that it will be promptly quelled, as the Susan affair was in Seville."

"Let us hope so," said Beatriz.

"My dear friend, Tomás de Torquemada, has sent two excellent men into Aragon. I know he has the utmost confidence in Arbues and Juglar."

"Let us hope that they are not over-stern — at first," said Beatrix quietly. "It is the sudden change from lethargy to iron discipline that seems to terrify the people."

"They cannot be too stern in the service of the Faith." Isabella spoke firmly.

Beatriz thought it might be wise to change the subject, and after a slight pause asked after the health of the Infanta Isabella.

The Queen frowned slightly. "Her health does give me cause for anxiety. She is not as strong, I fear, as the other three. In fact, our baby, young Maria, seems to be the healthiest member of the family. Do you think so, Beatriz?"

"I think that Maria has perfect health, but so have Juan and Juana. As for Isabella, she certainly has this tendency to catch cold. But I think that will pass as she grows older."

"Oh, Beatriz," said Isabella suddenly, "I do hope this one will be a boy."

"Because Ferdinand wishes it?" asked Beatriz.

"Yes, perhaps that is so. For myself, I would be content with another girl. Ferdinand wants sons."

"He has one."

"He has more than one," said Isabella after some hesitation. "And that is a great sorrow to me. I know of one illegitimate son. It is the Archbishop who succeeded to the See of Saragossa when he was but six years old. Ferdinand dotes on him. I have heard it whispered that there is another son. And I know there are daughters."

"These things will happen, Highness. They have always been so."

"I am foolish to think too much of them. We are often apart, and Ferdinand is not a man who could remain faithful to one woman."

Beatriz laid her hand on that of the Queen.

"Highness, may an old friend speak frankly?"

"You know you may."

"My thoughts are taken back to the days before your marriage. You made an ideal of Ferdinand. You made an image — a man who had all the virtues of a great soldier, king and statesman, and yet was as austere in his nature as you are yourself. You made an impossible ideal, Highness."

"You are right, Beatriz."

"Such a person as you conjured up is not to be found in Christendom."

"Then I should be content with what I have."

"Highness, you should be content indeed. You have a partner who has many qualities to bring to this governing of your country; you have children. Think of the kings who long for children and cannot get them."

"Beatriz, my dear, you have done me much good. I will be thankful for what I have. I will not ask for more. If God sees fit to give me another girl, I shall be happy. I shall forget that I longed for a son."

Isabella was smiling. She had decided that for the next few months she would give herself up to the enjoyment of her family; she would spend much time in the nurseries with her children; and it would be as though she were not Queen of Castile but merely the mother of a boy and three girls, awaiting the arrival of a new baby.

Ferdinand had returned from Aragon, reluctantly, Isabella believed.

It was natural, Isabella told herself, that his first thoughts should have been for Aragon, and she believed his presence had been needed there.

When he returned to her after a long absence he was always the passionate lover: a state of affairs which had delighted her in their earlier relationship, but which she now knew to be due to Ferdinand's love of change.

He was an adventurer in all respects. And she accepted him not as the embodiment of an ideal, but as the man he was.

He had risen from their bed, although only the first streaks of dawn were in the sky. He was restless, she saw, and found it difficult to lie still.

He sat on the bed, his embroidered robe about him, while she sat up and studied him gravely.

"Ferdinand," she said, "do you not think it would be better if you confided your troubles to me?"

He smiled at her ruefully. "Ours is a troublous realm, Isabella," he said. "We are sovereigns of two states, and it would seem that in order to serve one we must neglect the other."

Isabella said firmly: "Events in Castile are moving towards a climax. Since the capture of Boabdil we have made such great strides towards victory that surely it cannot be long delayed."

"Granada is a mighty kingdom which I have likened to a pomegranate. I have sworn to pluck the pomegranate dry, but there are still more juicy seeds to be taken. And meanwhile the French hold my provinces of Rousillon and Cerdagne."

Isabella was startled. "Ferdinand, we cannot face a war on two fronts."

"A war against the French would be a just one," urged Ferdinand.

"The war against the Moors is a holy one," Isabella replied.

Ferdinand was a little sullen. "My presence is needed in Aragon," he said.

She wondered then whether it was herself whom he wanted to leave for some other woman, whether he longed to be with another family, not the one he had through her. She felt sick at heart to contemplate his infidelity; yet as she looked at him, so handsome, so virile, she remembered Beatrix's words. She had greatly desired marriage with him. Young and handsome, he had appealed to her so strongly when she compared him with other suitors who had been selected for her.

No, she thought, it is not some other woman, some other family which calls him: it is Aragon. He is too firm a ruler, too clever a diplomatist ever to allow his personal emotions to interfere with his ambitions.

Not another woman, not the mother of the Archbishop of Saragossa, nor the Archbishop himself, nor any of those other mistresses whom he had doubtless found more to his taste than his chaste wife Isabella — it was Aragon.

As for herself, she longed to please him. There were times when she almost wished that she could have changed her nature, that she could have been more like what she imagined the others to be — voluptuously beautiful, as brimming over with sensual passion as he was himself. But she would suppress such thoughts.

Such a life was not for her. She was a queen — the Queen of Castile — and her duty came before any such carnal pleasure, the safety of her kingdom before a contented life.

She resisted an impulse to put out a hand and take his, to say to him: "Ferdinand, love me . . . me only; you may have anything in exchange that I could give you."

She thought then of Christ's temptation in the wilderness, and she said coldly: "The Holy War must be continued at the expense of all else."

And Ferdinand rose from the bed. He walked to the window and looked out, watching the dawn encroach on the darkness.

His back was towards her, but she saw that there was an angry gesture in the way he held his head.

It was a scene which had been repeated so many times in their life together. It was the Queen of Castile in command, not only of her own nature, but of the lesser ruler of Aragon.

The children, with the exception perhaps of Juana, were delighted to have their mother with them. Juana was the wild one, the one who could not conform to the high standard set by her mother, the one who fidgeted during church services, who refused to confess *all* her sins to her confessor, the one who struck a certain cold fear into her mother's heart on many occasions.

Isabella was six months pregnant, and it was during her pregnancies that she relaxed her stern hold upon herself to some extent.

I am, after all, a mother, she excused herself, and these children of mine will one day be rulers of some part of this earth. I must treat them as a very important part of my life.

If at this time it had been possible to continue with the war against the Moors with vigour, she would have neglected everything to do so. But it was not possible; it would take several years to build up the army they needed. There was nothing she could do at present to speed up matters in that direction. What she must think of was having a healthy pregnancy and recovering her strength as soon as possible. So for these few months

279

she gave herself to domesticity more whole-heartedly than she usually could.

She loved her children devotedly. She wanted to make sure that they were receiving the best education which could be provided for them — remembering how she herself had missed it. At the same time their spiritual education must not be neglected. She wanted the girls to be both good rulers and good wives and parents; she insisted that they sit with her and learn to embroider; and there was nothing which made her more contented than to have her children with her while she and the girls worked on an altar-cloth, and Juan sat on a stool close by and read aloud to them.

This they were now doing, and again and again her eyes would stray from her work to rest on one or other of her children. Her pale and lovely daughter, Isabella, her firstborn, who still coughed a little too frequently for her mother's comfort, was beautiful, bending over her work. They would have to find a husband for her soon.

It will be more than I can bear, to lose her, thought Isabella.

And there was Juan — perhaps the best loved of them all. Who could help loving Juan? He was the perfect child. Not only was he the boy for whom Ferdinand had longed, he had the sweetest nature of all the children; he was docile, yet excelled in all those sports in which Ferdinand wished to see him excel. His tutors discovered in him a desire to please, which meant that he learned his lessons quickly and well. He was beautiful — at least in the eyes of his mother. She felt her love overflowing as she looked at him. In her thoughts she had long called him Angel. She had even done so openly, and consequently he was beginning to be known in the family circle by that name.

There was Juana — little Suegra. Almost defiantly Isabella insisted on the nickname. It was as though she wished to emphasise the resemblance between this child and her grandmother, Ferdinand's sprightly and clever mother. Isabella tried not to see a subtler resemblance, that between her own sad mother and this child.

It was difficult to avoid this comparison. If there was trouble Juana would be in it. She had charm; it was in her very wildness. The others were serene children; perhaps they took after their mother. Yet little Juana, though she might have the features of Ferdinand's mother, had that in her — at least, so Isabella often told herself — which bore a terrifying similarity to the frailty of the poor sick lady at Arevalo.

And little Maria, the plain one, stolid, reliable, good little Maria! She would give her parents little concern, Isabella guessed. Strangely enough — for this very reason — she did not give her mother the same delight as did the others.

Isabella wondered whether she herself, when a child, had been rather like Maria — quiet, serene, docile . . . and not very attractive.

She saw that Juana was not working, and that her part of the altar-cloth was not as neat as that of the others.

Isabella leaned forward and tapped the child on her knee.

"Come, Suegra," she said, "there is work to be done."

"I do not like needlework," said Juana, which made young Isabella catch her breath in horror. Juana went on: "It is no use scowling at me, sister. I do not like needlework."

"This, my child," said the Queen, "is for the altar. Do you not wish to work for a holy purpose?"

"No, Highness," said Juana promptly.

"That is very wrong," said the Queen sternly.

"But Your Highness asked me what I wanted," Juana pointed out. "I must tell the truth, for if I did not that would be a lie, and I should have to confess it, and do a penance. It is very wrong to tell lies."

"Come here," said Isabella; and Juana came to her. Isabella held the child by her shoulders and drew her close to her. "It is true," she went on, "that you must not tell lies. But it is true also that you must discipline yourself. You must learn to like doing what is good."

Juana's eyes, which now bore a strong resemblance to those of Ferdinand, flashed in rebellion. "But Highness, if you do not like . . ." she began.

"That is enough," said Isabella. "Now you will work on this cloth tomorrow until you have completed your share of it, and if it is badly done you will unpick your stitches and do them again until it is well done."

Juana's lower lip protruded and she said defiantly: "I shall not be able to go to Mass if I must sit over my needlework."

282

The Queen was aware of a tension among the children, and she said: "What has been happening here?"

Her eldest daughter looked uncomfortable; so did Juan.

"Come," said Isabella, "I must know the truth. You, Angel, you tell me."

"Highness, I do not know of what you speak."

"I think you do, my son. Your sister Juana has been wicked in some way. I pray you tell me what she has done."

"I . . . I could not say, Highness," said Juan; but his beautiful face had turned a shade paler and he was afraid that he was going to be forced to say something which he would rather not.

Isabella could not bear to hurt him. His kindly nature would not allow him to betray his sister; and at the same time he was anxious not to disobey his mother.

She turned to Isabella; Isabella also did not wish to betray her sister.

The Queen was faintly irritated and yet proud of them. She would not have them tellers of tales against each other. She respected this family loyalty.

And fortunately she was saved from forcing an answer, by Juana herself — bold, fearless Juana, with the wild light in her eyes.

"I will tell you, Highness," she said. "I often do not go to church. I run away and hide, so that they cannot find me. I do not like to go to church. I like to dance and sing. So I hide . . . and they cannot find me, and so they go without me."

Isabella surveyed this defiant child with a stern expression which would have filled the others with terror. But Juana merely stood her ground, her handsome little head held high, her eyes brilliant.

"So," said Isabella slowly, "you have been guilty of this wickedness. I am ashamed that a child of mine could behave thus. You, the daughter of the Sovereigns of Castile and Aragon! You whose father is the greatest soldier in the world and who has brought peace within these kingdoms! You are a Princess of the royal house. You would seem to forget this."

"I do not forget," said Juana, "but it does not make me want to go to church."

"Juan," said the Queen to her son, "go and bring to me your sister's governess."

Juan, white-faced, obeyed. As for Juana, she stood regarding her mother with eyes that dilated with a certain fear. She believed that she was to be beaten, and she could not endure corporal punishment; not that she feared the pain; it was the attack upon her dignity which was so upsetting.

She turned and would have run from the room, but the Queen had caught her skirt. This was a very embarrassing situation for the Queen to encounter, and she felt a physical sickness which she found it difficult to control.

She told herself that it was due to her pregnancy; but there was a deep fear within her; and as she held the struggling child in a firm grip she felt a great love for this wild daughter come over her. She wanted to hold the child to her breast and weep over her; she wanted to comfort her, to soothe her, to beg the others to kneel with her and pray that Juana might not go the way of her grandmother.

"Let me go!" cried Juana. "Let me go! I don't want to stay here. I don't want to go to Mass."

Isabella held the child's head against her; she was aware of the shocked and wondering eyes of Isabella and Maria.

"Be quiet, my daughter," she warned. "Be still. It will be better for you if you are."

The quiet tones of her mother soothed the little girl somewhat, and she laid her head against the Queen's breast and stayed there. Isabella thought she was like an imprisoned bird, a wild bird who knew that it was hopeless to struggle.

Juan had returned with the governess, who looked very frightened to have been summoned thus to the presence of the Queen.

Isabella, still holding her daughter against her, acknowledged the governess's deep curtsey and said in a clear expressionless voice: "Is it true that the Infanta Juana has not been attending church?"

The governess stammered: "Highness, it was unavoidable."

"Unavoidable! I do not understand how that can be. It must not happen again. It must be avoided."

"Yes, Highness."

"How many times has this occurred?" asked the Queen.

The governess hesitated, and the Queen went on quickly: "But it is enough that it has occurred once. The soul of the Infanta has been put in jeopardy. It must never occur again. Take the Infanta away now. She is to be beaten severely. And if she attempts to absent herself from church again, I wish to be told. Her punishment then will be even more severe."

Juana had lifted her head and was staring at her mother pleadingly: "No!" she cried. "Please, Highness, no!"

"Take the Infanta away now and do my bidding. I shall satisfy myself that my orders have been carried out."

The governess dropped a deep curtsey and laid her hand on Juana's arm. Juana clung to the chair and would not move. The governess took her arm and pulled and Juana's face grew scarlet with exertion as she clung to the chair.

The Queen smartly slapped the small hand. Juana let out a great wail; then the governess seized her and dragged her from the room.

There was silence in the nursery as the door closed on them.

The Queen said: "Come, my daughters, we have this cloth to finish. Juan, continue to read to us."

And Juan obeyed, and the girls sewed, while in the distance they heard the loud protesting screams as Juana's strokes were administered.

The children took covert looks at their mother, but she was placidly sewing as though she did not hear.

They did not know that she was praying silently, and the words which kept repeating themselves in her brain were: "Holy Mother of God, save my darling child. Help me to preserve her from the fate of her grandmother. Guide me. Help me to do what is right for her."

A rider had come galloping to Cordova from Saragossa. There was news which he must impart immediately to Ferdinand.

Isabella knew of his arrival, but she did not seek out Ferdinand; she would wait until he told her what was happening. She herself was determined to remain the ruler of Castile; she left the governing of Aragon to him.

She knew that this trouble might well be concerned with the setting up of the Inquisition in Aragon. The first *auto de fé*, under the new Inquisition over which Torquemada presided, had taken place in May; this had been followed by another in June. She had heard that the people of Aragon regarded these ceremonies with the same sentiments as the people of Castile had done. They looked on in horrified bewilderment; they seemed stunned; they accepted the installation of the Inquisition almost meekly. But in Seville their meekness had been proved to be part of their shock; and, when that had subsided, men, such as Diego de Susan, had sought to rise against the Holy Office.

Isabella had warned Ferdinand that they must be equally watchful in Aragon.

287

She discovered that she had been right, for Ferdinand came quickly to tell her the news. She knew he was anxious and she always rejoiced that in times of crisis they stood together, all differences forgotten.

"Trouble," said Ferdinand, "trouble in Saragossa. A plot among the New Christians against the Inquisition."

"I trust that the Inquisitors are safe."

"Safe!" cried Ferdinand. "Murder has been done. By the Holy Mother of God, these criminals shall pay for their crimes."

He then told her the news which had been brought to him from Saragossa. It appeared that, as in Seville, the wealthy New Christians of Saragossa had believed that they could drive the Inquisition out of their town. Their plan was to assassinate the Inquisitors, Gaspar Juglar and Pedro Arbues de Epila, who had been working so zealously to provide victims for the hideous spectacles which had taken place in the town.

Several attempts had been made to murder these two men and they, being aware of this, had taken special precautions. They wore armour under their robes, but this had not saved them.

The conspirators had planned to murder their victims in the church, and had lain in wait for them there. Gaspar Juglar had not attended the church because he had become suddenly and mysteriously ill. It was evident that another plan had been put into action concerning him. So Arbues went to the Metropolitan church alone.

"It was quiet in the church," cried Ferdinand in anger, "and they waited as bloodthirsty wolves wait for the gentle lamb."

Isabella bowed her head in sorrow, and it did not occur to her that it was a little incongruous to describe as a gentle lamb, the man who had been hustling the people of Saragossa into the prisons of the Inquisition, into the dungeons where their bodies were racked and their limbs dislocated that they might inform on their friends.

She would have replied had this been put to her: the Inquisitors are working for Holy Church and the Holy Inquisition, and everything they do is in the name of the Christian Faith. If they find it necessary to inflict a little pain on those who have offended against Holy Church, of what importance can this be, since these people are destined for eternal damnation? The body suffers transient pain, but the soul is in danger of eternal torment. Moreover, there is always the hope that the heretic's soul may be saved through his earthly torments.

She said to Ferdinand: "I pray you tell me what evil deed was done in the church."

"He came into the church from the cloisters," said Ferdinand, his face working with emotion. "It was dark, for it was midnight, and there was no light except that from the altar lamp. These wicked men fell upon Arbues, and although he wore mail under his robes, although there was a steel lining to his cap, they wounded him . . . to death."

"They have been arrested?"

"Not yet, but we shall discover them."

A messenger came to the apartment to tell them that Tomás de Torquemada was outside and implored immediate admission.

"Bring him to us," said Ferdinand. "We need his help. We shall bring these criminals to justice. We will show them what punishment will be meted out to those who lay hands on God's elected."

Torquemada's emaciated face was twisted with emotion.

"Your Highnesses, this terrible news has been brought to me."

"The Queen and I are deeply distressed and determined that these murderers shall be brought to justice."

Torquemada said: "I am dispatching three of my most trusted Inquisitors to Saragossa with all speed. Fray Juan Colvera, Doctor Alonso de Alarcon and Fray Pedro de Monterubio . . . all good men. I trust this meets with Your Highnesses' approval."

"It has our approval," said Ferdinand.

"I fear," said Isabella, "that there will be some delay, and that these good servants cannot hope to arrive in time to prevent the escape of all the criminals."

"I shall discover them," said Torquemada, his lips tightly compressed. "If I have every man and woman in Saragossa on the rack, I'll discover them."

Isabella nodded.

Torquemada went on: "The people of Saragossa have been deeply shocked by this murder. The whole town is in an uproar."

290

"Yes," said Ferdinand; and quite suddenly all the anger went out of his voice, and it was soft, almost caressing. "I hear that riots were avoided by the prompt action of one of its citizens."

"Is that so?" said Isabella. "An important citizen, he must have been."

"Yes," said Ferdinand. "He left his palace and summoned the justices and grandees. He placed himself at the head of them and rode bravely to meet those who threatened to burn and pillage the city. He is but seventeen, and I fear he endangered his life; but he was very brave."

"He should be rewarded," Isabella declared.

"So shall he be," answered Ferdinand.

He had moved towards the window as though deep in thought, and that tender smile still curved his mouth.

Isabella turned to Torquemada. "You know who this young man is?" she asked.

"Why, yes, Highness. It is the young Archbishop of Saragossa."

"Oh," said Isabella. "I believe I have heard of this young man. It was a brave action and one which delights the King of Aragon."

And she thought: How he loves his son! Rarely have I seen his face so gentle as when he spoke of him; never have I seen him so quickly turned from anger.

She felt an impulse to ask questions about this young man, to demand of Ferdinand how often they met, what further honours he had showered upon him.

It is because of the child within me, she told herself. I am a very weak woman at these times.

Then she began to talk to Torquemada of this terrible occurrence in Saragossa, and how she was in complete agreement with his determination to meet opposition with greater severity.

Ferdinand joined them; he had recovered from the emotion which the mention of his beloved natural son had caused him.

The three of them talked earnestly of the manner in which they would deal with the rebels of Saragossa.

CHAPTER
ELEVEN

Cristobal Colon And Beatriz De Arana

In the nursery of the Palace at Cordova, Isabella sat holding a child a few months old, on her lap.

This was her daughter, Catalina, who had been born in the December of the preceding year. Her hopes had been in some way disappointed, for she had longed to present Ferdinand with another boy. But Juan was still her only son, and here was her fourth daughter.

Isabella could not continue to feel this disappointment as she looked at the tiny creature in her arms. She loved the child dearly and, on the birth of little Catalina, she had made up her mind that she would not allow herself to be so continually separated from her family.

She glanced up at Beatriz de Bobadilla, who was with her once more, bustling about the apartment as though she were mistress of it.

Isabella smiled at her friend. It was very pleasant to know that Beatriz was willing to leave everything to come to her when she was called. There was no one whom she could trust as she trusted Beatriz; and she realised that it was rare for one in her position to enjoy such a disinterested friendship.

She fancied today that Beatriz had something on her mind, for she was somewhat subdued — a rare state for Beatriz; Isabella waited for her friend to tell her what was the cause of her thoughtfulness, but Beatriz was evidently in no hurry to do so.

She came and knelt by Isabella's side and put out a hand to touch the baby's cheek.

"I declare," said Beatriz, "already the Infanta Catalina bears some resemblance to her august mother."

Isabella gave way to a rare gesture of affection; she lifted the child in her arms and kissed her forehead.

"I was thinking, Beatriz," she said, "how quickly time passes. Soon we shall be thinking of a husband for this little one, as we are for my dear Isabella."

"It will not be for many years yet."

"For this one," said Isabella. "But what of my young Isabella? I cannot bear to part with one of them. Beatriz, I think I love my children more fiercely than most mothers do because, since I have had them, I have been able to spend so little time with them. That will not be the case in future. When I go on my travels I shall take my family with me. It is a good thing that the people should know them, as they know their King and Queen."

"The children will enjoy it. They hate these partings as much as you do."

"Isabella will be leaving us soon," said the Queen.

"But now you have Catalina to take her place."

"Once Isabella is married we must think of marriages for the others. I fear they will take them far from us."

"The Infanta Isabella will go into Portugal, dearest Highness, but Portugal is not far away. Who will be next? Juan. Well, you will keep him here in Castile, will you not? You will not lose your son, Highness. Then Juana will have a husband and go away, I suppose."

A shadow crossed the Queen's face, and Beatriz, following her thoughts, said quickly: "But she is only six years old. It will be years yet."

The Queen was wondering what the years ahead held for wild Juana, and she tried hard to fight her rising fear.

"As for Maria and this little one," went on Beatriz, "marriage is far . . . far away. Why, Highness, you are indeed fortunate."

Isabella said: "Yes, I am fortunate. Isabella will be but a few miles across the border. She will be Queen of Portugal, and thus a very desirable alliance will be forged between our countries. Yet . . . her health worries me sometimes, Beatriz. She has that cough."

"It will pass. When she begins to bear children she will grow healthy. It happens so with some women."

Isabella smiled. "You are my comforter."

The baby began to whimper, and Isabella rocked her soothingly. "There, my little one. Perhaps you will go away from your home . . . Perhaps you will go to some country across the seas . . . but not yet . . . not for years . . . and here is your mother to love you."

Beatriz was thinking that now was the time to put her request. The Queen's mood was softened when she was with her children. Indeed, few were allowed to see her displays of tenderness.

Now is the time, thought Beatriz.

"Highness," she began tentatively.

"Yes," said Isabella, "you should tell me, Beatriz. I see there is something on your mind."

"I have had news from the Duke of Medina Sidonia, Highness."

"What sort of news? Good, I hope."

"I think it might be good . . . very good. It concerns a strange adventurer. A man who has impressed him deeply. He begs an audience with Your Highness. The Duke tells me that his attention was called to this man by Fray Juan Perez de Marchena, who is guardian of the convent of La Rabida. He has approached Your Highness's confessor, but doubtless Talavera has been unimpressed by the man's story. Talavera has his mind on one thing — ridding this country of heretics."

"And what could be better?" demanded Isabella. She was thinking placidly of the punishment which had been carried out on the murderers of Arbues in Saragossa. Six of them had been dragged through Saragossa on hurdles, and had had their hands cut off on the Cathedral steps before they had been castrated, hanged, drawn and quartered for the multitude to see. One of the prisoners had committed suicide by eating a glass lamp. A pity, thought Isabella, smoothing the down on her baby's head, for thus he had evaded punishment.

Beatriz said quickly: "Highness, this man has a fantastic story to tell. As yet it is but a dream; but I have seen him, Highness, and I believe in his dreams."

296

Isabella wrinkled her brows in some puzzlement. Beatriz was by nature a practical woman; it was unlike her to talk of dreams.

"He came originally from Italy and went to Lisbon in the hope of interesting the King of Portugal in his schemes. Apparently he considers he was cheated there and, because he believes you to be the greatest ruler in the world, he wishes to lay his gift at your feet."

"What is this gift?"

"A new world, Highness."

"A new world! What can this mean?"

"A land of great riches as yet undiscovered. He is certain that it exists beyond the Atlantic Ocean, and that he can find a new route to Asia without crossing the Eastern continent. Time and money would be saved if this were accomplished. The riches of Cathay could be easily brought to Spain. This man speaks so convincingly, Highness, that he convinces me."

"You have been caught in the dreams of a dreamer, Beatriz."

"As I feel sure Your Highness would be if you would receive him in audience."

"What does he ask of me?"

"In exchange for a new world, he asks for ships which will take him there. He needs three carvels, fitted out for a long journey. He needs the patronage and approval of yourself."

Isabella was silent. "This man has impressed you deeply," she said at length. "What manner of man is he?"

"He is tall, long limbed, with eyes which seem to look into the future. Red-haired, blue-eyed. Near Your Highness's own colouring. But it is not his physical features which impress me; it is his intensity, his certainty that his dream can be realised."

"His name, Beatriz?"

"It was Christoforo Colombo, but since he has been in Spain he has changed it to Cristobal Colon. Highness, will you receive him? I implore you to."

"My dear Beatriz, since you ask it, how could I refuse?"

Cristobal Colon was preparing to present himself to the Sovereigns, and in the small house in which he had lived since he came to Cordova, impatiently he awaited the moment to depart. It had been impressed upon him by his patrons that this was a great honour which was being bestowed upon him. Cristobal did not accept this. It was he who was bestowing the honour.

There was a knock on his door. A high feminine voice said: "Señor Colon, you have not left yet, then?"

Cristobal's face softened slightly. "No, I have not yet left. Pray come in, Señora."

She was a pretty little woman, and the fact that now there was a great anxiety in her eyes endeared her to the adventurer.

"I prayed for you last night and this morning, Señor Colon. May all go well. May they give you what you ask."

"That is good of you."

"And, Señor, when you return, would it be asking too much of you to step into my house? I will prepare a meal for you. You will be hungry after your ordeal. Oh, I know you will not be thinking of food. But you should, you know. You will need a good meal, and I will have it waiting for you."

"You have been a good neighbour to me, Señora de Arana."

"I was about to say that I hope I shall always be so, but of course I do not: I hope that you will be successful and that soon you will be sailing away. Pray let me look at you." She had a brush with her, and began brushing his coat. "Why, have you forgotten that you are to be in the presence of the King and Queen?"

"It is not my clothes I am taking to show them."

"Whatever else you show, you must first show respect."

She put her head on one side and smiled at him. Then he stooped and kissed her cheek.

She flushed a little and turned away. He took her chin in his hands and looked into her face. There were tears in her eyes.

He thought of this woman who had been his neighbour for some months; he thought of the pleasantness of their friendship. Then he understood; she had treated him with a certain motherly devotion; but she was a young woman, younger than he was.

His head had been so full of his schemes that he had not realised until this moment that those long months of waiting had only been made tolerable by this woman.

He said: "Señora de Arana, Beatriz . . . why . . . when I leave I shall be very sad because I must say goodbye to you."

"It will be some time before you are able to leave," she answered quickly. "So . . . the parting will not be yet."

He hesitated for only a second. He was a man of strong passions. Then he caught her to him, and the kiss he gave her was long and demanding.

She had changed subtly; she was flushed and happy.

"What now, Señor Colon!" she said. "At any moment you must leave for your audience at the Palace. That is what you have been waiting for."

He was astonished at himself. He was certain that he was about to achieve that for which he had longed for many years; and here, on the brink of achievement, he was dallying with a pretty woman.

He stood still while she continued to brush his coat. Then he knew the time had come.

He said a somewhat brusque farewell and left for the Palace.

Cristobal stood before the Queen.

Behind her stood Beatriz de Bobadilla, who encouraged him by her warm looks; seated beside the Queen was the King, her husband; and by the side of the King stood the Queen's confessor, Fernando de Talavera.

Cristobal held his head high. Even Isabella and Ferdinand were not more dignified than he, not more proud. His looks were impressive and, because he believed that he had a great gift to offer, he was lacking in humility.

This was noted by all present. On Ferdinand and Talavera it had an adverse effect. They would have preferred a humble supplicant. Isabella was as impressed by him as Beatriz had been. The man, it seemed, did not behave with the decorum to which she was accustomed in her Court, but she recognised the fine spirit in him, which had so impressed Beatriz, and she thought: This man may be mistaken, but he believes in himself; and in such belief lie the seeds of genius.

"Cristobal Colon," said Isabella, "you have a plan to lay before us. I pray you tell us what it is you think you can do."

"Your Highness," said Cristobal, "I would not have you think that I have no practical knowledge with which to back up my schemes. I was instructed at Pavia in the mathematical sciences, and since the age of fourteen I have led a seafaring life. I came to Portugal because I had heard that in that country I was more likely to receive a sympathetic hearing. It was said to be the country of maritime enterprise."

"And you did not find that sympathy," said Isabella. "Tell us what you hope to discover."

"A sea route to Cathay and Zipango. Highnesses, the great Atlantic Ocean has never been crossed. No one knows what lies beyond it. There may be rich lands as yet undiscovered. Highnesses, I ask you to make this expedition possible."

The Queen said slowly: "You speak with some conviction, yet the King of Portugal was unconvinced."

"Highness, he set up an ecclesiastical council. He asked monks to decide regarding a voyage of discovery!" Colon had drawn himself up to his great height, and his eyes flashed scorn.

Talavera's indignation rose. Talavera, whose life had been lived in the cloister, was afraid of new ideas. He was fanatically religious and deeply superstitious. He was telling himself that if God had wished man to know of the existence of certain continents He would not have made them so inaccessible that over many centuries they had remained unheard of. Talavera was wondering whether this foreigner's suggestions did not smack of heresy.

But Talavera was on the whole a mild man; it would give him no pleasure — as it would have given Torquemada — to put this man on the rack and make him confess that his suggestions came from the devil. Talavera showed his scepticism by cold indifference.

"So you failed to convince the King of Portugal," said the Queen. "And for this reason you come to me."

Ferdinand put in: "Doubtless you have charts which might help us to decide whether this journey would be a profitable one."

"I have certain charts," said Cristobal cautiously. He was remembering that the Bishop of Ceuta, having been made aware of nautical details, had dispatched his own explorers. Cristobal was not going to allow that to happen again. His most important charts he would keep to himself.

"We should have to give this matter great thought before committing ourselves," said Ferdinand. "We are engaged in a Holy War at the moment."

"But," said Isabella, "rest assured that your suggestions shall have our serious considerations. I shall appoint a council to consider them. They will be in touch with you; and if the report they bring to me is hopeful, I will then consider what can be done to provide you with what you need." She inclined her head. "You will be informed, Señor Colon, of the findings of the committee which I shall set up."

From beside the Queen, Beatriz de Bobadilla was smiling encouragement at him.

Cristobal knelt before the Sovereigns.

The audience was over.

The Señora Beatriz de Arana was waiting for him on his return. She looked at him expectantly; his expression was noncommittal.

"I do not know what will be the outcome," he said. "They are going to set up a commission."

"But that is hopeful, surely."

"They set up a commission in Lisbon, my dear lady. An ecclesiastical commission. The Queen's confessor was present at this interview. I did not much like his looks. But there was one there — a maid of honour of the Queen — and she . . . she seemed to think something of me."

"Was she handsome?" asked the Señora earnestly.

Cristobal smiled at her. "Very handsome," he said. "Very, very handsome."

Beatriz de Arana looked a little sad, and he went on quickly: "Yet haughty, forceful. I prefer a gentler woman."

She said: "I have a meal waiting for you. Come into my house and we will eat together. We will drink to the success of your enterprise. Come now, for the food is hot, and I would not have it spoilt."

So he followed her into her house and, when they had eaten the excellent food she had cooked and were flushed with the wine she provided, he leaned his arms on the table and talked to her of voyages of the past and voyages of the future.

He felt then what a comfort it was to have someone to talk to, as once he had talked to Filippa. This homely, comfortable widow reminded him of Filippa in many ways. She came and looked over his shoulder, for he had taken a chart from his pocket and was describing the routes to her; and as he felt her hair against his cheek, he turned to her suddenly and took her into his arms.

She lay across his knees smiling at him gently and hopefully. She had been lonely for so long.

He kissed her and she responded.

It was a strange day for Cristobal — the audience with the King and Queen, the acquisition of a mistress. It was the happiest day he had lived through for years. Diego was being well cared for in the Monastery of Santa Maria de la Rabida, and his mind was at rest concerning Filippa's son; and here was a woman ready to comfort him. For once in his life he would cease to

304

dream of the future and for a very short time enjoy the present.

Later, Beatriz de Arana said to him: "Why should you go back to your lonely house? Why should I be lonely in mine? Give up your house and let my house be our house during the weeks of waiting."

Ferdinand snapped his fingers when Colon had left and Beatriz de Bobadilla and Talavera had been dismissed.

"This is a dream," he said. "We have no money to finance a foreigner's dreams."

"It is true that there is little to spare," Isabella agreed.

Ferdinand turned to her, his eyes blazing. "We should prosecute the Holy War with every means at our disposal. Boabdil is ours to command. Never has the position been so favourable, yet we are prevented from making war by lack of money. Moreover, there are the affairs of Aragon to be considered. I have given all my energies to this war against the Infidel, when, were I able to work for Aragon, I should make myself master of the Mediterranean. I could defeat the French and win back that which they have taken from me."

"If we dismiss this man," said Isabella, "he will go to France and in that country ask for the means to make his discoveries."

"Let him!"

"And if he should be right? If his discoveries should bring great wealth to our rivals, what then?"

"The man is a dreamer! He'll discover nothing."

"I think you may be right, Ferdinand," said Isabella quietly, "but I have decided to set up a commission to consider the possibilities of his success in this enterprise."

Ferdinand lifted his shoulders. "That could do no harm. And whom will you put in charge of this commission?"

"I think Talavera is the man to conduct it."

Ferdinand smiled. He felt certain that if Talavera were at the head of the commission the result would be the refusal of the foreign adventurer's request.

Talavera sat at the head of the table; about him were ranged those who had been selected to help him arrive at a decision.

Cristobal Colon had stood before them; he had eloquently argued his case; he had shown them charts which were in his possession, but he had held back certain important details, remembering the perfidy of the Portuguese.

Then he had been dismissed, while the judges made their decision.

Talavera spoke first. "I believe this man's claims to be fantastic"

Cardinal Mendoza put in quickly: "I would not be so bold as to say that anything on this earth was fantastic until I had proved it to be."

Talavera looked with mild exasperation at the Cardinal, who had become Primate of Spain and who took such a large part in state affairs that he was beginning to be known as the Third King of Spain. It was like Mendoza to side with the adventurer. Lackadaisical in his religion, Talavera believed that, for all his undoubted talents, Mendoza was a menace to Castile. The Inquisition was firmly established, but Mendoza was not in favour of it. He was no zealot for either side, and he made no attempt to pit his love of toleration against the burning fanaticism of men such as Torquemada. He merely turned distastefully from the subject and devoted himself to state affairs.

Friar Diego Deza, a Dominican, who was of the commission, also spoke up in favour of the adventurer.

"The man has a zeal about him, a determination, which it is impossible to ignore," said Deza. "I believe he knows more than he tells us. I believe that if he were supported he would at least discover new sea routes, if he did not discover new lands."

Talavera said: "I sense the devil in his proposals. Had God wished us to know of this land, do you doubt that He would have told us? I am not certain that we should not pass this man over to the Holy House for questioning."

Mendoza inwardly shivered. Not that, he thought. That bold man, stretched on the rack, hanging on the pulley, subjected to the water torture . . . forced to admit . . . what! That he had strayed from the tenets of the Church, that he had committed the mortal sin of heresy?

Mendoza pictured him — boldly facing his accusers. No, no! It must not happen. Mendoza would bestir himself for such a man.

He rejoiced, for the sake of Cristobal Colon, that it was the comparatively mild Talavera and not the fanatical Torquemada who was at the head of this commission, as he, Mendoza, had decided what he would do. He would not press his point here. He would let Talavera have his way. He would agree that the voyage was impracticable and have a word with the Queen quietly afterwards, for Talavera would be contented if he prevented the Sovereigns' spending money on the enterprise. This unimaginative man would feel he had done his duty, and Cristobal Colon would then be of no more importance to him.

So Mendoza, subduing Deza with a look which conveyed that they would talk together later of this matter, allowed Talavera to carry the day.

The other members, mostly ecclesiastics of the same type as Talavera, were ready to follow him, and the news was taken to the Sovereigns. "The commission has questioned Cristobal Colon; they have weighed up the possibilities of success and have found them wanting. It would be quite impracticable to finance such a fantastic voyage which, it is the considered opinion of the commission, could only end in failure."

Beatriz de Bobadilla put aside her decorum and stormed into the Queen's apartment.

"That fool Talavera!" she cried. "So he has turned you against this adventurer."

"Beatriz!" Isabella exclaimed in pained surprise.

Beatriz's answer was to fling herself at Isabella's feet. "Highness, I believe he should be given a chance."

"My dear friend," said Isabella, "what can you know about this? A commission of learned men has decided that it would be a waste of money we need so badly to finance this man's expedition."

"A commission of idiots!" cried Beatriz.

"Beatriz, my dear, I suggest you retire and calm yourself," said Isabella quietly and firmly, in that tone which implied that immediate obedience was expected.

When Beatriz had left, the Cardinal of Mendoza arrived.

"Highness," he said, "I have come to tell you that I am not in entire agreement with the findings of the commission."

"You mean you have given way to Talavera?"

"I felt the bulk of opinion against me, Highness. May I tell you exactly what I feel?"

"That I expect you to tell me."

"I feel this, Highness. It may well be an impracticable dream, but it is equally certain that it may not be. If we dismiss this man he will go to another country . . . probably France or England. I ask Your Highness to consider what would happen if the King of France or England provided this man with what he asks. If he were successful, if he discovered a world of great riches for them . . . instead of for us . . . our position would be changed considerably. That is what I wish to avoid."

"But, my dear Cardinal, the commission does not believe this voyage would be a success."

"The commission is largely composed of ecclesiastics, Highness."

"Of whom you are one!"

"I am also a statesman; and I beg Your Highness to consider the possibility of the man's discoveries passing into hands other than your own."

"Thank you, Cardinal," she said. "I will consider this."

Cristobal Colon was summoned once more to the presence of the Sovereigns.

Ferdinand was delighted.

"I knew," he told Isabella, "that the man was a fanatic, from the moment I saw him. Three carvels! Men to man them! He asked us to provide these that we may waste our substance. So the commission has proved me right."

"There were a few voices raised in opposition," Isabella reminded him.

"The majority saw through my eyes," retorted Ferdinand.

Isabella said softly: "Ferdinand, can you visualise the riches that may exist in lands as yet undiscovered?"

Ferdinand was silent for a few moments; then he snapped his fingers. "Better to seek to regain the riches which we have lost than look for those which may not even exist. There are riches within Granada which we know to exist. Let us make sure of the substance before we seek to grasp the shadow."

Talavera and Mendoza arrived with the members of the commission, and news was brought that Cristobal Colon had arrived at the Palace and was seeking audience with the Sovereigns.

"Let him be brought to us at once," said Isabella.

Cristobal came in. With the air of a visiting king he bowed before the Sovereigns. His eyes were alight with fervour. He could not believe that they would be so foolish as to deny him the money he asked, in exchange for which he would bring them great riches.

"The commission has given us its answer concerning your project," said Isabella slowly.

He lifted those brilliant blue eyes to her face and she felt herself soften towards him. When he stood before her thus he could make her believe in his promises. She understood why he had produced the effect he had on Beatriz and Mendoza.

She said gently: "At this time we are greatly occupied with a grievous war; and it is for this reason that we find ourselves unable to embark on this new undertaking."

She saw the light die out of his eyes. She saw the droop of his shoulders; she saw the frustration on his face, and she went on quickly: "When our war is won, Señor Colon, we shall be ready to treat with you."

He did not answer. He was not aware of the amazement in Talavera's eyes, of the triumph in Mendoza's. He only knew that once again he had been bitterly disappointed.

He bowed and left the presence of the Sovereigns.

It was Beatriz de Arana who comforted him.

"At least," she said, "they have promised to do something."

"My dear," he answered, "I have heard such promises before. They come to nothing."

She told him then that she could not understand her feelings. She wept because she loved him and she could not bear to see his bitter disappointment; yet how could she help but rejoice that he was left to her a little longer!

But even as she spoke she saw the speculation in his eyes.

She knew he was wondering whether he might not find more sympathy at the Court of France.

Yet he turned to her and caressed her, and he too would have been sad if they had to part. But she understood. This dream of a great voyage was a part of himself; it must come to fruition. He had parted with his beloved son, Diego, for its sake. So would he part from Beatriz if and when the time should come.

There was at least this respite, she told herself; and as she felt his hands stroking her hair, she knew that all the comfort he could feel at this moment must come from her.

There was a visitor to the little house, and Beatriz ushered him in and called to Cristobal.

Beatriz left the two men together.

"Let me introduce myself," said the man. "I am Luis de Sant'angel and I am the Secretary of Supplies in Aragon to King Ferdinand."

"I am glad to know you," said Cristobal, "but what can your business be with me?"

"I come to tell you that you have friends at Court; there are many of us who believe in your enterprise and are going to do our utmost to persuade the Sovereigns to support you."

Cristobal smiled wanly. "I thank you. And if I seem ungrateful, let me tell you that for many years I have sought to make this journey, and again and again I have suffered the same frustration. I have had friends at Court, but they have not been able to persuade my detractors that I can achieve what I say I can."

"Do not despair. Let me tell you, Señor Colon, that you have friends in very high places. The great Cardinal Mendoza believes you should be given a chance. And he is said to be the most important man at Court, and to wield great influence over the Queen. Fray Diego de Deza, who is tutor to the Prince Don Juan, is also in your favour. And there is one other — a lady of great power. You see, Señor, you have your friends and supporters."

"I rejoice to hear this, but I would rejoice more if I might be allowed to fit out my carvels and make my plans."

"Come to the Palace this day. We have news for you."

He left shortly afterwards, and Cristobal hurried to tell Beatriz what had happened.

She stood at the window watching him as he left for the Palace; there was a spring in his step. The Aragonese Jew, Luis de Sant'angel, had revived his hopes.

Beatriz turned hurriedly away from the window.

When Cristobal presented himself at the Palace he was taken to the apartments of Beatriz de Bobadilla.

Beatriz, who was now Marchioness of Moya, was not alone. With her were Fray Diego de Deza, Alonso de Quintanilla, the Queen's secretary, Juan Cabrero, Ferdinand's chamberlain and Luis de Sant'angel.

Beatriz studied the man who stood before her, and she felt her spirits lifted. She wished in that moment that she could accompany him on his voyage, that she might be the one to stand beside him when he had his first sight of the new lands which he would discover.

I am being foolishly emotional, she thought. Merely because the man has such dignity, such character, such handsome looks; merely because he is a man of purpose, am I to forget my position, my common sense on his account?

It was so unlike her to be foolishly romantic. Yet this man moved her deeply as few men ever had; and she had determined that his cause should be her cause.

She had already begun to work for him, and it was for this reason that she had sent for him.

"Señor Colon," she said, "I would have you know that those of us who are gathered here today believe in you. We are sorry that there must be this delay, but in the meantime we would have you know that we are your friends and that we intend to help you."

"You are gracious, my lady," said Colon, inclining his head slightly.

"We have no doubt," said Beatriz, "that many have said these words to you."

"It is true."

314

"Yet," said Luis de Sant'angel, "we intend to show you our regard with more than words. That is so, my friends, is it not?"

"It is," agreed the others.

"We have therefore," went on Beatriz, "persuaded the Queen to give you some token of her regard during the waiting period. She has agreed that you shall receive a sum of 3,000 *maravedis*. It is not to be considered as something towards your expedition. That would be useless, we know. But while you remain here you must live, and this money is to help you, and to show that the Queen does not forget you."

"I am grateful to Her Highness."

Sant'angel touched his elbow. "Be grateful to the Marchioness," he murmured. "It is she who has the ear of the Queen. It is she who will work for you."

Beatriz laughed. "It is true," she said. "I shall see that in a few months' time more money is given you. Nor shall I allow the Queen to forget you."

"How can I express my thanks?"

Beatriz smiled almost gently. "By remaining firm in your resolve. By holding yourself in readiness. It may be necessary for you to follow the Court when it leaves Cordova. I shall arrange that you shall suffer no expense from these journeys. The Queen has given her consent to the proposal that you shall be provided with free lodging. You see, Señor Colon, we are your friends."

Cristobal looked from one to the other.

"My friends," he said, "your faith in me makes me a happy man."

★ ★ ★

For a few months his spirits were high. He had friends in high places. More money was paid to him; but the war with Granada went on in a series of sharp attacks and skirmishes. Cristobal knew that it would be long before it was brought to an end.

He would sit at dusk with Beatriz de Arana, looking out on the little street, always hoping that there would be a knock on the door to summon him to Court.

Once as they sat in the darkened room he said to her: "This is how it has always been. I wait here as I waited in Lisbon. Here I am happier because you are here, because I know my little Diego is being well cared for in his monastery. Sometimes I think I shall spend my whole life waiting."

"And if you do, Cristobal, could you not be happy? Have you not been happy here with me?"

"It is my destiny to sail the seas," he said. "It is my life. It sounds ungrateful to you who have been so good to me. Let me say this, that there is only one thing that has made these months of waiting tolerable: my life with you. But for this urge within me I could settle here and live happily with you for the rest of my days."

"But the time will come when you will go away, Cristobal."

"I shall come back to you."

"But you will be long away, and how can I be sure that you will come back? There are dangers on the seas."

"You must not be unhappy, Beatriz. I could not bear to think that I have brought unhappiness to you who have brought so much happiness to me."

"No," she said, "remember this. When you sail away — as you must — I shall not be alone."

He started and sought to look into her face, but it was too dark for him to see it clearly.

"I shall have my child then, Cristobal," she said softly, "your child, our child."

CHAPTER
TWELVE

Before Malaga

Isabella sat at her sewing with her eldest daughter, the
Infanta Isabella. She was conscious that now and then
the girl was casting covert glances at her, and that she
was on the verge of tears.

Isabella herself was fighting back her emotion. She
does not know it, she told herself, but the parting is
going to be even harder for me to bear than it is for her.
She is young and will quickly adjust herself to her new
surroundings . . . whereas I . . . I shall always miss her.

"Mother . . ." said the Infanta at length.

"My dear," murmured Isabella; she put aside her
needlework and beckoned to her daughter. The Infanta
threw hers aside and ran to her mother to kneel at her
feet and bury her face in her lap.

Isabella stroked her daughter's hair.

"My dearest," she said, "you will be happy, you
know. You must not fret."

"But to go away from you all! To go to strangers . . ."

"It is the fate of Infantas, my darling."

"You did not, Mother."

"No, I stayed here, but many efforts were made to
send me away. If my brother Alfonso had lived,

318

doubtless I should have married into a strange country. So much hangs on chance, my dearest; and we must accept what comes to us. We must not fight against our destinies."

"Oh, Mother, how fortunate you were, to stay in your home and marry my father."

Isabella thought fleetingly of the first time she had seen Ferdinand; young, handsome, virile. She thought of the ideal she had built up and the shock of discovering that she had married a sensual man. She had come to her marriage hoping for a great deal and had received less than she hoped for. She prayed that her daughter would find in marriage something more satisfying than she had thought possible.

"Your Alonso will be as beloved by you as Ferdinand is by me," Isabella told her daughter.

"Mother, must I marry at all? Why should I not stay here with you?"

"It is very necessary that you should marry, my darling. A marriage between you and the heir to the throne of Portugal could bring great stability to our two countries. You see, not very long ago there was war between us. It was at the time when I came to the throne and Portugal supported the claims of La Beltraneja. The threat of La Beltraneja has always been with us, for she still lives in Portugal. Now Alonso will one day be King of Portugal, and if you marry him, my darling, you will be its Queen; our two countries would be united and this threat removed. That is what we have to think of when making our marriages — not what good it will bring to us, but what good it will bring to our countries. But do not fret, my child. There is much to be arranged yet, and these matters are rarely settled quickly."

The Infanta shivered. "But they are settled . . . in time, Mother."

"Let us enjoy all the time that is left to us."

The Infanta threw her arms about her mother and clung to her.

As she embraced her daughter, Isabella heard the sounds of arrival below, and she put the Infanta from her, rose and went to the window. She saw a party of soldiers from Ferdinand's army, and she prepared to receive them immediately because she guessed that they brought news from the camp.

Ferdinand had taken possession of Velez Malaga, which was situated some five or six leagues from the great port of Malaga itself; and the King was now concentrating all his forces on the capture of this town.

The Christian armies were before Malaga, which was perhaps the most important town — next to Granada itself — in Moorish territory. It was a strongly defended fortress, rich and prosperous. The Moors were proud of Malaga, this beautiful city of handsome buildings with its fertile vineyards, olive groves and gardens of oranges and pomegranates.

They were determined to fight to the death to preserve it; thus Isabella knew that it would be no easy task for Ferdinand to take it.

Therefore she was impatient to hear what news these messengers brought from the front.

She commanded that they be brought to her presence immediately, and she did not dismiss the Infanta. She wished her daughter to know something of state matters; she did not want to send her, an ignoramus, into a strange country.

She took Ferdinand's letters and read that the siege of Malaga had begun and that he feared it would be long and arduous. There was no hope of an easy victory. If the Moors lost the port it would be a turning point in the war, and they knew this. They were therefore as determined to hold Malaga as the Christians were to take it.

The city had been placed in the hands of a certain Hamet Zeli, a general of outstanding courage and integrity, and he had sworn that he would hold Malaga for the Moors to the death.

Ferdinand wrote: "And I have determined to take it, no matter what the cost. But this will give some indication of the man we have to deal with. It was brought to my notice that many of the rich townsfolk were ready to make peace with me, in order to save Malaga from destruction. I sent Cadiz to offer concessions to Hamet Zeli and the most important of the citizens if they would surrender Malaga to me. I know that many of the burghers would have accepted my offer, but Hamet Zeli intervened. 'There is no bribe the Christians could offer me,' he retorted, 'which would be big enough to make me betray my trust.' That is the kind of man with whom we have to deal."

"Isabella, there is certain friction in our camp which causes me anxiety. There have been rumours of plague in some of the surrounding villages. These are unfounded, but I believe them to have been set in motion to distract our troops. There has been a shortage of water; and, I regret to say, several of the men have deserted."

"I can think of only one person who could stop this decadence. Yourself. Isabella, I am asking you to come to the camp. Your presence here will lift the spirits of the soldiers. You would give heart to them and, when the news reaches the people of Malaga that you are with us, I feel sure that their anxieties would be increased. They will know that we are determined to take Malaga. Isabella, leave everything and come to our camp before Malaga with all speed."

Isabella smiled as she read this dispatch.

She looked at the Infanta, who was watching her with curiosity.

"I am leaving immediately for the camp before Malaga," she said. "The King requests my presence there."

"Mother," said the Infanta, "you said that we should not be parted . . . that there may not be much time left to us. Dearest Mother, please stay here with us."

Isabella looked at her eldest daughter and said: "But of course I must go. There is work to do in the camp; but do not fret, my daughter. We shall not be parted, for you are coming with me."

Isabella arrived at the camp, accompanied by the Infanta and several of the ladies of the Court, among whom was Beatriz de Bobadilla.

They were greeted with enthusiasm, and the effect on the morale of the army was immediate.

Isabella's dignity never failed to have its effect, and when she turned several tents into a hospital and, with her women, cared for the sick and wounded, there was no doubt that her coming had saved a dangerous situation. Those soldiers who were wearying of the long war, who had been telling themselves that they could never conquer the well-fortified city of Malaga, now changed their minds. They were eager to perform feats of valour in order to win the respect of the Queen and her ladies.

Ferdinand had been right. What the army needed was the presence of its Queen.

There was little peace, for there were continual forays by the Moors who crept out of the besieged city under cover of darkness and made raids on the encamped army.

It might well have been that the Christian armies would have been defeated before Malaga, for El Zagal sent forces to help the town. Unfortunately for the Moors, and to the great advantage of the Christians, Boabdil's troops encountered the relieving force on its way, a battle ensued and there were so many casualties that it was impossible for El Zagal's men to come to the relief of Malaga.

When Isabella heard this she thanked God for the shrewdness of Ferdinand, who had insisted, instead of keeping Boabdil in captivity, on sending him back that he might do great damage to the Moorish cause.

Poor Boabdil was a bewildered young man. He hated war; he wished to end it as quickly as possible. He sought to placate the Christian Sovereigns by sending them presents, almost as though to remind them that through the recent treaty he was their vassal.

"We owe a great deal to Boabdil," said Ferdinand. "This war would have been longer and more bloody for us but for him. I will make him some return to show him that I am his friend. I shall allow his supporters to cultivate their fields in peace. After all, soon this land will be ours. It would be wise therefore to leave some of it in cultivation and at the same time reward Boabdil."

So the siege continued, and Ferdinand was confident of victory. He trusted his own shrewdness and his ability to get the best of any bargain; he had called his Master of Ordnance, Francisco Ramirez, to the front; this clever inventor with his powder mines could work miracles until now never used in warfare; and there was Isabella, with her dignity, piety and good works.

We cannot fail, thought Ferdinand; we have everything which makes for success.

It was afternoon when the prisoner was brought in. He was dragged before the Marquis of Cadiz; and he fell to his knees and begged the Marquis to spare his life. As the man could not speak Castilian, the Marquis spoke to him in the Moorish tongue.

"I come as a friend. I come as a friend," repeated the Moor. "I pray you listen to what I have to say. I will lead you into Malaga. I am the friend of the Christian King and Queen, as is my King, Boabdil."

324

The Marquis of Cadiz, who was about to order the Moor's execution, paused.

He signed to the two guards who stood on either side of the Moor to seize him.

"Follow me," said the Marquis, "and bring him with you."

He made his way to the royal tent, where Isabella was with Ferdinand. She came to the entrance, for she had heard the man shouting in his own language.

"Highness," said the Marquis, "this man was captured. He says he has escaped from the city because he has something he wishes to tell you. Will you and the King see him now?"

Isabella looked back into the tent, where Ferdinand, worn out with his recent exertions, was fast asleep.

"The King is asleep," she said. "I do not wish to waken him. He was quite exhausted. This man's story can wait. Take him into the next tent. There let him remain until the King awakes, when I will immediately tell him what has happened."

She indicated the tent next to her own, in which Beatriz de Bobadilla sat with Don Alvaro, a Portuguese nobleman, and son of the Duke of Braganza, who had joined the Holy War, as so many foreigners had, since they looked upon it as a crusade.

They were discussing the siege and, when Beatriz heard the Queen's words, she went to Isabella.

"I wish this man to be detained until the King awakes," said Isabella. "He says that he has news for us."

"We will detain him until it is your pleasure to receive him," said Beatriz; and when the guards, after having brought the Moor to her tent, stationed themselves outside, she continued her conversation with the Duke.

The Moor watched them. She was a very handsome woman and far more magnificently dressed than Isabella had been. He had glimpsed the sleeping Ferdinand, his doublet lying beside his pallet, and he had not thought for one moment that this could be the great King of whom he had heard so much.

But here was a courtly man in garments of scarlet and gold; and here was a lady, queenly in her bearing, with jewels at her throat and on her hands, her gown stiff with silken embroidery.

The Moor remained motionless, watching them slyly as they continued to talk together as though he were not there. He believed they were discussing how they would treat him, what questions they would ask.

He began to make soft moaning noises, and when they looked at him he gazed towards a jar of water with pleading eyes.

"The man is thirsty," said Beatriz. "Let us give him a draught of water."

The Duke poured water into a cup and handed it to the Moor, who drank it eagerly. As the Duke turned away, to put the cup by the jar, the Moor knew that the moment he had been waiting for had come.

He knew that death would doubtless be his reward, but he did not care. This day he was going to perform a deed which would make his name glorious in Arab history for evermore. There were two whose names struck terror into every citizen within the walls of Malaga — and of Granada also: Ferdinand, the great soldier, Isabella, the dedicated Queen.

He slipped his hand beneath his *albornoz* and his fingers closed round the dagger which he had secreted there.

The man should be first because, when he was dead, it would be easy to deal with the woman. He lifted the dagger as he sprang, and in a few seconds Don Alvaro, bleeding profusely from the head, sank to the floor. Beatriz screamed for help as the Moor then turned to her. Again he lifted the dagger, but Beatriz's arm shot up and the blow he struck at her breast was diverted.

"Help!" Beatriz shouted. "We are being murdered."

Again the Moor lifted the dagger, but Beatriz was ready for him. She slipped aside and the blow glanced off the encrusted embroidery of her gown. She was calling for help at the top of her voice. There was an answering shout and the guards entered the tent.

Again the Moor sought to strike at the woman whom he believed to be Isabella. But he was too late. He was caught by the guards, who seized him and dragged him from the tent.

Beatriz followed them shouting: "Send help at once. Don Alvaro has been badly wounded."

Then she turned back and knelt by the wounded man seeking to stem his bleeding.

Isabella came into the tent.

"Beatriz, what is this?" she asked; and she gasped with horror as she looked at the wounded man.

"He is not dead," said Beatriz. "With God's help we shall save him. It was the Moor, who said he had news for you."

"And I sent him to your tent!"

"Thank God you did."

Ferdinand had now appeared in the tent; he was pulling on his doublet as he came.

"An attempt, Highness," said Beatriz, "on the life of the Queen and yourself."

Ferdinand stared down at the wounded man.

"You see," said Beatriz later, "you are in danger here, Highness. You should not be in camp. It is no place for you."

"It is the only place for me," answered Isabella.

"That might have been the end of your lives. If you had taken that man into your tent he could have killed the King while he slept."

"And what should I have been doing to allow that?" asked Isabella with a smile. "Do you not think that I should have given as good an account of myself as you did?"

"I was fortunate. I am wearing this dress. I think his knife would have pierced me but for the heavy embroidery. You, Highness, are less vain of your personal appearance than I am. The knife might have penetrated your gown."

"God would have watched over me," said Isabella.

"But, Highness, will you not consider the danger, and return to safety?"

328

"Not long ago," said Isabella, "the King was reproved by his soldiers because he took great risks in battle and endangered his life. He told them he could not stop to consider the risk to himself while his subjects were putting their lives in peril for his cause, which was a holy one. That is the answer I make to you now, Beatriz."

Beatriz shivered. "I shall never cease to thank God that you sent that murderer into my tent."

Isabella smiled at her friend and, taking her hand, pressed it affectionately.

"We must take care of the Infanta," she said. "We must remember the dangers all about us."

All over the camp there was talk of the miraculous escape of the King and Queen, and the incident did much to lift the spirits of the soldiers. They believed that Divine power was guarding their Sovereigns, and this, they told themselves, was because the war they were prosecuting was a Holy War.

The Moor had been done to violent death by those guards who had dragged him from the tent, and there were cheers of derision as his mutilated body was taken to the cannon.

A great shout went up as the corpse was propelled by catapult over the walls and into the city.

Inside the city, faces were grim. Hunger was the lot of everyone and the once prosperous city was desolate.

From the mosques came the chant of voices appealing to Allah, but despair was apparent in those chants.

Some cursed Boabdil, who had been the friend of the Christians; some murmured against El Zagal, the valiant one, who waged war on Boabdil and the Christians. Some whispered that peace should be the aim of their leaders . . . peace for which they would be prepared to pay a price. Others shouted: "Death to the Christians! No surrender!"

And as they lifted the mangled remains of the intrepid Moor, an angry murmur arose.

One of their Christian prisoners was brought out. They slew him most cruelly; they tied his mutilated body astride a mule, which they drove out from Malaga into the Christian camp.

Inside the city the heat was intense. There was little to eat now. There were few dogs and cats left; they had long ago eaten their horses. They existed on vine leaves; they were emaciated, and in the streets men and women were dying of exhaustion or unspecified diseases. And outside the walls of the city the Christians still waited.

Several of the town's important men formed themselves into a band and presented themselves before Hamet Zeli.

"We cannot much longer endure this suffering," they told him.

He shook his head. "In time, help will come to us."

"When it comes, Hamet Zeli, it will be too late."

"I have sworn to El Zagal never to surrender."

"In the streets the people are dying of hunger and pestilence. No help will come to us. Our crops have been destroyed; our cattle stolen. What has become of our fertile vineyards? The Christians have left our land desolate and we are dying a slow death. Allah has turned his face against us. Open the gates of the city and let the Christians in."

"That is the wish of the people?" asked Hamet Zeli.

"It is the wish of all."

"Then I will take my forces into the Gebalfaro, and you may make your peace with Ferdinand."

The burghers looked at each other. "It is what we wished to do weeks ago," said one of them.

"That is true," said another. "You, Ali Dordux should lead a deputation to Ferdinand. He offered us special concessions some weeks ago if we would surrender the town to him. Tell him that we are now ready to do so."

"I will lead my deputation to him with all speed," said Ali Dordux. "It may be that the sooner we go, the more lives we shall save."

"Go from me now," said Hamet Zeli. "This is no affair of mine. I would never surrender. I would die rather than bow to the Christian invader."

"We are not soldiers, Hamet Zeli," said Ali Dordux. "We are men of peace. And no fate which the Christian can impose upon us could be worse than that which we have endured."

"You do not know Ferdinand," answered Hamet Zeli. "You do not know the Christians."

Ferdinand heard that the deputation had called upon him.

"Led, Highness," he was told, "by Ali Dordux, the most prominent and wealthy citizen. They beg an audience that they may discuss terms for surrendering the city to you."

Ferdinand smiled slowly.

"Pray return to them," he said, "and tell them this: I offered them peace and they refused it. Then they were in a position to bargain. Now they are a conquered people. It is not for them to make terms with me but to accept those on which I shall decide."

The deputation returned to Malaga, and when it was learned what Ferdinand had said there was loud wailing throughout the city.

"Now," the people whispered to each other, "we know that we can expect no mercy from the Christians."

There were many to exhort them to stand firm. "Let us die rather than surrender," they cried. They had a wonderful leader in Hamet Zeli; why did they not put their trust in him?

Because their families were starving, was the answer. They had seen their wives and children die of disease and hunger. There must be an end to the siege at any price.

A new embassy was sent to Ferdinand.

They would surrender their city to him in exchange for their lives and freedom. Let him refuse this offer and every Christian in Malaga — and they held six hundred Christian prisoners — should be hanged over the battlements. They would put the aged and the weak, the women and the children, into the fortress, set fire to the town and cut a way for themselves through the enemy. So that Ferdinand would lose the rich treasure of Malaga.

But Ferdinand was aware that he was dealing with a beaten people. He felt no pity; he would give no quarter. He was a hard man completely lacking in imagination. He saw only the advantage to his own cause.

He was making no compacts, he replied. If any Christian within the city was harmed he would slaughter every Moslem within the walls of Malaga.

This was the end of resistance. The gates of the city were thrown open to Ferdinand.

Isabella, richly gowned, rode beside Ferdinand into the conquered city of Malaga.

It had been purified before their arrival, and over all the principal buildings floated the flag of Christian Spain.

The great mosque was now the church of Santa Maria de la Encarnacion; and bells could be heard ringing throughout the city.

Isabella's first desire was to visit the new cathedral and there give thanks for the victory.

Afterwards she rode through the streets, but she did not see the terror in the eyes of the people; she did not see the cupidity in those of Ferdinand as he surveyed these rich treasures which had fallen into his hands. She heard only the bells; she could only rejoice.

Another great city for Christ, she told herself. The Moorish kingdom was depleted afresh. This was the greatest victory they had yet achieved, for the Moors in Granada would be seriously handicapped by the loss of their great port.

A cry of anger went up from the assembly as the Christian slaves tottered out into the streets; some could scarcely see, because they had been kept so long in darkness. They limped and dragged themselves along, to fall at the feet of the Sovereigns in order to kiss their hands in gratitude for their deliverance.

The sound of their chains being pulled along as they walked was audible, for as they approached the Sovereigns there was a deep silence among the spectators.

"No," cried Isabella; and she slipped from her horse and placed her hands on the shoulders of the blind old man who was seeking to kiss her hand. "You shall not kneel to me," she went on. And she raised him up. And those watching saw the tears in her eyes, a sight which moved those who knew her, as much as the spectacle of these poor slaves.

Ferdinand had joined her. He too embraced the slaves; he too wept; but he could weep more easily than Isabella, and he quickly allowed indignation to dry his tears.

Isabella said: "Let these people be taken from here. Let their chains be taken from them. Let a banquet be prepared for them. They must know that I shall not allow their sufferings to be forgotten. They shall be recompensed for their long captivity."

Then she mounted her horse and the procession continued.

Hamet Zeli was brought before them, proud, bold, though emaciated, and in heavy chains.

"You should have surrendered long ere this," Ferdinand told him. "You see how foolish you have been. You might once have bought concessions for your people."

"I was commanded to defend Malaga," said Hamet Zeli. "Had I been supported, I would have died before giving in."

"Thus you show your folly," said Ferdinand. "Now you will obey my commands. I would have the whole of the population of Malaga assembled in the courtyard of the *alcazaba* to hear the sentence I shall pass upon them."

"Great Ferdinand," said Hamet Zeli, "you have conquered Malaga. Take its treasures. They are yours."

"They are mine," said Ferdinand smiling; "and certainly I shall take them."

"But, Christian King, spare the people of Malaga."

"Should they be allowed to go free for all the inconvenience they have caused me? Many of my men have died at their hands."

"Do what you will with the soldiers, but the citizens played no part in this war."

"Their obstinacy has angered me," said Ferdinand. "Assemble them that they may hear their fate."

In the courtyard of the *alcazaba*, the people had assembled. All through the day the sound of wailing voices had filled the streets.

The people were calling on Allah not to desert them. They begged him to plant compassion and mercy in the heart of the Christian King.

335

But Allah ignored their cries, and the heart of the Christian King was hardened against them.

He told them what their fate would be in one word: slavery.

Every man, woman and child was to be sold or given in slavery. They had defied him and, because of this, they must pay for their foolishness with their freedom.

Slavery! The dreaded word fell on the still, hot air.

Where was the proud city of Malaga now? Lost to the Arabs for evermore. What would befall its people? They would be scattered throughout the world. Children would be torn from their parents, husbands from their wives. This was the decree of the Christian King: Slavery for the proud people of Malaga.

In the *alcazaba* Ferdinand rubbed his hands together. He could scarcely speak, so excited was he. He could only contemplate the treasures of this beautiful city which were now his . . . all his.

Then a certain fear came to him. How could he be sure that all the treasure would be handed to him? These Arabs were a cunning people. Might they not hide their most precious jewels, their richest treasures, hoping to preserve them for themselves?

It was an alarming thought. Yet how could he be sure that this would not happen?

Isabella was calculating what they would do with the slaves.

"We shall be able to redeem some of our own people," she told Ferdinand.

Ferdinand was not enthusiastic. He was thinking of selling the slaves. They would not help to fill the treasury, he pointed out.

But Isabella was determined. "We must not forget those of our people who have been taken into slavery. I propose that we send one-third of the people of Malaga into Africa in exchange for an equal number of our people held there as slaves."

"And sell the rest," said Ferdinand quickly.

"We might sell another third," Isabella replied. "This should bring us a goodly sum which will be very useful for prosecuting the war."

"And the remainder?"

"We must not forget the custom. We should send some to our friends. Do not forget that those who have worked with us and have helped us to win this great victory will expect some reward. The Pope should be presented with some, so should the Queen of Naples. And we must not forget that we hope for this marriage between Isabella and Alonso; so I would send some of the most beautiful of the girls to the Queen of Portugal."

"So," said Ferdinand, somewhat disgruntled, "we shall only sell a third of them for our own benefit."

But what was really worrying him was the thought that he could not be sure that all the treasures of Malaga would come to him, and he feared that some might be secreted away and he not know of their existence.

Hope suddenly sprang up in the desolate town of Malaga.

"There is a chance to regain our freedom!" The words were passed through the streets from mouth to mouth. A chance to evade this most dreadful of fates.

King Ferdinand had decreed that if they could pay a large enough ransom he would sell them their freedom.

And the amount demanded?

It was a sum of such a size that it seemed impossible that they could raise it. Yet every man, woman and child in Malaga must help to do so.

Nothing must be held back. Everything must be poured into the great fund which was to buy freedom for the people of Malaga.

The fund grew big, but it was still short of the figure demanded by Ferdinand.

In the streets the people called to each other: "Hold nothing back. Think of what depends upon it."

And the fund grew until it contained every treasure, great and small, for all agreed that no price was too great to pay for freedom.

Ferdinand received the treasure.

"Oh, great Christian King," he was implored, "this is not the large sum you asked. It falls a little short. We pray you accept it, and out of your magnanimity grant us our freedom."

Ferdinand smiled and accepted the treasure.

"Alas," he said, "it is not the figure I demanded. I am a man who keeps his word. This is not enough to buy freedom for the people of Malaga."

When he had dismissed the Arabs he laughed aloud.

Thus he had made sure that the people of Malaga would hold nothing back from him. Thus he had defeated them utterly and completely. He had all their wealth, and still they had not regained their freedom.

The capture of Malaga was a resounding victory.

There remained the last stronghold: Granada.

CHAPTER
THIRTEEN

Marriage Of An Infanta

The Queen crept into the bedchamber of her daughter, the Infanta Isabella. As she had expected, the girl was lying on her bed, her eyes wide open, staring into space.

"My dearest child," said the Queen, "you must not be unhappy."

"But to go far away from you all," murmured the Infanta.

"It is not so very far."

"It is too far," said the girl.

"You are nineteen years old, my daughter. That is no longer young."

Young Isabella shivered. "If I could only stay with you!"

The Queen shook her head. She was thinking how happy she would be if it were possible to find a husband for her eldest daughter here at the Court, and if they might enjoy the preparations for marriage together; if after the wedding, she, the mother, might be beside her daughter, advising, helping, sharing.

340

It was a foolish speculation, and they should be rejoicing. For years Portugal had represented a menace. It would always be so while La Beltraneja lived. And John, the King, had allowed her to live outside her convent! In Portugal there had been times when La Beltraneja had been known as Her Highness the Queen.

This could have been a cause for war. She and Ferdinand might have deemed it wise to make war on Portugal, had they not been so busily engaged elsewhere.

And now John saw the advantages of a match between his son Alonso and the Infanta of Castile. If this marriage took place he would no longer allow La Beltraneja to be called Her Highness the Queen, he would stop speculating as to whether it would be possible to put her back on the throne of Castile, and instead send her back to her convent.

"Oh, my darling," said the Queen, taking her daughter's limp hand and raising it to her lips, "with this marriage you are bringing great good to your country. Does that not comfort you?"

"Yes, dear mother," said the Infanta faintly. "It brings me comfort."

Then Isabella kissed her daughter's forehead and crept away.

It was April in Seville and there was *fiesta* in the streets.

The people had gathered to watch the coming and going of great personages. These were the streets which so frequently saw the grim processions of Inquisitors, and condemned men in their yellow *sanbenitos*, making their way to the Cathedral and the fields of Tablada. Now here was a different sort of entertainment; and the people threw themselves into it with an almost frenzied joy.

Their Infanta Isabella was to be married to the heir of Portugal. There were to be feasts and banquets, bullfights and dancing. This was a glorious occasion which would not end in death.

Tents had been set up along the banks of the Guadalquivir for the tourneys which were to take place. The buildings were decorated with flags and cloth of gold. The people had grown accustomed to seeing groups of horsemen magnificently caparisoned — the members of their royal family and that of Portugal.

They saw their King distinguish himself in the tournaments, and they shouted themselves hoarse in approval of the stalwart Ferdinand, who had recently won such resounding victories over the Moors and was even now preparing for what he hoped would be the final blow.

And there was the Queen, always gracious, always serene; and the people remembered that she had brought law and order to a state where it had been unsafe for travellers to ride out on their journeys. She had also brought this new Inquisition. But this was a time of rejoicing. They were determined to forget all that was unpleasant.

The Infanta, who looked younger than her nineteen years, was tall and stately, rather pale and delicate but very lovely, full of grace and charm — the happy bride.

The bridegroom did not come to Seville, but the news had spread that he was young, ardent and handsome. In his place was Don Fernando de Silveira, who appeared at the side of the Infanta on all public occasions — a proxy for his master.

Yes, this was a time of rejoicing. The marriage was approved by all. It was going to mean peace for ever with their western neighbours, and peace was something for which everybody longed.

So they tried to forget their friends and relations who were held by the Holy Office. They danced and sang in the streets, and cried: "Long live Isabella! Long live Ferdinand! Long life to the Infanta!"

To go from one's home to a new country! How often it had happened. It was the natural fate of an Infanta.

Does everyone suffer as I do? young Isabella asked herself.

But we have been so happy here. Our mother has been so kind, so gentle, so just to us all. Our father has loved us. Ours has been such a happy home. Am I now regretting that this has been so? Am I saying that, had we been a less happy family, I should not be suffering as I am now?

No. Any daughter should rejoice to have such a mother as the Queen.

They were dressing her in her bridal robes, and her women were exclaiming at her beauty.

"The Prince Alonso will be enchanted," they told her.

But will he? she asked herself. Can I believe them?

She had heard certain scandal at the Court concerning her own father. He had sons and daughters whom she did not know. Her mother must have heard this, yet she gave no sign of it. How could I ever be like her? the Infanta Isabella asked herself. And if *she* does not satisfy my father, how could I hope to satisfy Alonso?

There was so little she knew, so much she had to learn; she felt that she was being buffeted into a world of new sensations, new emotions, and she was unsure whether she would be able to deal with them.

"It is time, Infanta," she was told.

And she left her apartments to be joined by the seventy ladies, all brilliantly clad, and the hundred pages in similar magnificent attire, who were waiting to conduct her to the ceremony.

She placed her hand in that of Don Fernando de Silveira and the solemn words were spoken.

The ceremony was over; she was the wife of the heir of Portugal, the wife of a man whom she had never seen.

Out in the streets they were shouting her name. She smiled and acknowledged their applause in the manner in which she had been taught.

On to the banquets, on to the balls and fetes and tourneys — all given in honour of a frightened girl whose single prayer was that something would happen which would prevent her leaving the heart of the family she loved.

★ ★ ★

There was respite. All through the summer the festivities continued, and it was not until autumn that she rode out of Castile.

The people lined the roads to see her pass and cheer her.

It was said that Portugal had prepared to welcome her in a royal manner. They were delighted to receive her. She brought with her a larger dowry than that usually accorded to the Infantas of Castile, and it was said that she had such magnificent gowns which alone had cost twenty thousand golden florins.

And so, on she rode over the border, away from her old country into the new.

She was bewildered by the pomp which awaited her.

She saw one man standing by the throne of the King who smiled at her encouragingly. He was young and handsome, and his eyes lingered on her.

She thought: There is my husband. There is Alonso. And she averted her eyes because she was afraid that, out of her inexperience, she might betray her emotion.

She approached King John, and knelt before him, but he raised her up and embraced her. "Welcome, my daughter," he said. "We have long awaited your coming. I rejoice that you are safely with us."

"I thank Your Highness," she answered.

"There is one who waits most impatiently to greet you! My son, who is also your husband."

And there he was, Alonso — not the man she had at first noticed — young and handsome; and because she sensed that he also was a little nervous, she felt happier.

He embraced her before the Court and the people cried: "Long live the Prince and the Princess of Portugal!"

And so she came to happiness. Her mother had been right. If one grasped one's duty firmly, one was rewarded. She knew she was particularly fortunate, because she had been given a young and handsome husband, a kindly gentle husband, who admitted that marriage alarmed him even as it alarmed her.

Now they could comfort each other, they could laugh at their fears. And out of the intensity of their relief in having found each other, was born a great affection.

Isabella wrote home of her happiness.

Her mother wrote of her intense joy to receive such glad news from her daughter.

All was well. The important link had been forged between two old enemies, and at no cost to the happiness of the Queen's beloved daughter.

Now that she was away from her mother's supervision, the character of the Princess began to change. She discovered a love of dancing, a love of laughter. This was shared by Alonso.

One day Isabella woke up to the realisation that she had begun to live in a way which she had not thought possible. She had realised that life could be a gay affair, that one need not think all the time of the saving of one's soul.

"We are young," said Alonso, "we have our lives before us. There is plenty of time, twenty years hence, for us to think of the life to come."

And she laughed with him at what, such a short time ago, would have shocked her deeply.

She grew less pale; her cough worried her less, for she was spending a great deal of time out of doors. Alonso loved to hunt, and he was unhappy unless she accompanied him.

She understood that these months, since she had been the wife of Alonso, were the happiest she had ever known. It was a startling and wonderful discovery.

Her beauty was intensified. Many people watched her unfold. She was like a bud that opened to become a beautiful flower, slightly less fragile than had been expected.

"You are beautiful," she was often told; and she had learned to accept such compliments with grace.

"No one at Court is more beautiful than you," she was assured by Emmanuel, Alonso's cousin, the young man whom she had noticed when she had first come to the Court.

"When I arrived," she told him, "I thought you were Alonso."

Emmanuel's face glowed with sudden passion. "How I wish that had been so," he said.

Afterwards she said to herself that it was folly to expect such happiness to last.

347

A day arrived which began as other days began.

She awoke in the morning to find Alonso beside her ... handsome Alonso who woke so suddenly and in such high spirits, who embraced her and made love to her and then said: "Come, I want to hunt while the morning is young. We will leave as soon as we are ready. Come, Isabella, it is a beautiful morning."

So they summoned their huntsmen, mounted their horses and rode away into the forest.

Indeed it was a beautiful morning; the sun shone on them and they exchanged smiles and jokes as they rode along.

They were separated for a while in the hunt, so she did not see it happen.

She had been aware of a sudden stillness in the woods — a brief stillness, yet it seemed to her to last a long time, for it brought to her, like the scent of an animal on the wind, the consciousness of evil.

The silence was broken by shouting voices, by cries of alarm.

When she arrived on the scene of the accident the huntsmen had improvised a stretcher, and on it lay her beautiful, her beloved Alonso.

He was dead when they reached the Palace. She could not believe it. It was too sudden, too tragic. She had entered her new life, had learned to understand it and to find it contained more happiness than she had believed possible, only to lose it.

The Palace was plunged into mourning. The King's only son, the heir to the throne, was dead. But none mourned more sincerely, none was more broken-hearted than Alonso's young widow.

Now the young Emmanuel was treated with greater respect than had ever before come his way, for who would have believed that one so healthy and vital as Alonso would not live to take the crown.

But he had died in the space of a few hours, and now the more intellectual Emmanuel was heir to the throne.

Isabella was unaware of what was going on in the Palace. Everything else was obscured by this one overwhelming fact: she had lost Alonso.

The King sent for her, for her grief alarmed him. He had been warned that if she continued to shut herself away and mourn, she herself would soon join her husband.

What would Isabella and Ferdinand have to say to that? The Princess was a precious commodity. It was important that she be kept alive.

"My dear," he said to her, "you must not shut yourself away. This terrible thing has happened, and you cannot change it by continually grieving."

"He was my husband, and I loved him," said Isabella.

"I know. We loved him also. He was our son and our heir. We knew him longer than you did, so you see our grief is not small either. Come, I must command you to take more care of your health. Promise me you will do this."

"I promise," said Isabella.

She walked in the Palace gardens and asked that she might be alone. She looked with blank eyes at terraces and statues. There she had walked with Alonso. There they had sat and planned how they would spend the days.

There was nothing but memories.

Emmanuel joined her and walked beside her.

"I would rather be alone," she said.

"Forgive me. Allow me to talk with you for a minute or two. Oh, Isabella, how it grieves me to see you so unhappy."

"Sometimes I blame myself," she said. "I was too happy. I thought only of my happiness; and perhaps we are not meant to be happy."

"You suffered ill fortune, Isabella. We *are* meant to be happy. When, you have recovered from this shock, I would implore you to give me a chance to make you happy."

"I do not understand you."

"I am heir to my uncle's throne. Therefore your parents would consider me as worthy a match as Alonso."

She stood very still in horror.

"I could never think of marrying anyone else," she said. "Alonso is the only husband I shall ever want."

"You say that because you are young and your grief is so close."

"I say it because I know it to be true."

"Do not dismiss me so lightly, Isabella. Think of what I have said."

She was always conscious of him. He was so often at her side.

350

No, no, she cried with all her heart. This cannot be.

And she fretted and continued to mourn, so that the King of Portugal's alarm increased.

He wrote to the Sovereigns of Castile, to tell them how their daughter's grief alarmed him.

"Send our daughter home to us," said Isabella. "I myself will nurse her back to health."

So a few months after she had left her country Isabella returned to Castile.

And when she felt herself enfolded in her mother's embrace she cried out that she was happy to come home. She had lost her beloved husband, but her beloved mother was left to her — and only through the Queen and a life devoted to piety could she want to live.

CHAPTER FOURTEEN

The Last Sigh Of The Moor

The time had come for the onslaught on the capital of the Moorish kingdom, and Ferdinand's army was now ready to begin the attack.

He and Isabella were waiting to receive Boabdil. They had sent a messenger to him, reminding him of the terms he had agreed to in exchange for his release, and they now commanded him to leave Granada and present himself before them, that the terms of surrender might be discussed.

Ferdinand hoped that the people of Granada would remember the terrible fate which had overtaken Malaga, and that they would not be so foolish as to behave in such a way that Ferdinand would have no resort but to treat them similarly.

"He should be here ere this," Ferdinand was saying. "He should know better than to keep us waiting."

Isabella was silent. She was praying that the surrender of the last Moorish stronghold might be accomplished without the loss of much Christian blood.

But the time passed and Boabdil did not come.

Isabella looked at Ferdinand, and she knew that he was already making plans for the siege of Granada.

The messenger stood before the Sovereigns.

He handed the dispatch to Ferdinand, who, with Isabella, read what Boabdil had written.

"It is impossible for me to obey your summons. I am no longer able to control my own desires. It is my wish to keep my promises, but the city of Granada refuses to allow me to depart. It is full now, not only with its own population, but those who have come from all over the kingdom to defend it. Therefore I regret that I cannot keep my promise to you."

Ferdinand clenched his fists and the veins stood out at his temples.

"So," he said, "they will not surrender."

"It is hardly to be expected that they would," Isabella replied mildly. "When we have taken Granada, consider, Ferdinand, we shall have completed the reconquest. Could we expect it to fall into our hands like a ripe fruit? Nay, we must fight for this last, this greatest prize."

"He has spoken," said Ferdinand. "He has chosen his own fate and that of his people. We shall no longer hesitate. Now it shall be . . . to Granada!"

The Sovereigns called together the Council and, while it was sitting, news was brought that fresh revolts had broken out in many of the cities which had been captured from the Moors. There had been Moorish forays into Christian territory, and Christians had been slaughtered or carried away to be prisoners or slaves.

This was the answer to Ferdinand's imperious command to the Moorish King.

The war was not yet won. The Moors were ready to defend the last stronghold of the land which they had called their own for seven hundred years.

In the little house in Cordova, Cristobal continued to wait for a summons to Court. None came. From time to time he saw some of his friends at Court, particularly Luis de Sant'angel. Beatriz de Bobadilla sent messages to him, and occasionally he received sums of money through her, which she said came from the Queen.

But still there was no summons to Court, no news of the fitting out of the expedition.

Little Ferdinand, the son of Cristobal and Beatriz de Arana, would sit on his knee and be told tales of the sea, as once little Diego had.

Beatriz watched Cristobal uneasily. Once she had been secretly glad that the summons did not come; but she was glad no longer. How could she endure to see her Cristobal grow old and grey, fretting continually against the ill fortune which would not give him the chance he asked.

One day a friend of his early days called at the house.

Cristobal was delighted to see him, and Beatriz brought wine and refreshments. The visitor admired sturdy little Ferdinand — also Beatriz.

He came from France, he said; and he brought a message from Cristobal's brother, Bartholomew.

Bartholomew wished to know how Cristobal was faring in Spain, and whether he found the Spanish Sovereigns ready to help him in his enterprise.

"He says, if you do not find this assistance, you should consider coming to France, where there is a growing interest in maritime adventures."

"France," murmured Cristobal, and Beatriz saw the light leap into his eyes once more. "I had thought once of going to France."

When the visitor had left, Beatriz brought her chair close to that of Cristobal; she took his hand and smiled at him fondly.

"What is the use of waiting?" she said. "You must go, Cristobal. It is the whole meaning of life to you. Do not think I do not understand. Go to France. Perhaps you will be fortunate there. And if you must wait upon the French Sovereign as you have on those of Spain, then will I join you. But if they give you what you want, if you make your voyage, you will come back to us here in Cordova. Ferdinand and I can wait for you."

Then Cristobal rose and drawing her to her feet kissed her solemnly.

She knew that he had made his decision.

Ferdinand's troops were encamped on the banks of the Xenil, and before them lay the city of Granada. A natural fortress, it seemed impregnable, and even the most optimistic realised that its storming would be long and hazardous.

They could see the great walls which defended it on the side which faced the Christian armies; and on the east side the peaks of the Sierra Nevada made a natural barrier.

Ferdinand looked at that great fortress, and he swore to take it.

From the battlements the Moors looked down on the Christian armies; they saw that the fertile land before the city had been burned and pillaged, the crops destroyed; and they vowed vengeance on the Christians.

So the two combatants — Arab and Christian — stood face to face, and both decided to fight to the death.

Ferdinand, who had seen the effect Isabella could have on the troops at the time of the siege of Malaga, had suggested that she should accompany the army. Isabella's reply was that she had had no intention to do otherwise. This was her war, even more than it was Ferdinand's. It was she who had made her early vows that, should it ever be in her power to do so, she would make an all-Christian Spain.

So to the battle-front came Isabella. The Prince of the Asturias, although only thirteen years old, was with his father. He already considered himself to be a warrior, for in the spring of the previous year Ferdinand had conferred the honour of knighthood upon him, and the ceremony had been performed on the battlefield.

Isabella had brought with her her children and some of her ladies, for she had determined that she would not be parted from her family again. She believed that the presence of the entire royal family in camp was an inspiration to the army; as indeed it seemed to be.

Isabella herself was indefatigable. She nursed the sick, and even her youngest, the five-year-old Catalina, was given tasks to do. Her eldest, Isabella, worked with fervour; for since the death of Alonso, the piety of the young Isabella had rivalled that of the elder.

Ferdinand was delighted to have his family with him, for where the Queen was, dignity and decorum were not forgotten. There was neither gambling nor swearing in the camp when the Queen was present; instead there were continual prayers. Ferdinand was quick to realise the importance of a disciplined army, and the dignity of the Queen was more effective in ensuring this than any strict rules he could have enforced.

The weeks passed, but the great battle for Granada did not take place. There was deadlock between the two forces.

The great fortress remained impregnable.

Cristobal had said his farewells. He had left Cordova and travelled westward.

But before he could find his way to France there was one call he must make.

It was six years since he had seen Diego, and he could not leave Spain without seeing his son once more and explaining that he was leaving the country.

Thus it was that on a July day he arrived at the Monastery of Santa Maria de la Rabida, to find at the gate the lay brother who had been there on that day when Cristobal had come there with Diego. "I seek shelter," he said.

"Enter, my friend," was the answer. "It is denied no traveller within these walls."

And when he had entered, he said: "Tell me, is Fray Juan Perez de Marchena at the Monastery?"

"He is here, my friend."

"I greatly wish to speak with him."

Fray Juan embraced him and took him into the room where they had previously talked.

"You see a defeated man," said Cristobal. "Spain treats me even as Portugal has done. I have come to see my son, and to ask you if you will keep him here a little longer, or whether I should take him with me into France."

"You are leaving us, Cristobal Colon?"

"There is no point in staying."

"I did not think you were a man who would give in so easily."

"I am a man determined to embark on an enterprise."

"And you have decided to leave Spain."

"I am going to lay my proposition before the French. I have heard from my brother who is there. He tells me that there is some hope that there I might find more willing ears."

"This grieves me."

"You have been so good to me."

"I will send for Diego," said Fray Juan.

Cristobal beheld the tall youth with astonishment.

"Can it be?" he cried with emotion.

"I do not ask the same," answered the youth. "I know you, Father."

They embraced, and the bright blue eyes of the adventurer were misty with tears.

Finally, Cristobal released his son. He laid his hands on his shoulders and looked into his face.

"So, Father, you did not succeed."

"I do not give up hope, my son. I am leaving Spain. Will you come with me?"

Fray Juan had come forward. He said: "We have taken good care of Diego. We have educated him, as you will learn, Señor Colon. If he left us his education would be interrupted. I could wish that you had not decided to leave Spain for a while, and that Diego would stay with us."

"My mind is made up," said Cristobal.

"This day I feel prophetic," said the Friar. "Señor Colon, will you stay with us for a week . . . two weeks? Will you give me your company for that time?"

"You are hospitable; you have done much for me. One day I shall reward you. If the French support me, one day I shall be a rich man. I shall not forget your kindness."

"If you give me riches it would not be what I asked; and of what use is a gift which is not acceptable? I have cared for your son for six years. Give me this now. Stay here with us . . . two weeks . . . three . . . This is all I ask."

"For what reason do you ask this?"

"Obey me unquestioningly. I believe one day you will not regret it."

Diego said: "Father, you cannot deny Fray Juan this."

Cristobal looked at the earnest face of the Prior.

"If you would tell me . . ." he began.

"I will tell you this. I believe it is God's will that you stay here. Señor Colon, do not deny me what I ask."

"Since you put it like this, I will stay," said Cristobal.

Fray Juan was satisfied.

He left father and son together and went to his cell.

He wrote for some time; then destroyed what he had written.

He paced his cell. He knelt and prayed.

Then he made a sudden decision.

He went to Cristobal and Diego and said: "I have to leave the monastery on a most urgent matter. You have given me your word, Cristobal Colon, that you will stay here. I want you to promise me now that you will not leave until I return."

He looked so earnest that Cristobal gave his promise.

And that very day the Prior set out on his mule for the two-hundred-mile journey to Granada.

Isabella lay sleeping in her pavilion. These elaborate sleeping quarters were very different from the tents used by the soldiers, and had been provided for her by the Marquis of Cadiz.

She was weary, for the days in camp were exhausting. She was continually going among the troops, talking to them of their homes, urging them to valour; and as there were constant skirmishes, there were many wounded to be attended to.

But now the night was still, and she slept.

She awoke suddenly to a sense of alarm; it was some seconds before she realised that what had awakened her was the smell of burning.

She hastened from her bed, calling to her women, and as she ran from the pavilion she saw that draperies at one side of it were ablaze and that the fire had spread to the nearby tents.

Isabella immediately thought of her children, who were sleeping near the pavilion, and she found time in those seconds to visualise a hundred horrors which might befall them.

"Fire!" called Isabella. "Fire in the camp!"

Immediately the camp was awake, and Isabella made with all speed to those tents in which the royal children were sleeping; she found to her immense joy that the fire had not yet touched them, so she roused the children hastily and, throwing a few clothes about them, they hurried with her into the open.

There she found Ferdinand giving instructions.

"Be watchful," he called to the sentinels. "If the enemy see what is happening they might attack."

As Isabella, with her daughters, watched the soldiers dealing with the fire, she noticed that Juana's eyes were dancing with excitement and that the child seemed even a little disappointed when the fire was under control. Maria looked on with an expression which was almost one of indifference, while little Catalina grasped her mother's hand and clung to it tightly. Their sister

Isabella seemed listless, as she had habitually become since the death of Alonso.

The Marquis of Cadiz joined Isabella and explained that a lamp had evidently caught the draperies of the pavilion and the wind had carried the flame to the nearby and highly inflammable tents.

At length Isabella led the children into one of the tents which had been prepared for them. She lifted Catalina into her arms and the child was almost immediately asleep. She kept them with her for the rest of the night.

The elaborate pavilion and many of the costly tents and their furnishings had been destroyed; and in the morning Ferdinand estimated the damage with a frown. The loss of valuable property always upset him more than any other calamity.

"Ferdinand," said Isabella slowly, "this might have been a great disaster. We might have lost our lives, if the saints had not watched over us. How ironical if, on the eve of victory, we should have died through a fire caused accidentally."

Ferdinand nodded grimly. "The loss must amount to a small fortune," he grumbled.

"I have been thinking, Ferdinand. It is now July. Very soon the summer will be over. Suppose we do not take Granada before the winter is upon us?"

Ferdinand was silent.

"The advantage," she went on, "will be all on the side of our enemies. They will be in warm winter quarters in their town, while we shall be exposed to the weather in our encampment."

"You and the children will have to leave us."

"And what effect will that have, do you think? I prefer to remain with the army, Ferdinand. I think it is essential that I remain with the army."

"Then we shall have to retire and come back in the spring."

"And lose the advantage we now have! No! I have a plan. We will build ourselves a town here . . . here on the plain before Granada."

"A town! You cannot mean that."

"But I do mean it, Ferdinand. We will build houses of stone which will not take fire so easily as our tents. We will build a great garrison — houses, quarters for the soldiers and stables. And we shall not retreat from our position, but stay here all through the winter as comfortably housed as our enemies!"

"Is this possible?"

"With God's help everything is possible," she answered.

"It would have to be completed in three months."

"So shall it be."

Ferdinand looked at her with admiration. The previous day she had been exhausted by her work in the camp; her night had been disturbed by this disastrous fire; and here she sat, looking fresh and as energetic as ever, calmly proposing a plan which, had anyone but Isabella suggested it, he would have declared to be absurd.

★ ★ ★

Before Granada the work went on. The town grew up with a speed which astonished all who beheld it.

The Moors looked on in despair.

They understood the meaning of this. The Christians would remain there throughout the winter. The respite for which they had longed would be denied them.

"Allah has turned his face from us," wailed the people of Granada. And they cursed Boabdil, their King, who had brought civil war among them when he had challenged the rule of Muley Abul Hassan.

Isabella moved about among her workmen. They must work harder. The task was tremendous, but it must be accomplished. They must ignore the sporadic sallies of the Moors. They must build their town by winter.

There were two avenues traversing this new town as Isabella had planned that there should be.

"Thus," she said, "my new town is in the form of the cross — the cross for which we fight. It shall be the only town in Spain which has not been contaminated by Moslem heresy."

The town must have a name, it was decided; and a deputation of workers came to her and asked if she would honour the town by bestowing her name upon it.

She smiled graciously. "I thank you for the honour you have done me," she said. "I thank you for the good work you have done in this town. But I have decided on a more appropriate name than my own. We shall call this town Santa Fe."

And there was the town in the shape of a cross — a monument to the determination of the Christians not to rest until they had brought about the reconquest of every inch of Spanish soil.

Beatriz de Bobadilla was in her quarters within the fortifications of Santa Fe when one of her women came to her and told her that a friar had arrived and wished to speak to her on the most urgent business.

Beatriz received him at once.

"My lady," said Fray Juan, "it is kind of you to receive me so promptly."

"Why," she said, "you have made a long journey and you are exhausted."

"I have travelled two hundred miles from La Rabida, but the matter is one which needs urgent attention, and I beg you to give it. It concerns the explorer, Cristobal Colon."

"Ah," said Beatriz, "the explorer." She smiled almost tenderly. "How fares it with him?"

"He is frustrated, my lady; indignant and angry with Spain and himself. He is no longer a young man, and he bitterly resents the wasted years."

"There has been so much to occupy the mind of the Queen," she answered.

"It is true, and a tragedy for Spain. Unless something is done immediately, he will leave the country, and some other monarch will have the benefit of his genius."

"That must not be," said Beatriz.

"It will be, my lady, unless there is no more delay."

Beatriz made a quick decision. "I am going to see that you are given refreshment and an opportunity to wash the travel-stains from your person. I will go to the Queen immediately and, when I have returned, I will let you know whether Señor Colon is to be given help from Spain. I promise to let you know how I have fared with all speed."

The Prior smiled. He had done his part, and there was no more he could do.

Beatriz begged an audience with the Queen. Ferdinand was with Isabella, a fact which dismayed Beatriz.

But Ferdinand was friendly. He was pleased with the way events were moving, and was very much aware of the important part the women were playing before Granada.

"Highness," said Beatriz, "I come to you in great haste. Fray Juan Perez de Marchena has arrived in Santa Fe from La Rabida. Cristobal Colon is on the point of leaving Spain."

"I am sorry to hear this," said the Queen. "Was he not told to wait awhile, and that his schemes would have our attention when we had the time to devote to them?"

"Yes, Highness, he was, but he will wait no longer. He thinks that his expedition is of the greatest importance; and frankly, if your Highnesses will not help him, he has decided to find a Sovereign who will do so. He plans to go to France."

At the mention of the great enemy of Aragon, Ferdinand flushed with anger. His eyes narrowed, and with a certain delight Beatriz noticed the lights of cupidity shining there.

She went on to talk of the riches which he would bring back if he were successful. "For, Your Highnesses, even if he should fail in his discovery of a New World, he will have shown us a new route to the riches of Cathay and the East, of which Marco Polo wrote so glowingly."

"I thought," she finished, "that Your Highnesses would wish to stop him before he has an opportunity of bringing to another the riches which, would you but equip his expedition, he would lay at your feet."

"Willingly," said Isabella, "would we equip him for this expedition, but everything we possess must go into the prosecution of the war."

She looked at Ferdinand.

"Highness," pleaded Beatriz, "would it be so costly? It is unbearable to think that all that he might discover may go to another country."

"I was impressed by the man," said Isabella. She looked at Ferdinand as though expecting him to speak against asking the man to return, but Ferdinand said nothing; his eyes had that glazed look, and she realised that he was seeing the return of the explorer, his ships laden with treasures — gold, jewels, slaves.

Isabella continued: "I would be prepared to reconsider what might be done." She smiled towards Ferdinand. "Perhaps the King would agree with me in this."

Ferdinand was thinking: The man must be stopped from taking his plans to France. Even if he and the

Queen did not fit out his expedition, they must stop him from taking his plans to the enemy.

Ferdinand smiled at Isabella. "As usual, Your Highness speaks good sense. Let us recall this man and reconsider what he has to tell us."

Beatriz cried: "Thank you, Your Highnesses. I am sure your munificence will be rewarded." She turned to Isabella. "Highness, this man is poor. Would you agree that he might be sent money for his journey here, money to buy garments which would make him fit to appear before Your Highnesses?"

"By all means let that be done," said Isabella.

Within Granada conditions were deteriorating rapidly. The effect of the building of Santa Fe was disastrous to the morale of the besieged. The blockade, which the people had hoped would be lifted by the retirement of the Christian army during the winter, continued.

There were some who declared that there must be no surrender, that their fellow Moslems in Africa would never allow them to lose their grip on Spanish soil. But there were others who gazed out on the bustling and efficient fortifications of Santa Fe, who considered the destruction of the crops and knew that the end was near.

One of these was Boabdil. He called on Allah; he prostrated himself in his grief. He felt responsible for the plight into which his people had fallen, and he longed to save his country from the terrible fate which had befallen Malaga.

368

Under cover of darkness he sent messengers from the city to Ferdinand to ask what terms would be offered for the surrender of the town.

Ferdinand wrote:

"I am prepared to be magnanimous. Surrender the city, and the inhabitants of Granada shall keep possession of their mosques and shall be allowed to retain their own religion. They shall also retain their own laws and be judged by their own *cadis*, although there will be a Castilian governor of the town. They may continue to use their own language and the Arab dress. If they wish to leave the country they may dispose of their property on their own account. There would be no extra taxes for three years. King Boabdil would abdicate, but he should be given a territory in the Alpujarras which would be a protectorate of the Castilian crown. All the fortifications and artillery must be handed over to the Christians, and the surrender must take place in no more than sixty days."

Ferdinand stopped writing and smiled. If Boabdil and his counsellors accepted these terms he would be content. Lives and — what was more important to Ferdinand — money would be saved by a quick surrender. It was by no means certain how long the war would last, even though at the moment the Christians had all the advantages.

Eagerly he awaited the reply.

In his private apartments of the Alhambra, Boabdil read the Sovereigns' terms and rejoiced. He had saved the people of Granada from the fate which had befallen those of Malaga, and he believed that that was the best he could hope for.

The Sultana Zoraya was going about the town urging the people to stand firm. With flashing eyes and strong words she assured them that the battle against the Christian armies was not yet lost.

"You lose heart," she cried, "because you see them encamped outside our walls. But you should not lose heart. Allah will not desert us in our hour of need."

"Boabdil deserts us," was the answer. "So how can we expect Allah to smile upon us?"

They whispered among themselves. "Boabdil is a traitor. He is the friend of the Christian Sovereigns. He seeks concessions for himself, and will betray us to get them."

Revolt was stirring in the city, for it was rumoured that Boabdil was carrying on secret negotiations with the enemy.

Zoraya stormed into her son's apartment. She told him that the people were murmuring against him.

"They talk foolishly. They say you are negotiating with the enemy. These rumours do our cause great harm."

"They must be stopped, my mother," he said.

And later he sent word to Ferdinand.

All his terms were accepted; but there should be no delay. They must come with all speed to prevent revolt within the walls of Granada. If they did not, they might arrive to find their friend Boabdil assassinated, and the treaty flung in their faces.

There was rejoicing throughout Santa Fe.

Preparations had begun for the entry into Granada.

The Cardinal Mendoza, surrounded by troops, rode into the city that he might occupy the Alhambra and prepare it for the entry of the Sovereigns.

He ascended the Hill of Martyrs and to meet him rode Boabdil surrounded by fifty Moorish noblemen.

The vanquished Boabdil rode past the Cardinal towards Ferdinand, who, surrounded by his guards, had taken up a position in the rear of the Cardinal and his men.

On his black horse Boabdil was a pathetic figure; his tunic was green decorated with gold ornaments, his white *haik* flowed about his shoulders, and his gentle face wore an expression of infinite sadness.

He dismounted when he reached Ferdinand, and would have thrown himself at the conqueror's feet. Ferdinand, however, leaped from his horse and embraced Boabdil; he veiled the triumph in his eyes and assumed an expression of great sympathy.

Boabdil said that all might hear: "I bring you the keys of the Alhambra. They belong to you, O King of the Christians. Allah decrees that it should be so. I beg you to show clemency to my sorrowing people."

Boabdil then prostrated himself before Ferdinand, and turning went to Isabella, who was some short distance behind Ferdinand, and made similar obeisance to her.

He then left her and rode towards the sad group who were waiting for him. This was his family, at the head of which was the angry Zoraya.

"Come," said Boabdil. "Now is the time to say farewell to Granada and greatness."

Zoraya was about to speak, but, with a gesture full of dignity, Boabdil signed for all to fall in behind him; and spurring his horse, he galloped away in the direction of the Alpujarras.

On he rode, followed by his family and those of his courtiers and troops whom he had been allowed to take with him.

At the hill called Padul he stopped. This was the last point from which he could hope to see Granada in all its glory.

He looked back to that most beautiful of cities — the city which had once been the capital of his kingdom and was now lost to him.

His emotions overcame him, and the tears began to flow down his cheeks.

Zoraya pushed her horse beside his.

"Weep!" she cried. "Weep! It is what we expect of you. Weep like a woman for the city you could not defend like a man!"

Boabdil turned his horse, and the melancholy cavalcade moved on. Boabdil did not look back on the city he would never see again.

Meanwhile Isabella and Ferdinand, side by side, made their triumphant entry into the city, where the streets had already been anointed with holy water that it might be washed clean of the contamination of Infidels.

Magnificently clad, the Sovereigns rode at the head of the cavalcade. They both realised the need to impress with their grandeur the people of Granada, who had been used to the splendour of their Sultans. And although neither Isabella nor Ferdinand cared for fine clothing and outward displays of riches, they were determined to appear at their most magnificent on this progress through the city.

Christian troops lined the hill-road leading to the Alhambra and, raising her eyes, Isabella saw that which she had determined to see since, as a girl, she had made her solemn vows. The flag of Christian Spain was flying over the Alhambra; the last Moorish stronghold in Spain had capitulated, and the reconquest was complete.

Joyous shouts filled the air.

"Granada! Granada for the Kings — Isabella and Ferdinand!"

CHAPTER
FIFTEEN

Triumph Of The
Sovereigns

Cristobal Colon had arrived at Santa Fe in time to see the triumphant procession.

A day after the Sovereigns had made their entry and taken formal possession of the city he was brought to their presence by Beatriz de Bobadilla.

Cristobal's hopes were high, for the war was over, and it was the war which had made them hesitate.

Again he described all that he hoped to do; to Isabella he stressed the importance of conquering new lands that poor ignorant savages might be brought into the Christian fold; to Ferdinand he talked of the riches which these countries must contain.

The Sovereigns were excited.

"Your Highnesses will understand," said Cristobal, "that I must be granted certain concessions."

"These concessions are?" Ferdinand demanded.

"I should ask to be made Admiral of the lands I discover during my lifetime, and that on my death this title should be the right of my heirs."

Isabella, shocked, caught her breath. The title of Admiral was only bestowed on members of the nobility, and the Admiral of Castile was now Don Alonso Enriquez, Ferdinand's own uncle. Yet here was this humble sailor asking for a noble title!

Ferdinand's face had hardened also. It seemed to the Sovereigns that this man was insolent.

Cristobal went on serenely: "I should be Governor and Viceroy of the discovered lands."

"You do not know," said Ferdinand coldly, "but how could you — not being conversant with the ways of the Court — that it is the Sovereign's prerogative to choose and dismiss governors and viceroys."

"I know it, Highness," went on Cristobal stubbornly. "I should also need one-tenth of all the treasure I bring back, and one-eighth share in every expedition which leaves Spain for the Indies. If any dispute should arise concerning this, the right should be mine to appoint judges to try the case, and their decision should be final. I would also ask for a place at Court for my son."

The Sovereigns were dumbfounded. Isabella recovered her composure first.

"Señor Colon," she said, "these demands astonish us. You may leave us now, and we will discuss them; and in time you will hear our decision."

Cristobal bowed low. He said: "Highness, I would beg you not to delay the decision, for I have news that I should be very welcome at the Court of France."

He then left the presence of the Sovereigns.

★ ★ ★

"Impudence!" cried Ferdinand.

Talavera, who had been present, said: "Your Highnesses, the man should be sent about his business. Clearly he comes from the devil. Perhaps it would be advisable to hand him over to the Holy Office. They would discover what evil prompts him."

"He is a very bold man," commented Isabella, "but I think this boldness grows out of his certainty. I should like a little time to consider his claims, which we might induce him to modify."

"Your Highness heard what he said about the Court of France?" cried Talavera.

"Yes," answered Isabella. "But he will wait awhile, I think."

Ferdinand's anger seemed to abate suddenly, and Isabella, who knew him so well, realised that he was considering all the treasure which might be his.

"There is little money to spare for such an expedition," she said.

"Highness," insisted Talavera, "God has given a city of Infidels into our care. Should we not devote ourselves to bringing them to the true faith, rather than waste time and money on an adventurer?"

"I do not think it would be easy to find the money to equip the expedition," said Isabella. "But Cristobal Colon should be told that we still consider the matter."

The case of Cristobal Colon was temporarily forgotten by the Sovereigns, for another matter of the greatest importance had arisen.

376

Torquemada's campaign against the Jews had been relentlessly pursued since he had established his new form of Inquisition with himself as Inquisitor General, and the time had now come, he said, to make the supreme gesture against the Jews.

He wanted every Jew who would not accept Christianity to be driven from Spain.

Now, he declared, was the moment to do this. The Sovereigns had clearly been selected by the Divine will to create an all-Christian Spain. After seven hundred years they had recaptured the land from the Moors, so that the conquest was complete.

"This is a sign," said Torquemada.

Public opinion was ready. The Jews had never been so hated as they were at this time.

This was due to a case which had excited much public attention.

A year or so before, a Jew, named Benito Garcia, was travelling in the course of his business, when he had been robbed; and in his knapsack was found a consecrated wafer.

The robbers took this wafer to the magistrate and told him where they had found it. They were immediately forgiven *their* crime, and Garcia was arrested for what was considered an even greater one. He was cruelly tortured; in his agony he mentioned the names of other Jews, and a story emerged. It was the old story of a Christian boy who was kidnapped by Jews, taken to a cave where he had been subjected to ritual murder, his heart having been cut out, after which he was crucified in the manner in which Christ had been.

The case had excited public opinion, and Torquemada and his officials had seen that it received the utmost publicity. The Christian boy's body could not be found, but this, it was explained, was due to the fact that he had ascended to heaven as Christ had done. He became known then as Santo Niño, and miracles were said to have been performed in his name. Hysteria and superstition were intensified.

All those who were accused of being concerned in the case were tortured and met death at the stake. Two of them, however, had been considered too evil even for death by burning. These were an old man of eighty and his young son, who refused to accept the Christian faith and remained loyal to that of their forefathers to the end. Their flesh was torn with red-hot pincers, but before they died they were set over faggots which had been dampened that they might not burn too quickly, and these two — the old man and the youth — were finally killed by roasting over a slow fire.

Torquemada now believed the moment was ripe for the banishment of the Jews, and for this reason he came to Granada to see the Sovereigns.

Ferdinand's greed was now well known and, as the fury of the people had been whipped up against them, the anxious Jews met together to discuss what could be done.

It was suggested that they should collect a large sum of money which they would offer to Ferdinand in exchange for permission to keep their homes.

So, shortly after Torquemada reached Granada to obtain the consent of Ferdinand and Isabella to his plan, a deputation of Jews arrived and asked for an audience with the Sovereigns.

Ferdinand and Isabella received this deputation.

"Highnesses," they were told, "we could raise a sum of thirty thousand ducats which we would present to you in exchange for permission to stay in Spain and keep our homes. We implore Your Highnesses to allow us to set about collecting this money and to give us your sacred promise that when it is yours we shall be unmolested."

Even Isabella hesitated. The exchequer was perilously low, for the war had cost so much more than she had believed possible and there was still a great deal to be done. The need for money was desperate.

Thirty thousand ducats! The words were the sweetest music in Ferdinand's ears. And all they had to do was refuse to sign the Edict which Torquemada was preparing.

"I see that you are eager to become good citizens," said Ferdinand. "I believe that we might come to some arrangement."

The members of the deputation were almost weeping with relief; and Isabella felt a certain pleasure that she could agree to please both them and Ferdinand at the same time.

★ ★ ★

Meanwhile one of Torquemada's lieutenants had sought out his master.

"Holy Prior," he said, "a deputation is now in the presence of the Sovereigns. I have made it my business to discover theirs, and I have learned that they are offering thirty thousand ducats in exchange for the Sovereigns' promise that they may remain in Spain."

Torquemada's face was paler than usual.

He snatched up a crucifix and made his way to the royal apartments.

He did not ask for an audience but stormed into the chamber, where Ferdinand and Isabella sat at a table while the Jewish deputation stood by, presenting documents which the Sovereigns were about to sign.

Ferdinand looked at the Prior with astonishment.

"What means this?" he demanded.

"I will tell you what it means!" cried Torquemada. "The angels are weeping this day. And the reason! Judas Iscariot sold his Master for thirty pieces of silver. The Sovereigns of Christian Spain are preparing to sell Him for thirty thousand!"

He took the crucifix from under his robe and, holding it up, he raised his eyes to Heaven.

"Holy Mother of God," he went on, "you have interceded for us. Great victories have been granted us. Now you look down and see our unworthiness. I pray you do not hesitate to take our greatness from us. We have been granted grace, and in return we desecrate the holy name of God."

Then he threw the crucifix onto the table, and continued: "You are bartering Christ for your pieces of silver. Here He is. Barter Him away!"

Torquemada then strode out of the apartment.

Isabella and Ferdinand looked at each other, then at the crucifix on the table, and a terrible fear came to them.

They saw themselves as guilty of the great betrayal.

Isabella said: "Pray leave us. The Prior is right. The Edict shall go forth."

Thus was the fate of the Jews settled.

Meanwhile Cristobal waited.

Beatriz de Bobadilla and Luis de Sant'angel both implored the Queen not to allow him to go away again, while Talavera, on the other hand, was pointing out to the Sovereigns that the arrogance of Cristobal Colon was insupportable.

Luis de Sant'angel talked to Ferdinand of the explorer's prospects.

"Why, Highness," he said, "it is true the man demands a high price, but if he makes no discovery he receives nothing; and if he succeeds in making this discovery Spain will receive wealth as yet undreamed of."

Ferdinand listened intently. He had made up his mind that Cristobal Colon must make his discoveries for Spain and no other country.

"It is, however," he said to Luis de Sant'angel, "a question of providing the means. You know how the exchequer has been depleted since the Moorish wars.

381

Where could we find the money to finance such an expedition?"

Luis was staring carefully ahead of him, for he knew that Ferdinand did not wish to meet his eyes. As Aragonese Secretary of Supplies, Luis knew that there were ample funds in the Aragonese treasury to finance the expedition. But the affluence of the Aragonese treasury was a close secret which Ferdinand did not wish to be made known at the Court of Castile — and more especially to the Queen.

Ferdinand did not forget for a moment his Aragonese ambitions, which meant as much to him as the conquest of Granada itself. Therefore while Castile groaned in poverty, and the Queen had wondered how they could continue to prosecute the war, Ferdinand's Aragonese treasury had been in possession of these ample funds.

"I see," said Luis slowly, "that the Queen could not find the means to fit up this expedition."

"Alas, it is so," said Ferdinand, but he was thoughtful.

Ferdinand had now become convinced that there was too much at stake to allow Cristobal to offer his plans elsewhere.

He said to Isabella: "The man's demands are arrogant, but if he is unsuccessful he gets nothing. What harm would there be in making him our Admiral and Viceroy of lands he discovers? For if he discovers nothing the tide is an empty one."

Isabella was pleased; she had always been in favour of the man and was delighted as always when Ferdinand veered round to her way of thinking.

"Then," she said, "when we can muster the money we will send him out on his voyage of discovery."

"When will that be?" asked Ferdinand. "I do not think this man will remain here much longer. He has as good as said that if there is any more delay he will begin his journey into France."

The thought of the French's benefiting by new discoveries so agitated Ferdinand that Isabella said: "If I had not already pawned my jewels to pay for the war, readily would I do so to finance this expedition. The treasury is very low. I doubt whether there is enough money in it for what he will need."

Ferdinand, who had been walking agitatedly about the room, stopped short as though he had come to a sudden decision.

"There is something I have to tell you, Isabella," he said. He called to one of the pages: "Send for Don Luis de Sant'angel at once," he said.

"You think you know of a means to obtain this money?" Isabella asked him.

Ferdinand lifted a hand and slowly nodded his head. But he did not speak, and Isabella did not press him.

Within a few minutes Luis de Sant'angel was standing before them.

"You are very interested in this man, Cristobal Colon," said Ferdinand. "You feel certain that his voyage will be successful."

"I do, Highness," said Luis.

"You talked to me recently about money . . . money you have in Aragon."

Luis looked rather puzzled, but Ferdinand hurried on: "You would be prepared to help in financing this expedition which Colon wishes to make?"

Ferdinand was now looking intently into the face of his Secretary of Supplies, and Sant'angel, after long experience of his master, understood.

Ferdinand wished this voyage to be made; he knew that delay was dangerous. He was gong to finance it from the treasury of Aragon, but Isabella and Castile must not know that, during the time they had been urgently in need of money, Ferdinand had kept amounts of money separate from those of Castile to be used in the service of Aragon.

Any discoveries Cristobal Colon made would be for the good of Aragon as well as Castile. Therefore what Ferdinand was suggesting was that the money should be provided by Aragon, but that it should be advanced in the name of Luis de Sant'angel.

Luis felt a great uplifting of his spirits.

Cristobal Colon, he thought, at last you are about to have your chance!

"Since," said Ferdinand, "you are so generous, Sant'angel, you had better send Colon to us with all speed. We will grant his request, and he shall set about his preparations without further delay."

Luis retired as quickly as he could and went in search of Cristobal; but the explorer was nowhere to be found.

384

All through Granada, all through Santa Fe the question was being asked: "Have you seen Cristobal Colon?"

At last it was discovered that he had packed his few belongings and had left. He had said that he would not be back; he was leaving Spain, since Spain had no use for him.

Luis was nonplussed. It must not be that, when success was about to come to Cristobal after so many years of waiting, he was to lose it through giving in a day or so too soon. Luis was determined that it should not be so.

He wondered which way Colon had gone. He would go, he believed, in the direction of La Rabida, as he would certainly wish to see Diego before he left Spain. His other son, Ferdinand, had a mother to care for him, but he would want to make some provision for Diego.

Yet perhaps he had decided he could not afford to waste more time and was hurrying northwards to France!

Luis therefore dispatched riders in several directions and one of these overtook Cristobal six miles from Granada at the Puente de Piños.

Cristobal heard the sound of horses' hoofs thudding behind him as he made his way towards the bridge. He slackened his pace, and hearing his own name called, stopped.

"Cristobal Colon," he was told, "you must come back to the Court with all speed. You are to be granted all that you ask, and can make your preparations at once."

A smile touched Cristobal's face, and it was so dazzling that it made of him a young man again.

At last . . . success. The long waiting was over.

The roads to the coast were thick with bands of refugees. Old and young, those who had been accustomed to the utmost luxury, those who had been bred in poverty, now walked wearily together; they had been stripped of all they possessed, for although they had been allowed to sell their property, they had been cynically forbidden to take money out of the country.

This was the exodus of the Jews of Spain. Onward they trudged, hoping to find some humane creatures who would be kinder to them than those in the land which for centuries had been the home of their ancestors.

It was forbidden to help them. It was no crime to rob them.

The shipmasters looked upon them as legitimate prey. Some took these suffering people aboard, extracted payment for the voyage and then threw their passengers, who had trusted them, into the sea.

From all parts of this all-Christian Spain those Jews who refused to conform to the Christian Faith wandered on their wretched way to an unknown future.

Thousands died on many a perilous journey; some of plague, but many of barbaric murder. The rumour, that it had become a practice of these Jews to swallow their jewels in the hope of preserving them, was circulated and numbers of them, on arriving in Africa, were ripped up by barbarians, who hoped in this way to retrieve the jewels from their hiding-places.

Some, however, found refuge in other lands, and a few managed to survive the horror.

Torquemada was satisfied. He had had his way.

He knelt with the Sovereigns and they prayed together for the continued greatness of their all-Christian state.

In a room over a grocer's shop in the town of Seville a woman saw the Jews gathering together to leave their homes.

She looked from her window upon them, for she was too ill to leave her room, and she knew that only a few more weeks of life were left to her.

Those faces, on which were depicted blank despair and bewildered misery, took her mind back to the days when she, a Jewess, had lived in her father's luxurious house; and with a sudden, terrible fear she began to wonder what part she herself had played in bringing about this terrible crime which was taking place all over Spain.

What if she had not taken a lover; what if she had not been in fear that her father would discover her pregnancy? What if she had not betrayed him and his friends to the Inquisition — would this be happening now?

It was a terrible thought. She had not allowed herself to think of it before, although it had always been there hovering in her mind, hanging over her life like a dark shadow of doom which she could not escape for ever.

If Diego de Susan had not been betrayed by La Susanna, if his conspiracy against the Inquisition had succeeded, who knew, the Inquisition might not have taken hold in Spain as it had this day.

She clenched her hands and beat them against her wasted breasts.

And what a life had been hers, passing from one protector to another, moving down the scale as *la hermosa hembra* lost her beauty little by little.

At last she had found a man who really loved her — this humble grocer who had known her in the days of her pride, and was happy to be the protector of Diego de Susan's daughter — he who had been a millionaire of Seville — even though that man had been burned alive through La Susanna's betrayal of him.

He had looked after her, this little grocer, looked after her and the children she had had. And now this was the end. She could hear the suppressed sobbing of children in the crowd, little ones who sensed tragedy without understanding it.

Then she could bear no more. She stumbled back to her bed, but the effort of leaving it and the agony of remorse had been too much for her. She had shortened her life — but only by a few weeks.

Her lover came into the apartment, and there was anguish in his eyes. Ah, she thought, it is because he does not see me as I am; to him I am still the young girl who sat on the balcony of the house of Diego de Susan, then far out of the reach of a humble grocer.

"I am dying," she told him.

He helped her back to bed and sat beside her. He did not deny the truth of what she said, for he realised it would be futile to do so.

"Do something for me," she said. "When I die, put my skull over the door of this house, that all may know it is the skull of one whose passions led her to an evil life, and that she wishes a part of her to be left there as a warning to all. The skull of a woman who was a bawd and betrayer of those who loved her best."

The grocer shook his head. "You must not fret," he said. "I will take care of you till the end."

"This is the end," she said. "Promise me. Swear it on your Faith."

So he promised.

And, before the Jews had all left Spain, the skull of the woman who had once been judged the most beautiful in Seville was set up over the door of the grocer's house.

The reconquest secure, Isabella and Ferdinand appointed Talavera Archbishop of Granada, and the Count of Tendilla its Governor, and set off on a progress through the country, with their children, to receive the grateful thanks of the people.

They rode with all the splendour of royalty, and always beside them was Juan, the Prince of the Asturias. Isabella felt that all her subjects must agree that one of her greatest gifts to them was this bright and beautiful boy, the heir to a united Spain.

Ferdinand had said: "Castile is with us to a man, so is Aragon; but there has always been trouble in Catalonia since . . . the death of my half-brother. Now is the time to show the Catalans that we include them in our kingdom, that they mean as much to us as the Castilians and the Aragonese."

Isabella agreed that this was so and that now, in the full flush of their triumph, was the time to make the Catalans forget for ever the mysterious death of Carlos, Prince of Viana, who had been removed to make way for Ferdinand to take the throne of Aragon.

So into Catalonia rode the procession.

Ferdinand had been presiding at the hall of justice in Barcelona, and was leaving the building to rejoin Isabella at the Palace.

He was pleased, for never had he been so popular in Catalonia as he was at this time. Congratulations were coming to him from all over the world. He and Isabella were accepted as the hero and heroine of this great victory for Christianity. He was to be henceforth known as Ferdinand the Catholic, and Isabella as Isabella the Catholic. Even Catalonia, which had for so long set itself against Ferdinand, now cheered him wherever he went.

But no doubt there were some who did not share the general opinion. Ferdinand came face to face with one as he left the hall of justice, and suddenly he found himself looking into the face of a fanatic, while a knife gleamed before his startled eyes.

"Die . . . murderer!" cried a voice.

Ferdinand fell forward, and there was a shout of triumph from the man who held up the bloodstained knife.

Isabella was with her children when she received the news. Her daughter, Isabella, covered her face with her hands; the Prince was as one struck dumb; and the little girls ran to their mother and clung to her in terror.

"Highness, the King is being brought here to you. It was a madman outside the hall of justice."

Isabella felt her heart leap in fear.

"Not now," she prayed. "Not this. We have come through so much together. There is so much for us yet . . ."

Then she recovered her serenity.

She put the frightened children from her and said: "I will go to the King at once."

She was at his bedside, for she was determined that no one should nurse him but herself.

She prayed constantly, but she did not neglect to nurse him during those days while his life was in danger.

The would-be assassin had been captured, and had suffered the most cruel torture; but he could not be made to confess that he had had accomplices.

There was one fact which emerged from the torture chamber; the man was a lunatic, for he declared that he was the true heir to the throne of Aragon and that he expected to gain this on Ferdinand's death.

There came the day when Isabella knew that Ferdinand was out of danger and that this was not the end of their life together, as she had feared it might be. Outside the Palace the people were waiting for news. Never had Ferdinand been so popular in Catalonia as he was at this time. The people saw him as the hero of the reconquest, and they saw also a new life for themselves and their country through the greatness of their rulers.

Isabella was of Castile, and they had at first been suspicious of her; they believed that it was her careful nursing, her constant prayer, which had saved the life of Ferdinand.

The news was conveyed to them: "The King will live." And Isabella appeared on the balcony before the sickroom while the people shouted themselves hoarse with delight.

"Isabella and Ferdinand! Ferdinand and Isabella!" No longer for Castile, for Aragon, for Catalonia. But "Isabella and Ferdinand for Spain!"

She returned to Ferdinand's bed. He was smiling at her, for he had heard the shouts outside the Palace.

"It would seem," he said, "that they love us both with an equal fervour."

"They know," said Isabella, "that we are as one."

"It is true," said Ferdinand. "We are as one." And as he took her hand, he thought of the humiliation he had suffered when he had been forced to take second place in Castile; he thought of the women he had loved, so many of them, so much more accomplished in the arts of love than Isabella could ever be. But even as he considered them and all the differences of the past — and all those which no doubt were to come in the future — he knew that the most important person in his life was Isabella, and that in generations to come, when his name was mentioned, that of Isabella would be for ever linked with it.

She understood his thoughts and she was in complete harmony with them.

She said: "They are demanding the most painful death for your would-be assassin. It is to be in public that they all may see, that all may gloat over the agonies of one who might have caused the death of their beloved King."

Ferdinand nodded.

She went on: "I have given orders that he shall be strangled first. Secret orders. They will see his body taken out. They will not know that he is past pain, for he has been greatly tortured. But now I would let him die in peace."

Ferdinand restrained an oath. *She* had given orders in Catalonia . . . *his* province!

Again she read his thoughts, and for a moment that old hostility hovered between them.

Then she said: "Can you hear what they are shouting? It is 'Ferdinand and Isabella. Isabella and Ferdinand . . . for Spain!'"

The irritation vanished from his face and he smiled at her.

"We have done so much," Isabella said gently. "There is so much to do. But we shall do it . . . together."

Crowds had gathered in the streets of Barcelona, to take part in one of the great occasions in Spanish history.

It was April and the sun shone brilliantly as through the streets to the Palace came a brilliant procession.

Nuggets of gold were carried by brown-skinned men in robes decorated with gold ornaments; there were animals such as none had ever seen before.

And in the midst of this procession came the Admiral of the New World, Cristobal Colon, his head held high, his eyes gleaming, because now his dream of discovery had become a reality.

Among the crowd was a woman who held a young boy in her arms that he might see the hero of this occasion.

"See, Ferdinand," Beatriz de Arana whispered with pride, "there is your father."

"I see, Mother," cried the boy excitedly. "Mother, I see my father."

Isabella and Ferdinand were waiting to receive their Admiral, and with them were their family. There was one page, in the service of the Prince of the Asturias, who could scarcely bear to look, so strong was his emotion.

This was Diego, that other son of the explorer, who had waited so many years for the return of his father, first in the monastery of La Rabida, then at the Court.

Cristobal Colon knelt before the Sovereigns, and when Isabella offered him her hand to kiss, she knew that what he was offering her — and Spain — was a New World.

How happy I am in this moment, thought Isabella. Ferdinand has fully recovered his strength. I have all my beloved children with me. I have made not only a united Spain but a Christian Spain.

I have all this. I should be singularly blessed, even were this all.

But it was not all. And here is this adventurer, returned from his long journey with strange tales to tell. Here he comes, to lay a new world at my feet.

Isabella's smiling gaze embraced her beloved family; but she looked beyond them all into a future when men and women who were gathered together to discuss the greatness of a mighty Empire would say: "It was Isabella who made Spain great — Isabella . . . and Ferdinand."

Also available in ISIS Large Print:

The Concubine

Norah Lofts

"All eyes and hair" a courtier had said disparagingly of her — and certainly the younger daughter of Tom Boleyn lacked the bounteous charms of most ladies of Court. Black-haired, black eyes, she had a wild-sprite quality that was to prove more effective, more dangerous than conventional feminine appeal.

The King first noticed her when she was sixteen — and with imperial greed he smashed her youthful love-affair with Harry Percy and began the process of royal seduction . . .

But this was no ordinary woman, no maid-in-waiting to be possessed and discarded by a king. Against his will, his own common sense, Henry found himself bewitched — enthralled by the young girl who was to be known as the Concubine . . .

ISBN 978-0-7531-8330-4 (hb)
ISBN 978-0-7531-8331-1 (pb)

Castile for Isabella

Jean Plaidy

Fifteenth-century Spain is rent with intrigue and threatened by civil war. Here, the young Isabella becomes the pawn of her half-crazed mother and a virtual prisoner at the licentious court of her half-brother, Henry IV.

At just sixteen years old, is she already fated to be the victim of the Queen's revenge, the Archbishop's ambition and the lust of lecherous Don Pedro Girón? Numbed by grief and fear, Isabella remains steadfast in her determination to marry Ferdinand, the handsome young Prince of Aragon, her only true betrothed.

ISBN 978-0-7531-8344-1 (hb)
ISBN 978-0-7531-8345-8 (pb)

Lord Robert

Jean Plaidy

The greatest love story of all time

In the grim recesses of the Tower of London, two captives begin a passionate love affair that will last years but is destined to destroy them; one is Robert Dudley, the other is the future Queen of England, Elizabeth I.

Pardoned by Queen Mary, Dudley and Elizabeth are freed, but their mutual longing must be from a distance: Dudley is married and, as the next heir to the throne, Elizabeth must tread carefully . . .

ISBN 978-0-7531-8160-7 (hb)
ISBN 978-0-7531-8161-4 (pb)

Michael and All Angels

Norah Lofts

In the autumn of 1817, the arrival of the Ipswich coach and its occupants — a strange, ill-assorted company — changed the lives of those who lived at the Fleece Inn forever . . .

Will Oakley, landlord and host, with his two daughters, beautiful Myrtle, and the repellent Harriet, waited to receive his guests. Along with the usual farmers, merchants and the "quality", there were others who fitted into none of these categories. Like the handsome foreigner with the scarred face, and the fat man who appeared to be gloating over some malicious secret of his own . . .

ISBN 978-0-7531-8112-6 (hb)
ISBN 978-0-7531-8113-3 (pb)

The King's Secret Matter

Jean Plaidy

After twelve years of marriage, the once fortuitous union of Henry VIII and Katharine of Aragon has declined into a loveless stalemate. Their only child, Mary, is disregarded as a suitable heir, and Henry's need for a legitimate son to protect the Tudor throne has turned him into a callous and greatly feared ruler.

When the young and intriguing Anne Boleyn arrives from the French court, Henry is easily captivated by her dark beauty and bold spirit. But his desire to possess the wily girl leads to a deadly struggle for power that promises to tear apart the lives of Katharine and Mary, and forever change the religion of England.

ISBN 978-0-7531-7704-4 (hb)
ISBN 978-0-7531-7705-1 (pb)

ISIS publish a wide range of books in large print, from fiction to biography. Any suggestions for books you would like to see in large print or audio are always welcome. Please send to the Editorial Department at:

ISIS Publishing Limited
7 Centremead
Osney Mead
Oxford OX2 0ES

A full list of titles is available free of charge from:

Ulverscroft Large Print Books Limited

(UK)
The Green
Bradgate Road, Anstey
Leicester LE7 7FU
Tel: (0116) 236 4325

(Australia)
P.O. Box 314
St Leonards
NSW 1590
Tel: (02) 9436 2622

(USA)
P.O. Box 1230
West Seneca
N.Y. 14224-1230
Tel: (716) 674 4270

(Canada)
P.O. Box 80038
Burlington
Ontario L7L 6B1
Tel: (905) 637 8734

(New Zealand)
P.O. Box 456
Feilding
Tel: (06) 323 6828

Details of **ISIS** complete and unabridged audio books are also available from these offices. Alternatively, contact your local library for details of their collection of **ISIS** large print and unabridged audio books.